THE
Ex Talk

THE
Ex Talk

RACHEL LYNN SOLOMON

JOVE
NEW YORK

A JOVE BOOK
Published by Berkley
An imprint of Penguin Random House LLC
penguinrandomhouse.com

Library of Congress Cataloging-in-Publication Data

Names: Solomon, Rachel Lynn, author.
Title: The ex talk / Rachel Lynn Solomon.
Description: First edition. | New York: Jove, 2021.
Identifiers: LCCN 2020040938 (print) | LCCN 2020040939 (ebook) |
ISBN 9780593200124 (trade paperback) | ISBN 9780593200131 (ebook)
Subjects: GSAFD: Love stories.
Classification: LCC PS3619.O437236 E9 2021 (print) |
LCC PS3619.O437236 (ebook) | DDC 813/.6—dc23
LC record available at https://lccn.loc.gov/2020040938
LC ebook record available at https://lccn.loc.gov/2020040939

First Edition: January 2021

Printed in the United States of America
1 3 5 7 9 10 8 6 4 2

Cover art and design by Vi-An Nguyen
Book design by George Towne

For Ivan
Thank you for going on this journey with me, for the
unwavering support, and for loving stories as much as I do.
You always feel like home.

I don't go looking for stories with the idea of wrongness in my head, no. But the fact is, a lot of great stories hinge on people being wrong. —IRA GLASS

1

Dominic Yun is in my sound booth.

He knows it's my sound booth. He's been here four months, and there's no way he doesn't know it's my sound booth. It's on the station's shared calendar, the one connected to our email, in a blue bubble that reads BOOTH C: GOLDSTEIN, SHAY. REPEATS MONDAY–FRIDAY, 11 TO NOON. ENDS: NEVER.

I'd knock on the door, but—well, a sound booth's defining feature is that it's soundproof. And while I'm certain a list of my faults could fill a half hour of commercial-free radio, I'm not quite so awful that I'd storm inside and risk screwing up whatever Dominic is recording. He may be Pacific Public Radio's least qualified reporter, but I have too much respect for the art of audio mixing to do that. What happens inside that booth should be sacred.

Instead, I lean against the wall across from Booth C, quietly simmering, while the red **RECORDING** sign above the booth flashes on and off.

"Use another booth, Shay!" calls my show's host, Paloma Powers, on her way to lunch. (Veggie yakisoba from the hole-in-the-wall across the street, every Tuesday and Thursday for the past seven years. Ends: never.)

I could. But being passive-aggressive is much more fun.

Public radio is not solely filled with the kind of honey-voiced intellectuals who ask for money during pledge drives. For every job in this field, there are probably a hundred desperate journalism grads who "just *love This American Life*," and sometimes you have to be vicious if you want to survive.

I might be more stubborn than vicious. That stubbornness got me an internship here ten years ago, and now, at twenty-nine, I'm the station's youngest-ever senior producer. It's what I've wanted since I was a kid, even if, back then, I dreamed of being in front of a microphone instead of behind a computer.

It's eleven twenty when the sound booth door finally opens, after I've assured my assistant producer Ruthie Liao that the promos will be in before noon, and after environmental reporter Marlene Harrison-Yates takes one look at me and bursts out laughing before disappearing into the vastly inferior Booth B.

I see his shoe first, a shiny black oxford. The rest of his six-foot-something body follows, charcoal slacks and a maroon dress shirt with the top button undone. Framed in the doorway of Booth C and frowning down at his script, he could be a stock photo for business casual.

"Did you say all the right words in the right order?" I ask.

"I think so," Dominic says to the script instead of to me, completely serious. "Can I help you with anything?"

I fill my voice with as much sweetness as I can. "Just waiting for my booth."

Since he's blocking my path, I continue to scrutinize him. His sleeves are rolled to his elbows, and his black hair is slightly mussed. Maybe he dragged his hands through it, frustrated when his story didn't turn out precisely the way he wanted. It would be a refreshing contrast to his recent stories dominating our website, the ones that get clicks because of splashy headlines but lack any emotional depth. During those fateful twenty minutes he spent in Booth C, maybe he grew so fed up with public radio that he's on his way to tell Kent he's so sorry, but he wasn't cut out for this job.

He's barely been here long enough to understand the nuances between Booths A, B, and my beloved C: that the headphones in Booth C are perfectly broken in, that the weight of the faders on the board makes them easier to manipulate. He doesn't know the significance of Booth C, either—that it's where I mixed tracks for the first show I produced entirely solo, the one about being fatherless on Father's Day that tied up our phone lines for hours. Listening to those stories had made me feel, for the first time in years, a little less alone, had reminded me why I'd gone into radio in the first place.

I'd say it's not just about Booth C, but it's also possible that I've formed an unhealthy attachment to these twenty-four square feet of wires and knobs.

"It's all yours," he says, but he doesn't move, nor does he glance up from his script.

"It's supposed to be. Every weekday from eleven to noon. If your calendar isn't working, you should probably tell IT."

Finally, he wrenches his gaze from the script down to me. Way down. He settles into a lean against the doorframe, a slight hunch to his shoulders. He's always doing this, and I imagine it's because regular-size buildings are too small to confine him. I'm five two and never more aware of my height than when I'm standing next to him.

When our receptionist Emma took his photo for the website, she blushed the whole time, probably because he's the only guy here under thirty who isn't an intern. In the picture, he's serious except for one corner of his mouth, the tiniest parenthesis tugging his lips to one side. I stared at that corner for a long time when the photo was posted, wondering why Kent hired someone who'd never set foot inside a radio station. Kent swooned over Dominic's master's in journalism from Northwestern, consistently ranked the best program in the country, and the way he swept the collegiate journalism awards circuit.

Dominic gives me a tighter, more restrained version of that staff photo smile. "It was eleven oh five, and no one was in it. And I might have a big story to break later. Waiting on confirmation from one more source."

"Cool. I have to mix Paloma's intros, so—" I make a move to enter the booth, but he doesn't budge, his impossibly tall frame blocking me. I am a cub trying to get the attention of a grizzly.

That parenthesis pulls at his mouth a little more. "You're not going to ask what my story is?"

"I'm sure I'll read all about it in the *Seattle Times* tomorrow."

"Aw, where's your team spirit? Public radio *can* break news," he insists. We've had this argument a dozen times, dating back to his first week at the station, when he asked why none of our reporters regularly attended city council meetings. "Wouldn't it be great to get ahead of a story for once, instead of playing catch-up?"

Dominic can't seem to grasp that breaking news isn't our forte. When I told him during training that sometimes our reporters simply rewrite news briefs from the *Times*, he looked at me like I'd said we wouldn't be giving out tote bags during our next pledge drive. Our reporters do great work—important work—but I've always believed public radio is best when it focuses on longer features, deep dives, human-interest pieces. That's what my show, *Puget Sounds*, does, and we're good at it. Paloma came up with the name, a play on Puget Sound, the body of water along Washington's northwestern coast.

"People don't turn to us for breaking news," I say, trying to keep my voice down. "We've done studies. And it doesn't matter where local breaking news comes from. Tomorrow it'll be on every station, blog, and Twitter account with twenty-seven followers, and no one will care where they saw it first."

He crosses his arms over his chest, which draws more attention to his bare forearms and the pattern of dark hair that disappears into his sleeves. I've always been a forearm girl—a man rolling his shirt to the elbows is basically foreplay for me—and it's a crime that such nice ones are wasted on him.

"Right, right," he says. "I have to remember that real radio focuses on—what's your segment today?"

"Ask a Trainer," I say with a thrust of my chin that I hope projects confidence. I refuse to be embarrassed by it. It's one of our most popular segments, a live call-in show where renowned animal behaviorist Mary Beth Barkley—98 percent chance that's not her real name—answers listener questions. She always brings her corgi, and it's a fact that dogs make everything better.

"You're providing a real public service, analyzing cat vomit on air." He pushes away from the booth, and the door closes behind him with a thud. "I must have been sick that day in grad school. Not a lot of other people can capture that nuance the way your show can."

Before I can answer, Kent strides down the hall in his trademark suspenders and novelty tie. Today it's tiny slices of pepperoni pizza. Kent O'Grady: the station's program director, and owner of a radio voice that made him a Seattle legend decades ago.

He claps a hand on Dominic's shoulder, but since Kent's only a few inches taller than I am, it lands on his bicep. "Just the people I was looking for. Dom, how's that story coming along? Do we have a scandal on our hands?"

Dom. In ten years, I've never seen Kent bust out a nickname so quickly.

"Scandal?" I ask, interest piqued.

"We just might," Dominic says. "I'm waiting on one more call to confirm."

"Excellent." Kent runs a hand through his graying beard. "Shay, does Paloma have time at the top of the show for a live interview with Dom?"

"Live?" Dominic says. "As in . . . not prerecorded?"

"Of course," Kent says. "We want to be the first to break this story."

"Gotta get on that breaking news," I say as Dominic pales. While I don't love the idea of ceding time to Dominic, if he's uncomfortable, I am definitely on board. "I guess we can give you a few minutes of Ask a Trainer."

Kent snaps his fingers. "Remind me to catch Mary Beth before she leaves. The only way Meatball eats her food these days is if she transfers every single nugget from the dish to the floor."

"Only a few minutes, right?" Dominic's voice wobbles.

"Five, tops. You'll be great." Kent flashes us a grin and turns back to his office.

"Please don't mess up my show," I say to Dominic before I slip into Booth C.

Dominic Yun is in my studio.

Technically, it's three adjoining studios: the one I'm in with the announcer and mixing console—aka "the board"—the small call-in studio, and Studio A, where Paloma's sitting right now with her show notes, a bottle of kombucha, and an empty glass of water.

Dominic is next to her, wringing his hands after spilling said water on Paloma's notes. Ruthie had to race to print off another copy.

"Mary Beth's here," Ruthie says, coming into the studio behind me after mopping up Dominic's mess. "And yes, she has water, and her dog has water."

"Perfect. Thank you." I put on my headset and scan the show's rundown, my heart thumping its familiar preshow rhythm.

Puget Sounds is an hour-long burst of adrenaline every weekday from two to three p.m. As the senior producer, I direct the live show: cueing Paloma, calling guests and patching them through, tracking the time spent on each segment, and putting out any number of fires. Ruthie brings in the guests, and our intern, Griffin, works the call-in line in an adjoining booth.

Sometimes I can't believe I get to do this five times a week. Thousands of people across the city are turning their dials and apps and web browsers to 88.3 FM, and some of them will be so inspired, amused, or even furious that they'll call us to share a story or ask a question. That interactive element—hearing Paloma through your speakers one minute and chatting with her live the next—is why radio is the best form of journalism. It makes the world a little bit smaller. You can be listening to a show with hundreds of thousands of fans across the country, but it still feels like the host is talking directly to *you*. Almost, in some cases, like the two of you are friends.

I bounce my tan ankle boots up and down on the lowest rung of my usual stool. Next to me, Ruthie adjusts her headphones over her platinum blond pixie cut before placing a hand on my leg to stop my fidgeting.

"It's going to be fine," she says, nodding toward Dominic through the glass separating us. We try to keep our feud secret, but Ruthie, with all her brink-of-Gen-Z intuitiveness, picked up on it within weeks of his start date. "We've dealt with worse."

"True. You're my eternal hero after rebooking all four guests on our irrational fears show last minute."

I adore Ruthie, who came to us via commercial radio, which is faster paced despite the near constant ad breaks. Every so often, I catch her humming the 1-877-KARS-4-KIDS jingle under her breath. She says she's haunted by it.

In the center of the studio, Jason Burns rises from his announcer chair, an ergonomic contraption he specially ordered from Sweden. The board stretches in front of him.

"Quiet in the studio, please," he says in that warm maple syrup voice of his, hands lingering over a couple of faders. Jason's a sweet thirtyish guy I've only ever seen in plaid flannel and jeans, the uniform of both lumberjacks and Seattle natives.

The **ON AIR** sign next to the clock lights up.

"You're listening to 88.3 FM Pacific Public Radio," Jason says. "Coming up, a breaking local story on *Puget Sounds*. Plus, Paloma Powers asks a trainer your burning animal behavior questions. But first, here's your national news from NPR."

The **ON AIR** sign goes off. And then: *From NPR News in Washington, DC, I'm Shanti Gupta* . . .

There are few sounds more calming than the voice of an NPR news anchor, but Shanti Gupta doesn't soothe me the way she usually does. I'm too focused on the utter wrongness that is Dominic next to Paloma.

I hit the button on my line that connects me to Dominic. "Don't sit so close to the mic," I say, and he must be so startled by my voice in his ears that his eyebrows jump to his hairline. "Or all we'll hear is your heavy breathing."

His mouth moves, but I don't hear anything.

"You have to press the—"

"You really don't want me to be good at this, do you?"

The question lingers in my ears. If Paloma's paying attention, she doesn't show it, instead making notes in the margins of her rundown. My sweater suddenly feels too warm.

Ten years ago, I was the wunderkind, the intern who crafted perfect rundowns and researched riveting show topics and proved to Paloma and to her former producer, a guy who retired before I took his job, that I was something special. "This good, and she's only nineteen!" Kent would bellow. "She's going to run this place someday."

I didn't want to run the place. I only wanted to tell good stories.

And here's Dominic: our newest employee, fresh off a master's program, already on the air.

"Live in ten," Jason says before I can answer Dominic, and I push away my jealousy so I can focus on what's always been the best part of my job.

I slide off my stool and make eye contact with Paloma, holding my arm straight up at an imaginary twelve o'clock. "Five, four, three, two—" Then I lower my arm, aiming a finger at her, and she's *on*.

"I'm Paloma Powers, and you're listening to *Puget Sounds*," she says in her practiced way. Her voice is dark chocolate, low and mature with a hint of femininity. There's so much power in a voice like that, in the ability to make people not just listen but *care*.

A music bed plays underneath her, a bright piano melody that Jason will fade out as soon as she finishes her intro.

"Today we have renowned animal behavior expert Mary Beth Barkley in the studio for all your pet-related questions. Maybe you're wondering how to introduce a new kitten to your home, or whether you really can teach an old dog new tricks. We want to hear from you, so call 206-555-8803, and we'll try to get that question answered. But first, some breaking news from reporter Dominic Yun, who joins us live in-studio. Dominic, welcome to *Puget Sounds.*"

Dominic says nothing. He's not even looking at her, just staring down at his notes as though still waiting for a cue.

Dead air is not good. We can usually survive a few seconds of it without listener complaint, but any more than that, and we have a serious problem.

"Fuck," Ruthie says.

"*Say something,*" I mutter into his ear. I wave my arms, but he's completely frozen.

Well, if he destroys my show, at least he'll go down with it.

"Dominic," Paloma prompts, still perfectly cheery. "We're so happy to have you with us!"

Then something kicks in, as though the adrenaline has finally reached his bloodstream. Dominic blinks to life and leans into the mic.

"Thank you, Paloma," he says, rocky at first, but then evening out. "I'm thrilled to be here. Yours was actually the first show I listened to before I moved to Seattle for this job."

"Wonderful," Paloma says. "What do you have for us?"

He straightens. "It started with an anonymous tip. And I know what you're thinking. Sometimes an anonymous tip can be complete hearsay, but if you ask the right questions, you can find the real story. This one, I had a feeling—call it a reporter's intuition—that it was right on. I investigated something similar about a faculty member when I was at Northwestern." A dramatic pause, and then: "What I found out is that Mayor Scott Healey has a second family. And while his private life is his business, he used campaign funds to keep it quiet."

"Shiiiiiit," Jason says, spinning in his chair to face Ruthie and me. Behind the scenes, we're not exactly FCC compliant.

"I knew there was a reason I didn't vote for him," Ruthie says. "I didn't like his face."

"That—that is a big one, Dominic," Paloma says, clearly shocked, but recovering quickly. "We've had Mayor Healey on the show several times. Can you tell us how you figured this out?"

"It started at a council meeting last month . . ." He launches into the story—how he found the financial records and tracked where the money was going, how he eventually convinced the mayor's secret daughter to talk to him.

Two minutes go by. Three. As we approach five minutes, I try to signal Paloma to switch segments, but she's too focused on Dominic. I start to wonder if it's possible to sever a mic cord with my fingernails.

"I can't keep up with the phone lines," Griffin's voice says in my ear.

I press the button to talk directly to him. "Take down their questions and tell them Mary Beth will get to the ones she can."

"No—they're about the mayor. They want to talk to Dominic."

Oh. Okay. Gritting my teeth, I hop on our show chat.

Calls coming in, is D open to ?'s?

"It looks like we're getting a lot of questions," Paloma says after peeking at the screen. "Would you be open to taking some calls from listeners?"

"Sure, Paloma," Dominic says, with the ease of a seasoned reporter and not someone who played with a digital recorder a few times in college and decided why not go into radio.

When his eyes lock with mine through the glass barrier, all my loathing for him burns hot in my chest, turning my heart wild. The cut of his jaw makes him look more resolute than I've ever seen him, like he knows how badly I used to want this. His mouth tilts upward in a triumphant half smile. Delivering live commentary: another thing Dominic Yun is instantly perfect at.

Kent bursts through the door. "Shay, we're gonna have to reschedule Mary Beth. This is good motherfucking radio."

"Ruthie," I say, but she's already halfway out the door.

"Great work, everyone," Kent says, slapping Jason on the shoulder. "I'm glad we were able to get to this today."

I jostle my glasses as I rub at the space between my eyes where a headache is brewing. "This isn't right," I say after Kent leaves.

"It's good motherfucking radio," Jason says in a singsong, imitating Kent.

"It feels invasive."

"The public doesn't have a right to know that the mayor's a shady piece of shit?"

"They do, but not on our show."

Jason follows my gaze, glancing between Dominic and me. Jason and I were hired within a couple weeks of each other, and he knows me too well not to realize why I'm upset. "You hate that Dominic is so good at this," he says. "You hate that he's a natural, that he's live on the air a few months after he started working here."

"I'm—" I start, but stumble over my words. It makes me sound so shitty when he puts it that way. "It doesn't matter how I feel about it. I have no desire to be on air." Not anymore, at least. No point in wanting something I know will never happen.

Ruthie comes back in, cheeks flushed.

"Mary Beth's pissed." She clamps her headphones over her ears. "She says she had to cancel a private training session with one of Bill Gates's kids to be here."

"We'll send a groveling email later. No—I'll call her."

"I don't have enough lines," Griffin says in my ear.

"Ruthie, can you help Griffin? I'll pitch in if I need to."

"On it."

"Thank you."

Dominic reads off each illicit payment one by one. The numbers are staggering. It's not that this is a bad show—it's that somehow, it's become Dominic's show, and I'm no longer in control. He is the star.

So I sit back and let Paloma and Dominic take over. Dominic will win accolades and audiences, and I'll stay right here behind the scenes.

Ends: never.

2

Even though he was never on the air, my dad had the best radio voice. It was powerful but soft, a crackling fire on the coldest night of the year. He grew up fixing radios and owned an electronics repair shop, though of course he eventually learned how to fix laptops and phones, too. Goldstein Gadgets: my favorite place in the world.

I inherited his love for public radio but not his voice. Mine is the kind of high-pitched voice men love to weaponize against women. Shrill. Unintelligent. *Girly*, as though being a girl is the worst kind of insult. I've been teased my whole life, and I still brace myself for cleverly disguised insults when I'm talking to someone for the first time.

My dad never cared. We hosted radio shows in our kitchen ("Tell me, Shay Goldstein, what kind of cereal are you having this morning?") and on road trips ("Can you describe the scenery at this middle-of-nowhere rest stop?"). I'd spend afternoons with him at Goldstein Gadgets, doing my homework and listening to game shows, *Car Talk*, *This American Life*. All we needed was a great story.

I wanted him to hear me on the radio so badly, even if no one else did.

When he died my senior year of high school after a sudden cardiac arrest, it shattered me. Classes didn't matter. Friends didn't matter. I didn't turn on the radio for weeks. Somehow, I managed a B-minus average for the University of Washington, but I couldn't even celebrate getting in. I was still submerged in depression when I landed my internship at Pacific Public Radio, and slowly, slowly, I climbed out of darkness and into a conviction that the only way forward was to try to rebuild what I'd lost. Here I am, twenty-nine and clinging to that childish dream.

"Make people cry, and then make them laugh," my dad would say. "But most of all, make sure you're telling a good story."

I'm not sure how he would have felt about Ask a Trainer.

I'm the fifth wheel at dinner tonight. My mother and her boyfriend Phil, and my best friend, Ameena, and her boyfriend, TJ are already seated at a Capitol Hill French-Vietnamese fusion restaurant by the time I emerge from rush hour traffic. Ameena Chaudhry and I grew up across the street from each other, and she's been a constant in my life for more than twenty years.

"Only ten minutes late," Ameena says, jumping out of her chair to lasso me into a tight hug. "That's got to be a new record, right?"

TJ pulls out his phone to check the notes app. "There was one time last March we were all on time except for Shay, who was only three minutes late."

I roll my eyes at this, but guilt twists my stomach. "It's great to see you, too. And I really am sorry. I was rushing to finish one last thing and lost track of time."

We try to schedule dinners as regularly as we can, but my mother and Phil are violinists in the Seattle Symphony with regular evening performances, Ameena is a recruiter at Microsoft, and TJ does something important-sounding in finance that I've never fully understood. On occasion—fine, most occasions—I stay late at the station to make sure everything's prepped for the next day's show. Today I was on the phone apologizing to Mary Beth Barkley for an hour.

I hug my mom and TJ, then shake hands with Phil. I'm still not sure how to navigate my mother having a boyfriend. Until Phil, she didn't seem interested in dating. They'd been friends for ages, though, and he lost his wife a few years after we lost Dad. They supported each other during the grieving process, which of course never really ends, until they eventually became a different kind of support system.

I should be used to it by now, but by the time they started dating last year, I'd only just gotten used to the idea of my mother as a widow.

"As much as I love bullying Shay," my mother says with a half smile in my direction, "I'm starving. Appetizers?"

Phil points at the menu. "The chili cumin pork ribs are supposed to be incredible," he says in his Nigerian accent.

After we order and exchange how-was-your-days, Ameena and TJ share a quick sideways glance. Before they started dating, Ameena and I were the ones sharing sideways glances, inside jokes. Being the fifth wheel is only slightly crushing when I realize I'm not anyone's person. Ameena and TJ live together, so it's natural that she shares secrets with him before me, and my mother has Phil. I am a solid second, but I'm no one's first.

I'm on a dating app hiatus, something I implement every so often when swiping becomes especially frustrating. My relationships seem doomed to never last longer than a handful of months. I want so badly to get to that place where Ameena and TJ are, five years of dating after they accidentally swapped orders at a coffee shop, that it's possible I rush things. I've never not been the first to say *I love you*, and there are only so many times you can stomach total silence in response.

But I won't lie—I want to be that first person someone tells everything to.

"I have some news," Ameena says. "I'm interviewing with the Nature Conservancy tomorrow. So it's not news, exactly, but news adjacent. It's just the first phone interview, but . . ." She trails off with a shrug, but her dark eyes are bright with excitement.

When Ameena started at Microsoft, her goal was to gain enough experience to ultimately recruit for an organization that does good, ideally for the environment. She was the president and founder of our high school's Compost Club. By default, I was the vice president. She's a slow-fashion aficionado who buys all her clothes at thrift shops and rummage sales, and she and TJ have an impressive herb garden on their apartment balcony.

"Are you serious? That's incredible!" I say, reaching for a rib the server places in the center of the table. "They have a Seattle office?"

Her expression falters. "Well, no," she says. "They're in Virginia. I mean, I doubt I'll get the job."

"Don't reject yourself before you've even interviewed," Phil says. "Do you know how many people audition for the symphony? The odds were never in our favor, either, although I still claim it's nonsense Leanna had to audition three times."

My mother squeezes his arm, but she beams at the compliment.

"Virginia is . . . far," I say intelligently.

"Let's just ignore the Virginia part for now." Ameena brushes a stray thread from the vintage charcoal blazer we fought over at an estate sale last month. "I'm really not going to get it, though. I'm the youngest recruiter on my team. They're probably going to want someone with more experience."

"I miss being the youngest," I say, taking to heart Ameena's "let's just ignore the Virginia part" suggestion. Virginia isn't something I can even wrap my mind around. "It feels like the interns are getting younger and younger every year. And they're all so earnest and fresh faced. One of them actually told me the other day that he didn't know what a tape looked like."

"Like that reporter you're always going on about?" my mother says. "What's his name again?"

"Dominic something, right?" Phil says. "I did like that piece he did on arts funding in Seattle compared to other cities."

"He's not an intern, he's Kent's favorite reporter." And apparently the new star of *Puget Sounds*, based on the social media snooping I did after the show. Twitter loved him, which proves Twitter is a hellsite.

"Talk to me when you're thirty," Ameena says. We celebrated her thirtieth two months ago, in December, and it'll be my turn in October. I'm still in denial.

My mother waves a hand. "Please. You're both still babies." She says this, but my mother is gorgeous: dark red hair, sharp cheekbones, and a closet full of chic black dresses that would make Audrey Hepburn quietly, beautifully weep. In a symphony of fifty musicians, she steals the show every night.

I tug my hair out of its usual low ponytail and finger comb my long bangs that skim the top of my tortoiseshell glasses. *Thick*, *brown*, and *coarse*: the only adjectives that describe my hair, and all of them are tragic. I thought I'd have learned to style it by now, but some days I fight with a straightener and other days I fight with a curling iron before I resign myself to another ponytail.

It's only when I examine my mother, searching for the physical similarities between us—spoiler: there are none—that I notice she's acting strangely. She keeps rubbing at the hollow of her throat, one of her telltale signs of nerves, and when the food arrives, she pushes it around on her plate instead of eating it. She and Phil are usually pretty affectionate. We had a body language expert on the show a while back, and the way she talked about people falling in love described the two of them perfectly. Phil is always resting his hand in the small of her back, and she'll often cup the side of his face and skim her thumb along his cheek.

There's none of that tonight.

"How's the house?" Phil asks, and I respond with a dramatic groan. He holds up his hands and lets out a soft laugh. "Ah, I'm sorry. Didn't realize it was a sore subject."

"No, no," I say, even if it is a bit of a sore subject. "The house is fine, though I wish I'd waited for something smaller."

"Isn't it a three bedroom? One bath?"

"Yeah, but. . . ."

For years, Ameena and I shared an apartment in Ballard before she moved in with TJ. Buying a house seemed like the right next step: I was nearly thirty, had saved up enough money, and wasn't leaving Seattle anytime soon. Working in public radio is like serving on the Supreme Court—most people are there for a very long time. Even if I wanted to be on the air, I wouldn't be able to find a job at another station. It's impossible to get a hosting gig without experience, but you can't get that experience unless you already have some experience under your belt. The joys of job hunting as a millennial.

So because it seemed like the next step in the how-to-adult manual, I bought a house, a Wallingford Craftsman my real estate agent called cozy but more often feels too large for one person. It's always cold, and six months after picking out the kind of furniture I thought I wanted, it still feels empty. Lonely.

"I guess I just have a lot of work to do on it," I finish, though I'm unsure what exactly "it" means.

"It was a good financial decision," Phil says. "Buying a house is always a good investment. And one of my kids would be more than happy to help you out with any painting or repairs."

Phil has three sons and a daughter. All the Adelekes are tall and fit and happily married, most with kids of their own. A couple months ago, my mother and I had our first Christmas with Phil's large family, forgoing the Jewish tradition of Chinese food and a movie. I'd been hesitant at first, if only because I liked spending that time with my mother, but everyone had been warm and welcoming, and it was impossible to stay bitter.

"Thanks," I say. "Maybe I'll take you up on that."

A water glass shatters, and my mother offers up a sheepish grin. "Sorry," she says as a waiter rushes over to clean it up.

"Are you all right, Leanna?" Phil asks.

She presses her ruby lips together and nods. "All right. Yes. I'm great." Her hand is at her throat again. "Phil, I—there's something I want to say."

Oh no. She wouldn't be breaking up with him like this, would she? Not in front of a whole group, not in public. My mother is too classy to do something like that.

Ameena looks as puzzled as I do. All of us set down our forks, watching as my mother pushes out her chair and gets to her feet, visibly shaking. Oh god—is she sick? Maybe that's why she wanted to have this dinner, so she could tell all of us at once.

My stomach clenches, and I suddenly feel like I might throw up. My mother is all I have. I can't lose her, too.

But then she grins, and my shoulders sag with relief as she starts talking. "Phil," she says in this tone I don't think I've heard before. She places her hand on his arm. "I know it's only been eleven months, but they've been the best months I've had in a long, long time."

"For me, too," he says. A smile settles into the fine lines in his dark skin. As though maybe he knows what's coming, and now I think I might, too. She'll ask him to move in, I'm sure of it. Odd to do it in public, but my mother has always had a certain way of doing things. *That's just Leanna*, my dad would say with a shrug when she made soup in a blender before zapping it in the microwave or insisted on carving jack-o'-lanterns in early September.

"After Dan passed away, I didn't think I'd get a second chance. I thought I'd found my person, and he was gone, and I was done. But you were always right there, weren't you? Sitting next to me, playing the violin. I fell in love with your music, and then I fell in love with you. You know as well as I do that the grief never goes away, but you have made me realize love can live alongside grief. I don't want to spend any more time not being married to you. So . . ." Here she trails off, takes a breath. "Philip Adeleke, will you marry me?"

The room goes dead silent, everyone's eyes trained on our table, watching this proposal. My heart is pounding heavier than it does before a show, and in the corner of my vision, TJ clasps a hand over Ameena's.

Phil leaps out of his chair so quickly he knocks over his own glass of water, and maybe they really are meant for each other. "Yes, Leanna, yes," he says. "I love you so much. Yes, yes, yes."

When they kiss, the restaurant bursts into applause. A waiter brings out glasses of champagne. Ameena dabs at her eyes, asking if I knew this was going to happen, if I knew my mother was planning this, and no. No, I did not.

I force myself out of my seat to congratulate them, my mother and my—stepfather? Too many emotions swirl through me, and I can only name a few of them. I'm happy for them, of course I am. I want my mother to be happy. She deserves it.

I've just spent so many years convinced no one could replace my father that I never imagined anyone would.

Ameena peppers them with questions about the wedding. Turns out, Phil had been planning to propose this weekend, but my mother managed to beat him to it. They want it to happen soon, they say. Naturally, a quartet from the symphony will play the reception.

Eventually, Phil whisks my mother out of the restaurant to "celebrate"—like we don't all know exactly what that means—leaving Ameena and TJ and me to polish off the champagne.

"Leanna Goldstein is my hero," Ameena says. "I can't believe we got to be part of that."

I want to be able to say that too, that Leanna Goldstein is my hero—and she is, for so many reasons. For how she let me process Dad's death on my own time, with my own therapist, before the two of us went to family counseling together. For convincing me that we could still *be* a family even if it was just the two of us. Small but mighty, she'd say. She always knew I'd work in radio, though sometimes she jokes that I could have at least compromised and found a job at a classical music station.

"You okay?" TJ asks as we pack up. He tucks his blond hair into a knit beanie. "It's weird, I know. My parents are both remarried, and it definitely takes some getting used to."

"I guess I never thought I'd go to my mom's wedding before my own." In my head, it sounds like a joke. When I say it, it does not.

Ameena squeezes my hand. "This is a lot. Take the time you need to process it, okay?"

I nod. "Good luck on the interview," I tell her, digging into my bag for my keys as we step into the chilly Seattle night. My house is going to be so quiet when I get home. It always is. "Are you sure you don't want to come over and watch bad TV or something?"

"Shay. I love you, but you need to learn to be alone in your own house. Do I need to check for monsters under your bed again?

"Maybe."

Ameena shakes her head. "Get a dog."

The moment I get home, I flip on every single light and cue up the latest episode of my favorite comedy podcast. It's almost nine o'clock, and I've been away from my email for too long, despite the few times I checked it in the bathroom. (Enough that my mother asked me if I was okay, which is only slightly embarrassing as an adult, to think your mom is concerned about your bowels.)

I make some tea and settle onto the couch with my work laptop. I really am content helping others tell stories as opposed to telling them myself. Paloma does it better than I ever could, even if sometimes we're not telling the kinds of stories I love, sweeping epics about the human experience you can only hear on stations with a bigger budget. Sometimes I wonder if *content* is really just a synonym for *complacent*.

I try not to think about that, though.

After my dad died, I sought comfort anywhere I could. I smoked pot with Ameena, hooked up with the cute guy across the hall freshman year, had one bad experience with alcohol that taught me how much alcohol my body could handle. It wasn't anything outrageously unhealthy; I didn't want to go off the rails, but I wanted to get close enough to see what was on the other side of them.

The only thing that made me feel like myself again was my internship at PPR. That was when I realized the solution wasn't impulse—it was consistency. And of course it was; radio had always made me feel closer to my dad. I'd get the stable job, the house in a walkable neighborhood, and the devoted boyfriend, one day husband. Ameena remained my best friend; my mother remained single. With the exception of my dating life, everything's gone pretty much according to plan.

Phil becoming my stepfather, though—that's going to change things.

And historically, I have not been great at change.

A house was always part of my plan, and it should have felt like this tremendous accomplishment. I've had it six months, but I'm forever in the middle of making it *mine*. I'll spend hours scouring antique shops for the right kind of artwork before buying some mass-produced abstract blobs at Target, or try a dozen paint samples for the living room before realizing none of them feel quite right and never getting the energy to paint over them. In our early twenties, Ameena and I dreamed of hosting dinner parties when we had the space, but now we're always exhausted. Most of the time, I end up cooking something with prepackaged ingredients that show up on my doorstep twice a week.

Every time I imagined adulthood, it looked different from this reality. All the important people in my life have their person. I have an empty house and my supposed dream job that doesn't always love me back.

Against my better judgment, I listen to today's show. I did this all the time when I started out, eager for ways to improve, but I haven't done it in a while. Over and over, I rewind Dominic's answers, trying to pinpoint what, exactly, listeners found so appealing. It takes him a few minutes to find his footing; the cadence of his voice changes, and his words become smooth, buttercream frosting over red velvet cake. He's not a robot, the way I might have assumed before I heard him on the air. *It's almost like he didn't want someone to find out he was doing something illegal*, he says in such a mock-surprised tone that it makes me crack a smile. He responds to listener questions as though he genuinely cares about their concerns, and even when he doesn't know the answer, he does his best to convince them he's going to find out.

As much as I hate to admit it, Dominic Yun on *Puget Sounds* was good radio.

Even my dad would have agreed.

3

"Emergency meeting," Kent O'Grady announces the next morning, before I've even unzipped my coat. "Conference room. Five minutes. Senior staff only."

I've never been senior enough to go to a PPR emergency meeting. My promotion, in title and slight salary increase, happened a few months ago. The way Kent's M. C. Escher–patterned tie lies crooked, as though he was so frazzled this morning that he didn't notice, is troubling, but it still feels kind of great to be included.

I hang my coat on the hook next to my desk and remove the laptop, phone, and notepad from my messenger bag. My phone lights up with a notification from one of the dating apps I haven't gotten around to deleting.

We miss you! 27 matches are waiting

I swipe it away and drag the app to the trash. That's the only action I've had lately: Tinder and Bumble desperately trying to win me back.

Our newsroom has an open floor plan, offices reserved for the most senior of senior staff. My space is littered with empty coffee cups I'll definitely put in the dishwasher later today. The staff rotates kitchen duty, and for my first two years at PPR, I somehow got stuck cleaning it every Friday. I assumed I was just paying my dues as a newbie, but I've never seen Griffin, our *Puget Sounds* intern, on the schedule, which is drafted weekly by our office manager. It's never seemed important enough to bring up with HR.

Then there's my intricate filing system for past rundowns, and pinned next to my computer, a PodCon poster signed by the hosts of my favorite movie podcast. PodCon is an annual radio and podcasting festival, and if it sounds nerdy, that's because it is, and it's also the best. I went a couple of years ago when it was held in Seattle, and while it would be a dream to go as a presenter, obviously a local newsmagazine doesn't have national appeal.

At the desk across from mine, Paloma is adding flax and chia seeds to a cup of Icelandic yogurt. She's here at eight sharp every morning and out the door at four, right after we finish our afternoon show debrief.

"Emergency meeting?" I ask her. We're on a hiring freeze right now; Dominic was the last person brought on before it went into effect. I wonder if this meeting has to do with the station's finances.

She stirs her yogurt. "It's just Kent being dramatic. You know he loves a good show. We're probably pushing up a pledge drive or something." Paloma's been here for more than two decades, so if she isn't worried, maybe I shouldn't be. "You don't happen to have any extra chia seeds lying around, do you? Just ran out."

And although I have never eaten a chia seed in my life, I reach into the drawer beneath my desk and pull out a bag filled with them.

This is what a good producer does. I've trained myself to know what Paloma wants before even she does, to anticipate her every need. If your host isn't happy, your show can't be great. Paloma is the reason people love *Puget Sounds*, and I am the reason Paloma is able to put on a great show.

"You're a peach," she says, and gestures to her yogurt. "Literally. What would I do without you?"

"Eat subpar yogurt, obviously."

I used to be terrified of her. I'd grown up listening to her anchor the morning news, and when I met her the first day of my internship, I choked on my words, unable to believe she was real. *Puget Sounds* was her idea, and even today, there aren't a lot of female public radio hosts, and fewer queer women.

Paloma's in her late forties and doesn't have kids, and she and her art history professor wife spend two weeks every summer in a remote location I've never heard of, coming back with stories about how they got lost or ran out of food or narrowly escaped a wild animal. And yet while she's here, she operates on such a specific schedule that if I ever left, it would take weeks to train someone new on all her idiosyncrasies alone.

Paloma readjusts her shawl, a deep blue and green knit, and takes her yogurt down the hall to the conference room, where it becomes immediately clear that this is Very Serious Business. Everyone looks grim, and no one's on their phones. Even the early morning people, who are usually too peppy for their own good, are slightly less pepped than usual.

Paloma might not be worried, but I linger in the doorway, suddenly overcome by the *where do I sit?* feeling I knew so well in high school when Ameena and I didn't have the same lunch period. A senior staff meeting still feels a little like a club I tricked someone into letting me into.

A tall figure in a sky-blue-striped button-down approaches from the other side of the hall, and I tighten my grip on my notepad. Dominic's in jeans today, a rarity for him. They're perfectly pressed, not a wrinkle in sight. This is another reason his height is so frustrating: If he weren't a giant, I'd be able to more comfortably look him in the eye instead of cataloging his choice of legwear.

"Senior staff only," I tell him, plastering on a false-sympathetic smile. A place where I fit in and he does not. "Sorry."

"Dom! Come on in," Kent says from the head of the table, waving him inside.

And just like that, he brushes past me with his thermos of coffee, already inducted into this club it took me years to join. I hope the coffee burns his tongue.

"Stellar reporting," says senior editor Paul Wagner. "And the mayor resigned?" He lets out a low whistle.

"Thanks, Paul," Dominic says, running his free hand through his hair, which is looking a little flatter than usual. "It makes it worth getting here at five a.m., that's for sure." Ah. That explains it.

Paul gives a hearty laugh at this. "The news never sleeps."

I usually listen to PPR on my drive to work, but this morning I was finishing up a podcast. Dominic's investigation got the mayor to resign. No wonder he's been given a golden ticket to this meeting. It won't stop me from silently fuming about it, though.

I find a seat next to Paloma and flip to a fresh page in my notebook. *Emergency Meeting*, I write at the top of the page, feeling a bit less important now that Dominic is here.

"Good morning," Kent bellows when all eleven of us are seated. "Always a pleasure to see everyone's smiling faces bright and early." His M. C. Escher tie is hypnotic, and sometimes I forget how commanding he can be in front of a group. He's like Rob Lowe's character on *Parks and Rec*: positive to a fault. "Shay, do you mind taking notes? You're so great with details."

"Oh—sure," I say, scratching out *Emergency Meeting* and flipping to the next page to rewrite it more legibly. I wasn't expecting to be put to work at my first senior staff meeting, but I guess I *am* good with details. And I'm not about to argue with a compliment from Kent.

"First up," Kent continues, "I'd like to congratulate Dominic on his reporting yesterday, both live on *Puget Sounds* and into the evening as he tracked the story."

I fight the urge to roll my eyes, and make an executive decision not to record this particular tidbit. Dominic seems to make an attempt at looking humble, his cheeks even turning pink before he lifts a hand as though to remind all of us who he is.

"Cut to the chase, Kent," says Isabel Fernandez, our morning show producer. We've always been friendly acquaintances more than actual friends, but suddenly I adore her. "Are we moving up a pledge drive to bring in more money, or what?"

"Didn't we just finish a pledge drive?" Marlene Harrison-Yates asks.

"We're always either just finishing or just starting a pledge drive," Paloma mutters next to me, and I stifle a laugh because she's not wrong.

"No, no, nothing like that. Well." Kent clears his throat, straightens a stack of papers. "We're going to be rearranging our programming."

Now that's a euphemism if I've ever heard one.

"Please don't put me on mornings again," Paloma says.

"Well, I don't want afternoons," says our a.m. drive host, Mike Russo.

"Let him talk," I say, and Kent offers me a grateful smile that soothes, just a little, the churning in my stomach.

"The board and I were thinking . . . something along the lines of a new show."

The room erupts into chaos again. Across the table, Dominic catches my eye, one of his dark eyebrows lifting in a way I can't quite interpret. I don't know why we keep making eye contact like this when I spend so much of my day hoping we won't have to cross paths. I flick my gaze back to my notes.

"We have our morning show, our midday show, and our evening show," Kent says. "And the feedback we've been getting from listeners is that they're too similar." He presses a button, and a number of colorful pie charts appear on the projector screen. "They don't connect with hosts the way they used to, not like they do at the national level or for some of the really popular podcasts."

"Excuse me," Paloma says in a haughty voice, "*Puget Sounds* is nothing like *At the Moment*."

"And we can't exactly bring in a comedian to host the morning news," Isabel says.

But Kent's not wrong. As an NPR member station, we're in charge of our programming, and we're able to broadcast any of the national shows. Naturally, those are listened to more than our local shows. They have more name recognition, and as I'm always telling Dominic, it's an uphill battle getting people interested in local news.

"Does a new show mean we're getting rid of one of our flagship shows?" Mike asks.

Kent shakes his head. "I don't want anyone jumping to conclusions. This is solely an idea-generating meeting."

A brainstorming session with producers, hosts, and reporters usually goes a little like this: The hosts and reporters take control. The producers stay quiet. It's not easy to speak up in a room full of people whose job it is to speak.

"What about a news roundtable?" Dominic says. "We could invite local politicians and other leaders on every week to give updates on what's going on in their lines of work."

Snooze.

Isabel, bless her, shuts him down, which I underline in my

notes. "We tried that fifteen years ago. It lasted, what, a few months?"

"It was a different market fifteen years ago," Dominic says.

"Exactly. It was easier." Isabel thrusts an arm toward the screen, and the pie chart that shows how *Puget Sounds*' listenership has dropped over the years. It's not a nice pie chart—*Puget Sounds* has had the steepest drop of all the flagship shows. "Now everyone and their grandkids has their own podcast. There's too much out there. It's impossible to stand out."

"Something focused on the environment," Marlene suggests. "Everyone in the Northwest cares about the environment. Each show could focus on small actions people could take to reduce their carbon footprint. I already have a whole bunch of tape about sustainable farming."

"We're not thinking big enough," Kent says. "We're too hyperlocal already."

Mike suggests a cooking show and Paul suggests a storytelling show, which I love. But Kent says it sounds too much like *The Moth*, which is probably why I loved it. Dominic throws out a few more newsy ideas that somehow manage to sound less interesting than his first one. A real triumph.

"What about a dating show?" I mutter, more to a button on my corduroy skirt than to the group, assuming no one will pay attention to PPR's lowliest senior producer. It's not something anyone's talked about yet, and after my mother's engagement and my phone's reminder that I'm very single, it's been on my mind.

But Marlene hears me. "Public radio doesn't really go there. And for good reason: FCC regulations. Anything juicy would be tough to dig into."

"It's absolutely possible to do something about dating without pissing off the FCC," Paloma says, and I feel a burst of pride at her defense of me. "Last year we did a segment about reproductive health, and another one about sex education in high schools."

"Yes!" Isabel says. "But something new. Something fresh."

Across the table, Dominic rolls his eyes so hard I fear for his vision. Surely a dating show doesn't fall within his master's-degree-in-journalism idea of what public radio should be.

"What about a dating show hosted by people who are dating?" Paloma says.

"It's been done," Kent says. "About a dozen times on a dozen more podcasts."

"A dating show hosted by exes," I say, half as a joke.

The room goes silent.

"Go on," Paloma says. "A dating show hosted by exes?"

I didn't mean for it to sound that exciting—it's just a potential fresh take on a dating show. But maybe it's not a bad idea.

"Um," I say, feeling my face grow warm, the way it always does when I'm on the spot. Even in a room of people I know, people with incredible voices, I'm more conscious of the sound of my voice than ever. It's more high pitched, more nasal than usual. These people don't say *um* or *like*. They don't stumble over their words.

Dominic is watching me very intently, as though I'm the news ticker on a cable network. Even when he's sitting down, his posture is so stiff, the cut of his shoulders so sharp, that his muscles must ache when he gets home every day. I wish, not for the first time this meeting, that he hadn't picked the seat directly opposite mine.

"Well." An excellent start. I clear my throat. This is just like pitching a segment in my team's weekly pitch meeting. I can do this. They've all heard me speak before. No one's judging the way I sound, and if they are, they're not going to make snide comments about it. "A dating show hosted by exes. It's . . . exactly what it sounds like, really. We'd get the listeners invested in their relation-ship, in how they got together, and how it fell apart. We'd get them invested in the two of them as friends, as cohosts, as whatever they are now that they're broken up. It would be part storytelling and part informational. Each episode, they could share more about their past, and they'd also explore dating trends, or interview dating experts, or even do some live counseling on the air to figure out what went wrong."

And I'm surprised, hearing myself talk about it, that it actually sounds like something I'd love to listen to. Public radio can sometimes be fun averse, but something like this—my dad would have gotten a kick out of it. It would be like *This American Life* meets *Modern Love*. We could do a show that follows each side of a Tinder date, or one tracking down people who'd ghosted someone.

That's when I have to stop myself. I'm using *we* in my head, like I'm the producer of this show. I already have a show.

"Like Kent said, there are tons of relationship shows out there, plenty of them hosted by couples," I say, gaining more confidence. My coworkers, my fellow senior staffers plus Dominic, are still listening—to *me*. "But . . . but what if we really try to figure out what goes wrong in relationships by having two exes work through their issues? Because that's what people want to know, right? What they did wrong?"

It's a question I've had plenty of times. I allow myself to grin, to relax back in my seat.

"I kind of love that," says reporter Jacqueline Guillaumont, after the chatter in the room dies down. "I'd listen to it."

"It's unconventional," Mike says, "but I have to say, I like where Shay's head is at. Maybe that's what we need, something out of the box like that."

"We'd need two exes to host it," Isabel says. "But I guess we could figure that out?"

Paloma reaches over and scribbles on my notepad: *Great job,* and I feel myself glow from the inside out.

"I'm sorry, but I don't see how it would work," Dominic says, popping that bubble of pride. A wrinkle appears between his brows.

"Why not?" I'm so focused on him, on this sudden desire to press my thumb *hard* into that crease between his brows, that I can barely hear Paloma scraping the bottom of her yogurt next to me. The one time I get the courage to speak up in a meeting like this—a meeting he should never have been invited to—he rips apart my idea.

"It's not exactly groundbreaking reporting."

"Since when does everything need to be? It would get people talking, and it would have appeal beyond our regular listenership. Maybe it would even increase contributions to the station." I look directly at Kent when I say this. "We can't oust mayors every day."

"No, but we should at least conduct ourselves with a modicum of respect," Dominic says, spitting out that last word as he leans forward, gripping the edge of the table. "Exes bickering about why they broke up? Giving out relationship advice?" He scoffs. "This sounds like something on satellite radio, or god forbid, commercial radio. It sounds . . . *tawdry*."

"And exposing the mayor's private life isn't?"

"Not when it's news."

The rest of the room seems oddly captivated by us. Kent has been scribbling on his notepad, uncharacteristically silent. I've never seen anyone argue like this at a meeting, and I'm convinced he's going to let us have it. When he doesn't, I keep going.

"You think public radio is only this one thing, but it's not," I say, clutching my pen as tightly as I can. In my head, the cap flies off and splatters his chest with black ink, wrecking the shirt he must have picked out so carefully this morning. It drips down those blue stripes and onto his jeans. "And that's the beauty of it. It can be educational, but it can also be heartbreaking or thrilling or *fun*. We're not just delivering facts, we're telling stories. You've worked here four whole months, and you think you have this industry all figured out?"

"Well, I do have a master's in journalism. From Northwestern." He says the school name so casually, as though it wasn't at all difficult to get into or didn't cost sixty grand. "So I happen to think that degree hanging by my desk does qualify me to talk about journalism."

Finally, Kent lifts one hand, indicating for us to calm down.

"A lot of food for thought," he says, and then with two words, makes me lose all hope. "Other ideas?"

After another twenty minutes, Kent calls the meeting to a close, doing his best to reassure us about the future of the station.

"This is early stages," he says. "We're not making any programming changes quite yet."

Still, it's hard to ignore the subtle sheen of worry on my coworkers' faces as they leave with their mugs of cold coffee. I linger until I'm the last one out of the room, hoping to avoid Dominic. Unfortunately, he's waiting in the hall, ready to pounce.

"Jesus Christ," I say when he startles me, holding my notepad over my skittering heart. "What, you didn't finish educating me on the job I've had for ten years?"

That wrinkle reappears between his brows, and he looks softer than he did in the meeting. "Shay, I'm—"

"Dom! Shay!" Kent interrupts, and I'm a little annoyed because for a second, it seemed like Dominic was actually about to apologize.

But that would be about as likely as Terry Gross stepping down from hosting *Fresh Air*.

"Kent," I say, ready with an apology of my own. "I'm so sorry about what happened in there. It got out of hand."

All he says is, "I have a few meetings to get to, but I want to talk to both of you at the end of the day. Can you meet me in my office at five thirty? Great." With that, he turns and heads down the hall, leaving me with Dominic.

"And I've got an interview to record." He half smiles before he morphs back into his demonic self and adds: "Booth A. In case you were wondering."

4

Kent's office is a veritable public radio shrine. There are photos of him shaking hands with every major NPR personality, rows of framed awards, and a shelf filled with antique audio recording equipment.

I've been distracted all day. Ruthie eventually pulled me into a sound booth before lunch, desperate for gossip after hearing murmurs all morning. I told her about the morning's emergency meeting and, with some reluctance after my argument with Dominic, my idea.

Her eyes grew wide behind her clear-framed glasses. "A show like that is just begging for a catchy name. Something like . . . *The Ex Cast*, or *The Ex Talk*."

I snorted, but I kind of immediately loved it. "Like sex talk?"

"Exactly. Too risqué for NPR?"

"Maybe," I said, but truthfully, I didn't know. And it's only an idea I threw out in a brainstorming meeting, unlikely to become more than that. Public radio can be slow to innovate.

Once we're seated in the chairs in front of Kent's desk, he excuses himself to brew another pot of tea. Dominic gets to his feet and begins pacing.

"You're making me dizzy," I tell him.

"You don't have to watch." Still, he stops beneath the photo of a very young Kent sandwiched between Tom and Ray Magliozzi, the *Car Talk* guys. He settles into a lean—of course. We get it, you're tall. "Nervous?"

I shrug, not wanting to let on how uneasy this meeting makes me. I have no idea what to expect when it comes to Kent. He used to intimidate me, and while we're far from friends, we've always gotten along. Or at least I've always done exactly what he's asked of me, and we've never had a reason for prolonged interactions. I picked up extra pledge drive production shifts at his request, and back when I was still eligible, I never bothered him about overtime pay even when I worked late into the night. Now those late hours have become a habit I can't break.

"I've been here for almost ten years. I don't get nervous anymore."

"Ten years, and you're still doing the same thing," he says. "You don't get bored?"

"Fortunately, you're here to shake things up. It's not boring to have to reschedule a guest at the last minute who we booked months in advance and who missed out on business of her own as a result."

"Oh," he says, as though this thought truly never occurred to him. "I didn't realize. Shit. I'm sorry about that. Is she upset?"

"I was able to smooth things over," I say, thrown by his response. Was he about to apologize earlier, too? "We're going to do a whole show dedicated to animal behavior next month to make up for it. And before you can say anything about it, yes, I know it's not news, but those shows are really popular. Especially during pledge drives."

He holds up his hands. "I wasn't going to say anything. We had a class in grad school about how to grovel if you pissed off a source."

I pause. "Wait, are you serious?"

Then his armor cracks, and he lets out a laugh. A sharp, breathy *ha* that would sound distorted if he did it into a microphone. Number of times I've heard Dominic laugh in the past four months: fewer than ten. News is never funny, apparently.

"No, but you definitely believed me for a second."

Huh. It's an odd moment of self-awareness. Does he know that he brings up grad school every chance he can?

Kent reenters with a steaming mug of tea. "Shay, Dom," he says, nodding to each of us.

Dominic slides back into the chair next to me, and it's then that I notice our chairs are a little too close together. There's only a foot of space between us. His legs are so long that his knees bump against Kent's desk, and I can smell his cologne. Ocean salt, and something else—sage?

It would be awkward to move my chair. I shall suffer in silence.

Kent takes a slow sip of his tea and closes his eyes for a moment, as though savoring it. When he opens them, his face splits into a grin, and I am deeply, thoroughly confused.

"It's so obvious," he says. "It's right in front of us." Another sip of tea, and then he presses his lips together. "It's almost simple, really."

"What is?" Dominic asks, a note of irritation in his voice. It's slight, but it's there.

"The two of you. Cohosting Shay's dating show."

There's a brief silence before we both burst out laughing. Nothing about Kent's declaration makes sense, and yet he says it with an air of nonchalance. My heart leaps at the word *hosting*, but this has to be a joke. *Producing*, he must have meant.

I chance a look at Dominic, and it might be the first time I've seen him look genuinely amused. He's usually so serious, so stoic, every bit the objective reporter. There's an openness to this new expression of his.

"I don't even know where to start," Dominic says between laughs, and okay, now it's becoming excessive. He doesn't need to laugh *quite* that hard about the show idea, does he? "Is this a joke?"

"Not a joke," Kent says, and maybe all three of us have lost our minds. "What do you think?"

"Aside from the obvious, like Shay never having hosted a show . . . we've never dated," Dominic says, and though I take some offense at that, he's not wrong. There are a thousand holes in Kent's suggestion, but despite the content of the show, I'm not a host. I don't have the right training or the right experience or the right *voice*.

"You've never hosted a show either," I point out.

"But I've been on the air."

I don't want to spar with Dominic in front of Kent, but I can't deal with his smugness. "You were live for the first time yesterday." I give him some exaggerated applause. "I guess you picked up everything about journalism in one year of grad school, and then everything about live radio during a single hour-long show. Yeah, that checks out."

Kent's grin is terrifying. "See? This is it. This is what I'm talking about. This . . . thing you two have. It's fascinating. I see the way you two act around the newsroom. I know I spend a lot of time in this office, but I'm perceptive. You two have this great chemistry, this natural conflict. Dominic is all about the news and the hard facts, and Shay, you like the softer, more human-centered pieces."

I don't love the way he says *softer*, as though implying what I like is more feminine.

"Listeners are going to take one side or the other," Kent continues. "Team Dom, or Team Shay. We could get some hashtags going, really capitalize on the social media angle."

"But I'm a reporter," Dominic says. "A damn good one, based on what's happened over the past couple days."

"And I know you can do human interest, too," Kent says. "That piece you wrote in college, that personal narrative? We all read it when you applied here. It was compelling, and it was *beautiful*."

He must be talking about Dominic's most lauded piece, a story about traveling to South Korea and meeting his grandparents for the first time. I didn't cry, like everyone else in the newsroom did, but I kept a box of tissues next to me. Just in case.

"I think we're missing the biggest issue here," I say, too much of a snap to my voice for a conversation with my boss, but I've also never talked to a superior about my dating (or non-dating) life. All of this is surreal. "Dominic and I aren't exes. We've never had any kind of relationship."

Kent waves his hand. "You two are private about your lives at work, which of course I appreciate. And HR does, too. But anyone who's been around you both wouldn't be surprised to hear that you've been dealing with the aftermath of a breakup. Especially after what they saw in the conference room."

"I'm not sure I understand what you're saying."

"We create a relationship," Kent says, as though it's so simple. "We create a breakup. And then we create a show."

Silence. Again.

I can't wrap my mind around it. The pieces are there, but every one of them seems to belong to a different puzzle. Kent wants us to pretend to date—no, to pretend to *have dated*. My boss, Seattle radio legend Kent O'Grady, wants to pretend we had a relationship and then talk about dating on public radio.

Someone wants me to be on the radio.

"So we lie." Dominic folds his arms across his chest. His shirt-sleeves are pushed up again, exposing his lean forearms, and he jerks his head toward Kent's wall of awards. "All of that, and you want us to lie."

"I've got to keep this station afloat," Kent says. "We need a hit show, and we need one fast. No one wants to listen to career hosts anymore. They want fresh blood, and that might be you two." He taps the desk between us. "We don't have the time or the budget to train two new people, or to bring on someone else's ex. You two have the chemistry. And we're all storytellers, aren't we? So we tell the best breakup story. We're not lying—we're bending the truth."

Storytelling. Lying. There's a blurry line between them.

"Picture it: an hour-long weekly show. A podcast. A hashtag. Branded swag, even. We could make this big." Kent has become a salesman. "How incredible would it be to have a show with national appeal attached to the KPPR name? WHYY has *Fresh Air*, WBEZ has *This American Life* . . . we could have whatever this show is."

For a moment, I do allow myself to picture it: sitting in the big studio, a microphone in front of me, callers waiting on the line.

"*The Ex Talk*," I say quietly.

"What was that?" Kent says.

I repeat it, a little more conviction in my voice.

"*The Ex Talk* . . . yes. *Yes.* I like that a lot."

The way he talks about it, this show that was only an idea a few hours ago, feels almost *real*, like something I could reach out and touch. He's clearly spent the day figuring out the best way to spin this. Maybe that's how a program director's mind works, or maybe he really is that desperate for something new.

Kent wants me to lie.

Kent wants me to host a show.

"My voice," I say. The two men turn to me, as though they know exactly what's wrong with my voice, but they're unwilling to acknowledge it unless I explain it. As though it's okay to insult someone if they insult themselves first. "What? You both know what I sound like. Me on the air would be a disaster."

"You're being too hard on yourself," Kent says. "Public radio loves unique voices. Sarah Vowell, Starlee Kine. Shocking, but there are even people who don't like Ira Glass. And you want to be on the air." He says it like he knows the way I gaze longingly at Paloma during *Puget Sounds*.

"Well . . . yes," I say. "But this isn't about what I want." Is it? I'm no longer sure.

This can't be a real conversation. We're not really talking about me on the air—with Dominic of all people, hosting a show based on a relationship we never had. I must have tumbled into an alternate reality yesterday: Ameena's job interview she's positive won't lead to a job, my mother's engagement, my fake relationship and fake breakup with Pacific Public Radio's newest star reporter. Any moment, Carl Kasell will come back to life and record a message for my voice mail.

"I'm sorry, I don't understand," Dominic says, and he looks so upset, so perplexed that I actually feel a little sympathy for him. It's about the size of one of Paloma's chia seeds. "The mayor resigned. We had this massive story, and now—now you want to pull me off news to do a fluff show?

"And you did an incredible job with that piece." Kent sips his tea. "But it was also only one piece, and one piece does not a career make. Being a reporter, that's a lot of pressure. Those investigations are exhausting. You think you can turn out piece after piece like that?"

Dominic plants his elbows on his knees and stares at the floor, a blush creeping onto his cheeks, and there's another new emotion: embarrassment. He wants Kent to believe in him, the way he's grown accustomed to since he started. I'm reminded in that mo-

ment just how young he is. His master's program was only a
year—he could be as young as twenty-three.

Kent offers up a sympathetic smile. "People loved you yesterday, Dominic," he says, and this is what makes Kent a good manager: He knows exactly how to butter us up when he wants
something, even if it means poking at our insecurities first. "And
people would love you, too, Shay. They just have to get to know
you. I didn't want to say this to the whole staff, not yet, but . . ." He
lets out a slow, measured breath. "There are going to be layoffs. It
kills me to say that, it really does."

Layoffs. The force of that word pins me to my chair. He's talking
about new programming when they've already planned on layoffs?

"Shit," Dominic says, and I narrow my eyes at Kent.

"So that meeting was, what, a way for us to fight for our jobs?"
I say. "Without even realizing it?"

"Lucky for you, you may have landed on some job security."

"Lucky," Dominic says under his breath. "Right."

"What about my show?" I ask. The meeting's pie charts flash
through my mind. I already know what he's going to say, and it feels
like he's shoved his desk right into my chest. I didn't realize this
potential new show came at the cost of gutting Paloma's.

"I'm so sorry, Shay. The numbers don't lie. It's the lowest-
performing of all our shows, and we're going to have to cancel it. I
wish I didn't have to do this. The board has been talking about this
for months, and my hands are tied. I was planning to tell you and
Paloma tomorrow."

"What's going to happen to her?"

"She's being offered a very generous severance package," Kent
says. "I hate that we have to do this. I hate the layoffs. Absolutely
hate it—it's the worst part of my job. But it's unavoidable." His face
brightens. "If you two agree to this, I want to do whatever I can to
make you happy. You can pick your producer, in fact."

"Ruthie," I say immediately. "She's the one who came up with the name."

"Perfect. I wasn't looking forward to letting her go—she's a good one. You want Ruthie, she's yours."

Dominic stands, stretching up to his full height. "The board isn't going to sign off on this."

"You let me take care of that," Kent says. "Next Friday. That's when I need an answer, or I'll give you both glowing recommendations and you can start working on your résumés." He gazes settles on Dominic. "Because we have to cut some reporters, too."

Dominic lets out a sharp breath, as though he's been punched. I want to feel sorry for him. I want to feel sorry for Paloma, for everyone who's going to lose their job. And I do, I swear, but—

People would love you, *Shay*, Kent said.

They would *listen*.

To *me*.

"Forget it," Dominic says, his shoulders rigid as he heads to the door. "I'm not doing it."

5

I drag a paintbrush across a canvas, squinting at the photo of an apple orchard and then at my rendition of it. A few red blobs, a few green blobs. Not exactly a masterpiece.

"And then he basically insinuated you'd lose your jobs if don't do the show?" Ameena asks, dipping her brush in forest green.

"Yep. Brutal, right?"

She lets out a low whistle. "More like borderline illegal. I should talk to some of my friends in HR."

We're at Blush 'n Brush, a monthly paint night at a local wine bar. We've been going after work for a while now as a way to relieve stress, though Ameena is much more talented than I am. It may actually be increasing my stress. As a result, I have a handful of mediocre paintings of trees taking up space in my guest room. Who's visiting? Why do I have a guest room? Everyone I know lives in Seattle, but I didn't know what else to do with my house's third bedroom.

"It's not like that," I insist. "He just really cares about the station. But none of it matters, since Dominic said he won't do it." Which means unless he has a change of heart in the next ten days, we're both jobless.

"Shit. I am so sorry."

The reality of the layoffs hasn't sunk in yet. It's only been a couple hours since our meeting with Kent, and I must be clinging to *The Ex Talk* like a life raft. My chance to be on the air, to explore something fresh and exciting and different, is in the hands of someone who has made it clear I'm not his favorite person. And sure, he's never been mine, but I imagine I could tolerate him if it meant hosting my own show.

"I know you," Ameena continues. "You really want this, don't you?"

"I really, really do." I let out a sigh and dip my brush into water before swishing it into light blue paint. A sky—surely I can manage not to fuck that up too badly. It's only when I swipe it across the canvas that I realize it's the same shade as the shirt Dominic wore today. "It's stupid, I know. I've already come up with individual show ideas, and then I started brainstorming a logo on my drive here . . . but it's pointless."

"Hey. It's not stupid." She bites down on her bottom lip. "But speaking hypothetically, you'd be lying, wouldn't you? Isn't that a little . . . anti-journalism?"

I use Kent's rationale: "It's storytelling. We'd be acting, in a sense. Most hosts put on a different personality. No one's exactly the way they are on the radio—so much of that is for show. You create this personality specifically for people to connect with."

"Makes sense when you put it that way, I guess," she says, but she doesn't sound convinced. "So. Dominic. You're at least going to try to persuade him, right?"

"No idea how, but yes."

"What is it about him that you dislike so much?"

I groan, both at her question and at how I've somehow turned the sky in my painting into a muddy brown mess. "He thinks he knows everything about radio, he waves his master's degree around like it makes him some authority on journalism, and the idea of cohosting with him, being on equal footing . . . well, at least it's better than him thinking I'm beneath him."

"Is he cute?"

"What?" I choke on my pinot. "What does that have to do with anything?"

Ameena shrugs and glances away, feigning disinterest. "Nothing, really. I'm just curious."

"I mean—objectively—he's not *bad*-looking," I manage to get out, trying not to think about his forearms or his height but instead about the way it feels when he has to crane his neck to look down at me. Could I really deal with that five days a week?

A slight smile curves her lips as she sips her glass of rosé.

"Shut up," I tell her.

"I didn't say a word."

The instructor walks by our row and gushes over Ameena's painting.

"Beautiful work as usual, Ameena," she says. She turns to me and her smile tightens. "It's coming along. You're really improving."

Ameena beams. I roll my eyes.

"Here's the weirdest part to me," Ameena says. "Are you sure you'd be okay with the idea of talking about your past relationships on the radio? Airing all that dirty laundry?"

I consider this. "I guess I'd have to be. My laundry isn't that dirty, is it? There hasn't been anyone serious since Trent."

Trent: a developer with kind eyes and prematurely gray hair I went out with for three months at the beginning of last year. He was a regular pledge drive supporter, which was what made me swipe right. On our first date, he told me how badly he wanted a family. We spent every weekend together, and I got attached fast. We went to farmers' markets and state parks and very serious plays.

I liked how he held me in bed, how he buried his face into the nape of my neck and told me how much he liked waking up next to me. I assumed love was the next step after like, but when I blurted it out on our way to meet my mother for brunch one Sunday, he nearly veered off the road.

"I don't know if I'm there yet," he said.

We were listening to *Wait Wait . . . Don't Tell Me!* and having our own contest, tallying up points based on getting the correct answers before the panelists did. I shut it off immediately, not wanting this experience to ruin the show for me.

We could still have a good time, he insisted. It wouldn't make things weird, knowing I loved him and he didn't. But he broke it off that night, after the most uncomfortable eggs Benedict of my life.

I've always been staunchly anti-brunch, and Trent confirmed that stance.

People say they want something serious, but as soon as it starts heading that way, they bolt. Either they're lying, or they realize they don't want something serious with *me*. Hence my hiatus. It doesn't stop me from wanting to get married someday. It's just that the "someday" sounded much further away when I was twenty-four versus twenty-nine.

"I've offered to clone TJ," Ameena says with a shrug. "Not my fault the technology isn't advanced enough yet."

I add more red to my tree. It looks gravely wounded, yikes. I'll have nightmares if I put this up in my house. "Honestly, my biggest worry, more than Dominic or the content, is my voice."

"Shay," Ameena says gently, because she knows my history with it. I even used to beg her to make important phone calls for me.

"Seriously, Ameena. Who wants Kristen Schaal when they could have, like, Emily Blunt?"

"I like a unique voice. Most of the old white NPR dudes sound the same to me. And I hate the sound of my voice, too. Voice mail is the worst."

"It's not just a voice mail. It would be an hour every week. And a podcast, too."

"What would a mediocre white man do?" she asks.

Ameena and I started saying this years ago, after she had a seminar about diversity in the workplace. Ameena is Indian, and she relayed that women, especially women of color, are statistically less likely to ask for things men don't think twice about. *WWAMWMD*, one of us will text the other when we need support.

"A mediocre white man would probably have a perfect radio voice," I say. "Enough about me. What's going on with that conservancy job?"

Ameena tries to look nonchalant. "They moved me forward. I have a second phone interview next week."

I let out a squeal. "Congratulations!"

"Thank you," she says, and then forces a laugh. "Still convinced they're throwing me a bone here, but I have to admit, it was a nice ego boost."

"And you really feel like leaving Seattle?"

"I like Seattle," she says after a brief hesitation, "but I might be ready for a change."

Ready for a change. Ameena might get that job, and my mother is getting remarried, and my show is disappearing at the end of next week. A change as dramatic as leaving PPR—I'm positive I'm not ready for that.

"Apparently my mom is, too."

"How . . . are you feeling about that?"

It's been twenty-four hours, and they've already set a date: July 14. It'll be mostly family, though my mother's family consists of me and by extension Ameena and TJ, while Phil has his kids and their spouses and their kids. I suppose they'll be my family soon enough.

"That's a great question," I say. "It feels so sudden, I guess."

"Maybe, but they're in their late fifties. There's no point in waiting."

"You'll be there with me, right? Even if"—my voice catches—"even if you have to come from Virginia?"

Ameena swipes my nose with the tip of her paintbrush. "Of course. I wouldn't miss it."

Home: lights on, podcast loud. I check each room, making sure I'm alone. It's not that I'm worried someone broke in and is hiding behind a door, waiting to murder me, it's just—well, there's no harm in knowing for sure.

This is normal. Everyone who lives alone must do this.

Once I've determined my home is murderer-free, I settle into the rest of my evening: pajamas, laptop, couch. I have a home office, but I prefer the living room. The TV makes the room feel a bit less lonely, even when it's not on. I'll probably spend some time with my newest vibrator later, if only because the conversation with Ameena made me realize it's been nearly a year since I've had sex. Going solo isn't quite the same, but I have a routine. Lord knows I've had enough time to perfect one.

It's when I unzip my laptop from my work bag that it hits me—by the end of next week, I may not have a job to overwork myself with.

Instead of opening my work email, I log on to my bank account. I have enough in savings to last me a few months, and I imagine I'd collect unemployment. However that works—I'm not entirely sure.

It feels like something I should know, but I've only ever had this one job. Does the government just . . . give you money? God, I am a disaster millennial. I pull up the *Puget Sounds* archives, convinced we did a show about this at some point, but our search function is painfully outdated, and I grow frustrated with it before finding the information I'm looking for.

My next stop is the public media jobs board some of my PPR colleagues have talked about. There's a producer job in Alaska. A reporter job in Colorado. A managing editor job in St. Louis.

Nothing in the entire state of Washington.

I knew jobs in public radio were hard to come by, but I didn't realize it was quite this bad. I press a hand to my chest, trying to calm my increasingly panicky breaths. If I'm not in public radio, I have no idea what I'd be doing. This is all I know, all I've ever known. And sure, some of those skills are transferable, but I'm not ready to leave this field. I love radio too much to let it go.

I have to convince Dominic to do this show with me. And in order to convince him, I'd have to know him, which I do not. Luckily, being a producer has made me great at social media stalking research.

His Facebook profile is public. Bless this generation and our lack of boundaries. Only—shit, am I in a different generation from Dominic? There's no birth year on his profile, but he went directly from undergrad to grad school. That puts him at twenty-three or twenty-four. I'm solidly a millennial, but he falls in two generations: mine and Gen Z.

Strangely, we don't have any mutual friends, which means he must not have added anyone at the station yet. I click through his photos. Here he is, my potential ex-boyfriend, with unfortunate haircuts and teenage acne and posing for awkward family photos. His face looks softer here, though there's that sharp cut of his jaw. I've been so focused on being annoyed by him that I haven't really registered that he *is* cute. Especially once he passed the unfortunate-haircut stage. Somewhere, a barber should be fired.

I could have dated a guy like this, I muse, lingering on a photo of him giving a presentation in front of a class, his arms stretched out in some kind of emphatic gesture. The photo was uploaded by someone else, with the caption *Typical Dominic Yun presentation: please keep your arms and legs inside the vehicle.* I smile at that. Must be an inside joke.

I've never dated a younger guy; all my boyfriends have been my age or slightly older. And even though we wouldn't actually *be* dating, I can't deny there's a bit of a thrill there, buried beneath the generational angst.

I keep scrolling, landing on a series of photos—a *lot* of photos—of Dominic with a redheaded girl, some of them as recent as this past June, at his Northwestern graduation. *Mia Dabrowski* says the photo tag. She's extremely cute, a spray of freckles across her nose, a penchant for bright colors. I watch them age backward. There's the two of them at a party, at the beach, on someone's boat. Most of the time, they're surrounded by a group of friends, but sometimes they're on their own, pressing their cheeks together and mugging for the camera. Then they're at their undergrad graduation in matching gowns. They're adorable together. I click on her, but her profile is private.

His relationship status is single, so it must have been a somewhat recent breakup, I deduce. I wonder if it has anything to do with Dominic's reluctance to do the show or with his move to Seattle. I really do know next to nothing about this guy, and I'm overcome with an unfamiliar pang: I *want* to know him. I want to know this guy who had a full life back in Illinois, who not just smiled but beamed in all his photos, and yet hasn't Facebook-friended any of his coworkers.

Does he have friends at PPR? I don't know if I've ever seen him grab drinks with anyone after work. Jason had lunch with him once in his first couple weeks, but then he was put on afternoons. I've only ever seen Dominic leave the station in one way: alone.

I'm scrolling back to the beginning of his photos when tragedy strikes.

My hand slips on my laptop, and I accidentally hit the like button. On a really old photo of him and his ex-girlfriend.

The only rational solution is to set myself and my laptop on fire.

"Shit," I say out loud, tossing the laptop onto the couch cushion. "Shit, shit, shit!"

I leap to my feet and shake out my traitorous hands. He's going to know that I was stalking him. And it might bring up weird feelings about this ex, and then he'll never want to cohost with me, and fuck, *fuck*, how could I have been so fucking stupid?

Deep breaths. I'll just unlike it. He'll never even get a notification. I pick up my laptop, realizing that in my panic, I closed out of the window. So I have to find his page again and scroll through his photos, only I can't remember how far back this particular photo was, and—

A new notification pops up:

1 new friend request: Dominic Yun

6

Over the next week, desks empty out. Arts reporter Jess Jorgensen, who was hired right before Dominic, leaves on Thursday, followed by weekend announcer Bryan Finch. Kent breaks the news to Paloma, Ruthie, and Griffin on Monday, and I pretend I'm hearing it for the first time.

The newsroom is typically a chatty place, but the layoffs have turned us quiet. No one knows how many people are being let go, and we're all on edge. I've never seen the station like this. I don't like it.

Kent's deadline looms closer. Whenever I try to catch Dominic, he's on his way into a sound booth or out to meet a source, a recording gear bag slanted across his body. I'm even more aware now that he's always, always alone when he leaves work. He doesn't grab lunch with anyone. No after-work happy hours. Despite the praise his fellow reporters heaped on him, he is a lone wolf, and I'm not sure whether it's by choice. The station is a slightly older crowd, and I was the youngest for so long that my only choice was to make friends with people who had kids close to my age. Then Ruthie started, and I couldn't believe I was older than she was.

By Wednesday, I'm stress-eating chia seeds by the handful, and those things are not cheap. I can't lose this job. Not when I'm so close to being on the air.

I manage to finally corner him after that day's show, during which Paloma interviewed a university professor about dream psychology. It's another popular segment, with listeners calling in to get their dreams analyzed. Though apparently it's not popular enough to keep us on the air. It's a testament to Paloma's professionalism that she's able to remain composed, though she made the announcement to our listeners early in the week that we'd be off the air soon. I expected an outpouring of support from the community, emails upon emails begging us not to go.

We got one. And they spelled Paloma's name wrong.

"We need to talk," I say to Dominic, who's in the break room microwaving a Hot Pocket. Collegiate eating habits die hard, I guess.

"Are you breaking up with me?"

"Ha, ha," I say. "How do you feel about that Korean place down the street?" I saw him and Kent go there for lunch last month. At the time, I'd been jealous. It had taken me years to get a one-on-one lunch invite. Fine, I'm still jealous.

The microwave beeps, and he pops it open. "I recommend it. I hope you enjoy."

"Have dinner with me?" I plead, aware it sounds like I'm asking him out. "My treat. Please. You don't have to commit to anything right now. I just want to have a conversation."

As much as it pains me to beg him for something, I'd get down on my knees in front of him if I had to. But Kent wasn't wrong: The two of us on the air could be really great radio. With my producing background and his reporting background, plus Ruthie behind the scenes, this show could be much better than *Puget Sounds* ever was.

It could be *mine*.

A few different emotions seem to pass over his face, as though he's fighting a mental battle. "Six fifteen. Right after work," he says at last.

"Thank you, thank you," I say, relieved I don't have to quite resort to groveling. I hold my hands out in a prayer position anyway. "Thank you."

He gives me a brusque nod, then slides the Hot Pocket onto a plate before making a move to leave the break room. For once, I'm blocking his way, even though I only come up to his collarbone. He could mow me down if he wanted to, knock me out of the way with his hips. Or maybe he'd push me to the side. Flatten me against the wall.

I inhale, and there's that ocean-sage scent again.

"If you'll excuse me," he says, "I'm going to take this back to my desk and finish my story. It might be my last one here."

Dominic gets there before I do, only because I linger in the bathroom on our floor, not wanting to increase the awkwardness by riding the elevator down together. I reapply lipstick and run my fingers through my thick bangs. I wore my favorite outfit on purpose: tan ankle boots, black jeans, vintage houndstooth blazer. I don't usually go for a bold red lip, but desperate times and all that.

With the exception of the holiday party, I've never seen him outside of work. They called it a holiday party even though it was essentially a Christmas party, complete with red-and-green decorations and a tree and a Secret Santa. I drew my own name, didn't tell anyone, and bought myself an electric menorah. Dominic had looked slightly less stiff than usual, in black pants and a hunter-green sweater. I only remember what he wore because when we were in line for the buffet, I had the strangest urge to reach out and touch his sweater, to see how soft it was.

He's wearing the same sweater today over a checkered button-down, and it still looks soft.

The restaurant is a hole-in-the-wall in the basement of an old house. When I'm trying to find it, I walk past the entrance twice by accident.

"Let's get this over with," he says when I sit down across from him. "Make your case."

"Jesus, can we at least order first?" I open the menu. "What's good here?"

"Everything."

The place is small, and there's only one other table occupied by two businessmen chatting with the waitress in Korean. The kitchen is a few feet away and smells incredible.

"I've never had Korean food," I admit.

"And you've lived in Seattle for how many years?"

"My whole life."

He lifts his eyebrows expectantly, as though waiting for me to elaborate on how many years "my whole life" has spanned.

"I'm twenty-nine," I say with a roll of my eyes. "We should probably know each other's ages if we're going to think about doing this."

"We're not doing anything."

"Then why are you here?"

The free dinner, he could say. But he doesn't. He's quiet for a moment, and then: "Twenty-four."

A tiny victory.

He opens his menu, too. "Bulgogi. Korean barbecue beef," he says, pointing to a row of menu items. "White people usually love it. No offense."

"Why would I be offended? I'm white."

"Some white people get weird when you point out they are, in fact, white. Like even talking about their own race makes them uncomfortable."

"I guess most of us don't really think about being white?"

He gives me a wry smile. "That's exactly it."

Oh. "Well. I don't feel weird about getting the white people thing, if that's what you recommend."

In the end, that's what I do, and he says I can try his bibimbap. It's strange, this offer, and even stranger is the reality that I am having dinner with Dominic Yun. This is the longest conversation we've had about something other than radio. I'm not sure what it says about us that it's easier to talk about race than about the jobs we supposedly love so much.

When the waitress leaves, we fall into silence, and I begin shredding a napkin. It's unnerving to be this close to him without any screens or microphones nearby. He is, like I confessed to Ameena, not bad-looking. Obviously I've been in the presence of attractive men at work before.

But Dominic Yun's level of attractiveness is a little intimidating. Under different circumstances, I'd have swiped right on him, and then probably fallen too hard before he unceremoniously dumped me. Maybe that's why it was so easy to argue with him. I didn't have to worry about wanting him to like me; I already knew he didn't.

Thank god his forearms are covered.

"I realize," I start, tearing off a particularly satisfying piece of napkin, "that you're under the impression that it's the news or nothing. But come on. You have to find some enjoyment in radio beyond the cold hard facts. You have to listen to podcasts, right? There are only about five million of them."

"You brought me here to educate me about podcasts?"

"I'm sure you could find one that suits your interests. *Life After*

Grad School, maybe? Or is there something for people whose idea of a well-balanced meal is a pepperoni pizza Hot Pocket?"

A corner of his mouth quirks up. The barest hint of a dimple. "You really don't know much about me. I guess that would explain the Facebook stalking."

"That was—research," I insist.

"I listen to podcasts," he says finally. "There's a great one about the US judicial system that—"

I groan. "Dominic. You are killing me."

He's full-on grinning now. "You make it absurdly easy." He stretches out his long legs beneath the table, and I wonder if he always has that problem: tables so small they can't contain him.

WWAMWMD, I think, summoning power from mediocre white men everywhere.

"I want this," I tell him. "Look, it's not how I wanted it to happen, either. I've wanted to be on the radio for as long as I've known NPR existed. And *The Ex Talk*, maybe it's not your ideal show. But it would open so many doors. We'd be breaking new ground in public radio, and trust me, public radio doesn't break new ground every day. This is an incredible opportunity."

"How do I know you're not just trying to save your job?"

"Because you're out of a job soon, too, same as me."

He crosses his arms. "Maybe I've gotten other offers."

I narrow my eyes at him. "Have you?"

We stay locked like that for a moment, until he blows out a breath, giving in. "No. I moved here to work in public radio. Or moved back, I should say. I grew up here, over in Bellevue."

"I didn't know that," I say. "So did I, but I was a city kid."

"I would have been high-key jealous of you," he says. "I wasn't allowed to drive on the freeway until I was eighteen."

I snort. "Poor little suburban boy." But I'm surprised by how naturally our conversation is flowing.

"Everyone else in my program, they were getting hired for digital journalism, or to run small-town newspapers that'll fold in a few years," Dominic continues. "I didn't land here by accident. I went to grad school because, well—" He breaks off, scratches behind his neck like he's embarrassed by what he's about to say. "You're going to think this is ridiculous, but you know what I've always wanted to do?"

"Jobs as a Hot Pockets spokesman might be scarce, but you shouldn't let that hold you back."

He picks up one of my napkin scraps and flings it back at me. "I want to use journalism to fix shit. That's why I want to be involved in investigations. I want to take down corporations that are fucking up people's lives, and I want bigots out of power."

"That's not ridiculous," I say, serious. I don't know why he'd be ashamed of something that noble.

"It's like saying you want to make the world a better place."

"Don't we all? We just have different ways of getting there," I say. "Why radio, though?"

"I like the idea of being able to talk directly to people. There's a real power to your words when they're not backed up by visuals. It's personal. You're fully in control of how you sound, and it's almost like you're telling a story to just one person."

"Even if hundreds or thousands are listening," I say quietly. "Yeah. I get that. I really do. I guess I assumed you got lucky with this job."

The dimple threatens to make a reappearance. "Well, I did. But I'm also fucking good at what I do."

I think about him on the radio with Paloma, about the narrative he wrote in college. About all the stories on our website that people really do seem to love.

He *is* good.

Maybe that's what I've hated the most.

"I didn't realize you wanted to be on the radio," he continues. "I assumed you were happy, you know. Producing. That's what you've always done here, right?"

I nod. Time to get personal. I had a feeling this was coming, that I'd be spilling my radio history to him, but that doesn't make it any easier. It doesn't ever really get easier. "My dad and I listened to NPR all the time when I was growing up. We would pretend we were on the radio, and it was honestly the best part of my childhood. I loved how radio could tell such a complete, immersive story. But it's competitive, and I was lucky enough to get an internship at PPR, which turned into a full-time job . . . and here I am."

"So you want your dad to hear you on the radio."

"Well—he can't," I say after a pause, unable to meet his eyes.

"Oh." He stares down at the table. "Shit. I'm so sorry. I didn't know."

"It was ten years ago," I say, but that doesn't mean I still don't think about him every day, about how he sometimes personified the electronics he fixed, mostly to make me laugh as a kid, but even as I got older, I never got sick of it. *It's a risky surgery*, he'd say about an ancient iPhone. *She might not make it through the night.*

I'm grateful when our food arrives, sizzling and steaming and looking delicious. Dominic thanks the waitress in Korean, and she dips her head before walking away.

"I asked her for another napkin," he says, gesturing to the confetti remains of mine.

"God, it's good," I say after the first bite.

"Try some of this." Dominic spoons some of his rice dish onto my plate.

We eat in appreciative silence for a few minutes.

"So. *The Ex Talk*," I say, summoning the courage to talk about why we're both here. "What's holding you back? Is it . . . is it me? The idea of dating me?"

His eyes widen, and he drops his spoon. "No. Not at all. Oh god—I'm not, like, *insulted* by the idea that you and I could have dated. Mildly shocked, yes, but not insulted. You're . . ." At that, his eyes scan my face and travel down my torso. His cheeks redden. It gives me a bit of a rush, knowing he's very obviously assessing me.

You're a catch. You're a ten. I wait for a compliment from this person who's only ever been vile to me.

He clears his throat. "Cool," he finally says.

Excuse me while I walk right into downtown rush-hour traffic. *Cool* is the Kevin Jonas of compliments. It's like saying your favorite color is beige.

"And you?" he asks. "Not too horrified by the idea that we dated, in this alternate reality?"

I shake my head. "And you're not dating anyone right now."

"Not since I moved here, no. Which I assume you know after your late-night stalking session."

I cover my face with my hands. "Would you believe me if I told you I dropped my glasses onto my laptop and they happened to hit that like button?"

"Not one bit."

"So it's that the show isn't news."

He nods. "I went to school for journalism—"

"Wait, *what*?" I ask, and he rolls his eyes.

"—and that's where I want to be. It's killing me that the mayor story will be passed along, that I won't be able to follow up on it." He polishes off the last bite of his food. "Not to mention, I can't even picture what this show would sound like. I wouldn't know where to start with it. Like you said, most of the podcasts I listen to are . . ."

"Boring?" I supply. "Lucky for you, I am a connoisseur of fun podcasts. I'll email you a list." I'm already mentally compiling one. I'll have him listen to *Not Another Star Wars Podcast* and *Culture Clash* and *Femme*, to start. All of them have great cohost banter.

"Can't wait."

"Maybe this show isn't typical public radio," I continue. "But it's the edge we need. If we do a good job with it, you can do anything in radio that you want. Hosts are at the top of the food chain. It's no small thing that Kent offered this to you. It's a big fucking deal."

"You don't think he was a little . . . manipulative?"

Ameena essentially said the same thing.

"That's just Kent. He knows what he wants. And he clearly loves you." I hope he doesn't catch the jealousy in my voice. "This is different from anything public radio has ever done. Sure, the national desk has done stories, sometimes series, about dating and relationships, and same with member stations. But there's never really been an entire show dedicated to them. Isn't it exciting, to think you could be part of that?" He shrugs, so I keep going. "I've been behind the scenes for so long that I want to see, I guess, if I can be more than that."

My confession sits heavy between us.

"I had no idea you felt that way," he says quietly.

"It's not something I tend to broadcast very often." I start ripping apart napkin number two. "But if you don't think you can do it . . ."

He leans forward across the table, his eyes flickering with an emotion I can't name. "Oh, I could definitely do it."

I force myself to match the intensity of his gaze. It feels like a challenge, and I don't want him to think I'm backing down. I hope I don't have lipstick on my chin. I hope he doesn't think I'm too old for him, at least in the hypothetical sense. I hope he realizes exactly how much I want this.

And that means wanting him, too.

"Three months," he says finally.

"Six."

"Shay—"

I hold up a hand, trying to ignore how much I like the way he said my name. It rumbled in his throat, sending an electric spark from my toes to some places that haven't gotten much attention lately. I wonder if it's how he says a woman's name in bed. A growl. A plea.

Jesus Christ, I'm thinking about Dominic *in bed* with someone. I am not well. If I'm turned on simply by the sound of his voice, we're going to have serious problems.

"Three months isn't long enough to build a devoted audience," I say. "Six months, enough for me to get the hosting experience I need, enough to elevate your name to the point where you can move on to something else when we're done."

"And if we're caught?"

"I'm not snitching. Are you?"

His jaw tightens, and I can tell he's thinking. "Fine," he says, and though that word makes my heart soar, what I really want is for him to say my name again.

"Thank you!" I leap up from the table, and it's only when I'm standing that I realize I'm not sure what I was going to do. Did I think I was going to hug him? "Thank you, thank you, thank you. You won't regret this. I promise. This show is going to be fucking amazing."

He's watching me with an expression of clear amusement. Instead of going in for a hug, I stick out my hand.

"I'm going to hold you to that." His hand is large, slender fingers fitting between mine and warming my skin. "It was a pleasure breaking up with you."

7

"His name is Steve," says the Seattle Humane Society volunteer when we stop in front of the last cage at the end of the row. "But I don't know if he'd be a great fit for you."

"Why not?" A tan Chihuahua mix sits in the far corner on a gray fleece blanket, watching me with big brown eyes. He has giant ears and a small black nose and an underbite. He is the cutest thing I've ever seen.

Initially, I hadn't given it much thought when Ameena suggested getting a dog. But my house has felt eerier than usual lately, and having a little animal waiting for me at the end of the day might be exactly what I need. Aside from a pair of guinea pigs Ameena and I had right out of college, I've never had a pet of my own. We had a dog named Prince when I was a kid, though I don't remember him much. My parents had him before I was born, and I was nine when he passed away. Still, I am a perpetual asker of "Can I pet your dog?"

Flora, the volunteer, *hmms* under her breath. "He . . . has a lot going on. We think he's about four years old, but we're not sure. He was found on the streets in Northern California, and he was brought up here to have a better chance of getting adopted. He was actually adopted at the end of the year, but he wasn't a good fit for the family. They had three young kids, and he's not aggressive, per se, but he can get a little territorial."

"Aren't we all?" I ask, forcing a laugh.

Flora doesn't return it. "We've had him here almost three months now, and we've had a lot of trouble placing him. We think he'd be better off as the only pet with an experienced owner. No kids."

Three months. Three months of this constant yapping and no human to cuddle up with. Three months of loneliness. I can't even imagine what it's like at night here, after all the volunteers go home.

"I don't have any pets or kids," I say.

"But you've never had a dog, right?"

I did mention that when I walked in. But after walking up and down the rows, I can't imagine going home with any of these dogs— except Steve.

"I had one growing up," I say, standing taller and trying my best to appear like a responsible dog owner, someone who can handle a supposedly "difficult" dog like Steve. He can't weigh more than ten pounds. "And I have a friend who's a trainer." Sort of. Mary Beth Barkley was sad to hear about *Puget Sounds* ending, and I promised I'd do my best to get her booked on another show.

"Well then," Flora says, "let's see how he does with you."

She unlocks the crate and bends to take him out, but he backs up into the corner. She has to get into the crate on her hands and knees and bring him out, and when she does, he's shaking. I can't imagine a creature that small being a problem dog.

"I'm right out there if you need anything," Flora says after leading us to a room filled with treats and toys. And she shuts the door, leaving Steve and me alone.

I crouch down. Steve sniffs the air tentatively.

"Hey, little guy," I say, holding out my hand, letting him know I'm safe. "It's okay."

He inches closer, his tan body still trembling. His underbite makes all his actions seem uncertain. Once he's within licking distance, his pink tongue darts out and gives my fingers a swipe.

"See, I'm not so bad, right?"

He comes even closer, letting me stroke his back. He's much softer than he looks, and his paws are white, like he's wearing tiny boots. I scratch behind his ears until his eyes half close and he drops his head to my knee like this is the best thing he's ever felt in his life.

Apparently I am doomed to fall quickly with dogs, too—because just like that, I am in love.

I sign the paperwork with Steve in my lap. I decide his full name is Steve Rogers. Steve Rogers Goldstein. A very traditional Jewish name. Flora gives me a leash and a collar and some information about local vets and obedience classes. I don't want to set him down, even when I have to take out my wallet to pay the $200 adoption fee.

Flora is overjoyed but hesitant. "The dogs are usually shyer here at the shelter," she says. "So don't be surprised if his personality changes a bit when you get home."

"Is the underbite anything I should be worried about?"

"He's perfectly healthy. It's just a little quirk."

"I love it," I say, and I turn to him. "I love you and your underbite."

They tell me I have two weeks to bring him back for a full refund if it doesn't work out. A full refund. For an animal. It feels cruel, like they're almost expecting me to bring him back.

On our drive home, Steve vomits in the car carrier. When we get inside, he vomits again on a rug I never really liked, pees on my coffee table, and poops on the living room carpet. If my house felt empty before, now it's teeming with chaotic energy. I set up his bed in my room, and he humps it for a solid forty-five minutes before turning around in a circle four and a half times and curling himself into a tight ball. When I try to get near him, he growls, baring his underbite.

Steve, it turns out, is kind of a hot mess.

"I am not taking you back," I say adamantly, more to myself than to him. "We are going to make this work."

I clean up the house, then chase him around for fifteen minutes before I manage to hook the leash onto his collar. But when I take him outside, he stands frozen in my driveway like he's never seen the outside world before.

It's nearly six o'clock, after he runs about a dozen laps around my yard, when he finally tires himself out and returns to his bed. He already knows it's his, which I decide to consider a win. Once I'm certain he's asleep, I take a photo and send it to Ameena. He starts making these little dreaming sounds, and I nearly die of cute.

Because I can't stare at my dog all evening, I head to the kitchen to make dinner and call my mother, which I've been putting off since Dominic and I agreed to do the show a few days ago. And maybe this is one benefit of a small family: I only have to awkwardly lie to one person about my fake ex-boyfriend.

As much as I want to be honest with her, we both know how much my dad valued truth in radio. The idea of my mother calling me out, telling me my dad would be disappointed . . . I can't go down that road. I have to stay in this place where imagining him hearing me through his car speakers would make him happier than I'd ever seen him. That means keeping the truth from her.

And I'm not sure I could handle the judgment if she knew I'll be lying to my future listeners, too. No—not lying. Bending the truth. That's what Kent said.

Besides, I can't help thinking that if I can prove myself on this show, then maybe one day I'll be part of something that doesn't bend the truth nearly as much. That once I have this hosting experience, the career I always wanted will finally be within reach. Or, since it's radio, within earshot.

"I was dating this guy and it didn't work out and we're going to be doing a radio show about it," I say in one breath when she asks how work is going.

There's a pause on the other end of the line. "A radio show about . . . what, exactly?"

I explain *The Ex Talk* to her on Bluetooth while unpacking one of this week's meal kits. A white bean and sweet potato chili on a bed of couscous. Opening this box of ingredients is the most exciting part of my week. Love being single. Love it.

"You never mentioned him," my mother says. "Dominic, you said? Isn't that the guy you're always complaining about?"

"The complaining, uh, may have been a side effect of our breakup." The lie slips out so easily, and she buys it.

"I'm sorry, Shay. But it must be okay if you're willing to do a show with him, right? It sounds like it could be a lot of fun."

"Right," I say through gritted teeth as I chop garlic, ginger, and a jalapeño. This will get easier, right? It has to. *It's for my career*, I remind myself. It's not forever.

I change the subject, asking her how wedding planning is going.

"You'll come dress shopping with me," she says, not even phrasing it like a question.

"You want me to?"

"Of course I do! I know it's a little unconventional, picking out a wedding dress for your mom, but it wouldn't feel right without you there."

Which of course makes me feel even worse about bending the truth.

"I can't wait to hear you on the radio," she says, and maybe we both decide not to say what I'm sure we're both thinking: that my dad would have been beside himself with joy.

"Oh," I say before we hang up. "And I got a dog."

Later, after I've portioned the chili leftovers to take to lunch this week, I get to my room and find Steve curled up on my bed.

"Steve, *no.*"

I am not sacrificing my bed to a seven-pound dog. *WWAMWMD*, I think, though surely this advice doesn't apply to anxious Chihuahuas.

When I inch closer to the bed, he growls.

So I change into pajamas and pad down the hall to the guest room, moving Blush 'n Brush paintings off the bed so I can slip inside. The sheets are scratchy and a lamp throws eerie shadows on the walls, making me feel like a guest in my own house.

There's probably a metaphor here.

Steve wakes me up at five in the morning by pawing at the guest room bed. I maybe should have splurged on a better mattress for all my "guests." My neck aches and my back is all twisted. I've never felt the signs of aging sneak up on me like right now. He left a couple presents in my bed, so I heave everything off and into the washing machine. When we go outside, he's slightly better on the leash, except then he doesn't want to come inside. By the time I get into the shower, I only have a few minutes left to dry my hair.

"I'll be back to walk you around lunch," I tell Steve before I shut the door. "Please be good."

So really, I'm in fine spirits by the time I get to work for our last day on the show.

"Is that cereal in your hair?" Ruthie asks as I drop my bag beneath my desk.

I pull it out, examining it before flicking it into a nearby trash can. "It's dog food. Lovely. I, um, adopted a dog yesterday."

Her eyes light up. "You did? We should have a doggie playdate! Joan Jett loves making friends." Photos of Joan Jett the goldendoodle cover Ruthie's desk.

Given Steve's current emotional state, I tell her it might be a while before he's ready for a playdate.

"Hi, team," Paloma says during our morning meeting. She got an offer to host a jazz show on a commercial station, and she insists she's excited about this new direction of her career. I want to believe her. "Well. Today's the day. We had a good run, I think. Eleven years? Most shows never get close to that long."

"You've been phenomenal," Ruthie says. "We were all lucky to learn from you."

Paloma smiles, but I can tell there's some pain there. "Thank you, Ruthie. I was ready to come in here and make a grand speech, but I think all I can do at this point is thank all of you for being so wonderful to work with. You're as much a part of this show as I am." With that, she sniffs, as though holding back tears. "Ready for our last rodeo?"

Paloma, Ruthie, and I designed this show to be something of a retrospective. We spent hours finding clips of Paloma's best shows, the funniest moments and most heart-tugging ones. The driveway moments—the ones where you can't bear to go inside until you finish the story.

On Monday, Dominic and I will take the next steps forward in planning *The Ex Talk*. The real work will begin. But today, I am still a producer, and this is still my show.

An hour has never gone by so quickly. Toward the end, our coworkers crowd into the studio with champagne. Ten minutes left, and then five minutes left, and then Paloma takes the mic for her farewell.

"To the listeners who've been with us since the beginning, and to the listeners who maybe only recently discovered us, thank you for your support all these years. Starting next week, you'll be able to hear me on 610 AM Jumpin' Jazz radio. And our senior producer Shay Goldstein has a new show, so keep your ear out for that." She catches my eye through the glass, and I hold a hand to my heart, mouthing a silent *thank-you*.

Then it's time for her final sign-off:

"And that's a wrap on *Puget Sounds*. I've been Paloma Powers, and you're listening to Pacific Public Radio."

Over to Jason for the time and the weather, and we're officially off the air.

The studio erupts into applause, and on the other side of the glass, Paloma wipes away a tear.

We're done. *Puget Sounds* has been my entire public radio career, and now it's over.

An ending, and soon, a new beginning.

Our coworkers rush her studio, trading hugs and reminiscing, I'm sure. I can't hear any of it, and I'm not certain I should be part of it. Paloma's leaving. I'm staying. In a few days, I'll feel better, but right now, it's bittersweet.

Dominic's waiting in the hall, leaning in the doorway of the break room. My brain's so weird that I can't even appreciate his forearms today. He tips his thermos of coffee at me as I head back to my desk.

"Good show," he says, and he must be ill because I think he means it.

8

It's late the next Wednesday evening after work that Dominic and I craft both our relationship and our breakup.

In preparation for tonight, I printed a bunch of "how well do you know your significant other?" quizzes and borrowed a couple board games from Ameena and TJ. Everyone's left for the day, with the exception of the evening announcer running NPR content with occasional breaks for the weather. (Partly cloudy. It is always partly cloudy.) The only lights in the newsroom are the few directly above our heads, and it's already dark outside.

Dominic and I spent all of Monday and most of Tuesday in meetings with Kent and the station's board of directors. All public radio stations have them to handle ethics and finances, and they own the station's license. To them, our relationship was real—Kent's the only one who knows the truth. Earlier today, Kent announced the show to the rest of the station. And exactly as he'd predicted, they ate it up.

"I thought there was something going on between them!" Marlene Harrison-Yates said. "They were always either nonstop bickering or going out of their way to avoid each other."

"No wonder Dominic was so opposed to the show during that brainstorm," Isabel Fernandez said with a knowing smile. I tried to smile back.

I haven't finished mourning *Puget Sounds*, but I can't let myself get stuck thinking about it. *The Ex Talk* launches at the end of March as a weekly Thursday show, giving us a few weeks to create content and solidify our backstory. Our lie isn't hurting anyone. That's what I keep telling myself.

"Let's start with the basics," I say, turning my desk chair to face him and flipping open a notepad. "How did we start dating?"

Dominic leans against the desk across from mine, tossing a rubber Koosh ball into the air. The newsroom has been shuffled around so that our desks are next to each other. Where mine is organized chaos, his desk is wiped clean, with the exception of a pair of headphones on one side. I've never seen a desk that spotless.

"You heard my irresistible radio voice," he says drolly, catching the ball. After-Hours Dominic is only slightly less stiff than Eight-to-Five Dominic. His jeans are the darkest blue, his shirt a gray plaid with one and a half buttons undone. That second one is fighting with all its might to stay buttoned, but every time Dominic moves, it slips a little more.

"Are you going to do that all the time?" I ask, pointing at the Koosh.

He throws the ball and catches it again. "It relaxes me."

"You're not going to take notes?"

"I have an excellent memory."

I give him a hard look. He rolls his eyes, but he drops the ball onto his desk, slides into his chair, and opens a Word document.

"Thank you."

"I listened to your podcasts, by the way," he says. "I liked *Culture Clash*."

"Yeah?" Maybe I should give him more credit. I didn't think

he'd actually do it, but I guess he was committed to the research. "Which episode did you listen to?"

He levels me with a stare. "All of them."

"You . . . what?" I wasn't expecting that. "*All* of them? There must be more than fifty episodes!"

"Fifty-seven." His expression turns sheepish. "I had some time."

"Huh. Guess so."

I scrutinize him as a strange feeling works its way through me. It's not quite pride, though it's validating that Dominic agrees *Culture Clash* is good. I think I might be touched.

Dominic gestures to his computer screen. "Can we at least acknowledge how ridiculous this whole thing is?"

"Acknowledged. So I think what we have to do is establish that we were—ugh, I know this is horrifying—flirting pretty early on when you started working here, and that our relationship was solidified by your second or third week, though obviously we kept it secret from everyone at the station. New city, new job, and a new relationship all at once. You think you can handle that?"

"Guess I have to," he says. "What did this flirting look like?"

"I—I don't know," I say, caught a bit off guard by the question. "How . . . do you usually flirt with someone?"

He balances his index and middle fingers on his chin. "Hmm. I guess it's not always a conscious thing, is it? If it were someone at work, I'd find excuses to walk by their desk, to talk to them. I'd joke around, try to make them laugh. Maybe I'd touch them, just a little, but only if I was positive they'd be into it, and if they weren't, I'd stop immediately."

I let myself picture this. Dominic not just leering down at someone, but brushing her arm with the back of his hand, passing it off as an accident with a shy smile. Dominic placing a palm on someone's shoulder, telling her how much he loved her show or her story. Dominic trying to make someone laugh. I'm half tempted to ask him to tell me a joke.

The Dominic Yun who flirts with a hypothetical coworker is not the Dominic Yun I've known since October.

"Right," I say. "And—apparently I'd have liked all of that." I clear my throat. "How long did our relationship last?"

"Three months." He says it so matter-of-factly, as though he's put thought into it.

"Why three?"

"Fewer than that might not be seen as serious enough, and any more than that, I wouldn't have been back in Seattle yet. The longer the relationship, the more serious we were, the less likely people will believe it."

I lift my eyebrows. "I'm impressed."

"Like you said. We nail this, and then we can do anything we want."

We order pizza and continue plotting. Our first date: dinner at Dominic's favorite Korean place, easy, since I've already been there. Our second date: getting lost in a pumpkin patch corn maze the weekend before Halloween. We spent the holiday together, our first one, forgoing costumes while we handed out candy at my place. That was the night we made our relationship official, deciding to keep it from our coworkers for obvious reasons. The station was small, and we didn't want to make anyone uncomfortable.

We liked the idea of having a Halloween anniversary, since weren't relationships a little spooky?

"Do I call you Dom?" I ask.

His face darkens. "No. Never Dom."

"You don't correct Kent."

"You're not in charge of my paychecks."

Fair point.

I shove uneaten pizza crusts to the side of my plate and pick up my pen again, tapping it a few times against my notepad. "This isn't about the relationship, exactly, but do you think I should do some kind of vocal coaching?"

Dominic's mouth twists to one side. "Your voice is fine. Maybe it's a little higher than other people's, but it's your voice. That's not something you should have to change."

He's wrong, of course. Everyone has always made sure I'm aware of exactly how grating my voice is. He'll find out soon enough—I'm sure we'll be flooded with emails from opinionated listeners.

"What I'm more concerned about is keeping this from everyone," he continues. "We don't have any social media record."

"It's not too out of the ordinary," I say, "especially since we weren't telling coworkers. Have you told anyone about it? About what we're doing?"

He shakes his head. "Not the truth, no. It's not that I don't trust my parents, but they can get pretty chatty with their friends. What about you?"

"Only my best friend, but I trust her completely. We've known each other since we were in kindergarten." I'm not sure I can explain to him why it was easier to tell Ameena than it would be to tell my mother.

I turn back to my notes. It's nearing nine o'clock. I walked and fed Steve earlier this evening before running back to the station, but that doesn't mean I don't want to wrap this up as quickly as possible. "So. Moving on. The reason we broke up . . . it has to be something that would enable us to stay friends. Or at least friendly enough to host a show together. I don't want it to cast either of us in too negative a light."

"Huh," he says, "I was expecting you to paint me as the villain."

"Guess I'm full of surprises," I say. "Let's think back to why our last relationships ended. I haven't dated anyone seriously since early last year."

"What happened?"

"I was . . . more invested than he was," I say, not wanting to completely embarrass myself. "What about you?"

"Next question."

"Come on. You know I saw her on your Facebook. She dated you before I did. I should probably know *something* about her."

I try to imagine it, Dominic and cute redhead Mia Dabrowski. She must have really broken his heart if he's still this uncomfortable about it.

He swipes his keys from a drawer below his desk. "I'm gonna need alcohol to get through the rest of this. Any requests?"

Dominic Yun and I are drunk at work and playing catch.

He walks backward toward the bank of windows looking out onto a darkened Seattle street, laughing when he stumbles against someone's desk. He recovers, tosses the Koosh to me. Twin pairs of empty beer bottles sit on our desks. I don't know where my hair tie is—probably somewhere on the other side of the newsroom after I tried flinging it at him but overshot by a significant amount. His second shirt button lost the battle a while ago, and his hair is rumpled. He's wearing only one shoe, revealing a polka-dotted sock on his other foot. This is a version of Dominic I never thought I'd see, and I don't hate it.

Alcohol was a very good idea.

"What we really need," I say, fumbling with the ball, "is a catchphrase."

"A catchphrase? Like what . . . WHAAA-ZOOOOM?" He says it in his best AM radio talk show host voice.

I snort, beer coming up my throat and burning a little. "No

no no. Not a catchphrase. A whatchamacallit. An intro. Like"—
I put on a 1950s White Man Radio Voice—" 'Hi, I'm Shay and
this is Dominic, and we definitely used to date.' But you know.
Catchier."

"I don't know, I really like 'wha-zoom.' "

I hurl the ball at him as hard as I can, and he somehow catches
it. I fold my legs up onto my chair, having kicked off my boots a
while ago. I have tights on underneath my skirt, so hopefully I'm
not too indecent, sitting like this.

A bit of scruff has grown in along his jaw—an eleven-o'clock
shadow—and I find myself wondering what it would feel like to run
my hand over it. If it would be rough like sandpaper. He's usually
so clean-shaven. I can't decide which look I like best, and sure,
while it's concerning to mentally debate whether Dominic is more
attractive with stubble or without, there's nothing wrong with ac-
knowledging that he's an aesthetically pleasing human being.

I am perfectly capable of having a fake relationship—a fake
breakup—with an attractive coworker. I am a professional.

He walks back over to our desks and drops into his chair. "I'm
sorry about *Puget Sounds*," he says, stretching out his long legs until they touch the base of my chair. He nudges his foot against it,
spinning my chair a couple of inches in one direction. "Your last
show really was good."

"Thanks. It's been . . . kind of hard to let it go."

"I get that. You've only worked on that show," he says, and I
nod. "Look. I know why you don't like me."

"What? I don't—I don't not like you," I say, getting stuck on the
double negative.

"Shay, Shay, Shay," he says, slurring my name. "Come on. I took
a class on nonverbal communication in grad school, and even if I
hadn't, I'm not an idiot. It drives you wild that you're not the young
hotshot anymore, doesn't it?"

"What do you mean?"

"The intern who worked her way up to senior staff faster than anyone else in the station's history. You were the overachiever, and now you're . . ."

"*Old?*"

His eyes go wide, and his feet land hard on the floor. "No! Shit, no, I didn't mean that."

"We're only five years apart. You're technically a millennial, too." A very young one.

"I know. I know. I'm trying to figure out how to say this. It's hard when you feel like you can't impress the people you want to."

"And what would you know about that?" Despite the relationship we've crafted tonight, I have to remind myself he doesn't *really* know me, even if this conversation indicates otherwise.

"I'm the youngest of five kids," he says. "Everything I did, one of my siblings had already done, and usually better than I had."

And although he's still tight-lipped about why he and Mia Dabrowski broke up, this feels much more real than anything he's said all night. Shortly after he started drinking, he told me it was the distance. He was leaving Illinois, and she wanted to stay. But I can't shake the feeling that there's more to the story.

"I've been . . . not the nicest person to you. And I'm sorry. It's possible I've also been a little bit jealous." I hold my thumb and forefinger an inch apart.

"More like—" He reaches for my hand and pushes my fingers farther apart. The brush of skin on skin is gentle, despite how much larger his hand is. "But I probably haven't been the easiest to get along with, either. You're good at what you do. I've thought so since I started."

That compliment warps my boozy brain, drawing out another one of my fears.

"What if this doesn't work?" I ask quietly.

He inches his chair closer, until he's directly in front of me. He doesn't smell like his usual ocean-sage cologne. Tonight's scent is something woodsy. Earthier. Maybe even . . . better?

I need a paramedic.

He places one hand on each of my armrests, giving me an up-close and personal view of his forearms. The muscles in his arms flex as he grips the armrests, and I have to wrench my gaze away—up to his face, which is maybe more dangerous.

While I've noticed his crooked smile, his single dimple on the left side, I've never paid attention to how lovely his mouth is, his bottom lip just barely thicker than his top.

You're good at what you do.

"It's going to," he says, matching my soft tone. "I didn't play Curly McLain in my middle school's production of *Oklahoma!* for nothing."

"You didn't tell me you were a theater kid." I try to picture him in a cowboy hat—anything to keep me from wondering what his mouth would taste like. His knees are right up against the edge of my chair. If my legs weren't tucked, I'd be in his lap.

"No, the theater kids hated me. I killed my audition, but I've always had terrible stage fright. I'd have panic attacks before I went onstage every night."

Might have been helpful to know that before agreeing to do a live radio show with the guy. It's tough to wrap my mind around. He's never not seemed confident at work, except when he froze up on *Puget Sounds.*

"You have terrible stage fright," I echo, the beer in my stomach sloshing around. "And yet you're cool to host a radio show?"

He shakes his head. "This is fine. There's no audience—well, not one that you can see, anyway. I'm okay with smaller groups, but anything more than a dozen people, and my lungs suddenly decide not to work. Once I found my footing with Paloma, it felt like I was talking just to her." With his legs, he pushes off my chair, putting a foot of space between us. I let out a shaky breath. *Space. Yes. That's probably good.* "You must really be a lightweight. Your face is bright red."

I fling my hands up to cover it. "Ughhhhhh, I'm gonna get some water. This happens every time. The downside of not being six two."

"Six three."

"Jesus."

I make my way toward the break room, surprised when he follows me. Inside, I turn on one of the four light switches.

When I can't reach the water glasses on the top shelf, he easily grabs one and hands it to me, showing off one of his particularly enviable six-three superpowers. I mutter a thank-you as I hold it under the refrigerator tap.

"We still haven't figured out why we broke up," he says, leaning against the counter opposite the fridge.

"Maybe we should keep it simple. Working together and dating got to be too much for us?"

"That's not very exciting," he says. It's fitting that we can't agree. "Maybe you were intimidated by my raw sexual energy."

I nearly choke on a sip of water—that's how unexpected this is, coming from him.

But hey, I can play this game, too, especially with alcohol loosening my lips. "Or you were never able to get me to orgasm."

"I've never had that problem before," he says without missing a beat.

With just the two of us in this darkened space, I'm aware of how small the break room actually is. He shouldn't have followed me in here. I could have climbed onto the counter and grabbed a glass myself because short people are nothing if not skilled counter climbers.

But then he wouldn't be standing there in one of his Top Ten Most Infuriating Leans, eyeing me from beneath a truly impeccable pair of lashes.

The alcohol takes over. "So . . . we had a good sex life, then?"

One corner of his mouth kicks upward. "Maybe we weren't having sex."

Something horrific happens then: I let out this completely non-human sound, a mix between a snort and a laugh and a gulp. I shrink back until my shoulder blades hit the wall.

"What, you thought sleeping with me was a given?" he says. "Is my fictional self really that quick to put out?"

"Oh my god, no no no," I say. "I was just—if we were dating for three months, then we probably—I mean, maybe we didn't, but—"

He's full-on smiling now, as though amused by my incoherent babbling. I bring the water glass to my face so I can hide behind it. My sweater is draped across my desk, and I'm too warm in a thin black T-shirt. He's a six-three heat lamp.

"Shay," he says in a low voice. Teasing. He inches closer, reaching forward to take the water glass away from my face and holding it level with my shoulder. "Honestly, I'm flattered."

Then he taps the cold rim of the glass against my cheek gently, *gently*. A friendly little pat that sends my heart into overdrive. When he moves it away, I reach toward my face, holding a few fingers against the cold spot there.

His gaze is so intense that I have to close my eyes for a moment. My instinct is to back away, to put more space between us, but when I try, I'm reminded that I'm against the wall. I don't know where to look. Normally, I'm level with his pectorals, but he's hunched, the curve of his shoulders soft in this semi-light. Close enough to reach out and touch—if I wanted to. I watch the rise and fall of his chest. That's safe. Safer than eye contact, at least.

I've never had that problem before.

"I'm glad, because I'm really wishing the floor would open up and suck me into the Hellmouth right now."

"*Buffy* fan?"

"Oh yeah. I grew up with it. You?"

He at least has the decency to look sheepish. "Watched it on Netflix."

Of course he did. He's twenty-four, young enough to never have seen it live and sliced up by commercials. "By 'grew up with it,' I meant, you know, I was still *very young* during the early seasons, and I didn't understand most of what was going on . . ." I break off with a groan, though I'm relieved the conversation has turned away from sex. "God, don't make me feel like a grandma."

A laugh from deep in his throat turns my legs to jelly. That rumble—I feel it in the last possible place I want to feel it.

It is deeply concerning.

That's what catches me off guard, more than anything else tonight. I don't want to think about doing anything with Dominic besides cohosting a show about our fake relationship. I don't want to think about the way that rough laugh would sound pressed against my ear while other parts of him pressed against other parts of me.

And I really don't want to imagine him holding that cold glass to my bare skin again.

I swallow hard, forcing away these delusions. Sober Shay would not be fantasizing about Dominic Yun when he's right in front of her. My imagination is too creative, and my yearlong drought can't be helping.

Dominic passes the glass back to me and straightens to his full height. *Oh.* It's only then that I realize how easy it would have been for him to trap my hands over my head and push me against the wall, tell me with his mouth on my neck how journalism will save the world.

Of course, he doesn't do any of this, opting instead to take a step back. Then two. At three steps, the temperature in the room dips. At four, I can breathe again.

"For what it's worth," he says when he's halfway to the door, "I think it would have been good, too."

9

My mother turns, glancing at her reflection in the three-way mirror.

"You look gorgeous," I tell her from the cream leather couch. It's been true of the past five dresses she's tried on, confirming my theory: Leanna Goldstein is incapable of looking bad, even in twelve yards of chartreuse taffeta. Meanwhile, I have *my dog made me sleep in the creepy guest room again* circles under my eyes and darkened break room corners on the brain.

"It's not a mistake, not doing white, is it?" She sweeps her auburn hair off her neck, exposing the dress's plunging back. "I want to go nontraditional, but I don't want anything *too* mature."

She and my dad went nontraditional too, eloping in Colorado's Rocky Mountain National Park. The photos are breathtaking, the two of them pinned against teal mountains and Douglas firs. "All my friends said they spent so much money on food and never got to eat any of it," she'd say when I used to ask why my parents didn't have a wedding. Then she'd laugh her musical laugh. "And I couldn't imagine anything more tragic."

When she and I walked inside the bridal boutique, the saleswoman gushed over how exciting it is to shop for your daughter's wedding. My mother had to correct her, and the saleswoman apologized profusely.

It isn't the fact that we're here for my mother and not for me that makes it feel strange, though. It's that it's her second time, and now she wants to have the wedding.

"More and more brides are opting for nontraditional gowns these days," chirps the saleswoman, standing by with a pincushion and measuring tape. "I didn't think that green would work with your hair, but you look stunning."

Still, my mother frowns. "Something about it isn't feeling quite right. Do you have anything that's a little less"—she holds up the many layers of fluffy skirts—"well, a little less *dress*?"

"Absolutely. I'll be right back with some shorter styles." The saleswoman disappears, and I tip back the rest of my champagne.

I'm trying my best to focus, but my mind is back at the station. Thursday morning, Dominic strode in like nothing had happened between us, with the exception of one of those half smiles he shot my way when he picked up his Koosh ball to toss up and down. And . . . nothing *had* happened between us, right? That moment in the break room may have felt charged to me, but maybe he looms over women all the time, his pheromones and broad shoulders messing with their brains. It wasn't like he pushed me up against the wall because he needed to have his way with me and couldn't waste any time. I backed myself into the wall, and then he simply stood in front of me. Completely different.

We were drunk and exhausted and talking about sex. My mind ran wild with it, showing off the "overactive imagination" my elementary school teachers wrote about on my report cards. It doesn't mean I'm attracted to him.

The saleswoman returns with an armful of blush and mint and powder-blue dresses, and my mother thanks her.

"First show in two weeks," my mother says from the other side of the dressing room door. "How are you feeling?"

"Oddly okay," I say. "It hasn't hit me yet that I'm actually going to be on the air." I could say it a hundred times, and I probably won't believe it until I'm in that studio I've grown so used to being on the other side of.

"Your dad would have been telling absolutely everyone," my mother says, and then I hear her musical laugh. "People would have found him so obnoxious."

"Didn't they anyway?" I say, because it's true.

When someone dies, you don't only remember their good parts. You remember the difficult parts, too, like how if you asked a question he didn't know the answer to, my dad simply ignored it instead of responding. Or how he was in a perennial fight with our neighbors over the trees that drooped into our yard, and he passive-aggressively retaliated by mowing our lawn early every morning for months. The deceased don't immediately become flawless human beings. And it wouldn't be right to turn him into one. We loved him, faults and all.

"Sometimes," my mother says, emerging from the dressing room in a pink tulip-hemmed dress. "I've made my fair share of enemies in my career, I'm sure. No, no, this one isn't right."

I claw a hand through my low ponytail, covering my mouth with it before letting it flop back onto my shoulder. "I thought, I don't know, with Phil, and this wedding . . . that maybe you were finally doing it right this time."

The door opens again, and my mother appears in a nude bra, a navy dress around her waist. She has freckles along her arms and across her stomach. When I was younger, her wrinkles might have frightened me, but now they make her look strong. "Shay. No. Not at all." She hurries over to me, apparently not caring that she's half-dressed. "I know this has to be weird for you."

"A little," I say, because *a lot* might worry her. I want to be the cool, open-minded daughter, but I'm not sure how. I've gotten so used to our tiny family.

But I also got used to *Puget Sounds*. My job is changing, and with the exception of whatever happened in the break room, I've been okay.

"Your dad and I had exactly the kind of wedding we wanted," my mother continues, letting my hair out of its ponytail and running her fingers through it the way she used to do when I was a kid. "Our parents didn't get along, and they had different ideas of what the wedding should be. Mine insisted on a traditional Jewish wedding, while Dan's nonpracticing parents didn't want it to be religious." My paternal grandparents live in Arizona, but my mother's parents passed away when I was little. "And now that I'm older, now that it's just the two of us involved, we can do exactly what we want."

"Maybe that's the thing I'm getting hung up on," I say, trying to sound more confident than I feel. "That it's just the two of you, when I've always felt like it was just the two of *us*."

That lingers in the space between us for a while, and when my mother's face crumples, I immediately regret what I've said.

"Shit, that was really self-centered, I'm sorry. I'm so sorry. I was just thinking about how I had no idea that proposal was coming, and Ameena asked if I'd known about it, and—"

But my mother shakes her head, rubbing at the hollow of her throat the way she does when she's anxious. "No. You're right. We've been a unit for the past ten years, haven't we? I should have talked to you first. I'm sorry about that." She glances down, and then back up at me, and for a moment I see not just my mother, but a woman who's made a mistake and wants desperately to be forgiven. "But you're happy about it, right? You like Phil?"

"Oh my god, Mom, yes. *Yes.* I love Phil." I squeeze her hand. "I'm not mad. At all. I swear. I'm just . . . adjusting."

"I think we all will be, for a while," she says. "I want you to be part of this in any way you want, okay?"

"Okay, but if you try to get me to wear chartreuse, I am definitely standing up when the officiant asks if anyone objects."

She nods solemnly. "And I'd deserve that." Then she turns to the mirror, as though remembering she's only half-dressed. She gets to her feet and straightens herself out, and I see she's wearing not a dress but a sleek navy jumpsuit. It's sleeveless with a wrap front and long, clean lines. It's both age appropriate and nontraditional, commanding but understated.

Her face splits into a grin, and I realize for the first time we have the same exact smile.

Maybe I haven't seen it enough on either of us.

"This is the one," she says.

On Sunday afternoon, Mary Beth Barkley stands in my living room, locked in a staring contest with Steve.

"Thank you so much for doing this," I say. "He's been a bit of a nightmare. An adorable nightmare."

Mary Beth waves this off. "Aren't you the cutest little thing?" she said when she got here, and gave him a hunk of cheese from the pack around her waist. "What he needs are some boundaries and some discipline. I see it all the time with first-time dog owners, especially with dogs that haven't been socialized. He needs to know that you're the alpha."

She begins by calling his name, rewarding him when he responds to it. Then we practice some basic commands and leash training.

"He's walking you," Mary Beth says when we go outside and

Steve tugs me toward his favorite pee tree. "How much does he weigh?"

"Um. Seven pounds."

"*You* are the alpha," she repeats, and I decide not to tell her I've been sleeping in the guest room. "Make sure he knows that. He's not the one in charge. This walk is your choice, not his. You're leading him, not the other way around."

So I'm the producer of his life, essentially, and I more than know how to do that.

He pulls toward the end of his leash, but I stand firm. After a few moments of straining, he trots back to me, loosening the leash, and when I make a move to go in the other direction, he actually follows.

"Good boy!" I practically shriek it, which scares him, but a treat makes everything okay.

After about an hour, we head back inside, exhausted but victorious.

Mary Beth reaches down to scratch behind his ears. "You're gonna be a good boy," she says. "You just needed a little help."

I thank Mary Beth, but she refuses payment.

"Your show sent so much business my way," she says, which makes a bittersweet warmth bloom in my chest. We were doing something important. I always knew it, despite those moments Dominic made me doubt myself. "I'll look forward to catching your new show, even if it does have considerable less emphasis on dogs."

The training session makes me useless the rest of the day, which is probably good because the impending *Ex Talk* nerves have fully sunk their claws in me. Steve naps—in his bed, not mine—while I catch up on the handful of dating podcasts I now subscribe to, idly texting with Ameena.

A text from an unknown number arrives at a quarter to eight.

I'm in the bathroom painting my nails gray, and it's so startling I nearly drop my phone in the bathroom sink.

> It's Dominic. Got your number from the staff directory.
>
> I had this idea. What if we did a show about people who met someone through a rideshare? Someone I know from grad school is dating a guy who was her Lyft driver.

Dominic Yun. Texting me about a show idea. For *our show*.

> YES! I love that. Admit it. You're excited about this.

I screw the cap back on the nail polish bottle, wondering where he's texting me from and how he spends his weekends. Maybe he goes to the farmers' market or out to meals with friends. Maybe he hikes or bikes or reads classic novels by himself in a coffee shop. I don't know where in Seattle he lives, if it's in a studio apartment or a house with a bunch of friends or at home with his parents.

Of course, he might not even be at home. He's not currently in a relationship, but that doesn't mean he's not casually dating. Sure, Sundays aren't prime hookup nights, but that doesn't stop me from imagining his trademark lean against the bedroom door of a stranger's apartment. Pinning someone else against a wall for real this time, bracing his hands on either side of her. It makes my stomach twist in a strange, foreign way.

> Yeah. Guess I am. You worked some kind of magic on me.

Our words flowed so smoothly that night at the station, but now I'm not sure how to keep the conversation going. It hits me that I *want* to know him, where he lives and what he's doing on a Sunday night and what kinds of books he likes to read. Probably nonfiction with drab covers and tiny print. Exposés.

Why we don't have any mutual Facebook friends.

I've always been interested in stories, and yet I can't exactly journalism my way into Dominic's life. Especially when I can't decide what to text back.

Still, I'm disappointed when my phone doesn't light up for the rest of the night.

10

The next couple weeks are a promo whirlwind. We send press releases, take new photos for the website, and make a guest appearance on Pacific Public Radio's morning show. Our first three shows are booked solid with content and guests, and even that meant late nights and early mornings. It's hard to believe that a few weeks ago, I was producing a live show every day.

"You're popping your P's. Again."

We've been in Booth C for twenty minutes trying to record a fifteen-second promo, during which it's become increasingly clear to me that these booths were not meant for two people. Sure, there are two chairs, two microphones. But Dominic's height shrinks the booth by half. Today he's in khakis, which could so easily look horrifying on the wrong person. (He is not the wrong person.) They're paired with brown oxfords and a gray cardigan with elbow patches. One of his more casual looks, and it's only because we're working so closely together that I notice these details.

Dominic switches off the **RECORD** button. "Would it kill you to help me instead of making fun of me?"

"Oh, I assumed you had a class about this in grad school." I bite the inside of my cheek. "Sorry. That's not helping, either, is it?"

He lets out a long-suffering sigh. "You could start by telling me what the hell a popped P is."

That, I can do. It takes me back to the early weeks of my internship, the one-on-one coaching I got from Paloma. Back then, I thought it was ridiculous—I'd never be on the radio anyway. Still, I learned to avoid P-pops and the less common B-pops and hissing S's, just in case.

"It's called a plosive," I say, trying not to wonder if his sea salt cologne will linger in the booth after we leave. "You're sending a blast of air from your mouth right into the mic when you make that *p* sound." I hold my hand in front of my mouth, indicating that he should do the same. "Pacific Public Radio. Can you feel the difference against your hand when you say a *p* word versus an *r* word? There's more air with the *p*'s, right?"

"Pacific Public Radio. Pacific Public Radio." Dominic tries this a few times and nods. It's both funny and validating, watching this six-three giant taking direction from me.

"And the thing you feel is going to sound distorted on the recording," I say. "Aside from having better recording technology, which we're not going to be able to afford anytime soon, you can practice better breath control. It takes some time, and you'll probably be thinking about it a lot at the beginning, but it'll get easier."

He repeats the phrase into his hand several more times, sounding smoother. When he finally drops his arm, his sweater sleeve brushes my shoulder. I wonder if it's wool or cotton, soft or rough. Maybe I don't hate the way he dresses at all.

"Thank you," he says. "That's actually really helpful."

We try the promo again.

I'm Shay Goldstein—

And I'm Dominic Yun. This Thursday at three o'clock on Pacific Pub-

lic Radio, tune in to our new show, The Ex Talk. *It's all about dating, breaking up, and making up from two people who managed to stay friends after their own relationship ended.*

We can't wait to share our story and hear yours.

"Better," I say. But I can't get the sound of my own voice out of my head. With the show premiering so soon, it's the last place I want to linger. "*Culture Clash* was good this week."

"Don't tell me! I haven't listened yet."

"Okaaaay, but there's this one part where—"

He makes a show of clutching at his ears. "Has anyone ever told you that you're terrible?"

"Most people." I give him an angelic smile. "There's also this newish *Buffy* podcast I've been meaning to check out."

"*Five by Five*? It's great. First episode was a little shaky, but they found their footing by the third."

"So you don't only listen to the news," I say with a lift of my eyebrows.

"You mean, I'm a complex and layered human being?"

"Jury's still out."

His mouth twitches, like he's trying not to smile. "Now *that*'s a good podcast."

I snort. He doesn't need to know that I subscribed to one of his Supreme Court podcasts, *Justice Makes Perfect*. I haven't listened to any of the episodes yet, but I might. It's only fair—he listened to mine. I am a firm believer in reciprocation.

A few more run-throughs of the promo. If possible, my voice sounds more grating each time. I sigh, pushing the microphone out of the way and dropping into one of the two sound booth chairs. It's always better to record standing up—less pressure on your diaphragm.

"Are you sure my voice sounds okay?"

"For the nine hundredth time, yes."

"You've clearly never had anyone laugh in your face about it."

"No, but I've gotten anonymous emails telling me to go back to China," he says. "Which is especially hilarious, given I'm not Chinese."

"Oh." *Shit*. That is not even on the same planet as my issues. "Wow. That is really fucked up. I'm sorry."

"Thanks." He runs a hand through his hair, abandoning his lean to take the chair next to mine. "I want to say I've gotten used to it because it's happened often enough, but you really don't. You let it fuel you. You do even better because you know there are people out there who are waiting for you to fail."

At that, he lets his brown oxford tap the leg of my chair in a way that's maybe meant to be comforting.

Huh. We might be getting along.

I don't hate his company, not entirely, and I've mostly forgotten what happened in the break room. (Even if my throat went dry when I saw him filling a glass of water yesterday. I'm gonna be pissed if this turns into a fetish thing.) Maybe there's a way for the two of us to be friends. It won't be the relationship I had with Paloma, which was off balance from the beginning. But we could be something like *equals*. A real novelty in the public radio world.

I stare down at his shoe. The polished leather, the crisp laces. He's a little less intimidating when he's sitting next to me, but possibly even more of a mystery.

"One more time, then?" I say, and he hits **RECORD** again.

None of our listeners will see me, but I decide to dress up for show day. I wear a structured gray minidress, patterned tights, and lavender Mary Jane heels I found at a rummage sale with Ameena last year. My thick hair goes into its regular ponytail, but I straighten my bangs, which makes them sleek and shiny. I debate wearing contacts, but it's been forever, and I'm so attached to my tortoise-shell glasses that I don't want to risk any minor change to my vision.

You have a face for radio, my dad used to tell me with a grin. An A-plus dad joke. God, I still miss those.

The morning creeps by. It's about as agonizing as getting a root canal followed by a Pap smear. At lunch, my stomach can only handle a third of a sandwich from the shop on the first floor while Ruthie reviews the rundown next to me. I manage to get mustard on the skirt of my dress, and I spend fifteen minutes in the bathroom scrubbing at it.

Kent comes by our cubes as Dominic and I are practicing our intro.

"My favorite couple," he says, not-so-subtly gesturing to the Cupid-printed tie he wore in our honor. "Or favorite former couple. You two are going to knock it out of the park. We're all really excited about this."

But there's an undercurrent to his words:

Don't fuck this up.

Ruthie prints our most updated rundowns. This first show has no guest. It's Dominic and me, telling our fake stories, waiting for calls to roll in.

I stumble over literally just carpet on our walk down the hall to the studio.

"You okay?" Dominic asks, reaching out to grab my elbow, helping steady me. My dress is short sleeved, and his fingers are warm against my skin.

Well, now I'm not. "Five by five," I manage to say.

Ruthie breezes into the studio, setting a glass in front of each of us. "Water for my favorite cohosts," she sings.

"Thank you. I would've forgotten." Though I did it so many times for Paloma, I don't want Ruthie to feel like she needs to wait on us. "How do you seem so calm? I reapplied deodorant half an hour ago and I'm still sweating buckets."

"I'm your producer," she says. "It's my job to stay calm."

And she's right—it would be so much worse if she were freaking the fuck out, too.

I wonder how much worse it would be if she knew we'd never actually dated.

Fortunately, my nerves don't leave any room for guilt. Not today. Not when I am five minutes from a lifelong dream. Ruthie disappears into the adjoining studio, and Dominic and I sit together on one side of the table with our twin water glasses and spinny chairs, clamping headphones over our ears.

The **RECORDING** sign blinks on.

"Coming up next, the premiere of our brand-new show, *The Ex Talk*," Jason Burns says. "But first, these headlines from NPR."

It's happening. We're really about to do this.

My own show.

"I have some prescription-strength antiperspirant in my gym bag," Dominic says. "I could ask Ruthie to get it."

I give him a horrified look. We're in a small enclosed space together. I might die if he thinks I smell bad. I will definitely die if I have pit stains. "Do I need it?"

"Oh—shit. No. *No.* You seemed stressed about it, so I thought I'd offer. You smell normal. Sort of . . . citrusy. It's nice."

It's nice. Not *you smell nice.* An important distinction.

"Thanks," I say with some hesitation, accepting the compliment on behalf of my Burt's Bees shampoo.

His leg bounces up and down underneath the table. Dark jeans today.

"And what's going on there?" I ask, pointing.

His stage fright confession comes back to me. He said he'd be fine on the radio, without a visible audience. God, he better be right.

"Ah. That's me trying to hide how nervous I am. How am I doing?"

"Terrible," I say. "We both are."

The corner of his mouth twitches. This is something he does often, I'm beginning to realize. Like he doesn't want me to know he finds something funny, or a real laugh might mess up his stoic facade.

"There's one thing we're good at doing together, then," he says. He takes a drink of water, and my heart speeds up for an entirely different reason.

Focus. I flip through my stack of papers. How did Paloma make it look so effortless? Our choreographed intro, our fictional anecdotes, the sponsor breaks . . . And yet it's impossible to prepare for everything. If someone calls with a question not in my notes, will I have an answer?

WWAMWMD?

Ruthie comes through our headsets. "Thirty seconds," she says, a little breathless.

I cross and uncross my legs. Scratch at the mustard stain. Attempt a sip of water and dribble some down my chin.

"Hey," Dominic says right before the ten-second countdown. Finally, his leg pauses its frenzied jiggling, and he knocks my knee with his. "Shay. It's just like the two of us having a conversation."

"Right. Right. We can do that."

His gaze locks on mine. "And I'm really glad you talked me into this."

Then Ruthie points to us.

And we're live.

The Ex Talk, Episode 1: Why We Broke Up

Transcript

<Fade in audio clips while "Breaking Up Is Hard to Do" plays underneath>

"You call yourself a free spirit, a wild thing, and you're terrified somebody's gonna stick you in a cage. Well, baby, you're already in that cage . . ." (Breakfast at Tiffany's)

"Where I'm going, you can't follow. What I've got to do, you can't be any part of . . ." (Casablanca)

"Frankly, my dear, I don't give a damn." (Gone with the Wind)

"If I want to be a senator, I need to marry a Jackie, not a Marilyn . . ." (Legally Blonde)

"We should break up or whatever." (Scott Pilgrim vs. the World)

<Fade out>

DOMINIC YUN: It was a cold December day—

SHAY GOLDSTEIN: Pretty sure it was the beginning of January.

DOMINIC YUN: It was sometime in the winter. You were wearing that blue sweater—

SHAY GOLDSTEIN: Green.

DOMINIC YUN: And I was wearing my favorite gray beanie.

SHAY GOLDSTEIN: I really hated that beanie.

DOMINIC YUN: I hated that you hated that beanie.

SHAY GOLDSTEIN: Obviously, that's not why we broke up, but poor communication is one of the top reasons relationships don't last.

DOMINIC YUN: I'm Dominic Yun.

SHAY GOLDSTEIN: And I'm Shay Goldstein, and this is *The Ex Talk*, a brand-new show from Pacific Public Radio. Thanks for joining us. We're coming to you live from Seattle, or if you're listening by podcast, somewhere in the somewhat recent past. Full honesty: This is not just our first episode but also our first time on the air like this. I've been a producer at the station for ten years, and Dominic's been working as a reporter since October, which was also around the time we started dating. And earlier this year, we broke up.

DOMINIC YUN: But we still had to face each other at work every day, which I think made it easier for us to stay friends. Or at the very least, passive-aggressive acquaintances.

SHAY GOLDSTEIN: We've both been really excited about getting behind a microphone like this and having a chance to talk about something that public radio has never devoted an entire show to: dating and relationships. That's what *The Ex Talk* is about, with an emphasis on sharing stories—your stories. We're hoping to break down stereotypes and gender roles when it comes to relationships, and in the next few weeks, we'll have experts on the show to help us out.

DOMINIC YUN: On this first episode, we're talking about why we broke up. We'll take some calls a little later, but we wanted to start with our story, because clearly it's something even Shay and I can't agree on. Here are some other reasons couples break up these days: jealousy, broken promises, insecurity, infidelity—

SHAY GOLDSTEIN: Working too closely with your partner.

DOMINIC YUN: Or maybe interrupting them constantly.

SHAY GOLDSTEIN: I thought this was friendly banter?

DOMINIC YUN: I feel like that would require you being friendly.

SHAY GOLDSTEIN: I'm friendly! To my friends!

DOMINIC YUN: Okay, then—one friend to another, can I ask you a question?

SHAY GOLDSTEIN: Um . . .

Sound of papers shuffling.

DOMINIC YUN: It's not in our notes. Because I want to hear your honest answer.

SHAY GOLDSTEIN: Perfect. You want to ad-lib during our first three minutes on the air?

DOMINC YUN: Never mind. You're building it up too much. There's too much suspense.

SHAY GOLDSTEIN: Dominic Yun, I will walk out of this studio right now if you don't—

Dominic laughs.

DOMINIC YUN: Okay, okay. What I really want to know, since we're talking about, you know, our relationship, is what you'd change about me, if you could. Assuming I'm not a flawless human being.

SHAY GOLDSTEIN: Oh, I definitely don't need notes for that. Okay. So the first thing is that you'd only be able to talk about your master's degree, like, once a month. Preferably never, but I'm not sure your ego could take it.

DOMINIC YUN: My master's degree in journalism from Northwestern?

SHAY GOLDSTEIN: Yep, that's the one. You also—you do this thing where you lean against a wall and crane your neck to talk to people, and it feels really condescending sometimes. Like you're literally talking down to them.

DOMINIC YUN: You do realize you're, like, five feet tall, right? Am I not supposed to look at you when we're talking?

SHAY GOLDSTEIN: I am five *two*. Respect those two inches. No, but this is my special magical world where I can change anything about you. You didn't say it had to make sense.

DOMINIC YUN: You could just make me shorter.

SHAY GOLDSTEIN: I like how tall you are. I mean—so you can reach things for me when I don't feel like climbing up on a counter.

DOMINIC YUN: So my worst traits are my height and my advanced education? This is *scathing*.

SHAY GOLDSTEIN: You also have that ball on your desk you're always throwing around when you're thinking, and it drives me bonkers. So I'd take that away. And now you're going to tell me what you'd change about me?

DOMINIC YUN: Only if you can handle it.

SHAY GOLDSTEIN: You know I don't have emotions while I'm at work.

Dominic snorts.

DOMINIC YUN: Well, first, you'd have to get taller. It's just creepy for an adult to be as small as you are.

SHAY GOLDSTEIN: I got carded at an R-rated movie last weekend.

DOMINIC YUN: And you didn't you tell me? I could have spent the past week making fun of you.

SHAY GOLDSTEIN: We're getting off track. Tell me more things you don't like about me. Drag me, Dominic. That's what the cool kids say these days, right?

DOMINIC YUN: Yeah, the cool kids in 2016. Okay, I'll drag you. Let's see . . . sometimes you think there's only one right way to do things, so I guess I'd make you a little more flexible.

Shay coughs.

DOMINIC YUN: Do you need some water? Or do you need help reaching it?

Shay coughs more violently.

SHAY GOLDSTEIN: No, I—okay. I'm fine.

DOMINIC YUN: So, any of those things you wanted to change about me—do you think if I'd changed, we wouldn't have broken up?

SHAY GOLDSTEIN: Well . . . no. And I think I see what you're getting at. You're trying to say that even if we changed those things, we still wouldn't be right together. And as much as I hate to admit it, you make a good point. If you're expecting your partner to change, you may not be in the right relationship. Smart.

DOMINIC YUN: Well, I do have a master's degree.

I wake up the next morning scrunched on the edge of my bed. Steve is spread out in the middle, tiny whiskers twitching in his sleep. Progress. How such a small dog takes up so much space, I'll never know.

He usually wakes me before my alarm, so we're often on a walk before I have a chance to check social media. Today I relish the extra few minutes with my phone, arranging myself so I'm semi-spooning my dog, trying not to disturb him.

And . . . *wow*.

I was just shy of a thousand followers on Twitter, but now I'm past 2K. My mentions are a mess, and I wince as I swipe over to them, waiting for what I've always feared would happen if I ever got on the radio.

But that doesn't happen.

Because they're *nice*.

There's a bit of unavoidable internet vitriol, but overall, people loved the show. *Loved*. I'm not exaggerating—the word is all over social media.

Relief sinks me deeper into my mattress, and I fight a smile. For weeks, I've been carrying around this panic that we wouldn't be good enough, that no one would listen, that I'd screw up live on air. But this—this is a powerful feeling, and it's much stronger than I thought it would be.

The hour started slowly. Dominic sounded calm, smooth, completely anxiety-free. Either he's great at hiding it, or his stage fright really did go away once we went live. I was shaky at first, laughed a little too much, but then I gained my bearings. We had our intro scripted out, a he-said, she-said choreographed dance that he immediately threw a wrench into. Improvising with him wasn't as difficult as I worried it might be, although the whole time, I was aware the stories we told about Dominic dropping a candle while lighting the menorah on his first Hanukkah and our very public fight at an Olive Garden, the one where we tested the limits of all-you-can-eat salad and breadsticks, weren't about us. That I never actually branded him an honorary Jew. That it wasn't Dominic in the story about ice-skating at Seattle Center when "The Time Warp" came over the speakers and both of us knew the dance.

But for a few minutes, it felt like it could have been.

I wasn't sure how long I could improvise with him like that, though, so I was relieved when calls started coming in. "You sound like me and my ex," Isaac from West Seattle had said with a laugh. "Although I don't think I'd have nearly enough chill to host a radio show with him."

Then Kayla in Bellevue called in to lament that she seemed to scare off potential dates by being too forward and making the first move.

"As women, we're told we're not supposed to initiate things," I said, realizing it was something I had a strong opinion about. "That it's more romantic for the guy to do it. Aside from how outdated and heteronormative that is, how else are you going to feel like you have any semblance of equality in a relationship? I never want to wait around, hoping someone else will decide to take control when I'm perfectly capable of doing it myself."

"I love when women make the first move. In fact," Dominic said with a glance at me, "Shay's the one who asked me out."

"That's right," I said, not even needing to flip to the place in my notes where we summarized our first date. "I walked right up to him in the break room and asked if he wanted to grab dinner after work. And my mom just proposed to her boyfriend."

Kayla pressed me for more details, and I realized I was happy to share them, to gush about my mother. After I'd had some space to process it, I could admit that it *had* been a great proposal.

I continue scrolling through Twitter, laughing at a tweet from someone who swears that if Dominic were her ex, she'd never have let him go. The sound of my joy startles Steve, and he leaps into action, licking my face until I surrender and peel myself out of bed.

On our walk, I check my phone with frozen hands. I lunge for it immediately after my shower, dripping water all over the screen. I refresh our hashtag while waiting for the toaster to release my multigrain bagel.

By the time I'm ready to leave for work, it's eight forty-five. I have never, in my history at Pacific Public Radio, gotten to work later than eight fifty-five. I may be perpetually late to dinners with my family and friends, but never, never to work.

I haven't had a chance to reply to the text Ameena sent after she listened to the podcast last night, unable to take a break at work. Holy shit! You and your fake ex-boyfriend sounded so good! So I call her on Bluetooth as I sit in I-5 traffic.

"Hello, radio star. It appears video hasn't killed you."

"Not yet, at least," I say. "Hi. Yesterday was a whirlwind. I didn't want you think I'd forgotten you in my rise to fame."

She snorts. "Two thousand Twitter followers, and you're suddenly too good for me?"

"I wasn't going to say it, but if you feel uncomfortable with my extremely low level of celebrity . . ."

"Seriously, though, you guys sounded great," she says. "Really natural. I forgot for a moment that you hadn't actually dated, and I was cursing you for breaking up with him."

"Ha," I say. "Thank you. It sounded sort of real to me, too. Dominic hasn't been entirely terrible to work with."

"TJ wanted me to tell you that he was all ready to call in with a fake story about breaking up with me in public to save you if you needed it, but he didn't have to. He was almost disappointed—he spent a lot of time coming up with it."

"Tell him I appreciate it anyway."

My speakers go staticky, like she's covering the phone. "Ack, I have to run into a meeting," she says. "Brunch on Sunday?"

"You know how I feel about brunch, but I'll do it for you."

The panic over being late sets in once I step into the elevator and hit the button for the fifth floor. I'm convinced Kent is going to yell at me as soon as I open the door, but that's not what happens.

First, Emma McCormick at reception: "I loved your show, Shay!" And in a lower voice: "I shouldn't ask this, but was he a good kisser? He seems like he would be. It's okay if you don't want to talk about it, but if you do . . . you know where to find me."

Then Isabel Fernandez: "You two sounded fantastic! We should have done this a long time ago."

Even senior editor Paul Wagner tells me he and his wife listened to the podcast during dinner last night and couldn't stop cracking up.

None of it feels real. At any moment, I'm convinced Kent will pop up and say, *Gotcha!* Or that someone at the station will ask a question about my relationship with Dominic I'm unable to answer. That's the part that makes my multigrain bagel threaten to come back up.

This is only how it begins, I try to convince myself. We're telling a story. That's what radio is. The show will grow beyond our story—it has to. It's the only way I can stomach our lie.

I need to talk to Dominic, with all his journalism do-gooder morals. I need to know how he's feeling, if he's overwhelmed by the social media response or withering under the weight of a lie he never thought he'd tell.

But I don't get the chance. He's already at his desk, laser-focused on his computer screen. The ends of his dark hair are damp and curling slightly against the back of his neck. If his hair is still wet, he must not have gotten here that much earlier than me.

As soon as my bag hits the floor beneath my desk, Kent swoops in.

"My office," he says with such urgency that we don't waste any time following him there.

"Ruthie should be here," I say when Dominic and I sit down in front of Kent's desk.

"Here!" She rushes inside with two mugs of coffee, which she places in front of Dominic and me.

"You didn't have to do that," I say, but she waves a dismissive hand. My mug is a relic. 2003 KPPR FALL PLEDGE DRIVE, it declares in blocky purple letters.

I'm not sure how I feel about this new dynamic between us. I don't want to be that kind of host.

There are only three chairs in here, so Ruthie sort of stands off to the side, making me feel even more awkward.

"Just a second." Dominic gets up and leaves the room. A moment later, he returns with an extra chair, which Ruthie gratefully accepts.

"Shay, Ruthie, could one of you take notes?" Kent asks. I wait for him to add, "Or Dominic." He does not.

"I've got it," Ruthie says.

"Thanks." Kent clicks a few buttons on his computer. "So. You may have seen a bit of an explosion about the show on social media." He turns the screen to face us. It's a Twitter search of our hashtag, with new results popping up every few seconds. Then he clicks over to our podcast page. "Look at the number of downloads. It's about four times higher than any of our other shows that aired this week. That's *huge* for a new podcast."

"Oh my god," I say.

"And we had a pretty steady stream of callers," Ruthie puts in. "Plenty of people to choose from. That girl who talked about breaking up with her boyfriend in the middle of a road trip? *Gold.*"

"Suffice it to say, I was not prepared for this to happen right away, but I'm thrilled," Kent says. "Really thrilled. These numbers could make a huge difference come pledge drive season. They could put us on the national map, too. Excellent work, you two."

"Three," I say.

"Right. Of course. Sorry, Ruthie." Kent offers her an apologetic look. "I know you'd typically conduct pitch meetings on your own, but given the interest the show has garnered, I think you'll agree it makes sense for me to be involved as well. I'd like to be part of them moving forward, at least for a while, if that's okay with you three."

A bit unconventional, but . . . "That makes sense," Ruthie says. "I'm fine with it if Shay and Dominic are."

We nod our agreement.

"I just—wow," Dominic says, and it's maybe the first time I've seen him struggle for words. "I didn't realize it would be happening so quickly."

"Believe it," Kent says, "and enjoy it. But we can't stop now. What do you guys have planned for your next show?"

"We were going to do live couples therapy to figure out what went wrong in our relationship," I say. "And then the week after, we have an academic and a psychologist couple booked to talk about recent relationship studies."

"Love it. What else?"

"Well . . . ," Ruthie starts. "I hadn't pitched this yet, but I thought it would be interesting to do something about interracial dating."

"Pitch it to me," Kent says.

Pink spots appear on her cheeks. "Every time I'm dating an Asian girl or guy, people look at me almost like it's expected . . . And if I'm dating a white girl, or a white guy, people look at me in a different way. Like they're wondering if the person's only with me because they're into Asian girls. Then if I'm dating someone who isn't white *or* Asian, they're completely confused."

It's the most personal she's ever been. Three years, and I barely know anything about her.

I vow to change that.

"I've never dated an Asian girl," Dominic says.

I think back to his Facebook. Mia Dabrowski. How many other girls has he dated? It was hard to tell how long they'd been together—at least a couple years.

"I'd be down to talk about that," I say, and then to Dominic: "if you're okay with it."

He nods. "I'd want to have some other people of color on the show, too."

"Great, great," Kent says. "So you're solid content-wise. Now with regard to promo . . ." He clicks through a few things on his computer. "We need to strategize. I have the two of you talking to the *Seattle Times* at noon today, and a few online outlets want to interview you, too—BuzzFeed, Vulture, Slate, Hype Factory . . ."

"What the hell is Hype Factory?" Dominic says.

"Clickbait site," I say. Not the most groundbreaking journalism, but *"Fifteen Cats That Look Like Adam Driver (#8 Will Shake You to Your Core)"* entertained me for a solid two minutes last week.

"We have to hop on this," Kent says. "We're in a unique position here. The podcast had an incredible premiere, and I applaud all of you for that. But it's also just one episode. I don't want anyone's heads getting too big yet. What we need to do is keep this going, continue to build hype around it.

"Do you know how long people's attention spans last today? Not long. People go wild over a new *Stranger Things* season for a week before a new Marvel trailer drops, and then there's a new Disney remake everyone's talking about. Nothing lasts. But we want to stay relevant as long as we can, really be part of the zeitgeist."

Ruthie shudders.

"What was that?" Kent asks.

"Sorry, I just have a visceral reaction to the word 'zeitgeist.'"

I muffle a laugh at this, but Kent doesn't even crack a smile.

"I understand what you're saying." Dominic pushes up the sleeves of his black sweater. "I just don't want any of it to feel disingenuous."

Kent's hand flies to his chest, as though insulted by what Dominic is insinuating. "I'm not asking any of you to be anything except yourselves," he says, with the slightest lift of his brows.

A bigger reality hits me, settles like acid in my stomach: Ruthie thinks Dominic and I really dated. Making a vow to get to know her better sounds absurd when I'm lying to her simply by sitting next to her.

"Then if we're good here," Dominic says, "I'm going to go listen back to the show. See how we can improve next time."

"Excellent idea," Kent says. "And truly: Congratulations, you three."

But I'm still stuck on the other thing he said:

Nothing lasts.

It probably lasts even less time if you're lying about it.

Twitter

@amandaosullivan
Who else is obsessed with #TheExTalk? Dominic and Shay are so cute I can't. If any of my exes were like Dom, I never would have let them go!

@elttaes_amadeus
i ship @goldsteinshayyy and @dominicyun on @TheExTalk so hard, can they get back together plz??? 🙏 #TheExTalk #shayminic

@MsMollieRae17
can i just say it's so refreshing to hear someone with a REAL sounding voice on NPR? #TheExTalk

@most_dolphinately_
Dominic Yun sounds like a pompous asshole #TheExTalk

@photography_by_shauna
OMG just finished #TheExTalk and I NEED episode 2! does anyone else kinda want shay and dominic to get back together?

@StanleyPowellPhD
This is what's on NPR these days? Wish you could take back a pledge drive donation. #TheExTalk #nothanks

@itsmenikkimartinez
His voice sounds hot. Have you SEEN his photo? Hey @BabesofNPR, take a look. #TheExTalk #voicecrush #thirst

@_dontquotemeonthis
@itsmenikkimartinez @BabesofNPR Add @goldsteinshayyy too
🔥🔥🔥

12

Passover seders used to be solemn affairs. They were small, just my parents and grandparents, until my mother's parents passed away and my dad's parents moved to Arizona to escape the Seattle gloom. And then for most of my twenties, it was just my mother making a joke about me asking the Four Questions, since I'd never not been the youngest person at the table.

Now the first night of Passover is something of a party. We're in the house I grew up in, but with fourteen of us around the table, it's never been this loud. The Manischewitz and various other drinks flow freely, and Phil's grandkids had fun hunting down the afikomen, a broken piece of matzah wrapped in a napkin and hidden somewhere in the house. This was always my dad's favorite part of a seder, and he'd get a kick out of hiding it in my mother's violin case, between books on a shelf, and once, taped underneath the table, which was so unexpected it took me almost an hour to think to look there. Since it's their first Passover, I gave the kids an easy one: on top of the refrigerator. But next year, I'm going to be ruthless.

I like this part: sharing our traditions, leaving space for new ones.

"We're loving your show," says Phil's son Anthony, and his husband Raj nods his agreement while trying to get a spoonful of mashed veggies into their toddler's mouth.

"The second episode was even better than the first," Raj says. "Especially when you stumped that poor couples counselor."

"Thank you," I say, meaning it. "It's been a lot of fun so far."

Our second episode aired a few days ago, and I've been refreshing our subscribers almost hourly. I thought we'd continue trending upward, but our download numbers seem to have kind of plateaued. We probably won't have a chance at sponsors until we have thousands more downloads per month. It's still early—that's how I'm reassuring myself, at least—but I guess I assumed the media blitz would be enough to get us out there. Unless, like Kent said, the landscape is already so saturated that buzz for a new podcast sounds like more of a hiss.

"And Dominic sounds adorable," says Phil's daughter, a midthirties dentist named Diana. She's sitting across from me, flashing pearly white teeth. "I can't believe you broke up with him."

"Even someone with a nice voice can be . . . a huge dick," I say, grasping for the right word and never quite landing on it. Lying to Phil's family—*my* family—takes a toll on my appetite, and I push around the brisket on my plate before realizing it's exactly what Diana's kids are doing.

"But was he a huge dick where it mattered?"

"Diana!" Phil says from one end of the table. "Your father is here. And there are children present."

"Dad. I have, in fact, had sex before." She gestures to her kids. "Exactly twice."

More laughter at this.

This was the kind of family I always wanted growing up, especially during our quiet seders. I wanted competition for the afikomen. I wanted someone else to ask the Four Questions. Except once my dad was gone, I realized I didn't want a giant, raucous family. All I wanted was him.

It surprises me, this ease with which they talk about sex. Ameena and I talk about it plenty, but I've never quite gained that comfort with my mother. Maybe it's because I discovered grief and sex at the same time. My earliest experiences are wrapped in that tightest of blankets, warped by sadness. I didn't know how to have either conversation with her.

"So what happened?" Diana asks. "You can trust us with the NSFW version."

"There's no NSFW version." I try to sound nonchalant. "We were just . . . incompatible."

"I know all about that. Every guy in my early twenties. So much awkward fumbling." She reaches out and clasps her husband Eric's chin. "Fortunately, you were willing to learn."

"Are we really having this conversation in front of our kids?" he says. Admittedly, they're not paying attention, bickering about who spotted the afikomen first.

"I mean, have you met me?" Diana bats her lashes at him. He chuckles and shakes his head.

Truthfully, I'd love to be able to have conversations like that with Diana. But the one time we tried to meet up for lunch, one of her kids was sick and she couldn't find a sitter, and we never rescheduled. Or maybe I'm completely inept at making adult friends.

"Tell us about the wedding," says James, Phil's youngest son, a chemistry grad student. "What do you have planned so far? How can we help?"

I'm grateful for the subject change. Now that it's mid-April, July 14 no longer seems that far away.

"It'll be small," Phil says. "Not like your cousin Hassana's wedding in Ibadan."

Anthony slaps the table and bursts into laughter. "Remember the groom's arrival in a helicopter? And the runaway peacock?"

Diana joins in. "I swear that peacock was out for blood."

My mother laughs at this, too, and I'm not sure if she's heard the story from Phil or just wants to feel like she's part of this. Of course it's natural for Phil's family to have a history of shared experiences. But this is when it hits me that my family is no longer my mother and me and the occasional appearance from Ameena and TJ. We will never have in this room what we used to have, and in some ways that's a good thing. I've sat through too many lonely, quiet dinners, counted down the minutes until I could escape.

I didn't appreciate those dinners that sometimes felt haunted by my father's ghost. I'm convinced of that now. Talking about him was hard, but not talking was worse. So often, I'm trapped between the pain of remembering and the fear of forgetting.

Dinner winds down slowly, and it's nearing nine thirty when young kids are taken home to be tucked into bed. I can't recall a Passover with my mother lasting past eight o'clock.

I help her in the kitchen, though Phil tells us he has it covered and tries to shoo us. He's a good one, he really is, and I'm happy that my mother is happy. I wish it were easier for me to accept this change as a wholly positive one, instead of lamenting what I'm losing. Which of course makes me feel like a selfish piece of garbage. Guess it wouldn't be a holiday without a healthy dose of self-loathing.

Finally, Phil gets my mother to agree to take a break. She retreats to the living room with a book about music, leaving Phil and me alone in the kitchen. There is definitely a lot more dishwashing involved with a family this big.

"You wash, I'll dry?" he says, and we work in silence for a few minutes.

I run a sponge along the antique serving dish that belonged to my grandmother. "This was—really nice," I say, stumbling over my words.

"We were happy to be part of it." More silent scrubbing and drying, and then: "Your dad loved radio, yes?"

"Yeah. He did."

"He'd be so proud of you." Ever so gently, Phil dries the serving dish, treating it with the same kind of respect my mother has for so many years. "I'm not trying to take his place. You know that, right?"

"I know you're not an evil stepfather. You don't have to worry about that."

He grins. "Perhaps not, but it's still an adjustment. You can't be used to"—he gestures to the dining room—"all of that madness yet."

I give a sheepish shrug. "Not really," I say before we plunge back into semi-quiet, the only sounds are the running water and the classical music my mother is playing in the next room. Brahms. Classical has never been my favorite, maybe because the lack of words forces me to stay in my own mind instead of listening to what's inside someone else's. Still, growing up with it ensured I knew my way around it.

I could be content with this. I could continue giving him superficial responses, or I could make a concrete attempt to get to know my future stepfather. Because regardless of what I do or don't say, it's happening. A few months from now, this man who's shown my mother and me nothing but kindness will be an even more permanent fixture.

Maybe there will always be a ghost in this house, but it doesn't mean that I need to disappear, too.

"You mentioned during dinner that there's a new conductor at the symphony?"

"Alejandro Montaño," Phil says with utmost reverence. "A living legend. He's a little quirky, to put it lightly, but he's damn brilliant."

"Quirky how?"

"Well, to start, he's been singing parts of Mozart's *Marriage of Figaro* overture *out loud*."

I gasp. "No."

"Yes," Phil says, and maybe a relationship with him really is this easy. "And . . ." He glances around, as though worried legendary conductor Alejandro Montaño might overhear us. "He has a *dreadful* voice."

"And, of course, no one can say anything." From my mother, I know that conductors can be dictators of the classical music world.

"Of course not." He accepts another bowl I pass to him. "You really are doing a great job with the show, Shay. It's a lot of fun."

"Thank you," I say. "My dad always talked about how radio was more than just one thing. It could make you laugh one minute and then break your heart the next. Actually . . ." I trail off, chewing the inside of my cheek. An idea is forming, and though Phil has always been easygoing, I'm not sure how he'll react to this. "I'd love to be able to do some heavier episodes. Maybe . . . something about grief."

Phil pauses in the middle of drying the bowl. "Connected to relationships?"

I nod, the idea gaining a little more weight. "Maybe it could be about finding love again after—after losing a spouse or partner."

He's quiet for a few moments, and I curse myself for saying the wrong thing. He and Diana can joke about things I'd never joke about with my mother, but this might be off-limits. Maybe I've crossed a line.

"You know," he says finally, "I would really enjoy listening to that."

I can feel my shoulders soften with relief. This could be how I make up for lying to our listeners—by producing something real and raw. By finding the truth, as Dominic is so fond of talking about.

"What if you two came on the show to talk about it?"

"The two of us? On *The Ex Talk*?" My mother reenters the kitchen, rubbing at her throat, her dark brows climbing nearly to her hairline. "You don't want me on the radio. I highly doubt I'd have anything interesting to say."

"You would," I insist.

Phil pats his hands dry and wraps an arm around her shoulder. "If Leanna doesn't want to, then I'm afraid I'm out as well."

"But—you both would sound so great." I'm suddenly deeply attached to this seconds-old idea. I can imagine it: violinists healing from loss and rediscovering love through music. In my head, I become their conductor and the show becomes a symphony, a mix of strings and voices, with pauses at just the right time for the listener to take it all in.

"I'll think about it," my mother says. "Chag sameach."

"Chag sameach," I echo, and I hug them both before I leave.

On the drive back to my house, I forgo a podcast for the first time in what feels like forever. Classical music swells from my speakers, wrapping its notes around my heart and guiding me home.

The Ex Talk, Episode 2: We Need to Talk

Transcript

SHAY GOLDSTEIN: Welcome to *The Ex Talk*! I'm your host, Shay Goldstein.

DOMINIC YUN: And I'm your other host, Dominic Yun.

SHAY GOLDSTEIN: And we are two people who dated, broke up, and now have a radio show about it. Is that how we should introduce ourselves every time? We're still working on it.

DOMINIC YUN: I like it, but you never seemed to want to listen to my opinions.

SHAY GOLDSTEIN: That's because mine were usually better. We want to thank everyone who listened to our first episode, posted about it online, or shared it with their friends. If I can get sappy for a second, I've always wanted to host a radio show, and I didn't think it was ever going to happen. So truly: Thank you.

DOMINIC YUN: We have something a little terrifying on today's show—well, terrifying for us. Ideally it'll be enjoyable for you, the listener. A bit of schadenfreude for your Thursday afternoon, or wherever in time you happen to be when you listen to this podcast.

SHAY GOLDSTEIN: We're thrilled to have Dr. Nina Flores in the studio with us. She's a renowned couples counselor who's here to help us figure out what went wrong in our relationship. Dr. Flores, thank you so much.

DR. NINA FLORES: Please, call me Nina. It's my pleasure.

SHAY GOLDSTEIN: Nina, we'd love for you to take some calls from listeners, but first, we want to get your take on our relationship.

DOMINIC YUN: Maybe you could have even saved it.

DR. NINA FLORES: Well, Dominic, I want to be clear that it's not my job to do the saving. I give couples the tools to have an open dialogue about whatever they're struggling with, the ability to step back and analyze their relationship, to ask themselves, "Is this the best thing I should do or say in this scenario?"

SHAY GOLDSTEIN: So there's no magic wand?

DR. NINA FLORES: Correct.

DOMINIC YUN: Let's say you break up, but you still have to work with your ex. I would imagine a lot of our listeners can relate to that as well. And in my situation, well, my ex was intent on making my job as difficult as possible. What kinds of tools would you give me in that scenario?

Nina laughs.

DOMINIC YUN: I'd also like to point out that Shay is rolling her eyes.

SHAY GOLDSTEIN: I am not! There was a smudge on my glasses.

DOMINIC YUN: I see. You wanted to have a better view of my face.

SHAY GOLDSTEIN: A better view of its flaws. Did you just stop halfway through shaving this morning and call it good?

DOMINIC YUN: It's already three o'clock. I have very powerful testosterone.

SHAY GOLDSTEIN: You heard him, folks, we have a great big strong

MAN in the studio today. However will the women be able to keep from fainting?

DOMINIC YUN: Keeping their sarcasm to themselves might be a good start.

SHAY GOLDSTEIN: I'm starting to feel it. I—I'm getting weak. I'm not sure how much longer I can be in your presence. The room is spinning, and I'm hot all over, and—and—

DR. NINA FLORES: You know . . . forgive me for saying this, but in the interest of getting everything out in the open and on the table—I've worked with a lot of couples, and I'm sensing something between you two. Something you two haven't talked about. Some lingering tension, perhaps?

SHAY GOLDSTEIN: What? Oh—no. No lingering tension here.

DOMINIC YUN: Definitely not. Everything is on the table, Nina. Trust me.

13

The master's jar starts during episode three, when a caller named Lydia tells us she met her ex in grad school.

"I don't like to talk about it, but I also have a master's degree," Dominic says, catching my gaze, half his mouth tilting into a smile. There's a self-awareness to it he didn't have a couple months ago, or if he did, I never noticed. It's too funny to bother me anymore, especially now that it's become a joke with the listeners. They latched onto what I said in the first episode and even found some of his old college articles and tweeted them out.

Lydia's laugh is a fuzzy burst through the phone line. "You guys should start a master's jar. Like a swear jar, except Dominic has to put in five dollars every time he mentions his master's degree."

It's wild, the way she talks about Dominic like she's known him for ages. My favorite podcasts have built up years and years of in-jokes, and I can't quite believe that we're already starting to have something like that. A vocabulary just for us and our listeners.

"That's perfect," I say. "I'm all for shaming Dominic."

"Five dollars?" Dominic says, incredulous. "How much do you think we make?"

So that's how the empty Costco jelly bean jar ends up on my desk with DOMINIC MASTER'S JAR written on it in Sharpie. Ruthie decorates it with blue and orange stickers, the colors of the University of Illinois—Northwestern's rival. At the end of every month, the listeners get to vote on the charity we donate the money to. By the end of the week, there's twenty-five bucks in there.

People at the station have been trying to bait him, too. Mike Russo mentioned his daughter will be applying to college in the fall and wondered if Dominic knew of any good schools in Illinois, and Jacqueline Guillaumont asked if he had an opinion on the piece about higher-education funding she was working on. The funniest thing of all, maybe, is that he's being such a good sport about it, shaking his head, offering a tight smile, and backing away from any question that could steal five dollars from his wallet.

In a landslide, the listeners vote to send our first donation to the University of Illinois alumni association. I film a video to post on social media while Dominic pretends to shed a tear as he makes out the check.

The next week, Dominic and I wind up at a trendy new downtown restaurant to collect some tape for an upcoming show about aphrodisiacs. At Oscura, we're completely in the dark, both literally and metaphorically: All the lights are off, and the dishes, a prix fixe menu based on whatever the chef is in the mood for, are made up of primarily aphrodisiacs. Ruthie went here on a date when it opened and said it was a trippy experience. Today they cleared out the restaurant for a private lunch for Dominic and me.

"This is a cold pomegranate-beet soup with maca root," says

Nathaniel, the maître d', and I hear a soft clink as two bowls are placed in front of us. "It's a plant that has been called the Peruvian Viagra."

A recording device sits on the table between us. We wanted to experiment with our segments, mix in some prerecorded elements. Since we can't see what we're doing, it'll make for great radio, and my inner audiophile is positively giddy. The first course was oysters with some kind of fancy cocktail sauce. I'm probably one of only a handful of people in Seattle who don't like seafood, so I couldn't tell if they were good or not. But Dominic said *wow* after his first one, so I assume they were. The second course was a potato galette with a pistachio crust, the third a chicken curry with heaps of fenu-greek, and now we're on the last course before dessert.

In the dark, my sense of smell is much stronger, and the Viagra soup smells incredible. Tart yet earthy, with a hint of sweetness from the maca. I dip my spoon and lift it to my mouth. "Oh my god. I could eat a vat of that."

"How much science is there behind all of this?" Dominic asks. "Because what I've read is that oysters aren't scientifically proven to be aphrodisiacs, though there's some evidence to back up some-thing like maca or fenugreek."

"Our goal is to provide our guests a fun, inventive dining expe-rience," Nathaniel says. "But our chef does have a master's degree in nutritional science. I can bring him out for an interview at the end of the meal."

"We'd love that, thank you," Dominic says. "About how long did it take you to get used to the dark?"

"There was a lot of stumbling at first, a lot of dropped plates." If I could see, I imagine he'd be smiling. "But we got the hang of it after a couple of weeks."

"Do you just have people ripping off each other's clothing by the end of the meal?" I ask. I am a Serious Professional Journalist.

Nathaniel laughs. "Not exactly," he says, "but if they were, we wouldn't notice."

He retreats to the kitchen.

"How are you feeling?" I ask Dominic. "The maca isn't too strong?"

"Are you asking if I'm horny?"

I choke on my next spoonful of soup. "Gross, no, I don't want to know that."

Truthfully, I feel a little *something* not unlike what I felt in the station kitchen. It could be entirely psychological, the dark playing tricks on me the way the alcohol did. The table is tiny, and our knees keep knocking together beneath it. It's only when he pulls his legs back that I realize we've been touching for the past one and a half courses.

"You're still anxious about the numbers," Dominic says.

"How can you tell? You can't even see my face."

"It's your tone."

I didn't realize we'd been spending so much time together that he'd be able to gauge my moods by the sound of my voice, but maybe we have.

"A little," I admit. "I don't want to disappoint anyone. Not that I thought we'd be this overnight smash hit, and our listeners really have been amazing. I guess I just crave validation," I half joke in a way I hope sounds self-deprecating.

Dominic's quiet for a few moments, and I curse the dark. Not that I'd be able to read his expression anyway. "I wasn't going to say anything unless it seemed like it was going to happen, but . . ." He takes a breath. "A friend of mine from undergrad, he works in PR with Saffron Shaw."

"Why does that name sound familiar?"

"She's on that CW show, *Oceanside*?"

"I've heard of it." I've watched a couple episodes. Fine, seven.

"One of those shows where all the actors are in their midtwenties playing teens?"

"James Marsters was in his midthirties when he started on *Buffy*," Dominic points out.

"Fair. Wait, how have we not talked about whether you're on Team Angel or Team Spike?"

"Team Riley."

"Please leave."

He laughs. "Just wanted to test you. I'm Team Angel to my core. The romantic in me, I guess."

Huh. I never would have pegged him as the romantic type. I confirm for him that I'm on the same team.

"Saffron has like, this rabid fan base," Dominic says, "and she does this thing on social media where she recommends something to her followers every week, a show or a book or something. My friend thought Saffron would be into *The Ex Talk*, so he was going to try to get it to her, but I haven't heard anything."

"That's—really awesome of you," I say. He cares about the show. It shouldn't come as a shock to me, and yet it does. He wants it to succeed as much as I do. "Thanks for doing that."

"I wanted to be able to surprise you with it," he says, and then wryly adds: "So thanks for ruining that."

I want to swat his arm, but I'm worried I'd miss and dump what I assume is fuchsia liquid into his lap instead, so I keep my hands to myself.

After we polish off the pomegranate soup, Nathaniel returns with the final course. "These are handcrafted dark chocolate cherry truffles." He pauses. "We always encourage the couple to feed each other."

"Oh, we're not a couple," I say.

"You must have the full experience," he insists.

"We should do what the man says," Dominic says, and louder, as though making sure the mic catches this: "Let the record show that Shay Goldstein did not want my hands anywhere near her mouth."

"I have no problem with your hands near my mouth. It's not the worst thing I've ever put there," I say sweetly.

"Too racy for public radio," Dominic says with a cluck of his tongue.

"Shay, go ahead," Nathaniel says, sounding as though he's trying to hold in a laugh.

My hand stumbles around on the table before I find one of the truffles. It's bite-size but probably deathly rich. "The airplane is preparing for landing," I say as I bring it up to where I imagine Dominic's mouth is.

"Ah, yes, nothing more romantic than imagining you're feeding a picky child," he says, and I must press the chocolate into the side of his face because he adds, "Runway's a little to the left."

Carefully, I maneuver it across his stubbled cheek and over to his mouth. *There.* He parts his lips to take a small bite, his teeth grazing my fingers. And *oh my god*, that is a feeling I've never before experienced during dinner. His lips are so smooth, contrasted with the roughness of his cheek, and I can feel the chocolate melting on my fingertips.

"Sorry," he says in a scratchy voice that makes my hand wobble against his mouth and my heart do something similar inside my chest. "God, that's *phenomenal*."

He goes for the chocolate again, his tongue slicking the pads of my fingers. *Breathe.* I can do this. I can feed Dominic Yun a truffle without losing my shit.

Except every time we make contact, I imagine us up against that wall again, him inching closer and closer until there's no space between our bodies. And the various other ways he'd use his tongue and his teeth, how he might savor a girl the way he savors this piece of chocolate.

I hope Nathaniel knows this place is dangerous. We may be in a darkened restaurant designed to get people in the mood to ravage each other, but this is our job. I cannot have these kinds of feelings at work.

Finally, it's his turn to—ugh—feed me. I'm convinced it won't be as disconcerting as the sensation of his teeth on my skin, but he reaches my closed mouth a second before I'm ready, before I've had the chance to process what's happening. He nudges my lips apart with one gentle finger before slipping me a bite of the most decadent piece of chocolate I've ever tasted.

"Good?" Dominic says, and suddenly he sounds much closer than just across the table.

No. This truffle is downright indecent. It's not good, the way my teeth scrape his fingers. It's not good, the sweetness of chocolate and the salt of his skin. It's not good, the way I have to press my thighs together to guard against the sensation building there and demanding relief.

This is not foreplay. It's *work*.

We might be tricking our listeners, and now the darkness and proximity are tricking me, morphing my annoyance with him into some kind of deranged attraction.

"Great," I manage, and it's really not good, the way I crave chocolate the rest of the week.

Twitter

Saffron Shaw (✓) @saff_shaw
happy friday, loves!!! today's #saffrec is a podcast called @TheExTalk!

they only have a few episodes out but the hosts are so so charming and REAL! give em a listen so they can make more, k? ✌️

Replies: 247 RTs: 9.2K Likes: 16K

14

The Apple Podcasts Top 100.

We slide into spot number ninety-seven on Friday afternoon, after Saffron Shaw's tweet, and we ride that high all weekend. The tweet gets picked up by the Mary Sue, by Vulture, by NPR's own pop culture podcast. My follower count jumps to three thousand, to five thousand, to eight thousand. I lose the ability to keep up with my notifications, and at one point, #shayminic might be trending.

It's *wild*.

Monday is basically a wash. Kent brings in donuts at nine, pops a bottle of champagne at ten, and takes us out to a long lunch at eleven thirty. We don't get much work done after that.

The whole time, my mind is spinning. From the shock of our sudden fame and the pressure to sustain it, yes, but there's something underneath. The station is treating Dominic like a hero, which would normally make me roll my eyes. But he did help make this happen—I have to give him credit for that. Leading up to episode 1, I figured I'd be most anxious about my voice. And while I probably won't ever love listening to myself, I thought our lie would be easy. We were storytelling.

Except when listener tweets make it so clear they buy every detail of our fake relationship and well-crafted breakup, I can't help wondering which side of this my dad would be on. People have so quickly become invested in this story that isn't real, regardless of how Kent pitched it to the board of directors.

And yet there was Dominic, purveyor of Truth in Journalism, basking in the attention and letting Kent buy him another beer.

"Going down?"

He shows up in front of the elevator just as I'm waiting for it. Oddly, this hasn't happened since the show began. I've always needed to rush home to walk Steve, while Dominic seems content to stay late.

"Actually, I've been meaning to pay the AI golf club startup on the sixth floor a visit," I tell him. "They seem like good people."

"Never pegged you as the golfing type."

"I'm a complex and layered human being."

That earns me a smirk. "You know, I'm hating this much less than I thought I would."

"You're not hating your nearly ten thousand followers?"

"Don't be bitter because you're only at nine thousand."

"Nine thousand five hundred."

And I'm sure we'll both be flooded with sponsorship opportunities soon. Still, I've had to limit looking at my mentions, since some people don't exactly respect the boundaries between our private and professional lives. Sure, the show blurs the two, and the images of famous movie breakup scenes one listener posted with my and Dominic's faces photoshopped onto the actors' bodies were entertaining. Yes, I retweeted it.

But some comments have strayed a little past PG-13. I was flattered by it at first—strangers finding me attractive is certainly an ego boost—but it stopped feeling innocent when someone tweeted at me asking if Dominic's circumcised. Then someone asked Dominic to rate my performance in bed. And those were some of the tamer ones.

I have enough unsavory thoughts on my own without the internet making it worse.

The elevator arrives, and when we both go to hit **P**, his hand gets there first. God, he looks even taller in here.

My brain does bad things in enclosed spaces with Dominic, but I want to take advantage of our alone time, ask him the questions I can't in the newsroom.

"It's weird, isn't it, that some people want us to get back together?"

"Apparently, both of us are in the right and in the wrong, and we deserve both better and worse."

"We should really stop reading the tweets." I settle into a much less impressive lean against the opposite side of the elevator, toying with the strap of my bag. "You don't feel . . . I don't know, dishonest?"

He pauses, and then: "You made it pretty clear when you begged me to do the show with you. We're telling a story."

"Right." I thought maybe he was wearing a facade for Kent—not that he'd abandoned his journalistic morals. Maybe they weren't that strong to begin with. It changes my opinion of him, just a little. I guess I liked that he had something he was so passionate about. So steadfast.

"How's your family handling all of this?" I ask. "Do they listen to the show?"

His mouth curves into that frustrating side smile. "They wonder what I did to drive you away."

"And you told them it was your insistence on falling asleep to the lullaby of a judicial-system podcast?"

"Naturally. I was going to tell one of my buddies from college. Undergrad," he adds. "But we're all spread out, and we don't talk as much as we used to. Sometimes I wish I'd stayed here for college," he says, and there's a hint of . . . nostalgia? in his voice. "But then I wouldn't have the master's degree."

"That's five dollars."

"We're off the clock," he says, feigning a look of innocence. "You're not going to let me off easy?"

I hold out my hand, and he groans and slides his wallet from his pocket.

This ease between us, it's very new. I don't entirely hate it, even if it makes me more aware of all the angles of him: the slant of his shoulders, the curve of his cheekbones. It's cruel that I can't go back to simply being annoyed by him.

A ding indicates we've reached the parking garage.

"This elevator's been so slow lately," I say. "Well. See you tomorrow."

I'm heading toward the booth with the security guard, where we swipe our badges every morning, when Dominic says, "Wait."

I turn around.

"Do you . . . maybe want to grab drinks? Mahoney's next door has a great happy hour. Half off everything. To celebrate the top one hundred," he adds. "It's a big milestone. I mean—I guess we celebrated most of the day, but there's no such thing as too much celebrating, right?" He finishes this with a sheepish laugh, a rake of his hand through his dark hair. Is he . . . nervous?

"Oh—" I start, caught off guard by the comment. Drinks. Drinks with Dominic. Dominic asked me to grab drinks with him. A friendly round of drinks between colleagues. Surely that's all it was intended to be. He's trying to prove we can be friends, just like our alternate-universe selves after our made-up breakup. "I, um, can't. I have to feed my dog."

"Let me guess, he also ate your show notes?"

I clap a hand over my mouth. "Oh my god. I just realized how that sounded. I swear, I really do have to feed my dog."

"You just adopted him, right?" Dominic's features soften, but I don't feel any less relaxed. "I love dogs. My apartment doesn't allow them."

"Last month. We're still getting into a routine. He's a bit of a weirdo, but it's like, he's *my* weirdo." Now I might start rambling. "I didn't realize I'd love him so much, but I do, despite all his idiosyncrasies. Or maybe because of them."

For a few seconds, I think I might want to invite him over to meet my dog.

But that would be ridiculous, wouldn't it? Dominic in my house, playing with Steve? That's too strange a visual to even imagine.

"Okay—well," he says, nodding toward the doors. "I'm off to drink alone."

I groan. "Please, don't make yourself sound that pathetic. I'll feel bad."

"You know you love it." He waves, and I wonder if he really is going to a bar to have half-off drinks by himself, and something about that strikes me as so incredibly sad. He said he'd considered telling his college friends about our fake past relationship, but he didn't mention any Seattle friends. Again, I find myself wondering how he spends his free time. If we've gained any kind of friendliness with each other, it isn't enough for me to feel comfortable asking.

I half expect him to say something like *another time*, as though promising we'll do drinks again when my dog's dinner isn't as urgent. But it doesn't come, and as I navigate the parking lot maze to my car, I realize I was waiting for it.

I dump a few capfuls of lavender bubble bath into my tub and pile my hair into a topknot. Steve lounges on the rug in the middle of my bathroom, chewing on a stuffed hippo, and a glass of rosé is perched on the edge of the tub. It's been ages since I took a bath, mainly because it hasn't always been easy to relax in my house. Typically, I'd turn on a podcast, but the silence feels kind of nice. Tonight it feels like I can turn off my mind and just *be*. (Or, I'm trying to.)

Our show is doing well. (For now.)

My mother is happily planning her wedding. (And still on the fence about my grief show, but I'm working on her.)

Ameena's been swamped at work, but we made dinner plans for this weekend. (And she's continuing to advance in the interview process for the Virginia job.)

And Dominic . . .

Nope, not going there.

I'm stepping into the bath when my phone vibrates on the counter. I'd planned to leave it in my bedroom, but it's possible I'm a little too married to it, to our subscriber numbers, to my Twitter feed.

Dominic: I trust your dog had a prompt and gourmet dinner.

I can't help smiling at that. I send a response before sinking into the hot water.

Shay: He has a sophisticated palate. I think his kibble is even made with some amount of real chicken. Or at least they have to legally put that on the package.

Shay: How was drinking alone?

Dominic: Is it drinking alone if you make awkward small talk with the old trucker guy at the other end of the bar who may or may not have invited you to a trucker party?

Shay: Dominic. Are you at a trucker party? Do you need help?

Shay: Related: what is a trucker party?

His replies come so quickly that I barely have time to set my phone down before it lights up again.

Dominic: I'm at home, so sadly, I may never find out.

Shay: It's 8:30. Go out and do whatever the young folk are doing these days.

Dominic: But I'm already in my comfy sweats.

Shay: If you're in comfy sweats at 8:30, you're no longer allowed to make fun of me for being old.

Dominic: Fine, what are you wearing?

I choke on a sip of wine, and Steve glances up from the floor, as though to make sure I haven't died. Not because he necessarily cares about me, but because I am his source of food. Once he's confirmed I'm still alive, he returns to his toy.

Dominic: oh

Dominic: oh god

Dominic: I didn't mean that the way it sounds

Dominic: 💀 💀 💀

Shay: Good, because the answer would have been weird for both of us.

I'm not flirting. I swear.

Dominic: A sexy Gritty costume?

Shay: Damn it, you weren't supposed to guess right on the first try.

He goes quiet for a while, and I return to my rosé like the millennial trash I am. Three dots appear, then disappear, then reappear. I overthink and overanalyze.

Dominic: You know what? You've convinced me. I'm young and sprightly. I'm going out.

Shay: No more comfy sweats?

Dominic: Comfy sweats off, party jeans on.

Shay: Ha. Have fun.

I stare down at the phone, wondering if my response doesn't convey enough enthusiasm. I'm not entirely sure what I encouraged him to go out and do or what level of enthusiasm I should have about it. After a few more seconds of deliberation, I send a party hat emoji. That makes me feel a little better.

It's an hour and a half later, once I'm getting in bed with a steamy romance novel and another glass of wine, that my phone buzzes again.

Dominic: have you ever wondered why pizzas come in square boxes even though they're round

The lack of capital letters and punctuation is a dead giveaway. He's got to be drinking.

Shay: UNSUBSCRIBE

Dominic: won't work, I'm not asking you for money or to vote for me

Shay: Fine then. I assume it's because it's easier to make square boxes. And the square stops the pizza from sliding all over the place.

Dominic: so smart

I wish I could explain why texting with him makes me grin at my phone like my favorite podcast just dropped a surprise bonus episode. I probably wouldn't like the answer. For now, I'll blame it on being tipsy.

Dominic: Shay Evelyn Goldstein

Dominic: I am very drnuk. too drunk for autocrrect

Shay: How do you know my middle name?

Dominic: we dated for three months, of course I know your middle name

Shay: It seems as though the party jeans are really living up to their name.

Dominic: oh yeah. everything's spinny and bouncy and beauuuuuutiful

Dominic: I'm even starting to forget where I live 🙃

This wipes the grin off my face. I'm sure it's a joke, but I'm the one who suggested he go out. He was so in control when we were drinking at the station. Depending on how drunk he is, he may actually need help.

Shay: Where are you right now?

Dominic: the nomad in cap hill

Dominic: why, u putting on party jeans too?? 😂 👖

I'm not going to be able to properly enjoy this romance novel or even fall asleep afterward if I'm worrying about him, damn it.

Shay: Stay there. I'm on my way.

15

"You didn't have to do this," Dominic slurs when I find him hunched over the bar, proving exactly why I had to do this. A few empty shot glasses are stacked next to him. He has one cheek pressed to the countertop, and I don't want to think about how sticky his face is going to be when he sits up. God, it's strange to see him like this outside of work, like seeing your middle school principal at the grocery with a cart full of Lean Cuisines.

"Maybe not," I say, sidestepping a beer puddle. "But I can't host the show alone if you fall in a ditch on your way home, so here I am."

He couldn't have picked a divier place to drink away his sorrows, if that was in fact what he was doing. Or maybe he was just being young and sprightly. The bar is small and dark and playing Nickelback, which should on its own be a reason to shut it down. It also just *feels* damp.

"Shay." He schools his features into this expression of utmost concentration. With one hand, he strokes the counter, his ear intimate enough with it to contract an STD. "Shay. Shhh. I think I can hear the ocean."

"I'm sure you can, buddy." I pat his back, and it's meant to be reassuring, maybe even a little patronizing. It's rare for me to feel any kind of power with Dominic, and I can't say I'm not enjoying this. But I can feel the flex of his shoulders beneath his shirt, the firmness of muscle. How warm he is.

I drop my hand.

"Careful. I might have cooties." He snickers at this.

My head is starting to throb. I should have stopped after one glass of wine, but at least I'm not as far gone as he is. If I'd said yes to drinks earlier, would we both be this plastered?

"I'm so sorry about him," I tell the bartender, a woman with full sleeves of tattoos who looks like she could probably bench-press two Dominics. "I didn't realize I'd be taking care of a six-year-old when I came to pick him up."

"Don't worry about it. I've seen much worse." She fills up a glass of water, plunks it in front of him.

"Drink," I instruct, and though he grumbles, he manages a few sips. "Have you eaten anything?" I interpret his shrug as a no. "Do you serve food?" I ask the bartender.

"Just fries and tots," she says, so I order one of each.

Since I don't want to leave until he has a bit of food in his stomach, I hoist myself onto the too-tall stool next to him. Our baskets of grease arrive, along with a bottle of ketchup with just enough inside to make it look like I'm doing something obscene when I slap it against my palm.

"Wow. You really just get right to it," Dominic says.

I give the bottle another hard shake before the ketchup comes out.

Despite this bar looking like you wouldn't trust anything that comes out of its kitchen, the food is crisp and salted to perfection. I am eating Tater Tots with my former nemesis in a dive bar at eleven o'clock on a Monday night. My life has ceased to make sense.

After he's had enough to stop swaying in his seat, I figure it's safe for us to leave. He struggles to extract his wallet from his back pocket, though, so I fish out my own. "I'll pay you back later," he says.

"Oh, I know you will."

The bartender passes back my credit card. "You two have a good night."

You two. It's not an implication that we're together, just that we are two human beings leaving a bar at the same time.

It might be a Monday, but that doesn't stop Capitol Hill. Hipsters loiter outside bars, the chilly April air thick with cigarette smoke and weed. Dominic isn't wearing a jacket, just the slate-gray button-down he had on at work that's come untucked.

He slings an arm around my shoulders and slumps against me, which, given our height difference, must look comical. After a moment's hesitation, I reach around his waist to steady him. It's the closest we've ever been—even closer when his shirt rides up, and for the briefest moment, my fingers graze the warm skin of his lower back.

I draw back so suddenly that he attempts to right himself, relying more on his own legs than on my five-two frame. "Sorry. I was probably putting too much weight on you." He pats the shoulder of my jacket. "You're *tiny*."

"The least you can do is try not to insult me after I rescue you from Nickelback and Jägermeister."

"It wasn't an insult." He stares down at me, his gaze impossible to read as always. I feel not just tiny but like I'm giving a presentation at a senior staff meeting wearing only nipple tassels and my favorite public radio socks—I wouldn't be Shay Goldstein if I didn't have multiple pairs—with a fish holding a microphone beneath the words *Ira Bass*. "What's the tallest guy you've dated?"

"I don't understand how that's relevant." And yet as I think through my dating history, my wine-jumbled mind snags on the memory of us in the station kitchen. The way he loomed over me, caging me in. Pressing the glass of water to my cheek. How I felt small but safe, and a whole lot of other feelings I never gave my body permission to feel. Feelings I am definitely not experiencing right now.

I guess it doesn't hurt to humor him. "I dated someone a few years ago who was six one."

"Silly," he says, and he boops my nose. He's going to die when I rub this in his face tomorrow. "You're supposed to say me. Where's the car?"

"Since I was in the middle of a glass of wine when you texted, I took a Lyft." I pull up my phone to order another one, then maneuver us to a bench facing the street. He flops onto it next to me, head dropping to my shoulder. With this lack of control over his limbs, he's like once of those inflatable tube creatures at car dealerships. But heavier. And smelling only a little like alcohol—much less than I'd think after spending a couple of hours in that bar—and a little like sweat, but mostly like *Dominic*. Woodsy and clean.

"Why did you drink this much?" I ask.

"Thassagoodstory." He stretches it into one long drunken word. "I was already buzzed after Mahoney's. I had to drink away my misery after you told me a story about a fake dog so you wouldn't have to hang out with me."

"He's real! His name is Steve! I have photos!" I rush to get out my phone again, but Dominic just holds up a hand, laughing.

"I know. I know. Then I got home, and you were in a sexy Gritty costume, and I guess I wasn't done celebrating the show. And you know. Being young and sprightly and everything." He waves a hand at this. "And then I started thinking about how there was no one I could ask to come out with me. I don't even like going out that much. Not enough to get in the habit of doing it alone. But there I was. Drinking alone at a bar on a Monday night, and I figured drinking more would help me feel less like shit about it."

At first, I can't formulate words. This isn't the Dominic who teased me about *Puget Sounds* or even the Dominic who fed me truffles in the dark, his teeth on the tips of my fingers. I try to picture a version of Dominic lying on a couch in his comfy sweats, idly scrolling through Netflix but not finding anything to watch, texting with me because he had no one else to text with. Going out alone because he had no one else to ask. He grew up here, so this makes me even more curious about his background. He said he's the youngest of five kids, and I'm not sure where his siblings live or if they're close. I don't know which Dominic this is, and it makes me both hesitant and curious.

His confession turns me serious, drags out a secret of my own. "I feel lonely sometimes, too," I say in a quiet voice. "I basically have one friend, and she might be getting a job on the other side of the country."

"I'm so sorry," he says, and it sounds like he means it. Then he brightens, straightening his posture. "I'll be your friend!"

"That sounds like the alcohol talking."

"We're not friends?" There's an odd vulnerability there. He seems hurt, maybe, that I wouldn't consider us friends.

"No, no," I hurry to say. *Are* we friends? "We can be friends. We're friends."

He drops his head to my shoulder again, and I make myself stay very, very still. "Good."

The Lyft shows up then, relief of reliefs, and I manage not to sprain anything while helping this giant into a Prius.

Once we're inside, the driver confirms the address before returning to an impassioned argument about soccer with whoever's on the other end of his Bluetooth. The throbbing in my head has become a maddening, insistent tattoo. I let out a long breath as I relax against the seat, shutting my eyes for a moment.

"You smell good," Dominic says, and my eyes fly open.

"Oh—I, uh, took a bath earlier. It's probably the lavender bubble bath."

"When we were texting?"

"Mm-hmm," I manage. Yep, this will be what keeps me up tonight. "Just a typical wild Monday night. Right up there with drinking alone."

"Have I said thank you yet?"

"Nope."

"Thank you," he says emphatically, seeming to come back to himself a bit more, at least, the part of him that's genuine. The part of him that's peeked through a few times since we started this whole charade. "I mean it. I know I could have found my own way home, but I'll probably feel a lot less like death tomorrow, thanks to you."

"You're welcome. I was the one who encouraged you to go out, so. I felt bad."

"Maybe, but I'm the one who decided to do Jägerbombs."

When a streetlamp catches his face, the light hangs on the cut of his jaw, the curve of his mouth. It's rude that he looks good even sloshed. Even with—especially with—his hair disheveled. I like messy Dominic, the Dominic who is literally less buttoned up than he is at work.

"I hope I didn't get in the way of you trying to get someone's number or anything." *Shit*. I hate myself the moment I say it. *Why why why why why.*

He lifts an eyebrow. "You didn't. It's been a very long drought."

"Your last relationship ended about a year ago?" I ask, and he nods. "It's been about the same amount of time for me, too."

A very long drought. Does that mean he hasn't slept with anyone since his relationship ended, or that he hasn't dated? It's not unrealistic, of course. Maybe he isn't one for casual hookups. I tend to get too attached for them to be healthy for me, a lesson I learned in my early twenties. Which is where he still is.

"You haven't dated at all?" he says.

"I'm on a dating app hiatus." I stare down at the floor, realizing that in my haste to leave, I put on one black shoe and one brown shoe. Jesus, speaking of messy. "In the meantime . . . there's always the fun drawer. Never lets me down and never wants to go to brunch in the morning."

"There's a whole drawer?"

I am never drinking again. Dominic is going to think my nightstand is overflowing with dildos.

I steal a glance up front, making sure the driver is still immersed in his phone call. "Well, half a drawer." I *am* still tipsy, right? Or I have a contact drunk from him. That has to be the explanation for why I'm talking to him like this.

"You could find someone if you wanted." A lazy roll of his head toward me, a lowering of his eyelashes to half-mast. "Someone who isn't battery powered, I mean. You're cute."

It's the first time he's complimented me outright, and I have no idea what it means. Drunk words, sober thoughts? Even if that's true, I shouldn't care if Dominic thinks I'm cute. I *am* cute. He's simply stating a fact.

Of course, I'm not going to tell him that the finding isn't the issue—it's the scaring away once I inevitably fall faster than the other person does.

"I thought I was 'cool,'" I say, trying to project a coolness I do not feel. An aloofness. A nonchalance. I am Meryl Streep as Margaret Thatcher! I am Meryl Streep in that movie with the nuns. My gaze falls to his mouth, to the hollow of this throat, to the triangle of skin exposed by his unbuttoned buttons, and all pretense of *cool* vanishes. I am Meryl Streep in *Mamma Mia! Here We Go Again*.

"Both."

"And once again, Drunk Dominic is much more fun than Sober Dominic."

"Sober Dominic wants to tell you that he's fun, too, but he's too busy shaking his head disapprovingly at Drunk Dominic."

I'm still laughing, heart still hammering, when the car stops outside his place. The bar wasn't very far from his place downtown, but the ride felt shorter than I thought it would.

"I like this area," I say as we get out of the car and I five-star Julius. The air against my face is a welcome respite from the heat of the back seat.

He shrugs. "It's not great. You don't have to sugarcoat it. I picked it because it was close to work."

Each step we take is heavier than the last. I'm just walking him to the door. Surely I'm not helping him inside. He already seems much less wasted than he was at the bar. Still buzzed, but perfectly capable of entering a building without me fearing for his life.

"Thank you," he says when we reach the front steps of his building, a newer construction that looks the same as all the other apartments on this street. He leans against the door, his trademark stance. Somehow, it doesn't bother me as much as it usually does. "Again. I'm sure I would have made it home okay, but it's nice to know, I guess . . . that you cared."

That lands across my heart in a way I didn't at all expect. "Of course I care." I shuffle my weight from side to side, run my hand up and down the strap of my bag. "Just because we broke up doesn't mean I stopped caring. I care about all my exes."

This earns me a half smile. He likes that I'm playing along. He makes a move to reach for his keys—at least, that's what I think he's doing, until his hand lands on my wrist instead. I swear it happens in slow motion as he pinches the hair elastic I have there, snapping it against my skin.

The whisper of a sting goes away in an instant, but the aftershocks are vicious. I swallow hard. I'd wear elastics up and down my arms if it meant he'd do that again.

When he speaks, his voice is low. "I like your hair down," he says, and it makes me grab at my hair on instinct. I was in such a rush that I didn't think to put it up. "I know you wear it up all the time, and I like it up, but this . . . I like this a lot."

"It's really coarse," I say quietly, awed that I'm able to make any sounds at all. "It can never decide if it's curly or straight. That's why I usually wear it up."

His hand travels to my hair, sliding into it, and *oh*. I sway closer to him as his fingers get lost in my curly-straight mess, grazing my scalp. I inhale his earthy, heady scent. God, it's been so long since someone touched me this way, even if it probably doesn't count, given he's my cohost slash fake ex slash possible friend. And drunk. Sober Dominic may be fun, according to him, but he would never do *this*.

"It feels pretty soft to me," he says, and that is when I perish.

He uses that hand in my hair to guide me closer to him. Then he leans down, and before I can process what's happening, his mouth is on mine.

And I'm kissing him back.

The press of his lips is firm but curious, a burst of warmth on a cold spring night. I can't figure out what to do with my hands, not yet, not when this is already sensory overload. The lovely scrape of his stubble against my chin. The way his fingers grasp at strands of my hair. The rumble of a groan in his throat.

We shouldn't do this, my brain screams at me.

Maybe he's the only one who hears because he suddenly pulls

away, leaving me desperate for air, gasping into the dark downtown. The kiss must have lasted less than three seconds. Three seconds that stole my bones and left me weightless.

The look on his face is abject horror. "Shit. *Shit*. I'm so sorry. I shouldn't have—"

"No, it's—" I break off, unsure what I was about to say. That it was fine? Because it's definitely not. Because now I'm wondering what a sober kiss would feel like, what might have happened if I'd opened my mouth. If he'd pushed me up against his front door. "I mean, I'm still pretty tipsy too, so . . ."

"Fuck, this is embarrassing," he says, shaking his head, scrubbing a hand down his face. *Mistake* is written all over it. "I'm clearly still a lot drunker than I thought. Let's just—"

"Forget that happened?" I let out a sound that might be a laugh, but it's much higher pitched than I'm used to hearing. I bring my fingertips to my mouth, as though grasping for the memory of his lips there.

His shoulders sag. Relief—that's what it is. "Please. I really am so sorry."

"Me too," I say, because didn't he realize I was kissing him back? Maybe he couldn't tell. Maybe that's for the best. Maybe I should quit *The Ex Talk*. It sounds about as rational as any of the other thoughts racing through my mind. "Then I should . . ." I nod toward the street, making this supremely dorky gesture with my thumbs.

"Right. Yeah. Thank you. Again. Let me know how much I owe you for the drinks, and the Lyft, and—"

"It's no problem."

"Okay. If you're sure." He scratches at his elbow, unable to meet my eyes. A minute ago, that hand was in my hair. "Do you want me to, uh, wait out here until your ride comes?"

"Nope!" I chirp back. I am a Disney character. An animated mouse. "I'm good. Thanks."

"Well—okay," he says, fumbling with his keys before fitting them in the lock. "See you tomorrow?"

If I haven't flung myself into Puget Sound by then. "See you," I echo, and when his door shuts, I sink to the ground and vow to never drink again.

16

It's a relief to see Ameena on Wednesday, even if it means subjecting my poor ego to another wine-and-paint night. Tonight's Blush 'n Brush subject is a bowl of artfully arranged trinkets: a locket, a mirror, a doll with a sad haircut and a single eyeball. She has definitely seen some shit.

"Where did they get that fucking doll?" I hiss to Ameena.

Ameena frowns at her canvas, where she's captured the essence of the doll in a way few people could. "I don't know, but I swear her one eye is following me." She peers over at my rendering of it. "What the hell, Shay, you made it worse!"

"I'm sorry!" I lob more paint onto the canvas. "My mind is in about a hundred places."

"I get it. I've barely been able to focus on work this week with all the interview prep the conservancy sent over."

A thing that is happening: Ameena flying to Virginia for a final interview.

She told me ten minutes ago. I'm still processing.

The wine helps, but it's also led me down a few questionable paths lately, so I'm not about to trust it completely. I've amended my vow: I am not drinking only if Dominic is nearby, since I can't be trusted to make good choices.

So far this week, we've stuck to our plan to pretend Monday night never happened. We've been polite, probably too polite as we dance around each other in a finely tuned choreography of avoidance. Our conversations are about work and work only. No late nights at the office, no more tidbits about our personal lives. His face is as stoic as it's ever been. For the first time, I'm dreading tomorrow's show, and painting with Ameena isn't as much of a distraction as I'd hoped it would be.

Part of me is relieved we've been able to put it behind us, but another part—a part that's growing larger each day—can't stop thinking about the kiss. Can't get his stupid nice face out of my head. That brush of lips was so brief that sometimes I'm convinced I imagined it. I haven't even told Ameena.

And it's not just the kiss. It's what we talked about, our shared loneliness, and how I felt we might be turning a corner in our relationship. Because if the kiss didn't happen, then none of that did, either. *We're not friends?* Dominic had asked. No. I suppose we're not.

"Do you want help with the interview?" I ask Ameena, banishing Dominic to the darkest corner of my brain and tying him to a chair. No. Wait. That's worse.

She shakes her head. "TJ's been really great about it." Then, without looking up from her painting, she says, "He said last night that he'd move with me if I get the job."

"Oh . . . oh wow." I let this sink in. At least if TJ were here, Ameena would have more of a reason to visit. I don't want to admit my biggest fear: that I am not enough of a reason on my own. "That's good, yeah?"

"Yes and no," she says. "It would make my decision easier if they offer me the job, but it's still going to be a tough one."

"I'd come see you. We could do Virginian things, like . . ."

"You don't know anything about Virginia, do you?"

"It's for lovers?"

"Supposedly." She sips her wine. "And are you still pretending your cohost isn't cute?"

My face heats up. *You're cute.* That was what he said Monday night. Then he said he liked my hair down—liked it a lot. In related news, I've worn ponytails the past two days.

"I can admit he's cute. But even if I liked him, and even if he liked *me*, which he doesn't, this wouldn't be able to be a thing." If he had any nonprofessional feelings for me, he wouldn't have been so eager to forget the kiss. Simple as that.

"Why not?"

I glance around, then lower my voice. "The whole point of the show is that we used to date, and that our breakup was amicable enough for us to host it together.

"So maybe you got back together."

Lies on top of lies. "It wouldn't work," I say. "You know how I get in relationships. How much of a nightmare would it be if I somehow fell for him, and he didn't feel the same way, and we were stuck still hosting the show together?"

"Okay, okay. You're right," she says, but in this way that sounds like she knows I won't listen to anyone but myself about this. And she's not wrong, but I'm not wrong, either. Dating Dominic Yun would be a catastrophe. Even the hypothetical is enough to turn my stomach inside out.

Ameena's staring at my painting. "Can you at least turn that thing away from me?"

I decide to wear my hair down the next day. Show day.

I wake up early, by which I mean I had a Dominic nightmare

around three a.m. and couldn't fall back asleep. I have plenty of time to shower, let my hair air-dry, and straighten my bangs.

And it doesn't look bad at all.

Even though I want to drag my chair away from his before we start recording, I sit down next to him the way I do every Thursday, fold my hands primly on the table in front of me. If he notices the lack of ponytail, he's not giving anything away. I shouldn't be disappointed.

For this episode, our fifth, it was Ruthie's idea for Dominic to quiz me on dating slang.

"Breadcrumbing," he says, glancing up from his notes and lifting his eyebrows at me. A challenge. It's the most personality he's shown me all week, and I try to ignore the shiver it sends down my spine.

"That one's obvious," I say. "It's when you're dating a cannibal who lives in the woods. In a gingerbread house."

Dominic cues Jason to play a buzzer sound effect.

"Submarining."

"When you and your partner watch *Yellow Submarine* to get in the mood. Also known as 'Beatles and chill.'"

"Cushioning."

"Oh, that's when you bring a cushion with you on every date so your partner doesn't have to sit on any hard surfaces."

Dominic is laughing now, a hand clasped over his mouth. I'm trying very hard not to look at his hands, though, since I can't seem to do it without thinking about what they did in my imagination last night. Which is something I've shoved firmly to the back of my mind, along with Ameena's final interview. Gotta love compartmentalization.

"Let's try something new," I say, moving on to the next bullet point on our rundown. Maybe one day, I'll barely glance at it, like Paloma used to do, but five episodes in, and while I'm okay going off script sometimes, it's still the best kind of security blanket. "If you think you can come up with the best definition of one of the slang words we tweeted out before the show, call us at 1-888-883-KPPR. We'll pick our favorites at the end of the show. You can also tweet them out using the hashtag ExTalkSlang."

Our first caller is Mindy in Pioneer Square. "Okay, so, roaching," she says. "It's when someone tries to create a relationship out of the situation where they're sleeping on your couch that you graciously offered to them when their apartment became infested with cockroaches."

"That sounds like maybe something you've had firsthand experience with?" I say.

Mindy groans. "It was the worst. I didn't want to send him back to his disgusting apartment, and I thought he might have feelings for me, but I figured, I'll just do this nice thing, I work long hours, we'll barely see each other. Well, imagine my surprise when I got home from work to find him in the bathtub surrounded by very strategically placed rose petals."

"Roaching at its finest," I say with a shudder.

"Dominic, reassure me," Mindy says. "You wouldn't do that, would you?"

"Definitely not. I'd use lavender."

My mouth goes dry. I chance a look over at him, but he's staring straight ahead, stoic as usual. The bath I told him about. *You smell good.* Is he messing with me?

"Stop," Mindy says with a laugh. "I love you both so much. I would *not* be able to do this with any of my exes. And Dominic . . . you seem like one of the good ones. I don't know if you're single . . ." She says it suggestively, and I really don't like what happens in my chest as a result.

"Sorry, Mindy," he says, "I'm interested in someone."

That hits me in a weird place. He didn't mention it Monday

when there was clearly an opportunity for it. Or maybe it's new. I should be happy for him, but instead I feel strangely hollow. Maybe that's why he wanted to forget the kiss: because he was trying to start something with someone else.

The lavender had to be coincidental. Now I'm sure of it.

"I can't say I'm not secretly hoping you'll find a way to make it work with Shay," Mindy says, "but whatever happens, I'm happy for both of you."

"Thanks for calling, Mindy," I say, aware I sound a little brusque, but she doesn't seem to notice.

Dominic hits the button for the next caller. "Now we have John calling from South Lake Union," he says.

"Yeah, hi," says a curt male voice. Midthirties or forties, if I had to guess. "I was listening to you in the car and had to pull over and call."

"Glad to hear the show made an impact," Dominic says, but I lift my eyebrows at him, unsure the caller meant this in a positive way.

A sharp laugh. "Not exactly. My girlfriend, she's been really into it, but I don't see it."

"Oh?" Dominic says.

"Seems pretty convenient to me that you two, on the heels of your breakup, just happened to be qualified to host this show," says John in South Lake Union. "And I use the word 'qualified' loosely. But I guess they'll put anyone on the radio these days if it means getting more clicks."

"Say what you will about me," Dominic says, sitting up straighter in his chair, his brows in a hard line, "but Shay's been at this station for ten years. I've never met someone more devoted to public radio or more knowledgeable about it. *Puget Sounds* wouldn't have lasted as long as it did without her. She's earned this, one hundred percent."

His words pin me to my chair. They're too forceful not to be genuine. He's staring straight into the other studio, which is probably a good thing. I'm not sure my heart would be able to handle the eye contact.

It's the nicest thing someone's said about me in a long time.

"Well, I did a little research, and I think your devoted listeners might be interested to know that not only do neither of you appear on each other's social media, but you became Facebook friends about a month ago. I find that fascinating."

"I'm very private on social media," Dominic says.

Recovering from his compliments, I add, "And we wanted to keep our relationship separate from work."

"Then what about the tweet Shay sent out in January about swiping left on a guy sitting on the toilet?"

"I—uh," I say, fumbling. Because I did tweet about that. *Shit*. I thought I'd combed my social media for anything that would indicate Dominic and I weren't together this winter, but I must have missed something. *Shit, shit, shit*. I steal a glance at Dominic, who still won't meet my gaze.

We were prepared for this possibility. We talked about what we'd do if it ever happened.

I just never thought it would happen on the air.

"Look, John," Dominic says. "You can find any piece of someone's social media history and use it to prove whatever agenda you have. We've seen it happen plenty of times to people with much more at stake than Shay and me. We're not here to convince you if you've already made up your mind about us. I can tell you I didn't go to journalism school to tell lies on the radio."

And just like that, he hits the button that ends the call.

I can't read his expression. While I'm utterly grateful for him, I wish I'd known what to say.

"We have to wrap up today's show," Dominic says. He continues our sign-off, giving out our social media handles, telling the audience we'll be back next week.

Then Jason Burns with the weather, and then an NPR newsbreak, and I'm still frozen in my chair.

Dominic takes off his headphones. "Hey," he says. "You okay?"

I nod, but my hands are shaking. Finally, I find my voice. "I think so. What you said about me. That was—you didn't have to do that. But thank you."

"You're my cohost," he says, as though it's that simple. As though that's the only connection we have.

I'm actually interested in someone.

And maybe it is.

17

"To handling assholes with grace and dignity," Ruthie says, and the three of us clink our glasses.

Desperate to recover from our nightmare of a show, we decided to grab drinks after work. It's not something I'm used to doing; Paloma and her wife had long ago settled into their routines that didn't include three-dollar cocktails at dive bars. I didn't think I was the team bonding type, but so far, I like this a lot.

"That guy," Dominic says, taking a swig of his beer. "I've never before wished I could reach into a phone and punch someone."

The top button of his shirt is undone, and he looks thoroughly wiped. And yet still hot, especially with his hair end-of-the-workday mussed. It's unfair, really, for someone that attractive to have that great a radio voice. Too often, I've googled my NPR crushes only to learn their faces didn't quite match up with their voices. Also unfair: the way my gaze keeps dropping to his mouth when he talks.

Stop. Stop thinking about it.

"Ah, you haven't been in radio long enough," I say. "Ruthie, do you remember the—"

"The heavy breather?" Ruthie finishes. "Oh my god. *Yes.* I'll be haunted by that until I die."

It must have been sometime last spring on *Puget Sounds*: a call from a guy who claimed to want advice on our semi-regular gardening segment, then proceeded to ask Paloma and her guest elaborate questions about rutabagas, punctuated by long, deep breaths.

"I swear I heard the sound of a zipper," I say.

"I'm not about to kink-shame anyone, but honestly . . . ," Ruthie says. "I really hope he was just, like, taking a shit."

We're still laughing when my phone buzzes with a text from Kent.

Can you and Dom come in early tomorrow?

I frown down at it. *Dom.* The nickname he doesn't like but won't say anything to Kent about. I don't love that Kent asked only me, as though I'm responsible for Dominic. As though I'm still just a producer and not someone with the same responsibilities as Dominic.

Just a producer. I need to stop saying that, or I'm as bad as everyone else who buys into the nonsense public radio hierarchy that puts hosts on a pedestal above everyone else. Ruthie isn't just a producer. She's . . . well, Ruthie.

I show them the text. "Kent wants to talk to us tomorrow."

"About that caller?" Dominic says.

"Probably." And since Ruthie doesn't have any reason to believe we'd be panicked about someone discovering the truth, I add, "He must just want to make sure we're not too rattled or anything."

Dominic's eyes briefly meet mine over the top of Ruthie's head. It's strange to be on the same side as him, the same team. We both want this to be okay. We both want to not have fucked up the show.

"I should get home," he says. "I'm having dinner with my parents tonight."

I want to scrutinize his tone of voice, figure out what exactly his relationship with his parents is like. But he says it casually, and his face doesn't give anything away, either. We swap goodbyes and he pays his tab, and I watch him slink out of the bar, messenger bag swaying at his hip.

"Kind of fucked up that Kent texted you and not Dominic," Ruthie says.

"Right?" I say, grateful to tear my eyes from Dominic. When he's gone, I can breathe easy again.

Ruthie gets it. Of course she does. "It's almost like Dominic has a penis and you don't. I mean—sorry. I shouldn't say that."

"You're not wrong. Kent seems to play favorites sometimes, and a lot of his favorites are dudes," I say with a shrug, though it's validating someone else has noticed it.

"It's going okay, though? The show? Aside from John in South Lake Union?"

If I ignore my cohost, yes. "It's going surprisingly well. I love being on the air. Once I got over the voice stuff, it felt natural. It sounds strange to say that I love talking, because it's probably not that apparent if you just randomly met me, but . . ." I pause, trying to figure out how to put it into words. "I like being in control of the conversation and making connections with listeners, hearing their stories. There's something incredible about being able to do that. Plus, this month's master's jar is getting close to fifty dollars, and I can't say I don't love draining Dominic's bank account." I pause, wondering if I'm ready to tell her this next part. "I also had this idea. For a show about grief."

I explain it to Ruthie. My mother and I talked about it on the phone last night, and she agreed to go on the radio as long as I'd be there next to her. I told her there was nowhere else I'd rather be to hear that story.

"Yes," Ruthie says automatically. "I'm into it. We should clear it with Kent, since it's a bit different from what we've been doing, but it's already breaking my heart and putting it back together."

"Have I told you lately that you're my favorite producer?"

"Not nearly enough," she says. "I sort of can't believe I'm producing my own show, to be honest. I didn't think I'd be doing this at twenty-five." She reaches across the small table and covers my hand with hers. "Seriously, Shay. Thank you. Kent could have cut me loose, and I know you fought for me."

"It wasn't a fight," I say. "There was no question about it. I was only doing the show if I had you."

"Stop, I really am gonna cry!" She takes another sip of her drink and gestures to the bartender for another.

Meanwhile, I'm racking my brain, trying to remember if Ruthie and I have ever spent time together just the two of us.

We have not.

"How'd you get into radio?" I ask, suddenly curious.

"Oh, is it story time?" Ruthie crosses one leg primly over the other. "Okay. I went to school for marketing, and I was working on the sales side at KZYO for a few months. Then they had this summer that all their producers took a vacation at the same time, and it was kind of all hands on deck, so I pitched in and helped out. And I was good at it. More important, I loved it. I liked pulling the strings and putting the show together, you know? So the next job that opened up, I was able to switch over. There were always a lot of job openings there—the benefit of commercial radio."

"I had no idea," I say.

"And I really lucked out with this job. Kent liked that I had commercial radio experience, and I was dying to work somewhere

I wouldn't be nonstop tortured by jingles for auto repair shops and pickle companies." She shudders. "I can never eat a Nalley pickle."

"That jingle is the worst. *Crispy crunchy yummy—*"

"*Nalley Pickles!*" we both cry out, before bursting into laughter.

"But aside from that," she says when we recover, "the commercial station covered a lot of semi-sensational stuff. Someone getting into a car accident was big news, and it was always so upsetting. Public radio is much better at deep dives and talking about the issues in a more nuanced way.

"I know a lot of people go into public radio thinking they'll bide their time as producers until they get promoted to being a reporter or a host, but I love being a producer. I'm happy here. I get to make cool radio every day, and I'm doing what I love with people I love. Maybe one day I'll wanna do something else, but for now, I feel like this is where I'm supposed to be."

"That's honestly really refreshing," I say. "When I started working as Paloma's assistant producer, my senior producer told me we had to do whatever Paloma wanted, make sure she had her kombucha and her chia seeds, that the studio wasn't too hot or too cold, and I was just like . . . seriously? We're colleagues. Not servants. I know Paloma respected me, but that was what I turned into."

"You never make me feel like that. In case you're worried."

"Good. If I ever tell you I need kombucha at exactly forty-four degrees, please tell me to shut the fuck up."

Ruthie tips her drink to me. "Duly noted."

We continue to talk about work before the conversations become more personal. Ruthie tells me she's been on a few dates with a guy named Marco, and that she might be ready to make it official. I tell her about my mom and the upcoming wedding.

The whole time, the truth rattles around inside me.

She deserves to know.

And yet, my desire for self-preservation wins out.

"Why don't we do this more?" she asks when we realize we've been sitting here for two hours without glancing at our phones.

"We should," I say, trying to ignore the sour guilt climbing up my throat. "We will."

The Ex Talk, Episode 5: Ghosting Whisperer

Transcript

SHAY GOLDSTEIN: This week's episode is brought to you by Archetype. If you're anything like me, you have trouble finding shoes that fit just right. The whole size is too big, but the half size is too small, and uncomfortable shoes can make the workday feel far too long.

DOMINIC YUN: That's where Archetype comes in. All you have to do is measure your feet using their patented molding system, send it in, and they'll create a custom memory foam arch support perfectly contoured to your foot that you can use in all your shoes.

SHAY GOLDSTEIN: I slipped them into some size sevens, and I couldn't believe the difference.

DOMINIC YUN: I did the same with my size thirteens.

SHAY GOLDSTEIN: And you know what they say about guys with big feet . . .

DOMINIC YUN: That they should try Archetype!

SHAY GOLDSTEIN: And right now, Archetype is offering a special discount for our listeners! For fifteen percent off at checkout, go to archetypesupport.us and enter offer code EX TALK. That's E-X-T-A-L-K at checkout for fifteen percent off.

18

I'm entering the elevator the next morning for our early meeting with Kent when Dominic calls for me to hold the door. He's jogging out of the parking lot with his Pacific Public Radio thermos, clad in khakis and his sky blue shirt.

It takes all my willpower not to smack the DOOR CLOSE button.

"Thanks," he says when the elevator traps us inside.

I manage a weak smile and inch away from him as inconspicuously as I can. Distance and professionalism. It's the only way to eliminate this inconvenient attraction I've developed. His hair is shower-damp, and he smells fresh and clean with a hint of spice. His aftershave, maybe?

"Did you and Ruthie have fun last night?" he asks, taking a sip of his coffee.

"Mm-hmm," I say to the floor. I don't need to watch the bob of his Adam's apple when he swallows.

"How late did you guys stay?"

"Eightish."

He lifts his eyebrows at me. Every time I dart my gaze away, he captures it again.

"Are you avoiding me?"

"No."

"Something's wrong," he says, crossing the invisible line I drew down the center of the elevator. Instinctively, I press my back harder against the padded wall. He mercifully stops about a foot in front of me, leaning down to scrutinize my face with his deep, dark eyes. In my traitorous imagination, he pins me to the wall, smashes the emergency stop button. Bends to drop his mouth to my neck. "What's going on?"

"Nothing."

"If this is about Monday—" He breaks off, blushing, putting a little more space between us.

It's the first time I've seen him blush, and it makes me want to cover my own face.

"No no no." I tighten my grip on my bag. "It's not. We were drunk. We were just—"

"Really drunk," he finishes with a swift nod of his head. "I normally don't—I mean, that wasn't—"

"You don't have to explain," I say, though all I want is a detailed explanation with an accompanying PowerPoint presentation. I reach out to graze his wrist with a fingertip—a gesture of reassurance—realizing when I make contact that it was a terribly unwise decision. I am out of control and must be stopped. I should have known better, but the guy is a fucking magnet. That brush of skin against skin is enough to bring heat to my cheeks and to a couple other locations. Moth, meet flame. Give flame the middle finger.

"Good." He visibly exhales, his shoulders dipping at least an inch. Now he can pursue the someone he mentioned on the air, guilt-free. "Then if it's not that—"

"Dominic. I'm fine. I'm spectacular," I say. "Nothing to investigate."

"I've never heard you use the word 'spectacular.'"

"Better take me to the hospital. It sounds serious."

The corner of his mouth twitches. "I'm going to figure it out," he says.

A ding indicates we've reached the fifth floor. I've got to talk to maintenance about how slow the elevator's been lately. There might be something wrong with it.

"I always feel like I'm in the principal's office," Dominic whispers as we wait for Kent to make his tea. It's some complicated five-step process. He explained it to me once, and I promptly forgot it.

I refocus on the meeting itself. What's at stake is far worse than the equivalent of detention.

Kent walks inside with his mug, smiling as always, but it's a little tight. "Well. I'm sure you two know why you're here."

"We tried to get him off the air as quickly as we could," Dominic says, and it's strange he says *we* when I was mostly silent. "We were near the end of the show, and I didn't know how else to fill for time, so . . ." He trails off with a sheepish shrug. "Couldn't we cut it from the podcast?"

"The fact remains that it's out there," Kent says. "If we cut it, it's going to look like we're hiding something. We have to take this seriously, do some hard-core damage control. People heard it, and now they're going to be scrutinizing you more than ever before."

Dominic runs a hand over his face. "Well . . . fuck," he says, and I'd laugh at him uttering the word in front of our boss in such a serious meeting if I weren't so worried about what's going to happen.

"Fuck is right." Kent blows over the top of his tea mug. "If more people latch onto this, if they call the show's premise into question, then we are deeply, deeply fucked." He sighs, and then: "I've heard murmurs. Nothing is a guarantee, but we could have some big things on the horizon."

I scoot to the edge of my chair. "Big how?"

"Big like PodCon," Kent says, and I have to fight to keep a straight face. "And there's been interest from some exciting sponsors. Again, nothing certain yet, but do you realize how huge that could be for the station?"

I'm dying to know more about PodCon, about those potential sponsors, but the show's integrity—or lack thereof—is the more pressing issue. "We could . . . stage some photos from the relationship?" I wince even as I suggest it. More lying. It reminds me that anything good I feel about the show is accompanied by this disappointed voice that sometimes sounds like Ameena and sometimes like my dad.

It's a bit of a relief when Kent shakes his head. "It's not a matter of creating evidence," he says. "It's in the way you two talk to each other. It's almost too scripted. Too staged. I can hear it sometimes, too. And I know part of this is on me. I'm the one who encouraged this, and neither of you had solid on-air experience yet. But we looked through some listener feedback, and it turns out some of them also feel the show was a little too carefully choreographed, which makes me worry it seems as though you two don't know each other well enough. Which, again, to be fair, you don't. We didn't give the two of you much time to get acquainted with each other, on top of creating both your relationship and your breakup."

Dominic and I are quiet for a few seconds. Kent's admonishing us, but not blaming us?

"I don't understand what you're asking of us, then," Dominic says, once again proving he has more courage than I do when it comes to our boss. He makes no attempt to curb his frustration, while I'm always eager to please Kent any way I can. Is it because he's been Kent's favorite since the beginning? Why, then, did Kent text me about this meeting and not both of us?

"This is what we're gonna do," Kent says. He gestures to the two of us, though we're the only two in the room. "You two are going to spend the night together."

I practically leap out of the chair. "Excuse me?"

"The weekend together, actually. Clear your schedules. This is urgent. We rented an Airbnb for you on Orcas Island, all on the station's dime. You're going to spend the weekend together, and you're going to figure this shit out. You're going to make me believe you spent three blissful months as a couple. I want you to know how the other person brushes their teeth. When they replace the toilet paper, if it's hanging over or under. If they snore. What they look like when they first wake up in the morning. I want you to know every fucking thing about each other so we don't get into another mess like this."

His words render me speechless. My jaw doesn't just drop to the floor—it hits the basement parking garage. Kent returns to his tea, deadly serious. He's always been a take-no-prisoners kind of boss, but one with a considerable amount of empathy. This . . . this is something different entirely.

I'm afraid to even look at Dominic, let alone spend a whole weekend with him.

"I assume all expenses will be covered?" Dominic asks.

"Within reason," Kent says. "You'll both have your company cards."

"Good. Because I tend to get really hungry on weekends. Thirsty, too." He stares Kent down. They look like two lions about to fight over a gazelle, though I'm not sure what exactly the gazelle is in this scenario.

"As I said, the station will cover it within reason." Kent stands.

"Emma will give you all the information. I have a meeting with the board. I trust we're done here for now?"

"Actually," I say, because some part of me thinks that if I give in, if I make this weekend mess easier, then maybe he'll give me something I want in return. "Hey, Kent, while I have you." I feel the weight of his gaze and Dominic's, and I try to power through my anxiety. "I wanted to talk to you about this *Ex Talk* idea I had about, um, about grief and loss. Ruthie wanted me to run it by you, since it's sort of a heavier topic for the show—"

"This really isn't the time, Shay."

A swift kick to my chest. It's the first time Kent has outright dismissed me. I've always assumed he liked me, or at least respected me.

It makes me wonder what he would have said if Dominic had suggested it.

"I—okay," I say, wishing Dominic hadn't heard me get shut down. "I guess we'll just go to work, then."

Kent smiles. "Good plan. And enjoy the weekend, really. You should probably head out this afternoon if you want to beat traffic."

My legs stop working as soon as we leave Kent's office.

"I was going to go to a cake tasting with my mom this weekend," I say, crumbling against the wall. "And—and I'd have to take Steve, but he's never been on that long of a car trip with me, and I'm not ready to leave him with someone else yet. I—" I suck in a deep breath. My lungs are tight. Panic mode. Shit, *shit*, I don't want him to see me like this.

"Shay." He stands in front of me, placing strong hands on my shoulders. I don't like what my name in his mouth does to me, and I like even less the way his palms settle so naturally into the fabric of my blazer. "This sucks, I know. I'm just as pissed as you are. But it's one weekend. We can do it. We do this, and maybe we can take some short days next week, and you can be with your mom. It's for the show, right? Neither of us wants to see this show go down."

We're not supposed to touch like this, and we're not supposed to take elevators together or long car rides or spend an entire weekend on an island together. Distance. Professionalism. That was supposed to be my strategy.

"Besides," he says with a half smile, "I want to meet your dog. Also, how many cases of beer do you think is 'within reason'?"

I roll my eyes, but his reassurance makes me feel a little better.

Except it's not going to be easy to avoid him while trapped in a house together all weekend.

I pray to my radio gods, the ones who act cool and collected in even the most hostile of interviews. If Terry Gross survived her nightmare interview with Gene Simmons, then I can do this.

Terry Gross, Rachel Martin, Audie Cornish—give me strength.

19

Three hours in Friday rush-hour traffic. One and a half hours on a ferry. Eleven minutes waiting for Dominic to pick the right snacks at the island mini-mart. Another half hour in the car. Twenty minutes arguing over the Google Maps directions telling us to swim across a body of water that would have taken us into Canadian territory.

That's how long it takes for Dominic and me to get to the Airbnb house the station rented for us on the northern tip of Orcas Island, a little horseshoe-shaped piece of land in the northwest corner of the state.

This is also when it starts raining.

"Gotta love the Pacific Northwest," Dominic mutters as we shut the car doors and make a run for the house with our luggage.

Steve pulls to the end of his leash, looking for the perfect tree to pee on. "This is Steve Rogers," I told Dominic when I picked him up. "The furriest Avenger?" he asked. It was the only moment of levity on our entire trip. Shortly thereafter, I learned that Dominic has horrendous taste in music. Even though I was driving, he kept insisting we listen to his favorite radio station from his teen years, which used to play alternative but now plays whatever the hell "adult contemporary" is. I am an adult, and adult contemporary is garbage. Finally, we agreed to turn my Spotify to random.

Inside, Dominic drops our bags in the entryway before manspreading across the couch in the living room.

"I guess this is where we bond," I say.

"Right," he says, an edge to his voice. "Because Kent assumes we can conjure a relationship from thin air."

That stings a little. Like we don't have any kind of relationship at all when the past couple of months, we've gained at least a modicum of closeness.

Though, to be fair, that drunken kiss might have obliterated it.

The house is cute and quaint, mahogany furniture with blue accents and a real wood fireplace. Hanging plants, sprawling landscapes by Orcas Island artists. Exactly the kind of place two people might enjoy spending time together if they enjoyed spending time with each other.

"So should I take notes on all the weird things you do?" I say, making my way over to the armchair opposite him. "Take photos of you in your sleep to use as blackmail?"

"I look adorable while I'm sleeping, thank you very much."

I roll my eyes at this. "Now I know you're someone who takes their shoes off as soon as they get inside."

He glances down at his socked feet. "Habit. My parents had these pristine white carpets, and they lost their minds if we tracked a speck of dirt onto them."

It's just past eight o'clock, and while it's not so late that I'm ready to turn in, after being in the car all day, I have no desire to leave this place. The rain is coming down even harder, pummeling the house like it has a score to settle. Thunder roars in the not-so-distance, and Steve races around the house, barking like mad.

"Steve," I call out, running after him, trying to soothe him, but he's possessed: jumping on and off the couch, zooming so fast he starts panting. He even ignores a handful of his favorite treats I present to him. I've never seen him like this, and I hate that he's so scared. That I can't fix it. "Steve, it's okay. You're okay."

Dominic heads for his suitcase, unzipping it and retrieving a white undershirt. At first I think he's going to change into it, but instead he kneels on the floor, stretching out his hand to a wildly barking Steve. Steve sniffs the air tentatively, and then, as though lured simply by the scent of Dominic, trots over to him.

"Good boy," Dominic says, petting his head. I can tell he's still trembling. "Can I try something?" he asks me.

"Go ahead."

Gently, he scoops Steve into the T-shirt, then wraps it around his body once, twice. "It's okay, little guy," he says. "Do you have anything to secure this?"

I lift my eyebrows at him, completely lost. But I grab a few hair bands from my bag, trying to forget the way Dominic snapped one against my skin. Trying to ignore the way my skin burns when he takes them from me.

He uses the hair bands to hold the T-shirt in place, not too tight, and . . . it works? Dominic lets go of Steve, who looks concerned but no longer batshit. He sits down, staring at us and wagging his tail.

"My sister had a small dog that got scared of fireworks, and he had this special shirt that calmed him down," he explains, scratching behind Steve's ears. "This is just a makeshift one. The pressure helps with the anxiety."

Watching him with Steve tugs at my heart in a way I've never quite felt before. It catches me off guard, turns my legs liquid.

"Thank you," I say, still dazed. I wobble my way into the kitchen. We're in the relative middle of nowhere, so we brought enough nonperishables to cook dinner. I open a cabinet, checking for cookware. "Well, I'm getting hungry. Should we just make some pasta or something?"

"Yeah, sure. Don't overcook it, though. I like it when the noodles are al dente. The way they're supposed to be."

I pause with one hand around a pot. It's a relief he's back to being obstinate. It makes disliking him much easier. "I'm not going to make it for you. If you want dinner, you can come help."

I hear a groan from the living room, and then he appears in the kitchen, settling into a lean against the doorframe. Did he have to bring that lean all the way out here?

"Noodles are in the blue bag," I tell him.

I've never viewed making pasta as a particularly volatile experience, but with Dominic, it turns into one. The first batch of noodles, we overcook, and Dominic refuses to eat, saying they're too slimy, so we dump them in the compost bin and start over. He's acting like a child about it. Then he fails to mention he's allergic to mushrooms, and it's a good thing the pantry was stocked with another jar of sauce. It feels like I'm back in college, or in my first apartment with Ameena, where we set off the smoke alarm every time we tried to cook something besides macaroni.

It's nine thirty by the time we carry our bowls to the couch, along with two bottles of hard pear cider. Rain batters the windows, but Steve seems content to wear Dominic's undershirt and chew his hippo toy. Dominic flicks on the TV to salt-and-pepper static and lets out a long-suffering sigh.

"Are you trying to get me to break up with you again?" I ask, twirling some noodles with my fork. At least he left some room on the couch this time.

"Sorry," he admits. "I guess I'm a little on edge."

I try a softer approach, because he really is, and I'm no longer sure it's from being forced on this trip with me. "Are you . . . okay?"

He places his bowl on the coffee table and takes a swig of cider. He picks up the bowl before putting it back down again, as though debating whether he wants to tell the truth or put up another shield. Steve waits on the floor for a noodle he knows I'll probably give him at some point.

"My ex is dating someone new," Dominic finally says. "It's all over social media, the two of them together, and it's been hard to see. And I've been a dick all day, haven't I?"

"A little more than usual, yeah," I say, and he whacks my arm with the couch pillow. I clutch my arm, feigning injury. "With the exception of making Steve less neurotic. I'm sorry, though. It's shitty, and I want to tell you as the Token Old that it gets easier, but it really does suck every time. Just in a slightly different way."

"That's the thing." At this, he waits again, spinning his fork through the spaghetti, taunting Steve. "She was my first girlfriend. My . . . only girlfriend."

"Your only serious girlfriend?" I ask, assuming he's not counting high school relationships or casual flings.

He shakes his head. "No. My only girlfriend, period. I didn't date in high school. We met at freshman orientation. We dated all through college, and then we broke up right before I moved out here."

Oh.

That is an interesting revelation.

And he's not even being obnoxious about making it a point to clarify they met during *undergrad*, not grad school, so I know he's serious.

The house creaks, and Steve whines.

"Steve, no," I say, and he lies down, wagging his tail. "Dominic. I'm so sorry. I had no idea."

"I should have told you when we were figuring out our relationship, but it still felt kind of raw." He lets out a sigh, and I get the feeling there's more to this story. He places his hands on his knees and inspects his knuckles, as though trying to distract himself from the reality of letting me into his private, personal history. "I'm not still in love with her. It's been about eight months at this point. It's more that we were together for so long, and we went through so much, that it's been a strange adjustment."

"And it was the distance? That ended it, I mean?" I ask, thinking back to the reason he gave me that night we fake broke up.

"Not exactly." He reaches down to scratch Steve behind the ears. Steve seems to have taken to him immediately, much to my dismay. "We were inseparable, and when you're together nearly five years, everyone assumes you'll get married. We were That Couple, the one everyone made fun of because we were always together and so wrapped up in each other, and we pretended to hate it, but we loved it. We loved being that couple."

My heart twinges. I recall always wanting to be part of a couple like that. The pictures I saw on Facebook—they really did look like that couple.

"So," he continues as Steve leaps onto the couch to lick Parmesan cheese off his fingers, "when I applied to grad schools during senior year, my goal was to be able to stay at Northwestern. Mia was from Chicago originally. She was premed, and she was taking a year off before applying to med school to gather experience. So it kind of worked out perfectly when I got into Northwestern, both of us sticking around. Except . . ." Here he takes a deep breath. "A couple months after I started grad school, Mia went skiing with some of her friends from high school and—and she was in an accident."

"Oh my god."

He's quick to hold up a hand. "She's okay now," he says, and I feel myself relax. "It was *bad*, but she was really fucking lucky. That whole year, every moment I wasn't in class or studying, I was with her. Helping her eat, taking her to physical therapy, making sure she was taking her meds. I practically moved into her family's house. But then a month after I graduated, when I was in the middle of interviewing for jobs all across the country, she said she'd been feeling for a while like she wanted to move on. That she didn't think she was in love with me anymore.

"It wasn't that I thought she owed it to me to stay with me after that. I was just completely blindsided. I really thought I was going to marry her. And all that time, she was trying to figure out how to break up with me."

"You were planning to propose?"

"No, no, but I'd thought about it," he says, more to the top of Steve's head than to me. "I guess I didn't know her as well as I thought I did."

"I really am sorry. That couldn't have been easy, doing interviews while that was going on. And then moving back here." I want to reach out and touch him, the way he did so effortlessly after our meeting with Kent, but I'm not sure how to make it look natural, so I keep my hands in my lap.

"As you can probably guess, she called me Dom, and it just feels *hers*. It's hard to let anyone else call me that now," he says, and I get it. "So you can understand why I wasn't particularly forthcoming with you before. Especially with someone who, no offense, seemed to really dislike me."

I hold a hand to my heart. "I don't dislike you. I find you annoying. It's different."

He cracks a smile, but it vanishes in an instant. I want to lean over and keep it affixed to his face. His heartbreak has been etched into him since he started at Pacific Public Radio—I can see that now.

"It's hard out here sometimes, and seeing Mia and those photos made it worse. All my friends from high school, we lost touch. I tried to get dinner with one guy, but he had to take a work call halfway through and we never rescheduled. And then one girl and I tried to meet up, but then her boyfriend got territorial and thought I was moving in on her. It's even weirder because it's not like it's a completely new city for me. You'd think it would be easier. But I don't have friends here, not really, and my siblings are all busy with their own families. I've tried at work, but almost everyone has a partner or kids and I just feel . . . lonely, sometimes."

It brings me back to Monday night. Not the kiss, but his drunken confession. I turn so my body is facing his, and then I graze his denim knee with a few fingertips. Touching him suddenly becomes easy, or I've become braver.

"Hey. You're not alone. You have your fake ex-girlfriend slash current cohost slash fellow inept pasta chef with you." I chew the inside of my cheek, debating how personal I want to get. He laid it all out there—I might as well, too. "I've never left Seattle, so it's even more pathetic that I feel this way, too. I've really just had my mom and my friend Ameena for the past ten years, and a few boyfriends that never turned serious. So maybe we can be alone together."

This time when he smiles, it lasts a little longer. "Thank you. It actually feels good to tell someone, after all this time. I guess I'll have to get used to it if I ever want to date again."

"Oh please, you're twenty-four. You're not a cat lady quite yet." I scrunch up my nose. "It's ridiculous that there's no cat lady equivalent for guys. Fucking misogyny."

"Cat man?"

"Sounds like a very gentle superhero."

He puts on a dramatic newscaster voice. "He flies! He catches bad guys! He saves cats from really tall trees!" A pause. "So. What's your hang-up, then? Why are you doing a show about our fake relationship instead of being out there having a real one?"

"It's not exactly an easy thing to admit, but . . . I tend to get attached. Extremely fast." I reach out a hand in hopes Steve will let me pet him while I tell this story, but apparently Dominic gives better scratches. "I was the first one to say 'I love you' to all my exes, and it was always too soon. They freaked out and bolted."

"And you meant it, every single time?"

That makes me hesitate. "Yes? I've never stopped to really analyze it."

I don't tell him my biggest fear: that I wasn't deeply in love with any of them. That I so badly wanted something beyond the small family my mother and I have that I was eager to jump into anything— even if it wasn't the right time or the right fit. I craved those three little words so much that maybe I forced them from my own lips, hoping to hear them in return.

"It's why I haven't gone on a date in a while. It can be exhausting, giving that much when the other person is barely giving anything."

"None of this sounds like a bad thing," he says. "Difficult, yes, but not some fatal personality flaw."

"Maybe not with the right person."

"Then I guess you haven't found him yet."

We sit in silence for a couple minutes, a not entirely uncomfortable one. So of course, I decide to make thing awkward.

"There's something else I want to ask, but I don't want to sound too forward."

"I doubt it can get more forward than what we've already talked about, so please, go ahead." He gestures with the cider bottle.

"You've only dated Mia." I bite down hard on my lower lip,

wondering if I'm going to regret this. "Is she . . . the only person you've slept with?"

He nods, a blush creeping onto his cheeks. Suddenly he looks very, very twenty-four.

"What about you?" he asks, taking a pull from his cider. "What's your . . . number? That's how they say it, right? Your number?"

"I don't know who 'they' are, but sure, I guess." I run through a mental list. "Seven."

"Ah," he says, his brows flat, his expression impossible to interpret.

"But all the bravado," I say. "That stuff you said at the station about your 'raw sexual energy.'" No, of course the exact wording wasn't imprinted on my brain.

He waves it off. "It's easy enough to lie about it when the world expects men to be a certain way about sex."

"The world is gross. I wouldn't have judged you. I swear. Your taste in music, yes, but your number . . . definitely not."

"I appreciate that."

I shake my head, still wrapping my mind around everything. "I honestly assumed for a while that you were a bit of a player."

"Sleeping with someone feels like a big deal to me," he says, settling back into the couch, as though he's grown more comfortable with the subject matter than he was fifteen minutes ago. "I don't think I could do it casually. Maybe it's because I've only been with one person, but I don't know if I could ever have sex without it feeling personal and intimate."

The temperature in the room climbs a bit. His eyes don't leave mine, and his words land heavy between us. Personal. *Thud.* Intimate. *Thud.* In my head, *personal and intimate* translates to languid kisses and the kind of pleasure that gets stretched to its limit before it breaks. Slow and torturous and satisfying. I can smell the sweet-

ness of cider on his breath. I barely know how his lips feel, and that
only increases my desire to kiss him again. How would they feel on
my collarbone, my throat, right behind my ear?

No.

I set my bowl down on the coffee table and cross my legs tight.
When I speak, my throat is dry. "That . . . must be nice."

"It's never been like that for you?"

It hasn't. Not with Trent, my most recent ex, or with Armand,
the guy I dated before him, and certainly not with David, my first.
Sex has always felt . . . not transactional, necessarily, but far from
the intense emotional experience he's talking about.

It's too warm in here. I'll have to see about turning down the
thermostat.

"I think we've been honest enough for one night," I say.

A corner of his mouth pulls up into a smile. There's that dimple.
"Aren't we supposed to be getting to know each other?"

Not like this. Not in a way that makes me imagine Dominic
having personal, intimate sex with someone. Probably by candlelight, in a remote cabin on a snowy evening.

"Yes," I say, getting up from the couch and heading toward the
kitchen. "I'm really interested in how you do the dishes."

20

Dominic stares me down in the mirror as we brush our teeth. The upstairs bathroom is too small, and when we bend down to spit into the sink, we bang elbows.

"I'll report back to Kent what your toothpaste spit looks like," I say.

"Fantastic." He places his toothbrush back in its travel case. "I don't think I've ever seen you without your glasses," he says to my reflection, and I feel immediately self-conscious.

With a hand holding back my hair, I spit one last time before rinsing my toothbrush. "I'm so used to them that I always worry my face looks asymmetrical without them."

"I like the glasses." He splashes some water on his face, then swipes a towel to pat it dry. Bedtime Dominic, in his sweatpants and a worn Northwestern T-shirt, might be my favorite version of him yet. The softest, most dangerous version of him, all his armor stripped away. "But you look fine both ways."

Fine. See, this is what happens: I spend hours on the couch next to him watching old episodes of *Buffy*, wondering if our legs are touching on purpose or if he thinks I'm just part of the couch, and then he says something like this. Something that convinces me I'm the only one who feels gravity shift between us. Our earlier conversation swims through my head. Something *has* changed, I'm sure of it.

Or maybe we really are just getting to know each other.

The bedroom poses an interesting dilemma.

"I can sleep on the couch," Dominic says, eyeing the bed. His breath is wonderfully minty fresh.

"We're adults. We can sleep in the same bed without it being weird." I hope he doesn't hear the tremor in my voice.

"I'm not sure I can sleep next to someone wearing such a ridiculous T-shirt."

I glance down at it. I packed quickly, and of course I happened to pick this shirt. I'M INTO FITNESS—FITNESS TACO IN MY MOUTH, it says, with an illustration of a smiling taco.

"It was five dollars at Target."

"They paid you five dollars to take it off their hands?"

"I think it's cute!" I cross my arms over my chest, hiding the taco from Dominic's judgy eyes. I don't usually wear a bra to bed, but I didn't want to prance around braless, so I figured I'd finagle it off once I got under the covers.

"*You* are cute," he says. "The shirt is not."

That is a definite compliment, and I'm not sure what to make of it. It's the same thing he said to me on the night we don't talk about. I hope it's dark enough in here to hide my blush.

We creep toward the bed as though it's a wild animal and we're afraid to make any sudden movements. Sleeping next to him sounds at once terrifying and thrilling, his long body inches from mine, dark hair fanning across the pillow.

Slowly, I peel back one side of the blankets.

"Did you bring anything from the fun drawer?" he asks. "Because that might make this awkward."

I gape at him. A few beats of silence pass before I start laughing, a full-body laugh that makes me bend over and clutch my stomach. Then he does, too, and we're both completely losing our minds. I have to grip the bedpost to keep from falling over.

And it eases, just a little, some of that tension between us. It makes me feel like maybe we can be okay. Maybe we *are* okay.

When I steal a look at his face, his expression is a mix of amusement and something else I can't name. I've never seen him like this, without that confidence shield he puts up for everyone else.

I like that he's allowing himself to be this whole person with me.

We slip into bed without any other major catastrophes, and I manage to safely wriggle out of my bra. I'm thinking I can finally relax when he turns to face me, propping his head on one arm. Maybe it's the lingering alcohol or the dim lamplight, but he looks even lovelier than usual, as though painted with soft brushstrokes.

"Hey," he says. "I wanted to say thank you. Again. For being so great about all of that earlier. I haven't been able talk like that in a while, and it meant a lot to have you listen."

"Like you said," I say, turning to match him. "You'll have to be able to open up if you don't want to end up a cat man."

I expect him to laugh. Maybe I imagine it, but he seems to stiffen at my words.

"Or you're just really easy to talk to." Beneath the sheets, his foot grazes mine, a friendly little touch that makes me think unfriendly thoughts.

It would be so easy to slide closer to him, to line up our bodies, to press my face into his neck. It's a good thing we're under the covers, because otherwise my nipples would be glad to let him know exactly how turned on I am.

I let out a slow breath, convinced he can hear the hammering of my heart.

"Since we're being honest," I say. "There's something I've been wanting to talk to you about." He lifts his eyebrows, as though encouraging me to continue. "When we started this whole thing, you were so against the lying aspect of it. You were going on about taking down bigots and using journalism to really help people. And yet . . . none of what we're doing seems to bother you."

He's quiet for a few moments. "Compartmentalization is a powerful drug," he finally says. "My mom actually learned English through NPR. That's kind of the reason I was so excited about getting a job out here. So I'm pretty desperate to stay there, even if it means . . ."

"Compromising your morals?"

A wry smile. "Well . . . yeah."

Huh. "Dominic Yun, you keep surprising me. I'm just—" I break off, take a deep breath. "I'm glad I'm not going through it alone."

"Me too." With a fingertip, he doodles on the sheets between us. "We've been talking too much about me. I want to know more about Shay Goldstein." He drags his finger over to my bent arm, tapping at my elbow. "Tell me about your dad?"

It's a question, and the way he says it makes it clear I could easily say no. But I find myself giving in, only marginally distracted by the rhythm of his finger on my skin.

"He had the absolute best radio voice," I say. "Like Kent times a hundred."

"He worked in radio?" Dominic pulls his hand back to his side of the bed.

I shake my head. "He owned an electronics repair shop. Goldstein Gadgets. He started it before I was born. I spent most of my afternoons there as a kid, and I loved watching him work. He had so much passion for it, not just for the technology itself but for the art of radio. We listened to everything together, pretended to host our own shows. So I guess we kind of have that in common—inheriting radio from our parents."

I worry, for a moment, that I've slipped too deep into nostalgia, but Dominic is listening intently.

"My mom plays in the symphony," I continue, "so I never had a quiet house, though sometimes they fought about what to listen to. Even today, I can't stand the quiet."

"Do you want to turn something on?" Dominic asks.

"No. This is . . . this is nice."

"Is it okay to ask what happened? How he—" He breaks off, as though unsure how to verbalize it.

"How he died?" I say. It's been a long time since I told this story. I roll over to stare at the ceiling, unsure if I want him to see my face as I tell it. "Sudden cardiac arrest while he was at work. No one could have done anything or detected it. A random horrible thing. I remember getting the call from my mom, but then my memory goes dark for like a week. I can't even remember the funeral.

"My life just . . . fell apart after that. People would tell me I was lucky to have eighteen years with him, lucky he didn't die when I was much younger. None of that made it any easier to lose him. So I lived in my bed for what felt like months, made some bad choices, then some slightly less bad ones. And it wasn't until I started interning at PPR that things finally started to feel like they could be okay."

I close my eyes, trying to fight off the worst of the memories. The days I cried until I lost my voice, the night I lost my virginity to someone who didn't know it was my first time. Hoping it would help me feel something again when all it did was make me feel worse.

I try to focus on something happier: the radio shows my dad and I hosted in the kitchen, how excited he'd be to show me a new recorder or microphone. It's how I used to feel all the time, every day coming into work.

When did I lose that?

"I don't even know what to say," he says after a while. "I'm so sorry, but an apology doesn't feel like nearly enough. I guess I'll say thank you. Thank you for telling me."

"Goldstein Gadgets is a vape shop now. Isn't that depressing?"

"Incredibly." And then he apologizes again: "I'm sorry, Shay."

My name sounds light as gossamer.

"I've spent most of my twenties chasing this idea of domestic bliss I grew up with. And I'm not even sure what that means anymore . . . just that I want that constancy and comfort so badly sometimes that it scares me."

His fingers are back on my arm, a gentle stroke. Back and forth and back and forth and then they're gone. "Being an adult sucks," he says, and the bluntness of it makes me laugh, in spite of everything.

"It really does," I agree. The ghost of his touch lingers on my skin. "What should we do tomorrow? Fewer soul-searching conversations? We could explore more of the island. If the rain stops, we could go hiking."

"I'd be down for a hike," he says. "There's supposed to be some great antiquing on the island, too."

"Antiquing?"

"Ah, maybe I never told you. My parents own an antiques shop. I have an incurable fondness for old kitchen gadgets. Cast-iron cookware, specifically."

"Then it's settled," I say around a yawn. Just when I think I'm figuring him out, Dominic reveals another layer. "We'll go antiquing, and then we'll go hiking." I roll over to check the time. "How is it one thirty?"

"You tired? I'll let you go to sleep. I've always been kind of a night owl."

And the thing is . . . I *am* tired, but I don't want to sleep. I want to stay up talking like this. I'd love to learn his mouth for real, for him to roll his hips over mine and press me down into the mattress, but I also want to hear more secrets, to tell more secrets.

But I don't know how to do any of that, so I switch off the lamp and plunge the two of us into darkness.

"Night, Shay," he says, and it breaks my heart, just a little, that I'll only get to hear those words from him one more time.

The first thing I feel when I wake up is *warmth*. Sunlight pours into the room, and there is a very tall, very stubbly guy next to me. He has one arm beneath his pillow, the other stretched out on the bed between us. And *god*, he looks cute. I've always been weak for morning-guy sleepiness. They're so soft, so innocent in a way they rarely are in real life.

Steve is at the foot of the bed, softly whining for a walk, as though he doesn't want to wake Dominic, either. The bed creaks when I lift myself off it, and Dominic stirs.

"Sorry, did I wake you?" I say.

"No, no," he says, but his eyes are still closed.

I can't help smiling at that. "You can go back to sleep if you want. I'm going to walk Steve and shower."

"I'm getting up," he says as he rolls over, face mashed into the pillow.

After I walk Steve, Dominic showers downstairs and I shower upstairs. I put on something much less dressy than my work outfits: black leggings, graphic tee, gray hoodie. He's similarly athletic-casual in jeans, a Northwestern sweatshirt—seriously, how much college apparel can one person own?—and a Mariners cap.

Our weather apps predict morning drizzle and afternoon sun, so we decide to antique first, hike later. We spend the morning at a farmers' market, grabbing pastries and fresh fruit. Maybe Kent was right about the two of us bonding because this really does feel like something I'd do with a boyfriend. We take Steve with us, who greets every stranger like he wants them to take him home.

"Steve, where is your loyalty?" I say, mock-offended.

Once we're adequately carbo-loaded, we get in my car to map directions to Dominic's antique shops.

"Here," I say, passing him my phone while I secure Steve in his crate. "Look up where you want to go."

When I get into the driver's seat, he's grinning down at my phone. "I see you've been listening to a certain judicial system podcast."

I grab for my phone, but he holds it out of reach. "It was just—research. You know. Had to learn more about you."

"Uh-huh." He scrolls down, smirks. "Then why does it show you've listened to . . . all twelve of their most recent episodes?"

"Steve and I take a lot of long walks," I insist, and he grins the rest of the drive.

I'm more interested in observing Dominic in an antique shop than the antiques themselves. It's as though he immediately knows where to go, despite never having been there. I follow him to a section full of kitchen supplies.

He unearths a cast-iron skillet and inspects it. "A Griswold number seven. Nice." Upon seeing my perplexed expression, he turns sheepish. "It's an addiction. I probably have about twenty of these in my apartment."

"And you cook with all of them?"

"I restore them first," he says. "You have to remove all the rust with some steel wool before seasoning it."

"Seasoning it? Like . . . adding oregano or rosemary or what?"

"Not that kind of seasoning. You rub it down with oil, then

place it in a hot oven for an hour or so, and after that, it's ready for cooking."

"Wow," I say, genuinely impressed. "Ameena and I go to estate sales sometimes, but that's mainly just for clothes."

"Yeah?" A corner of his mouth quirks up as he sorts through the cookware. I kneel next to him, trying to help, though I have no idea what I'm looking for. "I like the way you dress."

My face heats up hotter than that skillet probably could. "I thought you weren't a fan of the taco shirt."

"Oh, you should burn the taco shirt, don't get me wrong. I meant what you wear to work." He digs into another stack, obscuring his face.

"Oh. Um—thank you," I say, and then, in attempt to change the subject: "Show me what we're looking for?" And so begins my cast-iron education.

Dominic's pretty pleased with his haul: that Griswold number seven and a Wagner number five. After a quick café lunch, we head off on our hike. It's an easy one, fortunately, easy enough that we're able to talk without getting too out of breath. Which is good, because that's a sensation I tend to experience around Dominic regardless of physical activity. Steve trots along beside me like he's just happy to be here.

"I haven't hiked in forever," Dominic says. His strides are much longer than mine, and I can tell he purposefully goes slower so I can keep up. It's both sweet and infuriating. "I love having the time to just think."

"My mom and I used to go hiking a lot in the years after my dad died." Our therapist suggested it as a bonding activity. We never talked much on those hikes, but I think it helped.

"Was your dad into hiking?"

I snort. "God no. He hated the outdoors. It was more that it was therapeutic for my mom and me. My dad actually had this joke—that it was wild he'd wound up in the Pacific Northwest because he and nature didn't get along. I mean, sure, he could appreciate a sunset or a particularly nice tree, but he was super fair skinned, and he had to wear like SPF ninety, and he claimed mosquitoes loved his blood because he always wound up covered in bites."

"Was he a redhead?"

"No, he was blond. But my mom is. Why?"

"Your hair"—he gestures—"it's not all the way brown. In the right light, it has this reddish tint. Or are those highlights?"

"Oh." I smooth my hands over my ponytail. "No. I've never dyed my hair. But I usually just call it brown. Not that exciting. The red is really subtle. Anyway," I say, moving away from the topic of my hair. "I haven't gone hiking in a while, either. Been busy. You know, dating you."

When he smiles, it's a genuine-looking one. "I did tend to monopolize your time. All the dinners out, all the dumb shit I made you watch on Netflix with me, all my insisting that we spend our weekends at antique shops. And then . . . then there were those weekend mornings where we'd stay in bed for hours." At that, his smile turns crooked.

"Hours?" I say, my heart picking up speed as my shoes thud against the dirt path.

"Sometimes the whole weekend. We'd order takeout so we wouldn't have to leave the bed."

I'm not sure what, exactly, he's trying to pull here. Surely he's just messing with me. Again.

"Sometimes you'd even call in sick," I say. "Because you needed me that badly, and you'd have been too distracted all day at work."

"Except for that time in Booth C."

I tap my chin, trying to appear cool and nonchalant. It's ridiculous how much I want all of this to have been true. "Refresh my memory?"

"You remember." He knocks my arm with his elbow, and for a moment, I'm convinced I really do have that fake memory locked away somewhere. "You sent me an email, asking me to meet you in Booth C. I thought you wanted my input on something you were recording, but you just locked the door and . . . well, let's just say, I'd never done that in a sound booth before."

His words stop me in my tracks. I'm going to need a very long shower when we get to the house. This must be a joke to him—right? Or is he screwing with me because he wants all of it to have been real, too?

"Yeah," I say. "That was, um. Pretty wild."

We're quiet for the next ten minutes or so. I try to focus on the rhythm of my breaths, the jingling of Steve's collar. It's not my imagination that Dominic's flirting with me—at least, I don't think so. But I can't tell what's real and what isn't, what we manufactured in the studio and what's grown since then. God. Dominic Yun, who I despised the moment he started at Pacific Public Radio. The guy I'm beginning to like more than I ever planned.

When we reach the top, the puffed-cotton clouds and the endless trees feel more like home than Seattle sometimes does. Steve selects a rock for a triumphant pee.

Dominic pulls me in for a victory hug, and it's criminal that he still smells good after an hour spent trudging up a mountain.

"Take a picture with me?" he says, pulling out his phone.

I make a face. "I look gross right now." All sweaty and grimy, my hair coming out of its ponytail.

"I'm sure I'm gross, too."

I reach up to swipe an imaginary smudge off his cheek. "Absolutely filthy."

He stares down at me, and I wonder if this is the kind of light that makes my hair look more red than brown. "You just climbed a fucking mountain. You're beautiful, Shay. At work or in pajamas or at the top of a mountain."

"I . . . ," I start, because I am speechless. He said it so effortlessly, like it wasn't meant to affect me quite this way. "Fine. Take the photo."

I pick up Steve, and Dominic leans in close and holds out his selfie arm. I get another whiff of soap and sweat, and suddenly it's so intoxicating that I have to press my body against his so he can hold me up.

He turns the phone to me so I can see how the photo turned out, but all I see is his smiling face, his hand on my shoulder, the dimple in his left cheek. How he looks truly *happy*.

I don't think I've ever seen that on his face before.

21

In typical Pacific Northwest fashion, it starts raining on our way back down, and by the time we make it to the house, it's pouring.

"What do you think?" Dominic asks as we shuck off our muddy shoes. "Pasta again?"

"Only if you don't complain about the noodles," I say. "Besides, now that I know you're a cast-iron expert, I feel like we could do better."

"For the tenth time, they're not supposed to be that soft, they're supposed to be *al dente*," he says, though there's a teasing lilt to his voice. He unzips his jacket and hangs it in the hall. His T-shirt clings to his chest, showing off muscles I didn't know he had and am not displeased to see. "And those skillets aren't ready yet. You'll have to wait until we're back in Seattle for me to show off my cooking skills."

I want to press for more information on when, exactly, I'll be in a position to enjoy his cooking skills, but I'm not ready for the real world. I fill Steve's food bowl and try not to think about the wet T-shirt contest Dominic is currently winning. "I should shower first. Wash off all this nature."

"Sure," he says. "I'll take the downstairs, you take the upstairs?"

It should feel good to get a break from him. Some space for my mind to untangle. Except once I'm under the hot water, attempting to relax, I can't keep from imagining Dominic doing the same thing downstairs, running his hands through his hair and down his chest and along other choice body parts. The jokes he made today, the things we said last night . . . we're closer than we've ever been, the charge between us more electric.

I wrap my hair in a towel and spend far too long deciding what to wear. Ultimately, I settle on leggings and a boatneck tee, forgoing makeup since he's already seen me without it.

When I reach the kitchen, he's at the counter, chopping vegetables from the farmers' market while oil sizzles in a pan on the stove. His back muscles flex against the gray T-shirt he's wearing, his hair damp and curling at the ends. He must have brought his regular soap and shampoo because there's that scent I've come to associate with him.

"Pasta primavera," he says, dropping broccoli and peppers into the pan. "Slightly more advanced."

"Anything that involves more than one pot and no recipe is impressive to me." The sight and scent of him have turned me to overcooked spaghetti.

When I spot two glasses of wine waiting on the table, my heart beats triple time in my chest. This is Dominic Yun, arrogant co-host, too tall for his own good, who set this up for us. Dominic, who comforted my terrified dog. Dominic, who spilled his secrets to me last night and encouraged me to do the same.

Who kissed me and asked if we could forget about it.

It's our last night on the island, and I can't bear to later get in bed next to him without touching him. No more pretending this isn't something I've wanted since we started *The Ex Talk*. I need to know it isn't one-sided.

"We've been honest with each other, right?" I say to his back. "This whole weekend?"

"Right." He adds squash, zucchini, garlic.

"I know we were supposed to forget what happened after the bar." My pulse is roaring in my ears, louder than the rain outside. "But . . . I haven't."

Finally, he turns away from the counter, facing me. I didn't know sweatpants could be sexy, but that's the only way to describe how they hang on his hips. "I haven't, either," he says after a pause. "I haven't even tried."

I'm not sure if I'm more relieved or turned on. "Even though you wanted to pretend it didn't happen?" My voice is barely a whisper. I curse myself as I ask it, but I have to know.

"It seemed like it would be easier."

"Has it been? Easier?"

A wry smile. "Sometimes," he says, and there are only a thousand ways I could interpret that. He glances toward the sautéing vegetables, gives them a stir.

"If we're really supposed to be bonding this weekend, getting to know everything about each other . . . maybe we should know what it feels like for real. Sober."

He shakes his head. "No."

"No?" My heart drops to the floor. I've never been able to read him, but I didn't expect him to shoot me down like that.

"If I kissed you again," he says, stepping closer, an intensity in his gaze I've never seen before, "it wouldn't be for the show, or for research, or for any reason other than that I wanted to."

Oh. I have to grip the edge of the counter to keep myself upright. I'm not sure what the rules are now. The line between reality and fabrication is smudged, blurred, stamped out completely.

"Dominic." I try to put a question mark at the end of his name, but it comes out breathy and needy. If he doesn't touch me in the next few seconds, I might explode.

He must hear that neediness in my voice because he switches off the stove and *almost* closes the space between us, a few inches between his chest and mine. I want to devour each one of his labored breaths. When he looks down at me, there's none of the ego I used to see. Eyes dark, mouth slightly parted—maybe this is the expression I haven't been able to interpret. His hair is damp and messy, and I've just decided that is exactly the way I like it. I'll like it even more when it's between my fingers and brushing across my stomach, my thighs.

He lifts his hand, his thumb landing on my cheekbone, skimming across it before sliding into my wet hair. "I'd want to remember every detail. The way you taste. The way you smell. The sounds you'd make."

At that, I let out an involuntary whimper. It's the hottest thing anyone's ever said to me, and if I were able to speak, I'd tell him I wanted to learn his sounds, too.

"Shay. *God.* Do you have any idea—" He breaks off, like he's too overcome by want to finish the sentence. It's powerful, the realization that you can steal words from someone like that.

A crash of thunder rocks the house, but I don't flinch. I am only want and need and the spaces he's touching me. His other hand moves to my waist, where I can feel the press of each fingertip through the fabric of my shirt.

"What?" I say, desperate to know how that sentence ends. I plant my hands on his chest, the heather gray T-shirt. He is taut and warm beneath my palms. Slowly, slowly, I move them upward, and his eyes flutter shut when one of my hands reaches his cheek, feeling the stubble there. Letting it scrape against my skin. "Do I have any idea what?"

"How fucking perfect you are right now."

That's all it takes. My hands dive into his hair, and I tug his mouth down to mine. I am kissing Dominic Yun, and he feels incredible, so warm and slick and *right* as he parts my mouth with his. I thought this would feel like immediate relief, but it's the opposite, a deep and dizzying need that grows and grows. I need him to kiss me harder. And he does, matching the swipe of my tongue and the bite of my teeth. I'd forgotten that rush of adrenaline that comes with being this close to someone new. Someone I supposedly broke up with a few months ago.

He spins us so he can push me against the counter, then kisses a trail from my mouth to my neck as his hips roll against mine. He's so much taller than I am that I feel the hard length of him against my navel, and it turns me wilder. There's a low rumble in his throat when I press back against him.

We shouldn't be doing this.

We have to keep doing this.

I murmur an *oh my god* as he sucks at my neck, teeth on skin. I feel myself about to buckle, but he's there, holding me up. "Bedroom," I gasp out.

He pulls me forward, wrapping one of my legs around him, indicating I should do the same with the other. Then he's picking me up, gripping my thighs and then my ass as we stagger upstairs.

"You have *moves*," I say when he sets me down on the edge of the bed, giving me a moment to catch my breath and safely deposit my glasses on a nightstand.

"No moves," he says, sounding earnest as he slides onto the bed next to me. "Just something I've been wanting to do for a while." His mouth, back on my neck. His hands, roaming the sides of my body, lingering at the dip in my waist.

"Me too." I experience a flash of panic as his fingers graze my breasts. "I should warn you, I'm wearing a truly hideous sports bra." It used to be charcoal, but now it's an unfortunate watery gray, the elastic peeking through various holes in the seams. Really, I should win an award for packing the world's least sexy clothing.

A laugh gets caught in his throat. "I can one hundred percent guarantee I won't care."

I can't take my shirt and bra off fast enough.

"Don't tell me you prefer the bra," I say when he just stares at me.

"Gorgeous," he says, but he's looking at my face. He leans in to kiss me again, a thumb stroking the hardened peak of one nipple before he bends to take the other into his mouth.

Fuck he's good at this. At this rate, I'm half-convinced I could come before my leggings are off. I go for the hem of his shirt, and he helps me yank it off. I barely have time to appreciate the ridges of his chest before I'm tugging at his waistband. I'm so greedy that even with his pants half-off, I reach inside, desperate to feel him.

He groans in my ear as I close my hand around him. He's hot and smooth and rock-hard, pulsing in my fist. "Don't—don't go too fast," he says, and I'm reminded of the fact that he's only done this with one other person. That this is a big deal to him.

That it must mean *I'm* a big deal to him.

"I won't." I draw back. Not too fast. I can do that. I can savor this.

Because there's a nagging thought at the back of my mind that I don't know what *this* will mean when we're back at the station.

We readjust so he can remove his pants, and then he holds himself over me as he fumbles with the waistband of my leggings. Another terrible clothing choice.

"They're kind of tight, so—"

"Making me work for it," he says, but he's grinning "I don't mind. I have a master's degree, after all. I'm used to hard work."

I nod toward the impressive tent in his boxer briefs. "I can tell."

He slides my leggings off and kisses me from ankle to knee to thigh, stroking along the outside of my underwear, already wet with my need for him. This pair is granny panty–adjacent, and yet I've never felt sexier.

"This okay?" he asks, his breath ragged. A finger grazes the fabric, and my body focuses all its attention on that single piece of cotton. I hold tight to his shoulders, silently begging him to push aside my underwear, tear it off, anything to feel skin on skin.

"It must be pretty obvious that it is," I manage, but because I appreciate he asked, I add: "Yes. *Yes.*"

Except he pulls back into a seated position on the bed next to me. I'm still panting, half-embarrassed by how feral those few strokes of his finger turned me.

"I just realized I don't have a condom," he says, and the reality is louder than a thunderclap. He runs a hand through his hair, looking sheepish. In this moment, even his sheepishness is hot. Inconvenient, but hot. "Shit. I'm sorry. Do you—?"

I cut him off with a shake of my head, forcing myself up so I can lean against the headboard. My dating app hiatus evolved into a birth control hiatus. "No. Didn't really think this would happen, so . . ."

We're both quiet for a few moments. Enough for the awkwardness to set in, enough for me to feel a little exposed.

"I'm sorry," he repeats. "I could go get some?" But the rain only seems to pelt the tiny house's roof harder, reminding us of the storm and the fact that the nearest drugstore is at least twenty minutes away.

"I . . . kind of don't want to stop." I lean in, palming his erection. "There are other things we could do."

He closes his eyes and lets out another groan. I could get addicted to that sound—Dominic struggling to stay in control. I grab at the elastic of his boxer briefs and help him out of them. A naked Dominic is almost too much: the cut of his stomach muscles, the

V shape that drags my attention downward. He's more beautiful than I thought he'd be, and I have thought about him like this a lot.

"You are . . ." I gesture to him, struggling to come up with an adequate compliment. "You are an extremely attractive man."

That earns me another grin. I swing a leg over him and settle into his lap, feeling him through the fabric of my underwear.

"Christ. *Shay*," he says. A warning and a plea. His hands are on my hips, guiding me as I roll forward. He feels so goddamn good like this that I have to wrap my arms around his neck to steady myself. My breasts press against his chest and I grind into him harder, faster, the friction bringing me closer and closer to release. "You are killing me. I have to touch you. Please."

He waits for my exhaled *yes* before he takes charge, pushing me onto my back and inching off my underwear, letting it drop to the floor. He nips at my throat as he teases me with one finger. At first he's tentative, drawing soft circles everywhere but the place I need him most. He moves so achingly slowly that I buck my hips, trying to encourage him to go faster. This makes him laugh, a rough noise at the back of his throat.

Don't go too fast.

Distantly, I wonder if this is what Dominic is always like in bed: determined to make it last as long as possible. Maybe he wants to savor it, too. He slips a finger inside me, and I can't help it—I gasp. He picks up speed, and I let my head fall back against the pillow.

"You have no idea how hot you are right now," he says. "My imagination didn't do you justice."

Half his mouth curves into a smile, like he knows how close I am. Knowing he imagined this sends me right up to the edge. I let out a whimper and squeeze my eyes shut. The pressure turns ruthless, white-hot, shimmering as I come hard against his fingers.

When I blink myself back to earth, he's grinning like we just hit the Apple Podcasts Top 10.

"So smug," I say, trying to catch my breath even as I'm reaching for his cock.

He flinches. "Only if you want to."

"You think I'm not dying to see you go fucking wild after that?"

He's already lying back, letting me take control. I watch what I'm doing play across his face: the twitch in his jaw, the fluttering of his eyes, my name on his lips. And the sounds he makes, these growls and grunts that spark right to my core. I haven't done this—given a hand job as anything except foreplay—since college, and the power is intoxicating.

Suddenly, he turns, slipping out of my grasp. "I want you to come with me," he says, voice shredded, trailing a finger up my leg.

Those words alone nearly make me collapse. I spread my legs to help him find that perfect spot again, and then I ride his hand as he drives into my palm, each thrust of his hips more frenzied, more desperate as he chases his own release. It's almost too much, touching him like this while he's touching me, but somehow I manage to hold on.

"I'm close," I say, and that's when he brings his fingers to his mouth, licks them, and returns them to the ache between my legs. "*Dominic*—"

I fall apart a moment before he spills into my hand with a low moan.

I am boneless. Weightless. Wrecked.

Both of us go still, the only sounds the rain on the roof and the rhythm of our breaths.

Neither of us speaks when he excuses himself to clean up. I pull on a T-shirt, suddenly feeling a little cold. There's an awkward moment where we switch places so I can wash up in the bathroom too, one that makes me hyperaware of the fact that we are Shay and Dominic and definitely not a couple.

To thousands of people, we are the opposite.

When I get back to bed, he's slipped on a clean pair of sweatpants, but he remains shirtless. His face softens into a smile and he pats the bed next to him.

"Come here," he says, and my whole body sags with relief.

"That was . . ."

A half grin. "Better than the fun drawer?"

"Significantly."

I'm not sure why I assumed he wouldn't want to hold me afterward. Maybe because we haven't discussed what this is or what this means, if it's a onetime thing, or if not having a condom necessitates a redo once we're back in Seattle.

I settle against him, trying to ignore how natural it feels to rest my hand on his chest. His fingers play through my hair, feather across my back. We'll have to get up eventually—have to talk about this eventually—but for now, I want to curl up inside this moment of not-quite real life.

So I pull that moment tight around us, and I don't let in anything else for the rest of the night.

22

His side of the bed is empty when I wake up. I feel for him with my hand first, eyes closed, trying to ignore the knot of disappointment that settles in my stomach when I find cold sheets, a dip in his pillow but no Dominic.

Last night might have been the hottest night I've had in a long time, maybe ever, and it's been a while since I slept this soundly. And yet . . . waking up alone makes the whole thing feel dreamlike. Distant.

But I can't forget what he said about *personal and intimate* and the possibility that this meant something to him, even if I can't quite unravel what it means to me.

I hear distinctly breakfast-like noises from the kitchen, and then some of Steve's little snerfling sounds. I put on a hoodie and meet them there.

Dominic's standing beside the stove, fully dressed and freshly showered, moving a pan from a burner to the sink. I don't know if he forgot a razor or didn't bring one on purpose, but the scruffiness makes me itch to run my hands over his face again. Except it's been a while since I navigated a post-hookup breakfast, and I've never done it with a coworker.

I'm unsteady on my feet as I reach the table.

"Morning," Dominic says, sounding much too chipper. "Pancakes?"

And there they are, a stack of blueberry pancakes, a pot of coffee, and two plates.

"You made pancakes?" I bend down to scratch Steve behind the ears.

"I've been up for a couple hours," he admits. "Ran out to the store to get a few things. And I took Steve out. Hope that's okay. I wanted us to get an early start, if possible." As he says this, he glances pointedly at my pajamas.

I pause halfway to the bottle of syrup. He made pancakes, which feels like a point in the let's-do-this-again-soon column. But he wants to get back to Seattle as soon as we can, which doesn't. I'm not sure how to reconcile those two things. "Oh—yeah, that's fine. Thank you. I'll shower and pack as soon as we finish."

He smiles, but it's a little strained, and it makes the sugary breakfast turn to chalk in my mouth. Is that . . . regret?

The things he said to me last night don't match up with that smile. *You have no idea how hot you are. I want you to come with me.* A tangle of sighs and limbs and desperation.

I'm suddenly not hungry, but I force down as many bites of pancake as I can.

We talk about nearly everything else on the ride back—podcasts, our families, the weather. But we don't talk about what happened. I could easily bring it up—*nice orgasms last night, huh?*—but if I do, and if he tells me it was some kind of extended experiment brought about by our predicament, I'm not sure I could handle it. Not while trapped in a car with him. Not when we finally feel like friends. I'd rather hold on to the maybe, so I embrace the silence.

By the time we stop outside his place, I have two and a half hangnails and a raging stress headache. The street is only half-familiar, like I visited it in a dream, but I'm able to spot Dominic's apartment right away, tucked between the columns of identical buildings.

He unbuckles his seat belt, but he doesn't move to get out. "Hey," he says, and I turn to look at him, my heart pounding against my own seat belt. "I guess I'll see you tomorrow morning?"

I do my best to project an everything-is-fine tone. "Yep. Bright and early."

And then, in one swift motion, he leans over and slides a hand into my hair, dragging my mouth to his. The kiss starts out sweet until I part my lips, eager to taste more of him. He matches me, pressing back with an urgency that leaves me gasping for air.

A crooked smile, and then he's gone, the kiss convincing me that whatever we started on the island wasn't done yet.

"Something happened," Ameena says, and it's a good thing I didn't go into broadcast journalism because my face is utterly incapable of keeping a secret. My mouth twitches, or my nostrils flare, or my eyes dart back and forth.

It was early afternoon when Dominic and I got back to Seattle, so when Ameena texted about an estate sale, I jumped at the chance to meet her. And when she asked how it went, I couldn't keep a straight face.

"Something definitely happened," TJ agrees, holding up a pillowcase with a clown embroidered on it.

"Absolutely not," Ameena says, and he slowly sets it down.

I walk to the end of a row of kitchenware. Of course, it reminds me of the antique shops we went to, and I find myself wondering if there's any cast-iron here.

"Fine, fine, something happened, and I am maybe in the middle of a crisis," I say, and I try my best to put it all into words. Not just the parts that involved no clothes, but our conversation Friday night, and the hike, and the way he held my dog. After five years, I've gotten used to telling Ameena about my relationships with TJ around, which of course means TJ also knows Dominic and I are lying about the show.

"You do have a thing for guys and animals," Ameena muses. "Remember that guy Rodrigo and the kittens?"

Ah, yes: Rodrigo the data analyst, whose cat had just given birth to a litter of six little fluffballs. After a while, I had to admit I was more interested in cuddling with the kittens than with him.

"They couldn't even open their eyes yet, Ameena. They *couldn't open their eyes.*"

She snorts, pausing to dig through a box of shoes. This week she finds out about the Virginia job, and I can tell she's on edge by the way she passes up a pair of yellow T-strap sandals.

"Now it's a problem, though," I say. "Because I really want it to happen again."

"Is there a reason it can't? Or that it shouldn't?" TJ asks.

Ameena points at him. "What he said."

"Because the whole conceit of the show is that we're *not* dating? And besides, maybe I only like him because I'm not supposed to. Maybe that's what makes it exciting."

"People can get back together," TJ says. "The listeners might even love that."

"I thought about that," I admit. Fleetingly, on the ride home, while working on my second hangnail. "But things are going too well with the show to jeopardize it. Doing anything with Dominic . . .

being a real couple. I can't see how it wouldn't mess shit up. Unless—unless we somehow managed to keep it casual."

Casual—the thing that Dominic doesn't do. And given my history, there's a risk I'd cling, and he's only twenty-four. Simple relationship statistics, many of which fill up my computer's search history—hazard of hosting a dating show—indicate he wouldn't be clinging back.

"And you're good at it." Ameena frowns, tucking a strand of her long dark hair behind one ear. "This might be a stupid question, but is there any chance the two of you could come clean?"

"No. It would be a disaster. We've already hooked a couple sponsors, and Kent hinted that we might—" I swallow, trying not to get my hopes up. "That we might have a chance at PodCon."

TJ lets out a low whistle. "Shit, that's huge. You think you can get Marc Maron's autograph for me?"

Ameena whacks his arm with a circle skirt. "You haven't talked about someone like this in a while," she says quietly. "I know the whole thing is inconvenient, but you're already pretending to be exes. It sounds like a lot to keep pretending you feel differently about him on top of all that." There's something in her voice that sounds a little like judgment.

"It's my career," I say, harder edged than I intend. "I can't just throw it all away for a guy."

"You're right," she says, her words threaded with frustration, and though TJ and I try our best to distract her with vintage dresses, she's aloof the rest of the afternoon.

Steve is waiting at the door when I get home. Even after being with him all weekend, I've begun to look forward to his *you didn't abandon me* excitement. He'll run circles around the living room, and it takes a few laps for him to slow down enough for me to pet him.

I settle into the couch, scratching his ears, and it doesn't sink in until I've been there for a while that I'm no longer eager for background noise. Some new pillows I bought last weekend add a spot of brightness to the room, and I even unpacked the moment I got home, throwing my dirty clothes in the washing machine. Not to mention having Steve's stuff everywhere makes the place feel more lived-in, less sterile. Suddenly, I don't hate being here.

Maybe I really was lonely.

Of course, that makes me think of Dominic. It aches when I picture him in his own apartment eating alone, drinking alone, watching TV alone. Climbing into bed and sleeping alone after two nights next to me.

Determined not to think about last night, I throw myself into researching our upcoming episodes. We're planning one about jazzing up dating profiles, one about gender ratios in major cities, one about dating as a single parent, all with guests who are experts in their fields. I have to focus on the show. Like I told Ameena, I can't risk my job after finally getting the chance to be on the air.

For three and a half more months, at least, according to my initial handshake with Dominic. Deep down, of course I'm hoping he loves the show enough to want to keep it up longer, especially if we get bigger sponsorship opportunities.

And yet the more I look through my notes, the more I find myself drawn to the one show that hasn't been approved yet. I've done enough research to know that no topic in the dating landscape is truly unexplored. We're just one of many, many podcasts that have traversed it. But what has always made radio so special to me is its ability to turn something intangible into something personal. To let someone tell a story only they can.

This grief show wouldn't be breakthrough radio, I know that—but it would be *mine*.

23

"Why are there dildos in the newsroom?"

Marlene Harrison-Yates is waiting by my desk on Monday morning, hovering over a box of sex toys that seemingly appeared there overnight. There are matching boxes on Dominic's and Ruthie's desks.

"That is an excellent question," I say, pushing the box out of the way to make room for my coffee and nearly knocking over Dominic's master's jar in the process.

"Sponsors," Ruthie says, peeking up from her desk. "Well, hopeful sponsors. They sent this stuff so you'd, um, try it out"—she chokes on a laugh—"and then, if you like it, talk about it on the show."

It's not just sex toys. There's also a lube-of-the-month subscription box, a pair of shoes made almost entirely from corn, and a set of organic bedsheets. I'm pretty sure we can't talk about half this stuff on NPR.

Marlene purses her lips and returns to her desk.

I spent far too much time debating what to wear to work this morning. I wanted to strike the perfect balance between professional and *don't you want to see me naked again?* Ultimately, I went with something not much different from what I usually wear: my favorite dark-wash jeans, ankle boots, and a fitted black blazer over a V-neck blouse. It's still NPR, after all. And Dominic said he likes what I wear to work.

I was so on edge I couldn't even listen to the radio in the car. One of my hangnails got so bad that I have two Band-Aids wrapped around my thumb, and the multiple orgasms I had with Dominic may have ended my drought but only deepened my sexual frustration.

And the box o' dildos isn't helping.

"How was the weekend?" Ruthie asks as we sort through the boxes, grouping items into two piles labeled SAFE FOR NPR and FCC LAWSUIT. Dominic's not here yet, and I'm not sure if I'm disappointed or relieved. "Did you guys bond?"

I avoid her gaze, worried my face will give away all the ways in which we bonded. "He and my dog did." I hold up the lube-of-the-month subscription box. May's flavor is key lime pie. "Can we talk about lube on NPR?"

"My gut says no," Ruthie says. "But the corn shoes are kind of cute, right?"

When Dominic arrives at a quarter past nine, there are no more adult toys on his desk. "Morning," he says to me as he drops his bag by his desk and pulls out his chair. "Morning, Ruthie."

"Morning!" Ruthie chirps before returning to typing.

My words get stuck at the back of my throat. I'm not sure I can utter a basic *good morning* now that I know how his hands feel on my skin, between my legs. What he looks like on the verge of orgasm. What is proper etiquette the day after you hook up with the fake ex-boyfriend you're doing a radio show with? I would honestly love a podcast about that.

Dominic doesn't look at me, which gives me a chance to watch him unpack. He's clean-shaven this morning, weekend stubble gone, wearing a red plaid shirt and black jeans. It's not normal, is it, for me to be able to smell his soap from a full desk away? And I know there's something wrong with me when him tossing the Koosh ball up and down doesn't even annoy me.

He's the one who said he didn't think he could do casual. Maybe he has no idea how to handle this, either.

Even if nothing that happened on Saturday felt casual at all.

I try my best to focus on my Monday to-do list instead of imagining his fingers on my skin again. We're doing a guest appearance at ten o'clock on the podcast *Thanks I Hate It*, which is hosted by Audrey and Maya, two stand-up comedian best friends who talk about millennial dating culture and adulting. They're pretty popular, and they have a book coming out next year. I was over the moon when their producer reached out to Ruthie last week, but today I have to force myself to concentrate on the interview.

Ruthie engineers the interview for us in Booth A. Fortunately, Audrey and Maya are easy to talk to, even if I feel myself tense up when Audrey introduces us as "America's favorite exes."

I don't know if the weekend made Dominic and me more awkward or less awkward, but we manage to make them laugh plenty of times. By the end of the interview, though, I can't remember a thing I've said.

Kent is waiting for us in the hall after we finish recording.

"Great stuff, really great," he says. "That in there—that's exactly what I was talking about. You two felt much more natural. Guess the weekend away worked wonders, huh?"

Huh indeed.

"Guess it did. Thank you," I say. Then, since Kent's in a good mood, I decide to try something again. *WWAMWMD*, I remind myself when I'm worried I might chicken out, and I charge forward. "I wanted to run something by you."

"Sure," he says with a glance down at his watch. "I've only got a few minutes, though."

I'm extremely aware of Dominic next to me and positive my face is the color of his shirt.

"My grief show. I know I brought it up at sort of a weird time last week, but it's important to me, and I think we could do a lot with it."

He turns icy almost instantly. "I thought we discussed that."

"A little bit, but I've been thinking about it, and—"

"I'm just not sure it's the best path for the show right now," Kent says, cutting me off. "Too dark. We want to keep things light, keep things fun. Dom, you agree with me, right?"

"Actually, no," Dominic says, straightening to his full height, much taller than Kent. "I think it would be fantastic radio. I don't think there's any reason we need to box ourselves into one type of show."

Kent taps his chin, deep in thought for a moment. I'm too warm in my blazer, unsure where this conversation is going. "Well, I trust you," he finally says. To Dominic. "I trust both of you. Go ahead and get the ball rolling."

I'm still gaping when Kent disappears down the hall.

"Did you—you realize what just happened there, right?" I manage to ask Dominic. Another entry for the Kent O'Grady misogyny playbook. I'm more positive than I've ever been that that's what it is.

"Fucking prick," he says under his breath.

I have to hold in a laugh. "Thank you," I tell him. "For being on board with it.

"It's going to be a good show." I'm about to head back to our desks, but what he says next stops me in my tracks. "I think we, uh, accidentally swapped phone chargers over the weekend," he says, eyes darting around the hallway as though making sure we're alone. "Would you mind swinging by my place tonight so we can switch back?"

I must not have noticed. "Sure, or we can do it tomorrow at work."

"I need it tonight." He steps closer, a hand reaching out so he can brush a thumb across my hip. His voice drops another octave. "Or are you going to make me say that I want to see you?"

"I don't hate the sound of that," I say, biting back a grin. Even if this is a thinly veiled booty call, I decide I don't mind. I have to be alone with him again—every cell in my body is crying out for it. "That is, if you're saying it."

He smirks. "I'll see you tonight."

24

Dominic's apartment smells incredible. "Welcome," he says, holding open the door. He's changed out of his work shirt into a soft flannel rolled to the elbows—holy forearms, Batman—and his jeans hang low on his hips.

I take off my jacket and slip out of my shoes, trying not to look like I'm examining his apartment. It's a design aesthetic I'd call IKEA chic but tasteful: clean white furniture, a few succulents on the coffee table in his living room, that lantern floor lamp everyone has owned at some point in their lives.

I hold up my charger. "I brought this," I say. "But I'm guessing I probably don't need it?"

"Not very smooth, was I?"

"I'm here, so I'd call that a win."

As I follow him into the kitchen, his fingertips graze the small of my back. It's criminal, the things those small touches do to me.

Dominic's cast-iron skillets hang from the ceiling. "I restored the skillets from this weekend yesterday evening," he says. "And one of them is right in there." He gestures toward the oven.

"Pizza?"

"The best pizza of your fucking life," he corrects.

"This is a considerable step up from that Hot Pocket."

He shrugs. "It's not very fun cooking just for myself. And I figured I owed it to you after the pasta incident."

This feels like a date. This cannot feel like a date.

"Right. So that and the phone charger—those are the only reasons I'm here?"

Pink creeps onto his cheeks. "Pizza's almost ready. Can we eat first and then talk? I wanted a place where we could do it that wasn't at work."

"Sure," I say, but the knot of dread in my stomach tightens. After dinner, he'll break it to me gently that we can't have a repeat of this weekend, and I'll be so enamored with the pizza that I won't mind. That has to be his strategy.

He takes the pizza out of the oven, and it's bubbly and fragrant and perfect. Honestly, his strategy might work. He throws together a quick salad, bagged lettuce with those little carrot slivers, a dash of oil and vinegar. Then he grabs a bottle of wine from the top of his refrigerator, grimacing at the label.

"Tonight's wine pairing is a vintage bottle of Two-Buck Chuck," he says, fishing two wineglasses from a cupboard. "I hope you can handle that level of extravagance."

We sit down at his white IKEA table that has only two chairs.

"What do you think?" he asks, waiting for my assessment before he digs in.

I take a chewy, cheesy, saucy bite. "Oh. Oh *shit*, that's good."

"It's really just a hobby," he says, but I can tell he's pleased. "But I may listen to a cooking podcast or two. I do, however, have to apologize on behalf of this sad, sad salad. I wanted you to think I was, like, a halfway functioning adult and that I can make meals with more than one food group."

"What even is a functioning adult? I ate two bagels for dinner yesterday." The pizza nearly burns my tongue, but it's so good that I don't care.

To my surprise, the rest of dinner is far from the slog I worried it would be when Dominic asked to table our impending serious discussion. Maybe after Orcas, nothing about Dominic should surprise me.

"I was thinking of what we talked about this weekend, about not having many friends," I tell him when there are only crumbs left on our plates. "And I had this idea. We should challenge ourselves to each make a friend date with someone." Besides, I've been meaning to ask Ruthie to drinks again, or maybe dinner.

"A friend date?" he asks, but the corners of his mouth twitch upward. "Okay. You're on." He drags his index finger up and down the stem of his wineglass. "Speaking of this weekend . . . I had a lot of fun."

"I did, too," I say. "And . . . I wouldn't be opposed to it happening again. If you feel the same way."

In response, he reaches across the table, turns my hand over so he can run that finger up my palm. Up to my wrist, circling my pulse point. That small intentional touch is enough to make me shiver. He must be able to sense it, because he's tugging me out of my seat and over to him.

"Hi," I say when I'm standing in front of him, my legs against his knees. I am very, very happy to be wrong about the direction this conversation took.

"Hi." He strokes his fingers up the backs of my thighs, and when he cups my ass and pulls me onto his lap, it becomes clear that whatever talk we were about to have is going to need to wait.

It feels different, kissing him in his apartment, in his kitchen, his mouth wine-tart. Our lips fit together like they didn't learn each other's shape only two days ago. He runs his hands over my legs, up my back, tangles them in my hair. We kiss and we kiss and I press against his shirt's softness, searching for something rougher. Finally, I tug it open, button by button, exploring the muscles of his chest.

He's hard beneath me, and I position myself so I can feel him exactly where I want to. When I rock against him, he groans into my ear. I could listen to that groan on repeat for the rest of the night. Longer, probably.

"You're evil," he growls as I rub myself back and forth across the stiff front of his jeans.

He stands up with me wrapped around him, and I'm wondering if this is some signature move or if I just fit against him this perfectly. Once he's vertical, we stumble down the hall to his bedroom.

Gently, I push away from him to take it all in. His room is small, a queen bed in the corner with a plain navy comforter. The furniture is IKEA again, a basic bedframe and dresser—and propped up on top of it, a box of condoms. Like it's been waiting for us.

I can't help laughing at it, and yet knowing he planned for this makes me want him even more.

"I wanted to be prepared," he says against my mouth, but he's laughing, too.

"I have some in my bag, too."

"You know—" He puts a foot of space between us. His hair is wild, cheeks flushed. My blazer is somewhere in the hall and my jeans are half-unzipped. "You can change your mind at any time."

"If I didn't know any better, I'd think you were trying to get rid of me."

"No. I swear. I'm just . . . not good at this. I told you, I've only been with one person. I don't know how these things usually go. Or what we're supposed to talk about. I want to do this with you. A lot." When he laughs again, it lands somewhere in the center of my heart. "It's all I've been able to think about since Saturday night. But I just want you to know, if you decide you don't want to, it's okay."

I try not to notice how *I want to do this with you* is not *I want to be with you*. But god, I want this, too—so badly I can't think straight.

"Dominic," I say, closing the space between us and placing my hands on his chest, deciding to be as clear with him as I possibly can. "I want you to fuck me."

That's all it takes. He leans in and crushes his mouth to mine, propelling me backward until I hit the bed and drag him down on top of me. I changed into a black lace bra and panties after work, and it's worth it for the way he groans when he gets my shirt unbuttoned. Maybe he didn't care about my sports bra, but he definitely doesn't hate this one.

We're clawing at each other now, my shirt and bra dropping to the floor, his jeans and boxer briefs in a heap next to them.

He kisses my breasts as he works my jeans down my legs. "Can you say that thing again? About what you wanted me to do?"

"What thing—oh." I grin, dragging my fingers across his back. "I want you to fuck me."

His cock pulses against my bare thigh, and he casts off my jeans in one swift motion. "Yes. That."

So Dominic Yun likes dirty talk.

I can work with that.

Then he's on top of me again, kissing me hard and deep while his fingers stroke the silk of my underwear. I might die if I have to wear them for much longer.

"How do you feel even better than last time?" His mouth travels down my body, but when he lowers his head between my legs, I instinctively clench up. "What? Should I not—"

"No, no," I say quickly, trying to haul him back up to me, but he doesn't budge. "I just—you don't have to. I don't really—I'm not sure I can—" And now it's my turn to be awkward.

A sly smile curves his lips. "Shay Goldstein. Have you never had an orgasm from oral sex?"

I shake my head, feeling a flush creep up my neck. "I mean, I don't mind it. But if it doesn't happen," I add quickly, "it's okay. We can . . . you know. Skip it."

"You don't mind it," he says matter-of-factly, his finger brushing the damp silk between my thighs. "You don't think I could make you even wetter than you are right now?"

"I—I'm sure you could," I manage as he continues moving his finger in a torturous circle. *Christ*. He can't be some kind of oral sex savant, can he?

He bends to kiss along my inner thighs, gently at first. Then he removes my underwear, kisses beneath my navel before dipping lower. "So this is something you wouldn't mind?" His tongue starts slowly, a whisper of pleasure as he steadies me with a hand on my hip. He slips one finger inside me—but only for a moment before he draws it back out. I clutch at his hair as he does it again. "Should I stop?"

"Don't you dare."

He gives me this smirk as he lowers his head again. It's only when I'm desperate for release that he flattens his tongue against my clit, settling into a rhythm that makes my head spin.

I grab at anything I can wrap a fist around—his hair, the sheets, the top of his ear. He doesn't let up, single-minded in his mission. I'm dizzy and lost and *oh* and *yes* and then I'm coming hard against his tongue, not caring how I sound or if anyone in the neighboring apartments can hear.

"That," I say when I can make words again, "was really fucking amazing."

His mouth is glistening and he's grinning like he's given me the best gift I've ever received. I'm greedy for more, pointing helplessly at the condoms on his dresser. He sheaths himself quickly, then leans over me and positions himself at my entrance.

"You good?" he says between heavy breaths.

"I'll be even better when you're inside me." Slowly, slowly, he slides in—and then pulls back out. "God. You really like teasing."

"This is going to make me sound incredibly suave, but since it's been a while, and since watching you come like that was maybe the hottest thing I've ever seen, I'm not sure how long I can actually last," he admits. "So I'm trying not to . . . you know."

"I'll try to be less sexy?"

He chokes on a laugh as he guides himself back inside. Stretching me. "Just promise me you'll give me another chance if I only go ten seconds this time, because there are about twenty different ways I'd like to fuck you."

Jesus. I've never talked this much during sex. The occasional dirty talk, sure, but not the frankness we have with each other. The ability to laugh. It was always a race to shed our clothes, to put tab A into slot B. This is oddly freeing.

"I promise," I say, letting out a gasp as he fills me completely.

He feels so good, so *right* that I can't believe we've never done this before. At first I'm mesmerized by the sight of him pumping into me until I flick my gaze back to his, pull his face to mine so I can kiss him. Together we find a rhythm, and he must notice my hand drifting down between us because he meets me there. A muscle in his jaw and down his neck tightens, like he's trying to hold back.

I arch my back to take him deeper as he draws a nipple into his mouth, sucking hard until I'm coming again. After a few more thrusts, his body shakes on top of mine, and he lets out this raw, shattered sound, burying himself even deeper than I thought possible. I have no idea how long it lasts, only that I'm completely spent at the end of it.

He withdraws, removing the condom and tying it off before throwing it away in the bathroom. I miss his warmth almost immediately, but I'm not entirely sure what to do now. I'm not spending the night—that's not what this is. If I spend the night, if he even wanted me to . . . I'd be utterly and completely lost to him.

So I swing my legs to the side of the bed, which makes him frown when he gets back.

"You're leaving?" he says, and the surprise in his voice makes me regret moving so quickly.

"I don't have to." I sink back into the bed.

"Good." He slides in next to me, drawing me close against his chest. I press my face into the space where his neck meets his shoulder, listening to the rhythm of our breaths.

It kills me, how he goes from sexy to sweet in a matter of minutes. It feels too nice, this closeness, the heat of his body and the earthy smell of sex.

"Dominic," I start. "We should talk about this."

A pause, and then: "I guess we probably should." He pushes up next to me so we're both sitting. I don't want to have this conversation in the nude, so I grab my shirt, and he must get the hint because he pulls on a pair of boxers. "Okay," he says. "Let's talk."

"This"—I motion to the bed—"was extremely enjoyable."

"I agree."

The problem with this conversation is that I don't know where to go from here. I don't know what I want, and he's so tough to read that I couldn't even guess at what he wants.

When I'm silent for a beat too long, he says, "Maybe I could learn to do the casual thing."

"Oh," I say, unsure how to feel about that. "Yeah?" I can't say I'm not anxious about keeping the show out of jeopardy. This might be the only way to do it.

He nods. "We're adults. We're being safe. If we can act normal at work, I don't see why we should stop." He pauses, glancing down between us, where he links his fingers with mine. "If you're cool with it."

Casual. It didn't feel casual when he asked if I'd ever had an orgasm from oral sex. It didn't feel casual when he said there were about twenty different ways he wanted to fuck me. And it definitely didn't feel casual, the way he draped his arm over my back and toyed with the ends of my hair.

"Casual," I say, trying to picture it. Sneaking around at work, showing up at his apartment at night. "Yeah. Okay. So . . . should we come up with rules, then? I haven't really done this before either, but I—I'm not sleeping with anyone else."

He makes a face as though this never would have occurred to him. "I wouldn't."

I exhale with relief. "And no spending the night, I assume?"

"Oh. Okay," he says with another strange expression.

"Good," I say, hoping he doesn't hear how tentative I sound.

"Good," he agrees, squeezing my hand. "I'm glad we figured that out."

But I'm wondering why *casual* was his first instinct. If it didn't cross his mind that this should be anything other than casual, I'll have to make sure it doesn't cross mine, either. It's safer, really, to hook up with someone so clearly wrong for me. It'll have to prevent me from getting attached.

The way we were on the island, those late-night conversations—

that was friendship. It wasn't a prelude to a relationship. There isn't anything I can realistically have with him that isn't casual.

If this is the only way I can have him, then I have to be okay with it.

The Ex Talk, Episode 7: Love Me Tinder

Transcript

SHAY GOLDSTEIN: Here's a good one. Someone in a bright blue skin suit with a bio that just says, "Are you brave enough to find out what's underneath?"

DOMINIC YUN: How about this? "I'm spontaneous and impulsive. I have my ex's lip print tattooed somewhere on my body. I'll only show you on our third date."

SHAY GOLDSTEIN: And then a winking emoji?

DOMINIC YUN: There's always a winking emoji.

SHAY GOLDSTEIN: Unless there's a smirking emoji.

DOMINIC YUN: Is this a bad time to mention the tattoo of your name on my lower back? It's very tasteful.

25

Casual turns out to be more fun than I expected.

Later that week, Dominic sits next to me during a meeting, placing his hand on my thigh underneath the table. Every so often, his thumb brushes the bare skin beneath my skirt.

The following week, when we find ourselves alone in that wonderfully slow-moving elevator, I drop to my knees and see how close I can get him before we hit the bottom floor.

When we get out of the elevator like nothing happened, Dominic surreptitiously buckling his belt, I trail his car to his apartment, and we try three and a half of his aforementioned twenty positions.

It's for the best that I don't have to worry about whether this thing with Dominic is anything other than casual because Ameena gets the job offer Friday afternoon. By the time she calls to tell me about it, she's already accepted. Ameena is stellar at what she does, so I'm not surprised that she got the offer. Nor am I surprised that she accepted, given that this is her dream job.

What does surprise me: that when I get to her Capitol Hill

apartment on Saturday evening before we head out for a celebratory dinner, there are already boxes everywhere.

"I might have been a little overeager," she says. "They want me to start next month, which is soon, I know, so we're flying out next weekend to look at apartments. Maybe even a house—the cost of living is much lower than it is here."

"It's not *that* bad here," I say feebly, even though it is. But some part of me is wounded that she's had the job for less than twenty-four hours and she's already dumping on the city we both grew up in.

She lifts a penciled eyebrow. As kids, we used to stare at ourselves in the mirror, practicing trying to raise one eyebrow and then the other. I could never pull it off, but Ameena mastered it. "Our rent is nearly three thousand a month."

It's midsixties and breezy, typical for May in Seattle, so Ameena grabs a cardigan before she and TJ follow me out the door of their early twentieth-century building. It was a steal when they signed the lease a couple years ago. They live within walking distance of numerous bars, restaurants, music venues, and cute boutiques. Things that seem important in your early twenties but maybe not as crucial in your late twenties, even less so when you're past thirty, I imagine. The only thing within walking distance of my house is a gas station. And, you know, other houses.

TJ slings an arm around her shoulder as we pass groups of Capitol Hill hipsters vaping outside bars. I try not to think about how if Dominic were my boyfriend, I'd be bringing him to this dinner instead of going alone, awkwardly clomping along behind them since the sidewalk isn't wide enough for three people.

"God, it's loud in here," Ameena says when we settle into a booth at a tapas bar we've been to a few times. "I've never realize how *loud* it is in Seattle."

"Pretty sure they have bars in Virginia, too," I say under my breath, not trying to sound like a dick, but doesn't she realize that I'm still going to be living here in this loud, expensive place? Without her?

We order drinks and a handful of small plates to start. At the booth next to us, a trio of tech bros are talking about a Tesla one of them bought. He has the nerve to say he can't believe he had to wait so long for it to be delivered.

"Imagine complaining about your Tesla," TJ says, taking a sip of an overpriced purple drink.

"Add that to my list of things I won't miss," Ameena says.

This hits a nerve. "Okay, seriously?" I say.

Her eyebrow leaps up in that practiced way again. "What?" she asks, voice threaded with frustration.

"You. Shitting on Seattle all of a sudden. I'm thrilled for you, I really am, and I know we're supposed to be celebrating. But do you know how hard it is to sit next to you while you talk about how happy you are to be getting out of this place?"

"Shay—I wasn't—I mean," she says, trying to backtrack. "Shit. I'm sorry. I . . . went a little too far. You know I've hated corporate recruiting. And I've been sick of Seattle for a while."

"Could've fooled me."

Ameena stares down at her drink, fiddling with the straw. "Look. Maybe you're happy here, doing the same thing you've always done. Working the same place you've worked since college. But I always wanted to get out. Right after college—" She breaks off, as though realizing she was about to say something she didn't want to.

"Ameena," TJ says quietly, covering his hand with hers. "Are you sure you—"

She gives him a half smile, as though reassuring him that she'll be okay after she drops whatever bomb she's about to drop, which puts me on edge. "I'm sure." She turns back to me. "Right out of college, I had a job offer from an environmental group in New York."

This is news to me. "You . . . what?"

"Yeah." She grimaces, maybe already regretting spilling this. "But I turned it down. You were still struggling with—with everything, and I felt awful about the idea of leaving you."

Her words drop like bricks to the floor of the bar.

"I—I didn't make you stay," I say, unable to process what she's saying. "I had no idea. If you'd told me, I would have encouraged you to take it!"

The fact that she talked about this with TJ, that the two of them decided it was wise to keep this from me, at least until now—that rattles me. And of course he knows. TJ's her number one. That's what happens when you find that person. They're moving to Virginia together, leaving me behind. And this time, she doesn't have to worry about me holding her back.

"Maybe you would have, but I'm still not sure I'd have taken it."

The alcohol burns going down my throat. "I'm sorry you pitied me so much that I kept you from your dream job."

My dad had been gone for four years at that point. I wasn't still a mess. I wasn't. I'd just started at Pacific Public Radio. That had made me happy.

Hadn't it?

"You only had me," Ameena says. "You only had me, and I felt . . . I don't know, tethered to you."

Tethered. The word lands as harshly across TJ's face as it does on my heart.

"You felt tethered to me?"

"No no no. Terrible word choice. Not tethered, I just—"

I don't let her finish. "I didn't just have you," I fire back. The tech bros at the next table are watching us, apparently more interested in this than their Tesla. "I had my mom. I had my job." I hope by the time the words leave my lips that they'll sound less pathetic, less plastic, but nope. They do not.

"Right, your job. The one that consumes you, that makes you late for everything, that's become your whole freaking personality."

"Ameena," TJ starts, as though sensing she's going too far. But her expression is intense in a way I haven't seen before, brows drawn, jaw set. Ameena and I don't yell. We don't fight.

Maybe we've been saving up for this one.

"No, she needs to hear this. It's for her own good." Her features soften, but her words remain sharp. "I love you. I do. But have you ever thought that maybe your dad is holding you back? That you're still at PPR to live out some dream your dad wanted, but you've never stopped to think about whether *you* still want it? You're lying to yourself, Shay," she continues. "You're lying to your listeners about Dominic, and you're lying to yourself. You're telling yourself whatever's happening with him isn't real so nothing has to change."

But I want things to change. I think it, but I can't bring myself to say it. That was why I took this hosting job, wasn't it?

"As much as I'd like to continue publicly fighting in this hipster bar that represents everything wrong with Seattle," I say, grabbing my bag, "I'm going to go."

"Shay, wait," TJ says, but it's no use. I'm already halfway to the door.

Fortunately, I make it outside before the tears start to fall, and I swipe them away as fast as I can, not wanting to be the woman crying in public.

And even though I'm not supposed to, even though it probably defies the definition of casual, I text Dominic on my way back to my car.

Can you come over? I really need to talk to someone.

It's a relief when his reply appears a few moments later.

I'll be right there.

26

"You didn't have to bring anything," I say when Dominic arrives, weekend casual in a black T-shirt and faded jeans, holding a plastic takeout bag. My stomach growls, reminding me I left Ameena's dinner without eating anything.

He puts on a grimace. "Shit, this is awkward. It's not for you."

I pull him inside, and Steve paws at his ankles until Dominic bends down to scratch behind his ears.

"I didn't know if you'd eaten dinner," he says, passing me the bag, "but I figured at the very least, you could have the leftovers tomorrow morning. Or afternoon, if you're someone who doesn't think leftovers taste better cold at ten a.m. on a Sunday."

"Wait. You are?"

"Yeah, because I'm not a monster who wants to obliterate the flavor of restaurant food with a microwave."

"Cold pizza, sure. But you're telling me you would willingly eat, like, cold lasagna? Or a cold plate of enchiladas?"

"I would, and I have."

I open up the bag. "Is this Thai? From Bangkok Bistro? All is forgiven."

"You mentioned a couple weeks ago that it was your favorite takeout," he says with a shrug, like it isn't a big deal.

He brought food for me. For us. It's sweet, maybe too sweet for whatever this fuck buddies situation is. Then again, maybe my desperate text already blurred that line. Right now, I'm too hungry and emotional to care.

We head into the kitchen, and I get us plates and silverware while he unpacks chicken pad thai and green curry and tom yum soup.

"I could bathe in this soup," I say. "Thank you for doing this. I'm starving."

He grazes my arm with his fingertips as I stack plates near the takeout containers. "It's no problem."

Since the food is still hot, I give Dominic a quick tour of my house, pointing out all the cozy spots Steve has claimed as his own. Dominic leans against the doorway of my bedroom while I show him the walls I finally decided to paint mint last weekend, looking so natural there that I can't bring myself to meet his eyes.

"Can I get you anything to drink?" I ask, steering him back to the kitchen. "Water, beer, wine? I'm afraid I don't have any Charles Shaw. A little too classy for my tastes."

He offers a half smile in response, but he appears unsettled. "Water's fine," he says. "And this is a great house. You should be proud of it. You own a house in Seattle, and you're not even thirty. The housing market is—"

"I *am* proud," I say, cutting him off before he treads too close to any of Ameena's talking points. As I pour him a glass of water, I realize that it's true: I'm proud of this place I've managed to make my own.

We carry our plates into the living room, where I collapse onto the couch next to him. His presence makes me feel a little less heavy than I did with Ameena. It's too easy to kick off my shoes and cross my legs so my knees are touching his. And I wonder if it's easy for him to place a hand on my knee, his thumb brushing back and forth. I wonder if he even knows how soothing that is.

"Is Steve okay?" he asks. He gestures with his fork to where Steve is standing on the other side of the living room, locked in a staring contest with the wall.

I stop myself from inhaling my soup. "Oh. That. He's been doing this thing where he, like, glitches. That's the only way I can think to describe it. His leg gets stuck in midscratch and he stares out into empty space for a while. Or he goes into the bathroom and stares at the wall for ten minutes. It's absurd."

"Weird little dog."

"*Perfect* weird little dog," I correct, and then call Steve over. He snaps out of his trance and jumps onto the couch between us, practically pushing me out of the way to get himself some of Dominic's superior head scratches. Disloyal weird little dog.

"Are *you* okay?" Dominic asks me between scratches. Now Steve is in a new kind of trance. "We can talk, if you want. Your text seemed a bit . . ."

"Panicky?"

"Well . . . yeah."

I take a long sip of water before setting it down on the coffee table. "You know how some schools do those senior superlatives? Biggest flirt, best dressed, and all that?"

Dominic sheepishly rubs the back of his neck. "I was, uh, voted most likely to succeed."

I whack him with a pillow. "Oh my god, of course you were. Well. So I told you my dad died senior year of high school. And unofficially, but officially enough for me to know everyone was talking about it, I became the Girl Whose Dad Died Senior Year.

That's how everyone from high school remembers me, with that sad story. I know I'm not the only person who's ever lost a parent, but it feels like I've never been able to shake that label."

"I'm sorry," he says. "I can't pretend to know what that's like. But why is this coming up now? What happened?"

I explain what was supposed to be Ameena's celebration dinner, and he sucks in a long, slow breath.

"She can't blame you for that," he says. "You know that, right?"

"Logically, yes. But . . ." I take a breath, uttering what I've been worried about since Ameena brought it up, or quite possibly for longer than I'd like to admit. "Sometimes I wonder if I'm too close to radio. In case you haven't realized, it's kind of my whole life." It doesn't feel like work, though, when I'm prepping for our grief show, scheduled for two Thursdays from now.

He's quiet for a moment. "You love hosting, though. And you're good at it."

"You're already sleeping with me. No need to butter me up."

"I wasn't buttering. You really are. You have this great way of thinking on your feet, and you're funny in this effortless way, and you're just—you're *fun* to listen to."

I want to bask in those compliments, but I'm stuck back at the bar with Ameena and TJ. "I do love being on the air. It's not so much hosting as it is the fact that I've had the same job since I graduated from college. Is that even normal?"

"If you find the right fit, sure." He stares at me hard. "I'll be your ex as long as you want me to be. I know we said six months, but I'm fully in this with you. I hope you know that."

"I—I didn't," I say. The relief is warm and immediate. "But thank you. I guess I just thought I'd have everything figured out by now. I'm almost thirty, and I don't know if I feel any closer than when I was twenty-one or even twenty-five. There's so much pressure to have all of this shit figured out, and I don't have a clue what

I'm doing. I wanted the kind of marriage my parents had, and I maybe wanted a family, but that's not something I can even wrap my mind around yet. I can only cook, like, two things competently. Most of what I eat comes from meal kits. I have a gym membership, but I never go to the gym. I work most weekends. Sometimes I feel like I'm playing at being an adult, like I'm constantly looking around, waiting for a real adult to tell me what to do if my garbage disposal starts making a weird sound or if I should be putting more money in my Roth IRA. I am just . . . I feel like a complete mess." I laugh in spite of myself, even as tears sting behind my eyes.

I shove up my glasses and wipe at my face, trying not to let him see. Crying in front of the guy you're casually dating—probably also not allowed. But of course he sees, and when he pulls me close on the couch, I let him.

"I think you're incredible," he says. "You've intimidated me ever since I started at PPR."

"Right."

"I'm serious." His fingers weave through my hair, and I realize with a tightening of my heart that he's softly untangling it. "You were so sure of yourself, spoke the language of radio so fluently, made it seem like I was an idiot for not getting it."

"Sorry about that," I say, cringing.

"I *was* an idiot, though," he says. "There was plenty I didn't know, and yet I came in with an ego just because I had some advanced degree. And besides, you're keeping a ten-pound dog alive. I'd say that's some measure of success. I barely remember to water my plants, and they only need to be watered once a week."

"Seven pounds. He has big dog energy, though."

He just laughs and holds me tighter, his fingers massaging my scalp. It's cruel how good it feels—because of course it's fleeting. I don't know our expiration date, but sometime soon, he will no longer be mine. He's barely mine now.

"I thought I had things figured out, too," he says. "Grad school, the long-term girlfriend. I thought we'd move somewhere together, that she'd be in med school and I'd be doing some noble reporting, bringing down an evil corporation, and I'd propose and we'd have the big expensive wedding."

"Do you wish you had that?" I ask.

He hesitates only a moment before responding. "No. I don't. For the first few months afterward, yes, absolutely. But it shaped me. I don't know if I'd have finished growing up without it, without knowing that kind of heartbreak. And now it's just something I carry with me, the same way you carry your dad."

I reach up a hand to stroke his cheek. The stubble is back—I missed it. He doesn't have all the answers because no one could, but at least he makes everything feel lighter.

I was convinced *casual* would be safe because he's so unlike anyone I dated in the past, guys who seemed to have their lives figured out. It's absurd that this guy who is supposed to be my ex could have been a great boyfriend. I thought I liked the danger of being with him, this little secret we've been keeping from the office for two weeks, but I might like this more.

I need to stop thinking like that.

"I had lunch with an old friend today, this guy Eddie," Dominic says suddenly. "We were the only two Korean kids in our sixth-grade class, and I thought that bonded us forever, but we lost touch after high school. He's working at some ultra-hip startup and will probably be a millionaire as soon as they get bought. He just broke up with his girlfriend, and he needed to talk to someone, too. And it was great. We might even do it again."

"You beat me. I've been meaning to ask Ruthie if she wants to grab drinks after work sometime, but I guess I've had . . . other things on my mind."

He nods, then kisses me, and I manage to yawn right in the middle of it.

"I'm sorry," I say, covering my mouth. "I promise, making out with you isn't boring." I check the time on my phone—almost midnight. I didn't realize we'd been talking for that long.

He gestures toward the door. "Should I . . . ?"

"No," I say, aware I'd be breaking the rules of our arrangement but not caring. "I'd hate for you to drive back this late. Maybe you could . . . stay the night?"

"You're sure?" The weight of his gaze pins me to the couch.

"You may have to fight Steve for a spot on the bed, but yes. If you want to."

"I'd like that," he says. Apparently he doesn't care, either, that we said no sleepovers.

I have Orcas flashbacks as I hand him a spare toothbrush. Nothing I own will fit his broad frame, so he folds his clothes neatly before placing them on top of my dresser and gets in bed next to me in just his boxers.

"I'm really tired," I say, turning to face him. The weariness drags me down. Maybe I really am getting old. "It's okay if you want to leave."

"You think I'm going to leave because we're not having sex tonight?"

"Well . . . yeah."

He looks disturbed by this. "We could be listening to Kent's old highlight reels, and I'd still want to be here with you," he says. "I'm here because of *you*."

But the worries pound against the walls of my brain. Now that we've done the casual thing, he probably wants to explore some more. It makes me a little ill, the idea of Dominic exploring other women.

I think back to what Ameena said, about clinging to my job and my comforts so nothing has to change. That's not true. At this point, I feel absolutely desperate for change. If I hadn't, I wouldn't have adopted Steve or started hosting or hooking up with Dominic. Keeping this casual—I'm protecting the show, yes, but more than that, I'm protecting myself.

"This might sound ridiculous, but . . . do you want to meet my family?" Dominic asks into the almost dark. My bedside lamp is still on, and I like the way the shadows hang on his face.

"What?"

"They've been a little worried about me. On account of the whole not-having-friends thing. So they asked if I wanted to invite my cohost over for dinner."

"But they can't know that we're . . ."

"No. They can't."

Bad idea. Bad idea. And yet I can't stop myself when an agreement tumbles out.

"Sure," I say. "I can't say I'm not curious about how all of this came about." I gesture down the length of his body, and he smirks, pouncing on me and pressing me deep into the mattress.

All we do is kiss, pausing every so often to laugh or talk or marvel at how excellent Steve is at managing to push both of us off the bed to make room for himself. I'm going to be exhausted tomorrow, but I don't care. Maybe I'm a masochist, liking him here in my bed and knowing we cannot be more than this. That even *this* is stretching the limits of what we are, and it's only a matter of time before we snap.

It's not real.

But I wonder, if it isn't, why we fall asleep with his face tucked against the back of my neck, his hand at my hip.

FROM: Yun, Dominic <d.yun@pacificpublicradio.org>
TO: Goldstein, Shay <s.goldstein@pacificpublicradio.org>
DATE: May 14, 3:52 p.m.
SUBJECT: Booth C

Hi Shay,

You'll see on our shared calendar that I reserved Booth C from 4 to 4:15 p.m. There's something I want you to listen to. I think you'll enjoy it quite a bit.

Regards,
Dominic

— — — — — — — —

FROM: Goldstein, Shay <s.goldstein@pacificpublicradio.org>
TO: Yun, Dominic <d.yun@pacificpublicradio.org>
DATE: May 14, 4:19 p.m.
SUBJECT: RE: Booth C

Dear Dominic,

You were right. That was an especially satisfying piece of audio.

All the best,
Shay

— — — — — — — —

27

"I want to say we've heard so much about you," Margot Yun says after taking my coat in the foyer of Dominic's childhood home. "But frankly, we've heard almost nothing at all."

I paste a smile on my face as I step out of the corn shoes a sponsor sent us a couple weeks ago. "My mom feels the same," I tell her. "Dominic and I are both just . . . private people."

"I think it's commendable." Dominic's father, Morris, stands about five inches shorter than his wife. It's clear which side of the family Dominic's height came from. "There's no need to post everything all over social media. There's not enough that people keep to themselves these days. Although I did just manage to figure out Snapchat. Tell them, Margot."

"He's been very proud of himself," Margot says. "He sends me photos from the shop when we're not working together, but I can't understand why they go away after only a few seconds. I can never seem to get them back."

"I tried to tell you, that's the whole point!"

"I don't have the heart to tell him no one uses Snapchat anymore," Dominic stage-whispers to me.

It's been a long week, and I haven't been entirely sure how to feel about meeting Dominic's parents. While I'm sure they're lovely people, my reluctance is tightly wrapped around my feelings for Dominic. The rest of my life isn't any easier to manage. Ameena and I haven't spoken since that night, though TJ has acted as an intermediary, letting me know they flew out to Virginia this morning to look at apartments. As much as I want things to go back to normal between us, I can't forget what she said. Though I know it's not my fault she didn't take that job all those years ago, her words sank their claws into me, stirring up an uncertainty that I come back to whenever work is slow.

We follow his parents into the living room. They're a little older than I expected, which I probably should have guessed, given that he's the youngest of five. Morris Yun is bald, with firm lines around his mouth and a slope to his shoulders that makes him appear even shorter. In contrast, Margot is willowy and regal, her gray hair chopped at her chin, and her clothes expertly tailored.

If I didn't already know they owned an antique shop, their house would give it away. It's a spacious two-story in Bellevue, a wealthy suburb of Seattle that becomes more and more yuppie by the day. Tapestries hang from the walls next to paintings in ornate frames, and every surface is decorated with small statues, vases, mirrors, clocks, and even an old gramophone in one corner. Still, it doesn't look cluttered. It gives off this museum vibe, but a museum you'd want to live in.

On the ride over, Dominic talked to me about growing up on the Eastside. "I remember going into Seattle was this exciting thing," he said. "I'd look forward to it for weeks."

"That is so cute," I said. As a born-and-raised city kid, I couldn't help teasing him. "Baby Dominic in the big city."

Now I sit next to him on the stunning Victorian couch, which looks like something out of a movie from the 1950s, wanting desperately for his parents to like me but not entirely sure why.

"You have a beautiful home," I say, and they both look pleased.

"We're proud of it," Margot says from a matching love seat. "It's sort of a living thing—we tend to change it up every so often when the mood strikes us, or when we find something we can't bear to give to the store quite yet. Dominic practically grew up there. I suppose you know all of that, even if we don't know anything about you."

"Mom," Dominic says under his breath, and it sounds like a warning.

I yearn for the alternate reality in which Margot isn't immediately on the defensive.

"You never used to be this private," Margot continues, smoothing the hem of her gauzy skirt. "He used to post all these updates on Facebook, and he'd get mad when I was the first like. He even called me up in college to ask me politely to stop doing it, since all his friends could see."

I have never seen Dominic's face this red.

"I don't do it anymore," Dominic says. "I can't remember the last time I went on Facebook."

"At least we have the chance to get to know you now," Margot says. "What does your mother do, Shay?"

I appreciate that Dominic must have warned them about my dad. "She's a violinist in the Seattle Symphony."

Her faces lights up, and I feel a burst of pride, grateful this has won me some points. "Is she really? We were there last week, for Mozart's *Jupiter Symphony*. Incredible. You must go all the time."

"Not as much as I used to," I admit. "But it was interesting, growing up with someone who's as much of a music snob as my mother. She took it as a personal attack when I started listening to the Backstreet Boys."

Dominic cracks a smile at this, and I don't love what it does to my heart.

"I could get you comp tickets, actually," I add.

"I wouldn't want to put anyone out."

"Really, it's no problem at all. My mom always has a ton."

"Well—thank you. That's too kind," she says, softening. "And you've been at the radio station for a while?"

"Since college." Not a sore subject. Nope. "How often is it just Dominic here?"

Morris slides his teal glasses higher up on his nose. "We usually see Kristina and Hugo at Christmas, since they're out of state. And then Monica and Janet usually every other month. But Dominic just can't seem to get enough of us."

"I'm not saying I'm their best kid because I come home more than the others, but . . ."

His mother winks at him, and seriously, what is happening to my heart? That wink makes me want so badly to be part of this—not as a friend or cohost or a fake anything, but as a girlfriend.

"Even if it's under strange circumstances," Morris says, "it's good to meet you. You and Dominic have clearly created something special, and even if it's not exactly something I'd listen to otherwise, a lot of people seem to be connecting with it. And it's great that the two of you have been able to stay friends." He gets to his feet. "We'll be finishing up dinner, if you feel like giving Shay a tour of the house."

"Can we help with anything?" I ask.

Margot waves a hand. "It's nearly ready." She grins as she adds, "And, well, we don't hate showing off our house."

"I think I'll show her my childhood bedroom," Dominic says. "Just so she can get in a few more laughs at my expense."

———

"This is a lot of Beanie Babies."

I gaze up at them: shelves upon shelves, each of them with their own personal bubble of space, some of them in collector's boxes. Bears and birds and monkeys and lions and lizards in every color, all with their trademark red tags still intact. And these shelves—they look like they were built for the express purpose of Beanie Baby storage.

"It's a sickness," Dominic says, hanging his head.

"How did this happen? How does one acquire this many Beanie Babies?"

"Three hundred and twenty, to be exact. Some of our relatives in Korea gave them to my sister Kristina as gifts when they visited us." He points to a blue bear with the Korean flag printed all over it. "They were really excited about this one. But Kristina wasn't into them, so she gave them to me, and for some reason, I loved them. I was one of those people who thought they'd be worth a lot someday. And I was one hundred percent wrong."

"Were they even still popular when you were a kid?"

"Barely. You can see, now, why I didn't lose my virginity until I was in college."

"I'm just . . ." I break off, shaking my head. It's hilarious but endearing, imagining a young Dominic painstakingly arranging them on these shelves. "I don't know if I can keep sleeping with someone who owns three hundred and twenty Beanie Babies."

"Alas. I knew it would come to this. Well, it was good while it—"

I interrupt him by pressing my mouth on his, kicking the door shut behind us. He draws me close, his hands on my hips. The warmth of his tongue, the woodsy scent of the soap I told him is much better than his cologne. I'm always waiting for the next moment we can be alone like this, and while we haven't had any more sleepovers, we've been together nearly every night since Orcas.

We're familiar enough with each other now to know exactly the ways we like to be touched, and when he goes for the spot where my neck meets my shoulder, I let out a soft moan that I also happen to know he loves the sound of. He's already hard against me, and it's always a bit of a rush, knowing he wants me.

A clang from the kitchen makes us spring apart.

He drops his fingers from my belt loops and takes a step back. The skin on my neck burns white-hot.

"Probably for the best," he says with a sheepish grin, pointing back up at the Beanies. "You'd have nightmares for days."

As I catch my breath, I examine the rest of his room. There's a collage of photos next to his desk, one that likely hasn't been updated in years. "Aww, was this your senior photo? You were cute in high school. I definitely would have had a crush on you." I flop down on his bed. "I can't believe I was out of college when you were still in high school. Way to make me feel ancient."

He sits down next to me. "Did you have dial-up? And CDs? What was your CD collection like?"

"Hmm . . . a lot of NSYNC, Mandy Moore, Blink-182, and a handful of Now That's What I Call Musics. And I will not apologize for any of it."

"Mandy Moore, like, from *This Is Us*?"

"Oh my god, don't even talk to me until you listen to 'Candy.'"

My room at home hasn't been nearly as preserved as his, but maybe that was more of a personal decision than a profound commentary on the passage of time. Also pinned to that corkboard is an old plane ticket to Seoul. A photo of him in front of a gorgeous green-and-red palace.

"So your mom was born in Korea, and your dad was born here?"

He nods. "She grew up in Yeoju, which is a smaller city outside of Seoul. Actually, it wasn't even a city when she was growing up there, just a county. I've only been there a few times—shockingly, it's pricey to do a lot of international travel with five kids. Especially if you're number five. But they're both only children, and they wanted a big family."

"It seems they're doing well now," I say. "Your house really is stunning."

"I know my mom appreciated that. And yeah, they are, but it took a while to get there."

The next time we kiss, it's not hard and fast, the way our kisses often are. It's a soft kiss, a reverent one, and it happens so slowly I'm convinced time stops, too. Then he brushes some of my hair out of the way so he can press a kiss to the shell of my ear. And another. It makes me shiver, the gentleness of his lips on my skin, the brush of his thumb along my jaw. My cheekbone. Like maybe he is memorizing me or even just . . . appreciating.

It terrifies me. All of this does—his parents and his bedroom and the parts of himself he doesn't share with anyone else. It makes me wonder if he's not that wrong for me after all. If he keeps touching me like this, like I am something precious, something delicate, I could really fall for him.

I might be halfway there already.

"Come over after dinner?" he says. His voice is honey sweet, tinged with a roughness that leaves no doubt as to what he's imagining us doing after dinner.

"I'm not sure if I can." I try to ignore the bitter sting of regret. "I have some plans with my mom early tomorrow. Wedding stuff." It's not a lie, at least.

His face falls, and the hand that stroked my face so tenderly drops to his lap. "Sure. That's fine."

It's for the best, I try to convince myself. Space. That's what we need.

Except . . . I don't get much space during dinner. Not when Dominic's foot nudges mine beneath the table, not when his mother admits, "I know you're not in a relationship, but you really do look cute together," and not when his parents ask for details about the "dates" we went on back in the fall, eager to know more about this part of their son's life he kept from them. It's a perfectly pleasant dinner, but if they knew the truth, I wouldn't be welcome here. I'm sure of it.

The low-key panic I've been nursing all evening turns into a full-fledged anxiety spiral, and by the time Dominic and I wave goodbye and head to his car, I'm stumbling over nonexistent cracks in the driveway.

"Thank you for tonight," I say. "Your parents are great. Your dad cracks me up."

"He's a character." Dominic swings his keys around his index finger. "You're sure you can't come over?" he asks, and there's so much control in his words that I'm convinced he's trying not to sound like he's begging. It kills me. "Just for a little?"

"I said I can't." The edge in my voice is too hard.

He holds up his hands. "Okay, okay. Sorry."

I need some space away from him to sort out my feelings. My work life and personal life are already muddied, now that I'm texting him about my problems and meeting his parents, and I can't have him in both. Casual has to end now if we have any hope of long-term success for the show.

When he drops me off after a silent drive, I don't lean over and kiss him. I don't look him in the eye. I'm not sure what's going to come out of my mouth when I open it, only that I'm probably going to regret it, but—

"I'm not sure if I can do casual anymore."

He pulls the parking brake. "What?"

God, don't make me repeat it. But I do, and when I feel his hand on my shoulder, I shrink against the seat. I hate how right it feels.

And that's the reason I have to end it, prevent something seemingly casual from warping my sense of reality when I fear it already has.

"Because . . . of my parents?" The confusion in his tone is evident.

"No. Not that. Well, kind of, but . . . no."

I like you too much to keep pretending I don't. I like you too much not to get attached because I'm already far more attached than I ever thought I'd be, and anything else is going to kill me.

"That makes a lot of sense."

"I'm sorry," I say. "I—I want to be able to explain it, but I'm not sure I can. With the show, it's just . . . too complicated." There. That can be my excuse.

He looks like I've just told him I'm breaking up with him— which, in a way, I am. His face is a mix of confusion and hurt, his brows knit together, his eyes wide. If I look at him a moment longer, I might try to take it all back.

"Shay," he says, "let's talk about this. Please."

I shake my head. "I can't. I'm sorry. I just—can't." And before he can say anything, I swing open the car door and head for my house.

I have to force myself not to look back.

28

Dominic has been a distraction.

By the end of the weekend, I've fully convinced myself of this. Ameena was wrong—it's not that I've outgrown public radio. It's that I've become complacent, letting Dominic and Kent speak for me when I have a microphone, too. I didn't even stand up for my own idea. That was all Dominic. I was grateful at the time, but it should have been me.

Now it will be.

After a soul-replenishing cake tasting, which my mother rescheduled after the unexpected Orcas trip, I dig back into work in a way I haven't in months. I camp out at a coffee shop, order a soup-bowl-size mug of chai, and clamp on my headphones.

We had a huge publicity push at the beginning, which I'll begrudgingly admit was thanks to Kent. Then there was Dominic's Saffron Shaw connection. I participated in all of that promo, sure. But it's almost like I was so used to being behind the scenes that once I wasn't, I didn't know what to do. We have some loyal listeners, but our early buzz has definitely dipped. Nothing lasts, Kent said. I'll prove him wrong. I'll find our momentum.

He said we had a chance at PodCon—I'm determined to make that happen. The full lineup hasn't been announced yet, and we sent over a handful of sample episodes last month. I'm going to make us impossible to ignore.

My social media following has scared me a little; even the blue checkmark by my name is something I'm not used to seeing. Still, I open Twitter and search our hashtag. People are still talking about us, discovering us every day. Our subscriber numbers have continued to climb.

I tweet out a shameless request for listeners to rate and review us on Apple Podcasts, Spotify, Stitcher. It gets twenty, thirty, fifty retweets within a few minutes, and it's hard to ignore the thrill of validation that brings me. I add a form on our section of the PPR website encouraging listeners to submit their dating stories, and I tweet that out, too.

Then I listen back to our most popular episodes, pull quotes from our guests, turn them into graphics for social media that Ruthie can post on our official Twitter and Instagram accounts this week. No—I'll do it. I schedule the tweets and posts, spacing them out so we don't bombard anyone.

I scroll through my friends lists, looking for people who have a connection to something bigger—former Pacific Public Radio employees who got snapped up by NPR, acquaintances with podcasts of their own. I send about a dozen messages. Hell, I even reach out to producers of some of the biggest dating podcasts, and I go back on social media and promote the shit out of their upcoming episodes.

It's not glamorous work, but radio often isn't. We don't see the people painstakingly stitching audio clips together, waiting for files to upload, refreshing their subscriber numbers. We see the shows that take off beyond anyone's wildest dreams, the *Serial*s and the

*My Favorite Murder*s and the podcasts hosted by whichever celebrity decided to start their own podcast that week.

Fortunately, I'm no stranger to the unglamorous, to the behind-the-scenes. I've been there for ten years. I'm producer-ing the shit out of this, and if there's anything I know for certain, it's that I was a damn good producer.

Slowly but surely, my producing works its magic.

On Monday, we have a few dozen new Apple Podcasts reviews and dating and breakup stories submitted by listeners.

On Tuesday, we sign a sponsorship deal with a major mattress company. And both Dominic and I get free mattresses.

On Wednesday, someone at NPR emails me back, apologizing for the short notice and asking if they can simulcast our grief episode this week.

That one makes me splash hot coffee all over my keyboard.

"Shit," I mutter, racing to the break room for some paper towels.

"Everything okay over there?" Dominic asks when I return.

I mop up the spill as best I can. "If by okay you mean, is NPR going to simulcast tomorrow's episode, then yes."

He glances up from his computer. We haven't exactly been doing sustained eye contact this week, and I've been immersing myself in the show as much as possible so I don't obsess over it. As long as I don't slow down, I don't have to think about his hands or his hips or his mouth. His scratchy voice in my ear, asking if I'm almost there.

Yes, of course this is healthy.

I tell him about NPR, and then we tell Kent and Ruthie and my mother and Phil, and oh my god. This could be it. This could be the thing that gets us to PodCon, the thing that turns us from cute local podcast to one of those massive success stories.

All we have to do is nail it.

My mother slips on a pair of headphones like she's worried they might bite.

"You're going to be wonderful," I tell her from across the table. "You go onstage in front of hundreds of people every night."

"Yes, but they don't have to hear me talk," she says. "And I'm not being broadcast live on NPR."

Ruthie pops her head in. "Need anything, Leanna, Phil? Water, coffee?"

"Water would be great," Phil says on my mother's other side. "Thanks."

Dominic is sitting next to me, as usual, and it feels like there's more space between our chairs than on past Thursdays. *Don't think about the way he smells. Or that he's wearing your favorite striped shirt. Or that it's rolled to his forearms.*

I wonder if this is how it would feel if we'd actually dated.

It's easier to reassure my mother than it is to reassure myself. When we chatted with the NPR producer, a woman named Kati Sanchez, she told us not to change a thing about the show. She'd write intro copy beamed out to member stations to use if they air our segment later. All we have to do is classic *Ex Talk*, be ourselves and all of that. With the knowledge that our listenership will be quite possibly multiplied by the thousands.

Ruthie returns with glasses of water, and Jason counts us down after the top-of-the-hour NPR newsbreak. I pile all my Dominic angst into a box at the back of my mind and nail it shut, determined to leave it there for the next hour.

When Dominic and I introduce ourselves, our voices aren't as light as they usually are.

"We're doing something a little different today," Dominic says. "We're talking about what happens after you lose a spouse or partner, and more specifically, stories about finding love after loss."

It feels even worse, lying to my mother on the air when she's sitting right next to me. But this isn't about me. Or at least, not entirely.

I take a deep breath and speak as solidly into the microphone as I can.

"This show is especially personal to me because I lost my dad when I was eighteen. My senior year of high school." I wait a beat—an unplanned beat because even though it doesn't feel, sitting here, like thousands of people are listening, I know they will be. They are right now, live, and they will later. Losing him again and again. "My dad is the person who got me into radio. He had this store where he fixed electronics. Goldstein Gadgets. Maybe some of you out there in Seattle remember it. And okay, you know my voice isn't the ideal radio voice"—I expect Dominic to maybe laugh at this, but he doesn't. I clear my throat and go on—"but my dad, he had this perfect radio voice."

"So if we're talking about love after loss, I thought, what better person to have on the show than my mother. She lost him, too—in a different way than I did. Um, Mom . . . thank you for being here. Feel free to introduce yourself."

Beneath the table, my mother squeezes my leg. "I'm Leanna Goldstein. I've played violin in the Seattle Symphony for about twenty-five years. And I'm a Sagittarius."

This earns a few soft laughs from the room.

"Can you talk about how you met my dad?"

"Dan Goldstein," she says, and she knew we'd start this way, but nothing about her feels rehearsed. She's natural but poised in this wonderful way, like she is onstage but better because this is her voice. "We met as his shop. I had this metronome that had been giving me trouble, and I figured it was a long shot, but I brought it in to see if he could fix it. And much to my surprise, he did. And looked pretty damn adorable doing it." Her expression morphs into panic. "Shoot, is it okay to say 'damn' on here?"

I assure her that she's okay—the FCC won't come after us for that.

"We're lucky enough to also have Phil Adeleke in the studio, another Seattle Symphony violinist," Dominic says.

"That's me," Phil says with his usual cheeriness.

"And you and Leanna have been sitting next to each other for—"

"Nearly twenty-five years," he finishes, and he and my mother laugh.

"Could you tell us about your wife?"

That cheeriness doesn't completely fade, but it does diminish a little. "Joy and I met in college in Boston, in a West African students association. We are both Nigerian, both came to the States for college. She was studying history, and I was studying music, and I proposed on our graduation day."

He talks about how it wasn't a perfect marriage because of course no marriage is. They didn't always have enough money, and her first bout with cancer a year into their marriage almost destroyed them. But she fought it into remission, and for a long time, they were okay. They moved to Seattle, where she worked in a university library and he in the symphony. Four kids. A mortgage. A cat. Unexpected kittens.

And then the cancer came back.

"I don't know how you went through all of that," my mother says to Phil. Like the two of them are having a conversation without either of us here, and this is where radio really becomes great. "For me, it was sudden. One day Dan was here, perfectly healthy, and the next, he was gone. It was unbelievably unfair, I know that. But my heart still breaks for what you went through."

"We don't have to play tragedy Olympics," Phil says. "What you went through was terrible. What I went through was terrible. Nothing makes any of it any less terrible."

Dominic and I sit back, letting them tell their intertwining stories.

"I truly thought I was done," my mother says. "I'd been lucky enough to have one great big love, and that was it for me. I didn't date. I didn't make any online profiles or go on any apps, like some of my friends wanted me to. Five years passed, and they thought it was time for me to 'get back out there.' Seven years, and still nothing." She shakes her head, and I want to tell her no one can see her doing that. "There was no getting back out there."

"We were sitting right next to each other," Phil says, "and we had no idea the other person was grieving the same way. For so many years."

It's at that moment that my eyes meet Dominic's for the first time the whole episode. There's a jolt in my chest that turns into a pang when he looks away first.

We take a few listener calls through the end. People want to talk to my mother, to Phil. A woman who lost her husband last month tells my mother how great it is to hear her so clearly happy. She says my mother gives her hope, and I wish we had more than an hour to talk about this. To listen to stories.

When we have a few minutes left on the clock, I gesture to where my mother and Phil's violins are already set up and mic'd in the corner of the studio.

"Since we happen to be in the presence of two of Seattle Symphony's finest," I say, "we thought you two could play us out."

The music is somber but not hopeless. Maybe I've never loved it, but my mother does, that's clear. We'll never have what I had with my dad, but we have something else.

Finally, the **RECORDING** sign blinks off. There's a burst of applause from the adjoining studio in our headphones. Ruthie's eyes are wet, and she asks both my mother and Phil for a hug. They're happy to oblige.

When it's over, I hate that the only person I want to celebrate with is Dominic.

And I hate even more how quickly he leaves the studio.

Apple Podcasts Reviews

Iconic duo

★★★★★

I've listened to every episode three times, and I can't stop humming the intro music. My friends are sick of it. My family is sick of it. Do I need professional help? MAYBE! Just give me more Shay + Dom.

Love love love

★★★★★

I don't know what I love more: Shay's cautious optimism or Dominic's endearing cynicism. Regardless, they're *chef kiss* perfection together. Five hundred stars.

Insightful and empowering

★★★★

Fun podcast, surprisingly insightful. Taking off a star because the live calls sometimes drag on too long.

Garbage

★

I tried so hard to like this, but their discussions are shallow and the hosts aren't as charming as they think they are. Am I the only one who doesn't care that they used to date? Why is that interesting? Hard pass.

otp

★★★★★

if shay and dominic don't somehow get back together, then i don't believe in love anymore

29

That Friday, we hit the Apple Podcasts Top 100 again at slot number fifty-five, and I'm so relieved, so grateful, so proud that I could cry. I do, a little, in the women's bathroom at lunch.

Even better, though, is that PodCon wants us in Austin next month. It's a last-minute addition to their lineup, but still. We'll be doing a live show, our very first, and we have a couple more big sponsors interested in coming on board. Dominic went pale when Kent announced it, and I remembered what he said about stage fright way back before our first episode. Well. He'll just have to deal with it, even if part of me is desperate to reassure him.

All of it feels unreal, which makes it easier to forget that we built it on a lie. This is what I wanted, wasn't it? I want to tell Ameena, but we're still not talking. See? Of course I want this. How can my dad be holding me back if I'm going to PodCon? Maybe if she sees this evidence that proves her wrong, she'll take back what she said.

Fortunately, tonight is my friend date with Ruthie. We decided to grab dinner at an Oaxacan restaurant in Ballard, this place with homemade tortillas and seven different kinds of salsa. After working until ten every night this week, I'm utterly exhausted, wrung out, in desperate need of salt.

"PodCon," Ruthie says, plunging a chip into pico de gallo. "I can't believe it. We haven't even had ten episodes, and we're going to be at fucking PodCon."

"It's pretty amazing," I agree. I drag a chip through salsa verde and chew it thoughtfully. Now that the initial excitement has dulled to a buzz, I'm feeling . . . strange. I want Ruthie's boundless enthusiasm to rub off on me.

"You look a little off." Ruthie frowns, as though weighing what she wants to say next. "Can I ask a kind of personal question?"

"Uh . . . maybe?"

She laughs. "You can one hundred percent say no. It's just, I'm around you and Dominic all day, five days a week. And the two of you have been acting especially weird lately."

"You've noticed that?"

She nods. "Did you—" She breaks off, shaking her head. "I can't believe I'm about to ask you this, but . . . has anything happened between the two of you? Since you broke up, I mean?"

When I'm silent, her jaw drops open.

"Shay," she whispers with a shake of her head, but it's not a judgmental one. "Oh my god. I had a feeling, and not to brag, but I'm never wrong about these things. Never. I swear I won't say anything to anyone."

"Thank you," I say. "I'm still a little mortified over the whole thing?" But that's not the right word. I'm not mortified when Dominic pushes a hand through his hair, and I'm not mortified when he bends to pick up his work bag and his shoulders flex beneath his shirt. "But I'm not sure we're anything anymore." I think about how Dominic was able to be brave with his childhood friend. If he could do that with someone he had so much history with, I should be able to do it here. "It really only happened a few times."

"A relapse," she says. "Maybe it was bound to happen, the two of you working so closely together. It happened after Orcas, didn't it? Or on Orcas?"

I'm quiet again, and she lets out a squeal.

"Part of me wants to say congratulations because, well, he's gorgeous. The boy does a good lean."

"He does indeed," I agree.

"But are you okay about it?"

Ruthie is too good. I don't deserve her—not when even this bit of truth is tinged with dishonesty.

"We're trying to be professional. I . . . sort of ended things last week. Again," I add quickly.

"Do you want to be together?"

"I'm not sure. No." Why does everyone keep asking me that, as though it matters? "How do you think people would react? If they knew?"

"I think it would be great fucking radio, first of all. The show bringing you two back together? People would lose their minds."

I hadn't thought of it that way.

"But it's tricky, you're right."

I take a sip of my sangria. "Well, I'm officially sick of talking about myself. Please feel free to talk about you for the rest of dinner."

"It's funny you think I'm that interesting," she says. "Well, I think Marco ghosted me, but I've been texting with this girl Tatum, and it's been going well . . ."

I listen. I really do. Ruthie is great, but I want this to be a salve to my loneliness in a way it can't possibly be. Not when I'm lying to her.

And definitely not when I'm lying to myself.

———

By the middle of next week, Dominic isn't looking great. I mean, yes, he is still a very attractive human male, but he shows up past nine thirty a couple of days, he's mostly unshaven, and when he smiles—which is rare—it barely touches his eyes. His Koosh ball is immobile on his desk, lonely and sad.

Truthfully, I'm not doing great, either. I'm crashing hard, a combination of overworking myself, prepping for PodCon, and checking my phone for nonexistent texts from him and Ameena.

I've gotten back into the habit of staying late at work, not wanting to risk ending up alone in the elevator again. So when he approaches me at my desk at six thirty on Wednesday and grazes my shoulder with his fingertips after I thought everyone else had gone home for the day, I nearly scream.

"Shit, I thought you'd left," I say, holding a hand to my heart. "You have some seriously light footsteps."

"Sorry." He leans against his desk. And he really does sound sorry.

"I know our desks are close," I say. "But sometimes I like to pretend there's an invisible line between them, and you just crossed into my bubble. I like my bubble."

"I'm sorry again," he says with a sigh. "Wow, okay, this is not going the way I hoped it would. Look, I just really want to talk to you."

"Okay. Talk," I tell my computer screen.

"Not here." The ache in his words wrenches my gaze over to him.

He looks nothing like the business casual stock photo I used to think of him as. His typically pristine shirt is sporting at least three whole wrinkles. If I look at him too long, then I start replaying what we did on the island, in his bed, in mine, on my couch . . . I only have so much willpower. And when he looks at me like that, I feel my resolve weakening.

"If we're going to go onstage at PodCon in a few weeks, I'd like to at least be on speaking terms," he says. "Please hear me out this one time, and if you don't want to talk after that, then I promise I won't bring it up again."

That's tough to say no to—so I don't.

It's approaching seventy-five degrees, a Seattle heat wave, so we pack up and head to Green Lake. Everyone else in Seattle seems to have had the same idea, given how many dog walkers, rollerbladers, and stroller-joggers we pass on our way to a bench facing the lake.

"Everyone's so polite today," Dominic says, sliding onto the bench next to me. "It gets above seventy degrees, and suddenly everyone's smiling. I've always liked that."

He's right—the nice weather changes people. Gloomy introversion is so built into our DNA as Seattleites that any bit of vitamin D turns us into strangely social creatures.

"You're stalling," I say lightly.

"Is it stalling if I tell you I really loved doing that episode with your mom? She seems pretty great."

"She is. Thank you. And yes."

His leg is jiggling up and down, the way it tends to do when he's nervous. "I've been such a mess lately," he says after about a minute of silence while we watch a flock of ducks swim farther out into the murky blue water. "I've gone over that night at my parents' house so many times, trying to figure out what I did wrong."

"You didn't do anything wrong." I'm not entirely sure what he wants here—if he wants to convince me we should do the casual thing again or if we should just forget all of it ever happened, wipe the slate clean. He can't miss the sex that much, can he? I'm not about to give my bedroom skills quite that much credit.

"I haven't been completely honest with you," he says. "When I told you that sex was a big deal to me . . . it wasn't just sex. It's the whole concept of a relationship."

"I—I figured that." It makes sense, but it doesn't exactly explain why we're having this conversation.

"And not just romantically. You know I don't have a ton of friends here. I mean, thank god for Eddie, who's even more awesome as an adult than he was when we were kids. I'm just—the idea of getting that close to someone again . . . it's terrifying."

"Wasn't that the whole point of being casual?" I cross one leg over the other, as though if I look appropriately casual, I'll be able to talk about it like it isn't a big deal. "Look, if you brought me out here to tell me that you miss getting off regularly with someone, do me a favor and tell me now, so we don't have to drag this out."

His expression morphs to horror. "Wait. What? That's what you thought this was?"

"Well . . . yeah. Kind of."

"I'd be lying if I said I didn't miss that," he says, lips curving into a grin that sends a shock of satisfaction through me, "but no. That's not what I wanted to talk about."

"Then I don't get it!" I throw my hands up, my frustration mounting. "You said you wanted something casual. So I don't see the problem with going from casual back to nothing. Why can't we just be nothing, Dominic?"

Even as I say it, it sounds wrong. My voice cracks and my heart stutters, and the word *nothing* bangs around in my head. I'm lying now, too. I haven't wanted nothing in a long time.

Dominic presses his lips together before letting a sigh slip past. "What I'm trying to tell you is that when we started this . . . it didn't feel casual to me."

And of course that starts the slow-motion replay behind my

eyelids. The adrenaline rush of those new touches, the incontrovertible fact that I have never had an orgasm as good as any with Dominic.

The incontrovertible fact that I have never talked so honestly with any man but Dominic.

"I only suggested it because you kept pushing to talk about it, and I figured it was because you didn't want me to get the wrong idea. And I knew how important the show was to you—is to you," he continues. "I didn't want to risk ruining the show if I didn't think you were on the same page."

"What same page?"

"That it's never felt casual to me." His fingers dance along the edge of the bench, a couple inches from my thigh. "Not back on the island, and not here. It's torture, sitting next to you right now and not being able to touch you. You're whip-smart and sexy and fun, and spending time with you just . . . makes everything else a little less difficult."

Now my pulse is roaring in my ears. I'm grasping for any bit of logic, all my defenses up. I want so badly to believe him. "But that time on the show, with that caller—you said you were interested in someone."

He rolls his eyes like I am the densest human on earth, and maybe I am. "Yeah. You."

A dam inside me breaks. Everything I've been holding in crashes out in one big emotional flood. I have been so tired—of making excuses, of lying, of trying to convince myself I can ignore these feelings for him.

"Oh," I say, feeling like a complete idiot. "Wow, you are really hard to read."

That makes him laugh, but it's a nervous laugh. His fingers make their way to my knee, thumb rubbing a slow circle.

"I brought you to meet my family," he continues. "You're the first person I've been with since Mia. The only person other than Mia. I've been giving you sign after sign."

"I told you how I tend to get too attached. And I'm older than you, and I didn't know if you wanted something serious. I didn't want to get my hopes up, I guess. I told myself that if we were just casual, then it wouldn't hurt to hear that you didn't want to be together for real."

"Shay. I showed you my fucking Beanie Babies."

I can't help laughing at that. "I don't know what to say."

"It would really help if you told me you like me, too."

I bite back a smile and scoot closer, leaning in to cup his face with my palm. "Dominic. I like you so much. I thought it was obvious. I like that the person you show me isn't the same as the one everyone else sees. You probably already know that I'm ridiculously attracted to you. And you care so deeply about the things in your life that are important to you—work, your family, Steve Rogers Goldstein."

"And Shay Goldstein," he says, adding to the list, and I might never want to leave this bench.

"It felt too real, being there at your house." I run my thumb along the stubble on his cheek. "That was why I had to end it. I didn't want to be there and not be your girlfriend."

One corner of his mouth quirks upward. I've missed his dimple. "You want to be my girlfriend."

"More than I want Ira Glass to personally ask me if I'll replace him on *This American Life*."

He breaks into a real, full grin then. And we're kissing, and it's like I've lived my whole life without chocolate and only now, at age twenty-nine, am discovering its sweetness.

His hands come up to my hair, messing up my ponytail. "God, I missed you," he says as I settle against his chest, pressing my ear to his strong, steady heartbeat.

30

Breaking news: Texas is hot. Texas in June deserves its own circle of hell. My poor Pacific Northwest body wasn't made for this.

It's been two weeks of keeping the kind of secret that makes me smile at random times: while spreading peanut butter onto a morning bagel, while brushing my teeth, while sitting in traffic on my way home.

Because most of the time, I am going home to him.

It's an early flight, and we luck out that Ruthie and Kent are on a later one. While I downloaded plenty of extra podcasts, I must end up passing out as soon as we get up in the air. When my eyes flutter open, the pilot is letting us know we've landed in Austin, where the local time is 1:40 p.m. and the weather is an incomprehensible ninety-five degrees.

"Were you watching me?" I ask Dominic as I return my seat to its upright position.

"You mumble in your sleep."

"I do not."

"It's cute," he says with a guilty half smile.

"I'm sure it would be, but I don't do it."

Because our live taping isn't until tomorrow afternoon, we check into our hotel, where the station booked two rooms for us, though of course we didn't tell them we'd only need one. Then we spend the day exploring Austin, since neither of us has been here before. We try the city's best barbecue, and then when we're hungry again a few hours later, stop at another place that claims to have the best barbecue, until we're certain we can't look at another pork product for as long as we live.

We hold hands as we walk down Sixth Street, taking in the dive bars and historic buildings. Bands are setting up, music pouring out of live venues. I'm positive we're not at risk of anyone recognizing us in such a big city, but we wear sunglasses just in case, and Dominic sports a Chicago Cubs baseball cap.

It feels like we're a real couple.

We stop for a while at a bar with outdoor seating, which is much rarer—and possibly less exciting for the locals—here than in Seattle. Here, life can be less complicated. Here, I can stop thinking about not having reconciled with Ameena and her first week of work and TJ packing up their apartment. He'll meet her in Virginia next week, and while they'll both be back for my mother's wedding, I'm not sure when I'll see them again after that.

"I had this idea," Dominic says when we're on our second beer, pulling me out of my spiraling thoughts. "So the whole appeal of the show is that we're exes. We can't suddenly start dating."

"Perish the thought."

"So . . . what if we got back together?"

I pause with my glass halfway to my mouth. "Like, publicly?"

He nods. "Think about it. It would be a real testament to the power radio has to connect us. The listeners would love it."

Of course it's appealing. TJ suggested the same thing after I got back from Orcas.

"Shay," Dominic says, poking my arm. "What do you think?"

"It's a good idea. But there's still a lie at the root of it. I know there isn't a way around it, not at this point, but I still feel shitty about that."

"I get it. But we wouldn't have to keep sneaking around. I like this so much, being with you. We don't know how long this show will realistically last, and I hate having to hide it, not being able to tell anyone. We'd still be exes. Exes who were brought back together by the power of radio and podcasting. And some shoes made from corn."

Maybe he's right. Maybe it wouldn't matter that we were exes before—just that we got back together.

I don't want to have to choose between the job I never thought I'd have and the guy I might be starting to love.

"What happens if—if we break up?" The relationship still feels so new, so delicate. I'm certain we can weather a frank question like this, but I hate asking it.

He's quiet for a few moments. "I know you're trying to be rational, but . . . I don't think we can possibly know that. I can't keep thinking that far into the future. All I know is that you make me so fucking happy, and not telling anyone is killing me."

I reach across the table and squeeze his hand. I want to believe him so badly. I want there to be a way to have this day every day.

"What if we do it tomorrow? At the festival? At the live taping?"

Dominic smirks. "Do you think Kent would lose his shit?"

"All the more reason to do it."

"Fair point."

"I am going to tell all our thousands of listeners how much I love the mumbling you do in your sleep."

"Then I'll tell them about your Beanie Baby collection."

"You wouldn't dare. The Beanies are sacred." He pushes up his sunglasses, his gaze both wild and full of longing. "Come here," he says, and I'm in his lap an instant later, wrapping my arms around him, not caring who sees us.

There's this moment, one where my heart is beating so in sync with his that *I love you* almost slips from my mouth.

But every other time it's happened in the past, that's when it's gotten messy. I don't want to risk not hearing it back if he's not there yet.

I go with three different words.

"Let's do it," I tell him, aware that once we do, we can't take it back.

We make it back to the hotel before eight o'clock, and in the elevator up to our floor, I make a joke about being old and having an early bedtime. Except when Dominic shuts the hotel room door behind us, he presses me against it and kisses me for a long, long time, these lazy swipes of his tongue that turn me to melted chocolate.

Every time I reach for his belt, he bats my hand away. I forgot how much he likes to tease and be teased.

"Slowly," he warns.

My lips are swollen and I got too much sun today, and I'm altogether too dizzy and shimmery to protest.

He runs a hand up my thigh, beneath my short skirt. A moan escapes my lips as he drags a finger along my damp underwear. I cup the stiff front of his jeans, rubbing back and forth, but he wraps his fingers around my wrist to get me to stop. I let out a frustrated sound and he laughs.

"I want to ask you something." Now he's not laughing. His gaze pins me to the door, his eyes molten black. "Did you ever get yourself off, thinking about me?"

"Yes," I say, not even embarrassed.

"Could you—could you show me?" he asks, his voice low. "It's kind of been . . . a fantasy of mine."

Somehow, I'm already breathless. "I could do that."

A beat passes between us, and he withdraws his hand from my skirt. I swallow hard, leading him over to the bed with its perfectly made hotel sheets. With trembling hands, I take off my sandals and skirt, slide my underwear down my legs. I've never done this in front of someone else. Something about it has always felt so intimate—more intimate than sex.

He sits next to me on the bed, fully clothed.

"You have to give me something," I insist, tugging at the hem of his shirt, and he obliges.

I lie down with my head on a pillow, my heart hammering. At first I'm not sure I can actually make myself come in front of him, or if he wants me to go that far. But the intensity in his gaze, the anticipation there, propels me forward. I have never been so open with my body with someone else, but with him, I want to be.

The entire time, I'm aware of his eyes on me, the way his jaw clenches, as though he's forcing himself not to react. That somehow makes it hotter, knowing he's holding himself back. It's what makes me stop holding myself back.

"God, yes," he says, wrapping a hand around my ankle as I quicken my rhythm. "You are so unbelievably sexy."

I let out a soft moan at that. I stretch my hand toward his mouth, and he sucks on my fingers before I plant them back between my thighs. The orgasm takes me by surprise, the pleasure cascading up my spine in a hard, fast burst. I'm still riding the waves of it when his mouth crashes into mine.

"That was the hottest thing I've ever seen," he says, and knowing it turned him on makes me greedy for more. "I need you to see how beautiful you are when you come." Then he's pulling me off the bed and over to the full-length mirror, undoing his jeans and stepping out of his boxer briefs.

He stands behind me, cupping my breasts, pushing kisses into my neck. My skin is flushed and my hair is already wild.

"We look good together," I say as his hand drifts down between my legs, and just like that, I'm ready again.

I watch in the mirror as he slides a finger along my slickness before dragging it up across my abdomen, leaving a wet streak there. The teasing is torture, and I fucking love it.

"You make me wild," he says. "I lose my mind when I'm with you like this."

When the pressure starts building, building, building, he draws back again. I let out something like a growl. Still, he doesn't enter me, continuing to use his fingers until I come again, my breath fogging up the mirror.

"You have amazing self-control."

A strangled-sounding laugh. "No. I don't. I'm dying. I just wanted to see you come at least a few times before I buried myself inside you for the rest of the night."

At this point, my legs are gelatinous, so I'm happy to collapse back onto the bed, even happier when he rolls me on top of him. I will never not love how he feels inside me, the heat and the pressure and the silk of him. We go slow for a while, languid movements that stretch me inch by inch, his eyes never leaving mine. *Deeper*. Despite his fondness for teasing, we never go slow like this, not when we're connected this way—we're usually too hungry for each other by that point. This new rhythm we find, it's torturous.

"Come with me, baby," he says, and maybe it's the command or the term of endearment or both that sends me over the edge with him.

We hold each other for a long time afterward, as though waiting for aftershocks. It smells like sweat and sex and some kind of pleasant hotel room air freshener, but no part of me wants a shower.

"That was—" I start, unsure how to verbalize it. I need to know he felt the same intensity I did. That it felt different to him, too.

He cups my head to his chest. "I know."

Eventually, we head into the bathroom to shower together, which takes significantly longer than any shower should and is, on a related note, the best shower of my life. We slip on plush white hotel robes and order room service, then climb into bed and find a bad movie on TV.

"Tomorrow," he says, squeezing my hand.

"It's only a day away, as they say. Are you nervous?"

"A bit of stage fright," he admits. "But as long as I know what I'm doing, and we've been planning this for weeks, then I'll be fine. And I know the show. I feel good about it. You're not having second thoughts, are you? About telling everyone?"

I shake my head. "No. This, between us . . . it's right."

His eyes crinkle at the edges, and he says, "I was so mad about hosting this with you at first. Not just because we weren't being completely truthful, but because you are so fucking cute, and I knew I'd be flustered around you."

"Stop," I say, pounding at his chest. "You did not!"

"I swear!" He crosses his heart. "You were the cute *Puget Sounds* producer, and I was this obnoxious reporter who only cared about the news, and you hated me."

"Reporter with a master's degree," I correct. Then I admit, "Fine, fine, I thought you were cute, too. But definitely still obnoxious, which made it annoying that you also happened to be cute. As soon as you rolled up the sleeves of your shirt, I was done. Toast." I run my hands along his arms. "Forearms are like . . . unspeakably sexy to me."

"Ah," he says. "If only I'd known sooner. I would have worn short-sleeved shirts to every *Ex Talk* taping to woo you."

"Psh," I scoff. "I'm not that easy."

"No," he agrees, "but so worth it."

We finish the movie and the two slices of red velvet cake room service delivers before shucking off our robes and slipping back into bed.

"We should go on vacation together somewhere." Dominic's fingers play through my hair, lingering on my neck, tracing my spine. "Not for work. Just for us."

It suddenly sounds so, so nice, and hearing him suggest it tugs at my heart. "We should," I say wistfully. "Where would you want to go?"

"Greece," he says without hesitation. "Maybe it's cliché, but I've been obsessed with the mythology since elementary school. I went as Hermes three Halloweens in a row."

"I'd be down for Greece. Or Spain. Or Australia."

"A whole world tour." He presses his lips to the top of my head. "It'll be perfect. No email, no internet . . . just you and me, exploring ancient ruins and eating excellent food."

"Perfect."

The weight of that desire feels heavy, especially with what we have to do tomorrow. I want to stay in this dreamworld as long as we can, this place where we can talk fearlessly about the future and know we fit into each other's visions of it. This is real. I have to keep reminding myself because otherwise I'm not sure I'd believe it.

He drifts off to sleep first, his fingers going still in my hair. I lie there quietly for a while, burrowing closer, listening to his breaths. I'm still half unsure how we got here but mesmerized by it nonetheless.

That love I thought I felt earlier—I'm certain of it now.

31

It doesn't take long for me to fall in love with PodCon, too. Our live taping is in one of the smaller auditoriums, since our fan base doesn't come close to matching some of the bigger podcasts'. Still, I've never seen anything quite like it, even the year it was in Seattle. Dominic and I wandered the exhibition area with Ruthie earlier this morning, playing with audio gear and other swag the festival sponsors had on display. We met producers and hosts of podcasts I've been listening to for years, and all of it was wildly surreal. It's one thing to scroll through our mentions on Twitter. It's another to see real live people waiting in line for us.

All of these people connected by something most of us do completely alone, with headphones on, blocking out the rest of the world—it's kind of magical.

"They're just about ready for us," Ruthie says, joining us backstage in the greenroom.

Dominic's doing some breathing exercises in a corner, and I'm on the couch, reviewing our show notes. Last night, I googled tips to combat stage fright and insisted he eat a banana before coming here, since they can soothe nausea. I also made sure we arrived an hour early. Of course I want the show to go well, but more than that, I want him to be comfortable up there. "I can't imagine not feeling comfortable with you onstage with me," he said this morning, and it made me want to tug him back into bed.

When he spots Ruthie, he heads over to the couch. And he really does look more relaxed.

"How's the stage fright?" I ask him.

He gives me a cheesy thumbs-up. "I should be able to make it through without vomiting."

"You both are going to be great," Ruthie says. "I was going to wait to show you until afterward, but I'm too excited. We have buttons! And T-shirts!" At that, she pulls a stack of buttons and a neon-blue shirt from her bag with a flourish. The shirt boasts the name of the show, plus a line drawing of a man and a woman's face, a microphone between them. The woman even has my swoopy bangs and glasses. The button has the same image, along with #publicradioturnsmeon, which Ruthie came up with a few weeks ago. "We're gonna sell them after the show."

Dominic points to illustrated Shay. "You look so cute," he says with a grin, which slips off his face the moment he glances up at Ruthie.

"It's okay," I say quickly. "She knows." It's not the whole truth, but these days, what is? It's close enough, though I should have told him earlier.

"Oh." A wrinkle of his brows. "Well . . . good. That's a relief."

"I support this a hundred and ten percent," Ruthie says.

"In that case," I say, gaining more confidence. "We're planning to tell the audience today. That we got back together." If Ruthie's on board, it has to be the right decision.

Ruthie's hand flies to her mouth. Her nails are the same neon blue as the T-shirt. "I love it. Oh my god. This is going to be incredible. Where's Kent? Does he know?"

"We, uh, haven't told him," Dominic says, a little sheepish.

"It's our decision," I say. "Not his."

"Okay," Ruthie says with a firm nod. "I'm with you, then."

Dominic squeezes my shoulder, and I can't help remembering last night. How we were open with each other in a way I've never been. How we fell asleep together and woke up together, and how suddenly the idea of waking up without him is too grim to imagine.

I'm in love with you, I think.

I might even be ready to tell him after the show.

The live show is going to revolve around storytelling. We scheduled a few local guests, and then we're going to encourage audience members to come up to the mic and share their own dating and breakup stories. We'll cut it up with ad breaks for the podcast later.

I'm not nervous—or at least, the nerves making my stomach sway are poised on the edge of relief. Once we let everyone know we're "back together," we can finally breathe. Finally have a normal relationship.

One of the festival volunteers knocks on the door. "Everyone ready?"

Kent's still not here, though he told me he'd meet us in the greenroom. He must be somewhere in the audience, playing spectator.

"We are," I say as Dominic smooths the collar of his shirt.

An Austin public radio host introduces us, and we wave as we walk out together. The audience isn't as loud as they were for earlier podcast tapings, but I'm sure my perception up here is distorted. Though the lights are bright, and at first I have to squint, I can tell nearly every seat is filled.

The stage has two orange chairs in the middle, two microphones angled toward them. The PodCon logo is splashed on a banner behind us.

We sit down, and I adjust the mic so it's at mouth level. "Hello, Austin!" I call out. I've waited so long for this, and I want to soak up every moment.

When the audience yells back, I'm convinced they're not just quieter than other audiences but tentative, too. At least one person in every row is on their phone.

I flash Dominic a worried glance, but he gives me a small shrug in return. In the wings, Ruthie is staring at us with an odd expression on her face, one that makes my stomach tighten with dread. Ruthie, who is always calm and always levelheaded, who always knows exactly how to reassure us.

And I immediately know something's wrong.

The show only gets weirder from there. Onstage, everything goes smoothly—Dominic seems at ease, maybe a sliver less confident than he is in the studio, and our guests, including a food critic who fell for a chef after writing a scathing review of her restaurant, are perfectly charming. But some audience members leave in the middle—just get right up and walk out, though I think this is some of our best material. Others continue scrolling through their phones, like it's not the rudest thing you can do at a live event like this.

Earlier, Dominic and I decided we'll announce our relationship at the very end. We'll say we spent all these long days together working on the show, it reminded us what we liked about each other. And that we appreciate our listeners' support but we want to try as best we can to keep our current relationship status separate from the show. Now I have no idea how the audience will respond.

By the time we invite the audience up to the mic to share stories and ask questions, the knot of dread has climbed up my throat, and Dominic's hands are visibly shaking.

One woman springs up from her seat in the third row, stalking toward the mic like she's on a mission.

"Yeah, I have a question," she says. "Did you think it was funny to deceive your listeners like this?"

A wave of murmurs rolls through the crowd. The woman is unfamiliar, a thirtysomething in a *Welcome to Night Vale* T-shirt. Dominic looks about as lost as I feel.

"Sorry, what?" I ask, my voice quaking. I hope she doesn't hear it. I hope none of them do.

She holds up her phone, gives it a wave, though of course I can't see the screen from here. "It's all over social media. Your little trick. You two were never actually dating—you were just coworkers who teamed up for a cheap gimmick."

It's a mad dash as the audience members not already on their phones dive for their bags and dig through pockets, hundreds of people now furiously swiping.

Never actually dating.

Just coworkers.

A cheap gimmick.

I grip the arms of the chair. If I don't, I'm worried I might bolt. I have to anchor myself, have to tell her it's not true, it's not true, it's not—

"We—uh—" Dominic tries, but he can't get out a full sentence. All the breathing exercises in the world couldn't have prepared us for this.

How the hell did this happen?

I look to the wings, to Ruthie. Our steadfast producer. I wait for her signal. I wait for her to tell us what to do, the way I signaled Paloma Powers so many times when we were hit with a hostile caller or a boring guest. But she looks stricken as she stares down at her phone, and I realize that whatever's out there, whatever's just exposed us—she's finding it out for the first time, too.

The audience is in chaos now, others storming toward the mic. The first woman, clearly pleased after her public takedown, returns to her seat.

A guy who appears to be in his late twenties steps up to the mic next. "I have a question, too," he says, and I relax a little, some ridiculous part of me preparing for a legitimate question, like maybe there's still a way to salvage this. "I'm curious, was it for money? Or was it some kind of messed-up social experiment?"

The audience goes wild again.

Kent.

It had to be him. I don't know why, and I don't know what he did, but the only other person who knows is Ameena and, by extension, TJ. Even if we're not currently on speaking terms, she would never do this. And as far as I know, Dominic still hasn't told anyone.

"If we could just, um, get the questioning on track," I say, but no one's listening to me. They're talking at us, but they're not expecting answers. They want the controversy, the outrage—but not the explanation. It's scary, watching them turn on us.

"And we fell for your lie," the next person says, "about being private on social media. And about how you were both so scared about starting a new relationship."

"That's true!" I say, wondering if this means I'm admitting the rest wasn't.

"So what if they bent the truth?" the next girl at the mic is saying. "It was good radio, right? It kept us entertained for an hour a week, helped us forget for a while that the world is on fire."

Yes, random person, thank you.

"We bought into the show because of them and their relationship," someone else says. "Can you imagine finding out that Karen Kilgariff and Georgia Hardstark weren't really friends?"

I can't take this. I can't have them control the narrative.

I wrench my mic off its stand and charge to the center of the stage. "Okay," I say. "Okay. You're right. Before we started working on this show, we hadn't actually dated."

When I turn to Dominic, his face is ashen. He's pinned to his chair, unable to make eye contact. *Help me*, I plead, but it doesn't reach him, and I can't help thinking not just about his stage fright but about his journalistic morals, the ones that the past few months have steamrolled and pulverized. This has to be his worst nightmare.

I take a slow, shaky breath. If I really am meant to tell stories, maybe there's still some way to spin this.

No—I'm done spinning it.

"At the beginning, we were just two coworkers who didn't really like each other, and it seemed like a great premise for a show. Two exes giving out relationship advice." I break off to half laugh for a moment, remembering the meeting where I first pitched it. "We weren't thrilled about the lying component. But what we saw was an opportunity to do something different on public radio, and to help save our station."

Maybe, maybe, I'm getting them back. Some of the people who were halfway to the door have paused, returned to their seats.

"And then, as we started working together, well . . ." I'm sweating in about a hundred different places, but I'm buoyed by a few whoops and whistles in the crowd. "We realized we liked each other. It was a difficult situation, but after a couple months of tiptoeing around it, we're together now. Officially."

Now there's more applause. It's scattered, but it's there. A few people on our side—that feels like enough.

Dominic was so sure our listeners would be happy for us. I'm not ready for the alternative: that this is over.

"Is that true, Dominic?" someone asks at the mic, and it's at this point I realize he still hasn't said anything. I wanted to fix this for us, but I can't do it alone. The story doesn't work if I'm the only one telling it.

I gesture for him to join me where I'm standing downstage. "Dominic?" I say, forcing more warmth into my voice than I feel. Anxiety is brutal, but I'm suffering up here, too. We are supposed to be a team. He has to realize how important this is. After all, he was the one who suggested going public because he couldn't bear keeping it a secret any longer.

Say something, I beg.

"She's—we—" he tries. He shakes his head, as though trying to calm himself. "I—" An attempt at a deep breath, a hand pressed to his chest. "The show—"

The crowd erupts into more shouting, more accusations. We've lost them.

Finally, Dominic gets to his feet. Without a microphone, he utters two words to me, so quietly that only I can hear him: "I'm sorry."

And then he rushes offstage.

32

In public radio, thirty seconds is a lifetime. Thirty seconds is long enough for someone to get bored, change the station, switch over to a different podcast. To unsubscribe. Thirty seconds can end a career.

It took less than thirty seconds for *The Ex Talk* to collapse.

Ruthie is the one who finds Kent up in his hotel room. To our shock, he welcomes us in.

Welcomes us.

I'm not entirely sure how I made it off the stage. I think Ruthie helped me into a Lyft. I think she directed it to the hotel. Despite knowing that we sucked her into this, Ruthie is still here.

Dominic is not.

I shouldn't be on social media, but I can't help it. I needed to see how all of this started. It took less than thirty seconds to pull up *The Ex Talk*'s Twitter feed and find the thread posted before we went live.

IMPORTANT LISTENER ANNOUNCEMENT

We're very sorry to say this, but now that the show has taken off, we feel compelled to tell the truth.

Shay Goldstein and Dominic Yun were never a real couple. They were coworkers who always had a bit of a friendly rivalry, and we thought it would be easy to pass them off as exes to enhance the premise of this new show. Everything about their past relationship was a complete fabrication.

Once again, our apologies, and we hope to still see you at our live #PodCon taping.

Months ago, I convinced myself lying was okay. It was storytelling, wasn't it? And now the truth's caught up with us. I'm not sure what's worse: that everyone knows we're frauds or that it's wrecked Dominic so much that he couldn't even be part of the conversation.

He and I had a plan. We were cohosts, partners, allies.

Onstage, we weren't.

I'm sitting on one of the hotel room's queen beds while Kent leans against the desk in the corner, Twitter frantically updating on the computer screen behind him.

"Look," Kent says, finally closing the lid of his laptop. "I just need a moment to explain."

I wave my arm. "The floor is yours. Start talking."

As though weighing exactly how to explain his betrayal, he tugs on his tie, which today is patterned with tiny microphones, each of them mocking me. Ruthie is cross-legged on the other bed, holding tight to her messenger bag.

"The show's been doing well," Kent says. "You and Dominic are great, and listeners clearly love you."

I don't bother telling him all of that should be in the past tense.

"The board has had some concerns for a while. It took some sweet-talking to get them interested in the show at first, but I was able to manage it. They were finally excited about getting something new on our airwaves, especially something that had appeal beyond our own little station." He sighs, pulling at his tie again. "But lately, the board has started to feel as though the show verges on a bit . . . suggestive for the station, for public radio in general. That it's much better suited as a podcast. We can't risk an FCC violation."

"Then fine," I say. "Why not just cut the live show and make us podcast only?" I have a hard time believing the board isn't made up of primarily old cishet white men.

He shakes his head. "They didn't want that, either. In their minds, the only option was to completely dissociate *The Ex Talk* name from Pacific Public Radio."

Ruthie speaks up. "But why—" She glances over at me, her eyes uncertain behind her clear-framed glasses. "I can't get past the fact that Shay and Dominic were okay with the lie from the beginning. That you all brought me onto this show without telling me."

"Ruthie, I'm so sorry," I say. "I know there's no excuse, but—I wanted to tell you. So many times."

"We were friends," she says, and it hurts more than anything Kent's said.

And yet something isn't quite adding up. "Why sabotage us, though? Why not just take us off the air? Let Dominic go back to being a reporter?" His name is sour on my tongue.

"There was . . . interest. From some big podcast distributors. I knew they'd be coming for you both and offering the kind of money we wouldn't be able to match." He runs a hand over his lined, weather-worn face. "I can see now this was a terrible mistake, but I didn't want the station to lose either of you. Whatever you're doing at the station, Shay, whether you're producing or hosting, you're an exceptional employee. We don't have anyone else like you."

Funny, he's never mentioned this to me before, not when I asked about my grief show or back when *Puget Sounds* was on the chopping block. How convenient that it's coming up now.

I wonder if exceptional really means obedient.

"And you wanted to keep Dominic."

A guilty smile. "Well—of course."

"So you sabotaged us, right before the biggest show of our careers. You made it so if PPR couldn't have us, then no one could? That wasn't your decision to make!" I've leapt to my feet, anger pulsing through my veins. I've never known rage like this. "How are you that vindictive?"

"I didn't know it would happen like this," he insists. He has the gall to look sheepish. "Shay, I really am sorry. I didn't think the audience would react the way they did."

I don't believe him. I think he planned for it to happen exactly like this. I've always viewed him as well-meaning—a little pushy, but ultimately a good guy. A good guy who wanted the best for his station and the best from his staff. And yet here he is, capable of destroying my career with a single click.

A single click after months of lying that I barely questioned.

"You don't know how rough it is to keep this station afloat," Kent says. "You think every media outlet is as noble as Dominic wants them to be? You think everyone in this field is motivated by doing good? All people want are clicks. No one wants content anymore. This is how we stay alive, Shay."

I stalk toward him, wishing I had at least a few inches of Dominic's height. "No. Not everyone. I refuse to believe that. That's not what journalism is."

"You agreed to this. If you still have some lofty idea of what journalism is, you're selling a lie to yourself just like you did to your audience. It's brutal out there, and all of us are just trying to fucking survive."

The show took that integrity away from Dominic, too. And maybe he was complicit, maybe he was backed into a corner, but he went along with it. We both did.

"What do we do now?" Ruthie asks quietly. I'd almost forgotten she was still here, and I hate myself for it.

Kent pulls out a chair and sits down as calmly as he can beneath a serene watercolor landscape. If I could redecorate this room, I'd drape it in reds and oranges, take a knife to the fluffy pillows. Tear everything apart. "This is where it gets trickier, and believe me, I hate to do this, but it's coming from the board. I'm just the messenger here." Another transparent fucking lie. "I can't keep all three of you on payroll. Not with the show gone. I could find a way to use Dominic as a researcher, at least until all of this blows over, then get him back on the air as a reporter. But I could probably only use one of you as a part-time producer . . ." His eyes flick expectantly between us.

I want to burn shit down. Apparently I'm not "exceptional" enough.

"Sure, you have space for Dominic," I spit. "Are you serious? You're saying Ruthie and I can choose who gets your special part-time producer job? I gave ten fucking years to this station, and you're content to give me a consolation prize, while Dominic gets this cushy job that hundreds of people would kill for? Did you ever think that maybe the station is suffering because of you, Kent, and the way you manage it?"

"I know you're a little fragile right now," Kent says in a level voice, like he's trying to reason with a toddler throwing a tantrum. "We're all feeling emotional—"

"I'm not fucking fragile, and you can take your coded sexist language all the way to hell." I head for the door. "I'm done. Even if you had more than half a job for me, I don't want it."

Ten years, and I no longer matter to the station. Kent's never had any allegiance to me.

I leave the room, ready to unleash my fury on the one person who should have.

He's in our hotel room.

He's in our hotel room, calmly packing clothes into his suitcase like our careers didn't just implode.

"Good news," I tell him, surprising myself with how steady my voice is. "You still have a job."

He drops the pair of socks he's holding and turns to face me. His cheeks are pink and his shoulders are stiff and he somehow looks so small, like he's folded himself into the suitcase alongside his button-down shirts and travel-size shampoo.

Last night, I thought I was in love with him.

Today, maybe the worst thing about all of this is that I still am.

"Shay," he says. "I am so fucking sorry. I—"

"I talked to Kent," I say, because as badly as I want an explanation, I have to catch him up on the meeting he missed because he fled the stage after embarrassing me in front of hundreds of people. Thousands on social media. "He was responsible for the tweets. Turns out, the board wanted to take the show off the air, and Kent was worried about us getting poached by a distributor. So he fucked us over. But like I said, you're still more than welcome to stay on board as a researcher, while Ruthie and I get to fight over a part-time producer job."

Dominic's mouth drops open. "I can't even—what?"

I head over to my own half-unzipped suitcase on the half-made bed we slept in last night and start throwing things into it haphazardly. I'm too jumbled, too furious to keep anything organized.

"That's not even the worst part. I don't care about the fucking show." Tears are stinging the backs of my eyes. "All I cared about was feeling like I wasn't alone up there while the audience destroyed us. And you could barely say a single word!"

"I'm so sorry," he repeats, still looking stricken, losing another inch of his height. As though if he can make himself small enough, he'll earn my forgiveness. But the apology feels flat, empty. "I really thought I was going to be okay. We had everything planned out, and you were being so great, and then—and then it went off the rails. And I didn't have a script. I didn't disagree with anything you were saying. You know that. I froze up. I wanted to say something, but I just—I couldn't. I couldn't even breathe up there once the accusations started."

"Neither could I!" I shout. "You humiliated me. Last night, we—" I break off, pushing up my glasses and pressing my fingers into my eyes to keep the tears from dripping down my face. "We said we were trying a real relationship. I know you're kind of new at this, but guess what, partners don't abandon each other like this."

The truth is this, though: Beneath the rage, I might be able to forgive him. Eventually. He is not his stage fright, and the more space I have from PodCon, the more I'd be able to see that. I'd need time to lick my wounds, but maybe we could get back a piece of what we had. We were so good together before today. I was so certain we would last.

"I could go back, talk to Kent . . ."

"You're going to take that job?" I ask. "You actually want to keep working for that piece of shit?"

And he just looks at me, like not taking the job is something that would never have crossed his mind.

It's a look that shatters any hope of reconciliation. This was why I didn't want to get too deep. I love too much, too soon, and the other person can't reciprocate. They always let me down. They just keep finding new ways of doing it, those innovative assholes.

"I—I don't know," he says. "Maybe? I can't think clearly right now."

"No, no, you should keep it. You're the real journalist, right? Go talk to your buddy Kent. Real stand-up guy, that one. He's always preferred you to me, anyway."

"Fuck." He rakes a hand through his hair, drags it down his face. His hair is the kind of mess I'd have loved to slide my hands into yesterday. "Fuck, Shay, I just want to make it up to you. Please tell me how to do that."

"Sure. Why don't you go run onstage and tell everyone you were part of this too, that I wasn't the only fucking idiot up there?" When he's silent, I shake my head. "The worst part is," I continue as I hurl a toothbrush into my suitcase, unsure if it's his or mine. "I thought I was falling for you. But I guess that was my stupid heart making me cling once again to someone who isn't worth it."

I watch his face, some masochistic part of me searching for an indication he felt the same way. There's a flicker of emotion, but I'm pretty sure it's just sadness. Not love.

"I don't know what to say." He sags onto the bed between our suitcases.

"Seems to be a common theme with you." I try to zip up my suitcase, but I've arranged everything so awkwardly that it won't close. "Maybe this was what you wanted all along. You were the one who was so uncertain about the show in the beginning. Now you don't have to do it anymore."

"I might have felt that way at first," he admits, "but I loved doing the show. I loved doing the show with you."

"Even if that's true, the show was a bad decision from the beginning." Another shove of my suitcase. *Come on, come on, just fucking zip. You have one job.* "All of it was a lie. Including us."

"You can't mean that. That we weren't real. Here, let me help—"

"I've got it," I say through gritted teeth, heaving all my weight on the suitcase to force the zipper closed, my breath rushing out of me once it's done.

I want so badly to tell him that of course I meant everything I said to him. Of course I want to climb back in bed and let him hold me until I no longer feel so utterly, hopelessly lost. Of course we were real.

But frankly, I'm not sure anymore.

"Let's go back to Seattle and give it some time," he says. "Can we talk about it when we're both calm?"

"I'm calm." I haul my suitcase to the floor with a thump. "And I'm done talking. So I guess the next time I hear you will be when you're back on PPR."

The tears start falling as soon as I slam the door behind me.

33

I don't remember the ride to the airport, the earlier flight I manage to catch, or the drive home. I'm numb as I pick up my suitcase from baggage claim, numb as I collect Steve from doggie daycare, numb as I refresh social media again and again until finally I have to disable my accounts because it's all too goddamn much.

My name is a hashtag.

I am a joke.

The laughingstock of public radio.

Dominic has the nerve to text me.

Shay, I can't even begin to tell you how sorry I am.

I want to make it up to you.

Can we talk?

Delete, delete, delete.

When I flip on the lights in my house, sponsorship products glare back at me from every surface. Those corn shoes, which by the way smell terrible. The custom arch support that felt great for a day but then fucked up my feet. And if I have to look at one more fruit-and-nut bar, I'll scream.

I crawl into bed—onto my free and actually somewhat life-changing memory foam mattress—and bury my face in Steve's fur. He seems to get that I'm feeling down because he's a muted version of his typically energetic self. I will throw my pity party alone and without shame. No one can judge me if no one knows about it.

"That includes you, Steve," I mutter when I catch him giving me a particularly savage side-eye.

I zombie through the next few days. I ignore texts and calls from my mother and Ameena and TJ and Ruthie, ignore more texts from Dominic. The wedding is next week, and I know I'll have to see Ameena and explain to everyone how big of a liar I am. But I'm not ready. Not yet.

I don't let any of my podcasts update, and I don't turn on the radio. I know our—their—pledge drive is soon, and I can't bear to listen to them asking for money. *If you call now and pledge a minimum of twenty dollars per month, you'll get a KPPR T-shirt . . .* I used to look forward to each year's T-shirt design. They're all in my drawer, from least to most recent, varying levels of softness as a result of countless wash-and-dry cycles. I love those shirts. I'm going to miss them.

Oh god. How many of those *Ex Talk* T-shirts will wind up at a Goodwill or in a Dumpster?

I devoted my twenties to public radio, and it feels wrong for it to have turned on me like this. And yet, the wild thing is . . . when I think about not having to go back to PPR, I feel something a little like relief. Sure, it's buried beneath the heartbreak and the humiliation, but it's there. The show is over. My public radio career might be, too, but not having to carry that lie makes me feel like I can stand up a bit straighter. I've been working myself to the bone, nights and weekends for years. Zero breaks. Maybe now I'll have the time to decide what I really want.

Maybe once the social media backlash fades, once I'm no longer going through a bottle of wine a day, I'll be able to see that this is actually a good thing.

After all, it saved me from the biggest relationship mistake of my life.

Day four post-PodCon, I finally turn on my laptop. I drag it over to the couch, push aside a takeout container to make room for another half bottle of wine. Instead of going straight to social media or the work email account I'm sure has been deleted, I open up a file I haven't touched in forever.

My dad had all kinds of recording devices, some from this century and plenty that weren't. We argued about analog versus digital in between recording our many "radio shows." Eventually, I uploaded everything to my computer, tucked away in a folder simply labeled with his initials, *DG*. Like only two letters would make it somehow easier to look at.

The thing about losing someone is that it doesn't happen just once. It happens every time you do something great you wish they could see, every time you're stuck and you need advice. Every time you fail. It erodes your sense of normal, and what grows back is decidedly not normal, and yet you still have to figure out how to trudge forward.

Ten years, and I am still losing him every day.

At first it's really fucking hard to hear his voice through my laptop speakers. Our recording equipment was too good—there's no static, nothing that makes it sound like the audio has aged even remotely.

"This is *Dan and Shay Do the News*," he says in that perfect voice, and I suck down more wine.

I hear my eleven-year-old self giggle. "No, no, you're supposed to say my name first."

"Whoops, sorry, I forgot. Let's try that again. This is *Dan and Shay Do the—*"

"Daaad, you did it again!"

"Oh shoot, did I? One more time—"

He was doing it on purpose, of course. I can hear it now.

I listen to the two of us spar, laugh, tell stories. It tugs at my heart, it aches, but it doesn't give me the kind of clarity I was hoping for.

Fact: I loved doing these shows with my dad.

Fact: I wanted to grow up and be on the radio.

I dreamed of telling stories that would make people feel something—the same way radio did for me. For a while, hosting a successful show felt like an answer to the questions I'd had my whole life. It was validation.

The Ex Talk gave me that, just for a while, but if I'm being honest with myself, I hadn't felt it on Paloma's show in a long, long time.

I keep clicking through files. I'm already at rock bottom, so what's a little more suffering?

The funny thing is, my dad would have gone wild for what happened at our live show. Oh, he'd absolutely be disappointed in me, but he loved when radio went off script. He craved those human moments, the times you got to see the people behind the personas.

Well, here you go, Dad. Here's how I ruined public radio.

34

My mother gets married in my childhood backyard on a clear July day.

It's just shy of eighty degrees, perfect for a Seattle summer, and she's radiant in her navy jumpsuit, red hair arranged in a sophisticated knot with a few curls tumbling onto her shoulders. Phil is in a charcoal linen suit and navy tie, and neither of them can stop smiling.

The wedding is small, only about thirty people. My parents were always proud of our backyard—lord knows my dad spent enough time maintaining it. Turns out, there's enough space for a chuppah, several rows of chairs, and a small dance floor. Everything is adorned with yellow roses and elegant calla lilies, a marriage of my mother's and Phil's favorite flowers, and we strung tea lights along the fence. There's a string quartet made up of their friends from the symphony, and later, the two of them will play, too.

It hits me that not everyone gets to see a parent so deeply in love like this, and that makes me feel lucky, that I'm privy to this side of my mother.

That I've seen her this in love not once but twice.

My new stepsiblings and their kids are enough to make a small party feel alive and electric, and while I'm wistful for the quiet celebrations I had with my parents, I think I could get used to, well, fun.

There's so much to set up that I don't get a chance to talk to Ameena and TJ, who arrive close to the start of the ceremony. I know I'll have to talk to them at some point, but I'm putting it off as long as I can. My mother is my first priority.

The ceremony itself is short and sweet. My mother and Phil wrote their own vows, and they're both appropriately sappy. They incorporate the Jewish tradition of breaking a glass—after which we yell out, "Mazel tov!"—and a Nigerian tradition where guests spray money at the bride and groom, which they opt to donate to a cancer charity in honor of Phil's late wife.

"How are you doing?" my new stepsister Diana asks after the ceremony, while we're in line at the small buffet next to the dance floor.

"Oh—I'm fine," I say, because we don't yet have the kind of closeness where I can be fully open about the fact that I'm drowning in self-pity with a healthy dash of self-loathing. But maybe one day we will. "Just . . . job hunting. Shockingly, no one's knocking down my door begging to hire me."

"It's rough out there. Hey, if you want to babysit," she says with a waggle of her eyebrows, "we're in the market for a new nanny."

I force a smile. While I like her kids, I don't think I could be around them for that many hours a day. I still don't even know if I want my own.

"Tempting offer, but I'm going to have to pass," I say, and she snaps her fingers.

"Damn. I was really hoping we could wrangle some kind of family discount. Nannies aren't cheap."

"Are you trying to trick Shay into becoming our nanny?" her husband Eric says, heading over with a glass of white wine.

"Yes, and it's not working. Who are the kids terrorizing now?"

"They're calmly eating ravioli. At least, for the next few minutes." He tips his glass at me. "Shay, can I get you anything?"

I've had enough wine in the past week to power ten weddings, so I probably shouldn't. "I'm good," I say. God, they really are so nice. I don't know why I was ever so reluctant. "Thank you."

Since I waited until everyone else had gone through the buffet line to take my turn, I carry my plate of food back to the only table with empty chairs. Of course it's the one Ameena and TJ are sitting at. She's in a lilac dress that I remember buying with her at an estate sale last year, and I wonder if she remembers the Capitol Hill boutique where I bought my powder-blue one. Everything else about her is so familiar that I can't believe it's been months since we spoke.

TJ gives her a gentle nudge forward.

And I just . . . crumble.

Ameena and I venture deeper into the garden to talk.

"I can't believe everything that happened," she says, sitting next to me on a stone bench my dad planted here so many years ago.

"I can't wrap my mind around it, either," I admit. "Sometimes it feels like a bad dream, but then I wake up and nope, I'm still extremely unemployable and extremely embarrassed."

She squeezes my shoulder, and I lean into her touch. "I wish I could have been there for you. I don't hate Seattle, I swear. I was just so eager for a change. Everything I said was completely out of line."

"Maybe," I agree, "but I don't think you were entirely wrong.

The weirdest thing about this is that I feel relieved underneath everything. Relieved I don't have to keep lying. And a little relieved that I can figure out if there's a job for me out there that isn't in public radio."

"Shay Goldstein not in public radio," she says with an exaggerated gasp. "What is the world coming to?"

That's the most terrifying part: that I've defined myself by public radio for so long that I've never wondered who I am without it.

Maybe the truth is that I've been scared to find out.

Ameena opens up her beaded clutch. "I know it's not traditional to give the daughter of the bride a gift," she says. "I actually had these made before our fight. I was going to give you yours before I left, but . . ."

"Holy shit. You didn't." I unwrap a custom-made silver bracelet with *WWAMWMD* printed on it. "You got me a WWAMWMD bracelet."

"So you never forget," she says with a grin.

"Tell me you have a matching one?"

She pulls out a second one and slips it on. "Duh."

We continue catching up. Ameena tells me more about her job, about Virginia, about the humidity her hair was completely unprepared for. After a while, TJ finds us and asks Ameena to dance. She lifts her eyebrows at me, and I gesture to her that it's okay. We'll be okay, too—or at the very least, we'll try to be.

I venture back to the wedding guests, sliding into an empty seat next to my mother.

"How have you been dancing for two hours and you still look flawless?" I ask her.

"Oh, stop," she says, but she's glowing. "I know you put on an act out there for the wedding, and I appreciate it, but you can be honest with me. How are you doing?"

I appreciate that she hasn't judged me for lying on air to thousands of listeners. She must have known I had enough of it from every corner of the internet.

"I'm not okay," I admit, running my fingers along the petals of a nearby calla lily. "But I'm trying to be."

"And Dominic?"

"He's back at PPR. As a researcher." His apologies must really have been empty if he was okay staying on their payroll, working with Kent. The fact that he's still there, siding with Kent over me, feels like a tremendous betrayal. If only my heart could realize it. "I think I got so caught up in the idea of the show that it didn't matter that we were lying to people, that they were giving us money because they bought into the lie, and when you think about it that way, it seems . . . really shitty."

"You wanted to make good radio," she says simply. "You made an error in judgment. From the sound of it, Dominic made the same one."

"It would all be fine if I could just stop loving him."

"You know how many times I thought things would be so much simpler if I could stop loving your dad?" She shakes her head, and maybe it's strange to bring him up on her wedding day, but this is the proof that he's never gone. "All the years of therapy, loneliness, grief . . . if I could flip a switch and just stop, it would have been easier, right?"

"That would have been awful," I say. "Easier, sure, but still awful."

Now I'm thinking back to all the times in my past relationships I said *I love you* too soon. I'm certain I meant it, but it didn't feel anything like loving Dominic. I crave the smallest, simplest things: his rare dimple, the jokes about our age gap, his passion for cast-iron cookware. The way he felt in my bed, yes, but also the way he trusted me with his painful memories, and the way I trusted him with mine.

Maybe not so small and simple after all.

The quartet transitions to a cover of "September," and more dancers rush onto the floor.

But my mother appears lost in thought. "You know, I used to be jealous of the two of you. You and Dan."

"You what?" I say, positive I heard her wrong.

"It's silly, isn't it? Or at least, it sounds silly now. You and your dad had this thing you were both so in love with. You'd fully inherited his passion for it, and it was fun to watch the two of you, but . . . sometimes I wished, just a little bit, that you could have liked music, too."

Oh. I had no idea my mother felt this way. It's reality shattering to hear your parent confess something so . . . human.

"Mom," I say quietly. "I—I'm sorry."

She waves this away. "It's not your fault! You liked what you liked. I couldn't force it on you. You tried piano lessons, and you tried violin lessons, and you tried choir, and you just didn't click with any of them. And that's okay."

She's being generous. I was terrible, no rhythm and no patience. Music on the radio, especially the kind of music my mother listened to, didn't excite me the way NPR did. And maybe I was the only nine-year-old geeking out over *Car Talk*, but I didn't care.

"I loved that the two of you had that special bond," my mother continues. "But you go into parenting hoping, maybe selfishly, that your kid will love the thing you love, and you can share that with them."

"And I let you down."

"No," she says firmly. "Especially now, I'm so, so glad you had that time with him."

I lean my head against her shoulder, and she combs her fingers through my hair until Phil tows her back onto the dance floor. I watch the couples as the sun dips low in the sky and the stars blink on, but I don't feel like the odd one out, the third or fifth or fourteenth wheel. I'm not lonely, exactly. I don't need someone next to me, and I'm not rushing to fill an emptiness. It's that I want one person in particular, and it's the person I don't know how to forgive.

I used to think that without my dad, I'd never be whole again. But maybe that's what we all are—halfway-broken people searching for things that will smooth our jagged edges.

35

Dominic eventually stops texting. I guess it confirms that whatever we had, it's really over.

I don't expect to miss it as much as I do, but the love lingers like a bruise, aching even when I'm not actively thinking about it. My past breakups never made me this miserable. Maybe it's because I was forcing those guys to fill a space I thought needed to be filled, while Dominic slid into my life so naturally. A want, not a need.

Every now and then, Ruthie texts to check in. She's still processing, but she says she wants to be there for me, wants to remain friends. I don't think I could have forgiven myself if I'd torched that relationship, too.

I have enough savings to last me through January if I manage to avoid any major crises, but I'm not used to being idle. So I focus on my job search. If Dominic can be content working at Pacific Public Radio, then I can at least send out a few résumés. I don't know what's out there for a disgraced public radio host. I try a TV station, a few PR firms, a handful of companies looking for whatever the hell a content creator is. But I don't get any bites. Maybe I'm unqualified, or maybe they're googling me and don't love what they find.

In mid-August, I get a text from Paloma Powers that nearly knocks me out of my kitchen chair.

Heard what happened. Kent's a fucknugget. Let me know if you need anything.

Before I can overthink it, I message her back, and just like that, we have lunch plans for the weekend. I'm not sure what I'm going to get out of meeting with her, but I've worked with her longer than anyone. The rapidly shrinking optimistic part of me wants to believe she can help.

Paloma and I meet at a new restaurant she claims does the best panzanella in Seattle. It's such a Paloma thing to say that it comforts me immediately.

She's in one of her lighter shawls for summer, and her hair is longer, skimming the tops of her shoulders.

"I can't seem to find a producer as attentive as you were," she says with a sigh between sips of her turmeric juice. "But it's going well. I thought I liked jazz, but turns out, I love jazz. So that was a relief. And it's much less stress than what I did on *Puget Sounds*. That's the last thing I want in my life at this point."

"That's good to hear," I say. It's strange, this lunch with her. When we worked together, I'd never have considered us friends. We never grabbed lunch. It wasn't that I didn't like working for her. I respected her, and there was a hierarchy. Or it felt like there was.

We both order the panzanella, which I'm thrilled to learn is a bread salad. It instantly becomes my favorite kind of salad.

She steers the conversation like a talk show. "Kent has been a sexist piece of shit as long as I've known him," she says. "He hides it well."

"I guess I was always quick to find an excuse for it, or I'd be afraid to say anything because, well, he was my boss." I think back to the way he trusted Dominic's opinion over mine, or how he'd ask a woman at a meeting to take notes, never a man. Because the woman was "so good at details." He made it seem like some special treatment we were getting. "But it was so clear he loved Dominic, and I felt like I was second tier, even though I'd been at the station so long."

"That's how he works, the sneaky fuck. He's overly nice to make up for the fact that he doesn't fundamentally respect women. He might not even be aware of it—internalized misogyny is a hell of a drug. But that doesn't excuse it. I've also heard him brag about hiring people of color, like he's single-handedly solving this industry's diversity issues." She leans in conspiratorially. "And did you know that he asked me out once?"

"What?"

"Yep. I wasn't out at work yet, and when I told him I wasn't interested, he played it off like it wasn't a big deal. He was head of the news department back then, and I was a reporter, and he started assigning me stories no one else wanted to cover. Stories so bland the station probably shouldn't have been covering them at all, and then sometimes he wouldn't even air them. I tried to talk to him about it, but he insisted I had to pay my dues. It went on for a year before I got tapped to host *Puget Sounds*—by the board, not Kent."

"Jesus," I say. "Paloma, I'm so sorry."

"What made it worse was that everyone else seemed to love him so much, respect him so much," she continues. "And because of that unspoken hierarchy, I couldn't say a damn thing."

Our food arrives, and we're quiet for a few minutes as we dig in.

Finally, I find the words to tell her about my own insecurities. "I felt some of that hierarchy when I was working with you," I admit.

"You did? Because of me?"

And she looks so stunned that I want to take it all back, but I push forward. "It's this strange dynamic between producers and hosts, I think. You're the 'talent,' and our jobs rely on making it easy for you to do your job."

I realize I say *our* like I'm still a producer, like I didn't just host a successful but doomed show. Maybe at my core, I still am.

"I'm sorry," Paloma says after a beat of silence. Then she a cracks a smile. "If it helps, I get my own chia seeds now. I've been humbled."

"Was it hard to leave public radio?"

"It was hard getting pushed out," she says. "I'm sure Kent had been looking for a reason to get rid of me for years. But I think it was time for me to move on, even if I was reluctant to do it at first. I definitely don't miss the pledge drives."

"Wait, you don't like begging strangers for money?" I say, and she laughs.

"Public radio doesn't have to be your identity," she says. "Ahem, speaking as someone for whom it was their whole identity. You're still at the beginning of your career, and people have short attention spans. If you want to go back to radio, you can. This doesn't have to take it away from you. I'd be happy to write you a recommendation, if you think that might help you out. But if you're not sure, and if you have the ability to do so . . . there's no harm in taking time to figure out your next step."

"I've just been doing radio for so long that I don't know what else I'm good at."

She gives me this strange look. "Shay Goldstein," she says, "if that's what you think about yourself, then you're not the person I thought you were."

36

I slide the WWAMWMD bracelet up and down my wrist. Ameena's been sending me photos of her new apartment, and yep, it's much bigger and cheaper than anything in Seattle. We've tentatively planned for me to visit in November, once she's more settled.

Ruthie's girlfriend Tatum works at a vegan café in North Seattle, and she supplies us with free food while Ruthie and I send out résumés and commiserate about unemployment. The free food helps. Free alcohol helps even more, but honestly, I should cut down on the day drinking.

My weekends don't feel as empty as I thought they might, though maybe it's because my weekdays are still a bit empty, too. I had a job interview earlier today as a copywriter at a marketing agency, which I was unsure I wanted—they just happened to be the first place that called me. In the middle of the interview, someone knocked on the door and asked to talk to the HR manager, and when she came back in, she was decidedly chillier than she'd been before.

"You could always come back to commercial radio with me," Ruthie says, swiping a sweet potato fry through sriracha aioli.

"KZYO offered me my old job, but I'm not sure yet if I'm going to take it. I'm trying to see what my options are."

I take a sip of my rosé. "Truthfully, I'm not sure I could handle the commercials."

"They're not that bad."

She launches into a familiar jingle and Tatum shouts from behind the counter, "Is she singing the pickle song again? Because she's not allowed to do it within fifteen feet of me, it's a relationship rule."

Ruthie holds a finger to her lips. "It pays really we-ell," she singsongs.

"I'll think about it," I promise.

We return to our laptops, the clacking of our keys mixing with the surfer girl pop punk playing through the café's speakers. The café isn't busy—in fact, we're the only two people here, plus Tatum and a cook in the kitchen.

"If there's anything I can do to help, you'll let me know, right?" I ask Ruthie after a couple minutes. It's still strange, sitting across from her after spending five months lying to her.

Ruthie's hands pause on her keyboard, her rings glittering in the afternoon light. "I've already told you a hundred times that I forgive you," she says. "I have a feeling whatever you're putting yourself through is enough. I don't need to add to it."

"You're too good for this world."

"I know," she says. "I almost don't wanna ask, but . . . any word from Dominic?"

I shake my head. "He was texting for a while, but then he stopped. To be fair, I wasn't exactly responding." I let out a sigh. "I can't talk to him if he's still working there."

"I get it," Ruthie says. "I'm so sorry. I really was rooting for you two."

Suddenly, Tatum gasps from behind the counter. "Oh my god,"

she says, racing over to our table, her long dark ponytail bouncing. She shoves her phone at Ruthie.

"Tweeting on the job?" Ruthie says, shaking her head and making a tsking sound. But her eyes grow wide as she sees what's on the screen. "Oh my god," Ruthie echoes. She wrenches the phone from Tatum's grasp and scrolls down the page.

I lean forward in my seat, trying to see what they're looking at. "What is it?" Working in a newsroom, you get used to these kinds of reactions when something terrible happens somewhere in the world: people crouched over a phone, hands over mouths. But the two of them seem shocked rather than upset.

"Turn on Pacific Public Radio," Ruthie says, patting my laptop. "My battery's dying."

I spit out a laugh. "No thanks. I'll just check Twit—"

"Shay. Turn on the fucking radio," Ruthie repeats, with so much vigor in her voice that I don't dare disobey her.

Begrudgingly, I navigate over to the PPR homepage and click the little microphone icon to start the livestream. Tatum turns down the café's sound, and we all lean in to listen to . . . An NPR newsbreak, featuring a story about an alligator in Florida that was finally caught after escaping from a zoo earlier this week.

"Are we . . . into alligators now?" I ask.

Ruthie rolls her eyes. "Just wait until the end of the newsbreak."

Tatum slides into the booth next to Ruthie, and we wait. When PPR comes back on the air, it immediately becomes clear they're in the middle of a pledge drive, which sparks an odd twinge in my chest. I didn't even register that it was happening this week.

"And we're back, talking about how you can support great local journalism," says a familiar voice. "Which also happens to be hour number two of my apology tour. If you're just tuning in, here's what happened."

I can't breathe.

"There was this girl," Dominic says, and I think my heart might actually stop. "That's the way these stories always tend to start, right? So. There was this girl, and she's the smartest, most interesting girl I've ever met. We worked together at this very station. She'd been at Pacific Public Radio for ten years, and she's fantastic at her job. She's basically an NPR encyclopedia. We even got lucky enough to host a show together . . . but that didn't exactly go as planned. The show was built on a lie—the notion that the two of us had dated in the past and were now teaming up to dole out relationship advice and hear tales of other dating misadventures. But it gets really, really complicated when you start falling for a girl all your listeners think you've already dated and moved on from. Especially when your desk is right next to hers."

"Shay," Ruthie says, grabbing my arm. "Shay."

"I—oh my god." The café disappears around me. I have tunnel vision, and it's definitely not just the rosé. All I see is the microphone icon on my screen, and all I hear is Dominic's voice. He sounds so natural on the air now, more than he ever has.

"But I messed up," Dominic continues, and then breaks off with a half laugh that jolts my heart, gets it beating again. "I've always had a little stage fright, and unfortunately, I froze up when she needed me most. I wasn't there for her, even after we'd promised to be a team. I'm here today to tell all of you that I'm so deeply sorry for the lie *The Ex Talk* was based on, but more than that, I'm sorry, Shay. I'm so incredibly sorry, and all I want is to talk to you again."

This is really happening. Dominic, apologizing on the radio.

"It's all over Twitter," Ruthie says, holding her phone to my face, but I can't process any of the text on it. "Apparently he was saying something about Beanie Babies earlier?"

"This is the most romantic thing I've ever seen," Tatum says. "Or heard, I guess."

"I don't know if she's listening," Dominic is saying, "but I can't think of another way to tell her how badly I screwed everything up. If she gives me a second chance, even if it's one I don't deserve, I will do whatever I can to make things up to her. And more than that . . . I need her to know that I love her. I've been in love with her since the island, maybe even before that. And I'm dying to tell her in person."

Another voice comes on the radio, one I recognize as Marlene Harrison-Yates'. "And if you'd like to call in with a donation to keep Dominic on the air, to keep us going, that number is 206-555-8803, or you can donate online at KPPR.org."

"Oh my god," I say again, unsure if I know any other words. My first instinct is to turn it off, shut him down, ignore it all. Insist that he can't sweet-talk his way back into my life. I close my eyes for a moment, trying to latch onto reality. "He's still at the station. He's still working for them. All of this is . . . wow, but it doesn't change the fact that he took that job after they practically kicked me out."

"Don't you think you owe it to him to hear him out?" Ruthie says.

Deep down, I know she's right. If there's any chance of fixing things between us, I have to talk to him. "He's still on the air. What should I do?"

"Go down there and tell him you're madly in love with him?" she suggests. "I mean, just an idea."

"I can't just go down there. I quit, remember? They practically fired me." With trembling hands, I pick up my phone. "I'll—I'll call." I have no idea what I'm going to say, but it's the only option that seems to make sense to my soupy brain right now.

The number is practically part of my DNA at this point, though I've never actually called it. Still, I'm so rattled that I miss a digit the first time.

"Pacific Public Radio call-in line, what's your comment?" Isabel Fernandez asks, and it's such a rush of emotion to hear her voice.

During pledge drives, they often have listeners call in to share a story about the station and why they support it. I can't believe I got through right away.

"Isabel, it's Shay. Shay Goldstein."

If I could hear someone's eyes bulge on the phone, it would probably sound the way Isabel's stunned silence does.

"Shay? Hold on, let me put you through. This is going to be amazing!"

"No, wait—" I say, but it's too late.

It's odd, hearing the radio streaming from my laptop and then listening through my phone as I wait to be live on the air. And the whole time, I can't believe I'm doing this, I'm really fucking doing this.

"It seems like we have a caller on the line," Dominic says in my ear now.

"Dominic." My voice is shaky.

Ruthie and Tatum are leaning across the booth to listen, Ruthie gripping my arm and Tatum gripping Ruthie.

Silence on the line. I want to admonish him, tell him dead air is deadly.

"Shay?" His voice shakes, too. "I didn't think you'd hear. I mean—I hoped you would, but I figured you'd been avoiding the radio, and . . . wow. Wow." I try to imagine him there in the studio, pacing back and forth, running a hand through his hair, pushing up the sleeves of his shirt. "It's so good to hear your voice."

I feel my face split into a grin. His voice isn't enough. I have to see him, and I have to see him now. "Stay there," I say. "I'm coming down."

"Wait," he says. "Wait—Shay—"

Ruthie and Tatum are gaping at me. "What is happening," Ruthie says.

"Hopefully the most romantic moment of my life."

———

I'm too jumbled to drive, so Tatum leaves the cook in charge of the café so she and Ruthie can drive me.

Ruthie's car is parked around the corner. I take the messy back seat, filled with receipts and canvas bags and two shoes that do not match and a handful of CDs.

"You have CDs?" I ask, moving my foot so I don't step on Hall and Oates's greatest hits.

"Old car," Ruthie says. "That's all it can handle."

"Besides, then she can act all hashtag retro," Tatum says.

"I hate that CDs are retro," I say as Ruthie speeds toward the freeway. It'll take us probably twenty minutes to get downtown. Twenty minutes of panicking in the back seat.

"Sorry it's so messy," Ruthie says. "But if you find a piece of gum back there, let me know."

"Let the girl breathe," Tatum says. "She just received a public declaration of love." She turns to me. "Do you want the radio on?"

"I don't know." It feels so personal that everyone's hearing this. But that's what we were doing with the show, weren't we? "If someone could convince me I won't manage to fuck this up, that would be awesome."

And, bless them, they try. By the time we pull up to the familiar building and Ruthie circles the block, unable to find a parking spot, my heart is in my throat.

"You've got this," Ruthie says firmly. "We'll be right down here if you need us. Partly because we can't find a parking spot, but mainly because I think you need to go up alone."

"Good luck," Tatum says. "We'll be listening."

I nod, swallowing hard. "Thank you. Thank you both so much."

On wobbly legs, I make my way to the security door, realizing

I don't even know if they'll let me in if I buzz up. I give the door a pathetic swipe of my key card, but of course, it's been deactivated. So with a shaky sigh, I hit the buzzer.

"Pacific Public Radio," chirps Emma McCormick's staticky voice.

"Hey—Emma," I say, holding down the button. "It's me, um, Shay Goldstein. I wanted to come up to talk to Dominic. He's on the air—"

"Shay, oh my god!" Emma squeals. "I can't get over it. I wish someone would do something like this for me. You are so lucky. The phone lines have been bananas, and we've already crushed our goals for the entire pledge drive. It's really—"

There's a scuffle in the background, and then another familiar voice. "Shay? It's Marlene Harrison-Yates. I'm letting you up."

"Oh—thank you," I say as the door clicks. Nothing makes sense today.

Then I am in the hall and the slowest of slow elevators, taking out my ponytail and then putting it back up, wiping the lenses of my glasses on my shirt, trying to make myself look less nightmarish. But Dominic has seen me at my worst, he's seen me panicked and without makeup and with tears streaming down my face, and he loves me.

He loves me.

When I get to the fifth floor, Marlene is holding open the station door. "I'm a sucker for true love," she says with a shrug. "And Emma wasn't getting you up here fast enough."

Emma offers an apologetic but still peppy shrug.

I barely have a chance to take in the station foyer with its warm hominess and vinyl-record-covered walls before Kent sprints toward me.

"Shay!" he says, so falsely cheery that it churns my stomach.

"We were wondering if you'd show up. I know it's a little unconventional, but social media is blowing up. I've never seen anything like it. It's really big of you to put all of this behind you and—"

"I'm not here for you." God, it feels incredible to interrupt him. I gesture to the hall. "And as much as I used to love this place, I'm not here for the station. I'm here for Dominic, and that's it. Then I'm gone."

Kent's mouth tightens, and he gives me a curt nod. Marlene's long skirts flutter as she steps in front of him, and when our eyes meet, a brief understanding passes over her face. "Go," she urges me, and I dip my head in gratitude.

My former coworkers seem to have realized what's happening, and they join us in the hall, staring, openmouthed, as I make my way to the place I used to feel most myself. *Deep breaths. One foot in front of the other. I can do this.*

I squeeze my eyes shut, and when I open them, there he is, standing in the middle of the studio like he's delivering a filibuster. His clothes are crisp but his hair is rumpled, just like I imagined it. Dark scruff along his jaw, studio headphones clamped over his ears. Beautiful and sexy and sweet and kind. The guy I was scared of falling too hard for.

When his eyes lock on me, his face completely changes. A smile spreads from one corner of his mouth to the other, drawing out his dimple, and then he's full-on grinning. His dark eyes brighten, and his posture seems to dip with relief. That shift is incredible to watch.

He heads for the door, and he must forget that he's wearing headphones because the cord tugs him back toward the table. It's adorable, watching him fiddle with it, trying to untangle himself.

"Get her mic'd up," someone is saying. I don't even know who.

And then I am being shoved into the studio with the man who just poured his heart out to me on live radio. Headphones are plugged in and wrangled onto my ears, and did they always feel this heavy?

"We're on a newsbreak," Jason Burns says in our ears. "You have four minutes before you go live again."

"Hi," Dominic says. The word is a breathy exhale.

"Hi."

I thought I'd run toward him, that he'd scoop me into his arms, kiss me passionately. That the outside world would fall away, fade out, end credits.

Except none of that happens. My feet turn to concrete. We stare each other down, as though we're both unsure what to do now.

"You look—you look great," he says, his voice a little hoarse. I should have brought lozenges.

"Thanks," I say, self-consciously running a hand through my hair again. "You—um. You do, too."

We still have so much to say, but now that I'm here with him, I don't know where to begin. Sure, I dreamed of us reconciling, but I never imagined it happening quite like this, with Dominic standing here like he has no idea what to do with his hands.

"You've been . . . okay?" I say. "Since the show went off the air?"

He nods, but then grimaces. "Work has been . . . you know. Fine. But I have to be honest. I've been fucking miserable."

And that makes me crack a smile—not because he was miserable, but because I've felt the same.

"Me too," I say in a small voice.

"Thirty-second warning," someone says.

"I have to go back on the air," he says.

Shit. Shit. We've barely even had a conversation.

"Are you—" He swallows. "You want to come on the air with me?"

We started this on the air. I want to finish it—whatever that conclusion is—on the air, too. "Yes," I say quietly.

The rest of PPR has gathered outside the studio, and Kent is scrolling through a tablet. I have to focus anywhere but on him.

"I'm back with Shay Goldstein," Dominic says when the **RECORDING** sign goes on, and woof, the nostalgia hits me with such force that I have to slide into a chair.

"Hi." I wave, though I know no one can see me.

Dominic sits down next to me. "So I've kind of been spilling my feelings here for the past two and a half hours."

"I've heard." I force a laugh. "I don't know why I'm laughing, actually."

"It's kind of funny," he concedes. "We were able to lie that we were exes because we argued so much. Then we fell for each other. And then we hid it from ourselves for a while, and when we finally admitted it to each other, we had to hide it from the audience. But then everything blew up, and now . . . now I don't know what we are."

"When you went silent onstage in Austin, and then when you disappeared afterward . . ." I shake my head, still unable to block out that humiliation. "I'd never felt like that before. 'Embarrassed' doesn't even begin to cover it. I've spent the past month trying to figure out if I'm supposed to work in radio, but being back here . . . I might be done with the station, but that doesn't mean I've stopped fucking loving it."

Whoops, FCC.

That's gonna cost the station.

I find I don't care one bit.

"And you're fucking good at it," he says, and I lift my eyebrows at that. He's the one who still works here, not me.

"I've been here since college," I say, speaking more to our audience than to him. "And so to have my dream job, to be onstage, and then to see my journalism career end so quickly . . . I wasn't ready for it."

"Your journalism career isn't over," he says. "Not if you don't want it to be."

"And I know that," I say, because deep down, I believe him. "I think what's been hurting the most is that after everything went to shit, you kept working here. You still had a job, a place here, but I didn't. That's what I can't get past."

He nods, letting this sink in. "I wanted to explain. I've needed to explain, and I don't blame you for not responding to my texts because I probably wouldn't have responded to them, either." He inches his chair closer to me, his shoe tapping mine, and it reminds me of that late night we spent at the station, creating a history for us. It was one of the first times I realized I might have feelings for him, though I was hell-bent on denying them.

"I'm not the best in front of big groups of people. I never have been. Doing the show with you in here, that was fine, but I had the worst stage fright of my life in Austin. And that's only a partial excuse, I realize that. You were going through shit onstage, too. You were being put through the wringer just as much as I was. But it's the truth. Anxiety made me freeze up, and somewhere deep in that thought spiral, I worried that whatever I said would destroy my journalism career. For the longest time, I wanted to be a serious reporter, and somewhere along the way, I lost sight of that. Except when I came back to work, everything felt wrong. It killed me to accept that job, to keep coming into work every day without you here. Any marginal amount of career success I have feels lackluster if the rest of my life is off-kilter. I embarrassed you, and I'm so sorry about that. If I could go back, I'd stand behind you one hundred percent. No doubt about that."

He takes a breath before continuing, and I have to hold a hand to my chest again to still my thumping heart. "My first day back at work, I wanted to quit. But I knew we had a pledge drive coming up, and so I thought this might be my last chance."

"Your last chance for what, exactly?"

A chat pops up on the computer screen next to us. **DONATIONS GOING WILD, KEEP GOING!** But we're not doing it for them.

Dominic's familiar half smile curves his lips. I want to feel that half smile pressed against my neck, my throat. I want to forgive him. "You know what I said on the air," he says.

"Say it to me." I shift forward so our knees are touching. "Tell me like I'm the only person here. Like there aren't hundreds of people listening."

"Thousands," he whispers, and I can't help smiling at that. "I want to try this again. No lies, no pretending. Everything completely out in the open."

His fingers graze mine.

"I have this history of telling people I love them and not hearing it back," I say. "It's a problem, maybe—I jump too quickly. But . . . I want to be brave this time."

"I do, too," he says, and then with one swift motion, he reaches forward and unplugs both our pairs of headphones, effectively taking us off the air.

Outside the studio, our coworkers throw their arms in the air and bang fists against the glass, but no one rushes inside.

"I love you," he says only to me, a hand cupping my cheek, thumb tracing along my jaw. "I'm in love with you, Shay."

"Dominic." We're breathing in time with each other now, as steady as my mother's metronome. "I love you. I love you so much. I love your radio voice and your cast-iron skillets and the way you wrapped my dog in a T-shirt when he was scared, and I even love your Beanie Baby collection."

He plugs his headphones back in with one hand, still holding on to me with the other. "I fucking quit, by the way," he says.

And then, because I'm feeling powerful: "Fuck you, Kent." I say it into the mic, crisp and clear, relishing the strength in my voice. "Enjoy your fucking fines!" Then I rip out the cord.

"I love you," I say again to Dominic, unable to stop. I grab the collar of his shirt and pull him close as his hands slide into my hair. "I love you, I love you, I—"

His mouth meets mine, warm and sweet and certain. My past and my future—because he has always felt like home.

And even though we're in a soundproof both, I swear I hear people cheering.

Epilogue

"You can take away my EKTORP and my MALM, but you can't take away my VITTSJÖ," Dominic says, wrapping a protective arm around the bookshelf in his living room.

"It doesn't match any of my furniture!"

"No no no," he says. "The beauty of IKEA's minimalist designs is that they go with everything."

I take a step back, assessing it, and relent. "I guess we could put it in our guest room." It might actually look nice in there. That room could use some sprucing up.

Dominic brightens, that lovely smile spreading across his face. He's been doing that a lot since I asked him to move in a couple weeks ago. "*Our*," he says, and it might be my new favorite word. "I like that a lot."

It takes us a few hours to load everything into the U-Haul, with a break for some Thai takeout we eat on the floor after realizing we maybe shouldn't have packed up all the chairs first.

"Ready to say goodbye to this place?" I ask as we stand in the doorway, giving it one last look. The walls are bare, everything either packed in the truck or donated to Goodwill.

"Truthfully? I've been ready since I moved in." He hooks his arm around my shoulders, drops a kiss on the top of my head. "But I'm really glad this is the reason it's happening now."

In the truck, Dominic flips through the radio presets, panic flashing in his eyes when one of them turns out to be 88.3 FM. I haven't been able to listen to PPR since I stormed the offices during their pledge drive three months ago. Not yet. It helps that Kent was let go, but there are still too many grim memories attached to it.

So I surprise both of us when I say, "Leave it," before he changes the station.

"You sure?"

I swallow around a lump in my throat and nod. It's the top of the hour, so we listen to an NPR newsbreak. And damn if those NPR voices aren't still the most soothing journalistic lullaby.

A few seconds into a local story from Paul Wagner about Seattle's housing market, I bail. "That's about all I can handle for today," I say, switching the station to Jumpin' Jazz with Paloma Powers. Apparently I like jazz now. Human beings really are capable of change.

Steve is waiting to greet us, pawing at our legs until he's received a sufficient amount of pets. Then I give him a new chew toy to keep him occupied while we unload boxes of Dominic's clothes, toiletries, and cookware.

"How did you manage to sneak this in?" I ask, holding up a collectible glass box with a Beanie Baby inside. A white bear with a heart on its chest.

"We hold on to Valentino for a few more years, and we've got it made." Dominic taps the box. "This guy's gonna put our kids through college. I can feel it."

After we've emptied the truck, I stand back and take a look at my living room—our living room. We have plenty of rearranging to keep us busy for the next few days, but I don't hate the moving-day messiness. We swapped my TV for his larger one, draped a fringed blanket of his across the couch. One of Ameena's Blush 'n Brush landscapes is hanging in the hallway next to a framed photo of Dominic and me hiking on Orcas Island. Even though we've taken plenty of photos since then and we weren't officially together in that shot, it's still my favorite one of us.

The guest room, too, is looking much less sad. Along with the VITTSJÖ bookshelf, we added a vintage lamp from his parents' antique shop, and we have plans to paint the whole house together once we're a bit more settled. We might host Ameena and TJ or Dominic's friends from college, many of whom he's rekindled relationships with, sometime soon. There's a novelty: guests for the guest room.

This house used to feel like some adulthood status symbol. Maybe I didn't have the rest of my life figured out, but I had these walls and windows, these objects without memory. That was all they were: things I hadn't attached meaning to yet. It became a home long before Dominic and I decided to move in together, and Steve helped, but more than anything, I think I just needed time to learn to love it on my own terms. I grew into that love, into this place, and I can't believe I wanted to rush it.

We're so wiped that we're in bed by nine o'clock. Our new larger dresser will arrive next week, but for now I like the way Dominic's clothes live next to mine. All of this is new to me, and I tell him as much when we slide beneath the sheets.

"It's going to be good, though," he says. "I can't wait to learn all the weird things you do when you're alone."

"They can't be worse than you wearing a blanket as a cape and pretending to cast spells on Steve."

"That was one time! And I really thought you were still in the shower."

I snuggle closer, laughing into his shoulder. His arms come around me, a thumb stroking the space between my shoulder blades. It hasn't sunk in that we get to fall asleep together like this every night, that I'll wake up next to him every morning.

"I love you in this house," I say. "I've thought so since the first time you came over. I was too scared to say anything, but you just felt so right here. It was the worst, feeling all those things and not knowing if you were feeling them, too."

He grasps me tighter. "I was. I was feeling them so much that it killed me to leave. It killed me to leave every time."

Even now, hearing that does something to my heart. "Can you believe we hated each other a year ago?"

"I think you mean a year ago, we were on our third or fourth date. I believe that was the one where I demonstrated some of my raw sexual energy."

"I might need a refresher," I say, but he's already rolling me on top of him, his hands on my hips, and together we discover maybe we weren't that exhausted after all.

The doorbell rings at ten thirty the next morning, while Dominic's in the kitchen breaking in one of his new cast-iron skillets. A spinach and red pepper frittata. I've already canceled my meal delivery service.

"Sorry I'm early, I was just so excited," Ruthie says when I answer the door. She sniffs the air. "That smells amazing."

"Hey, Ruthie," Dominic calls. "Help yourself."

The three of us settle in at the kitchen table, catching up. Ruthie's working in public relations and loving it, which is a huge relief.

"But I'm still not sure if it's my forever job," she says.

I lift my glass of orange juice. "Join the club."

"You're going to find something," Dominic says with a squeeze of my shoulder. "It's okay to want to wait for the right thing."

And I know he's right. That's what I'm doing: taking this time to explore in a way I've never done before.

"You two seem to be nesting quite nicely." Ruthie stands up, craning her neck to look down the hall. "But are you gonna make me beg to see it?"

Dominic and I exchange a glance, his mouth slipping into a half smile. "Okay," he says, and we lead Ruthie into the room that used to be my office. The one I used probably less frequently than the guest room.

Her hand flies to her mouth. "Holy shit, it's beautiful."

There are twin microphones at the desk, giant headphones connected to a brand-new recording system. Acoustic panels on the walls for soundproofing.

Our own little studio.

Dominic ducks out to grab a few glasses of water and the notes we've spent the past month working on. Ruthie makes herself comfortable in the chair closest to the computer.

"Are we ready?" she asks.

I take a deep breath, my gaze snagging on Dominic's. The determination on his face makes me brave, and the warmth in his eyes makes me certain. I am. I'm ready because this has always been in my blood. Because for me, radio has never been about the hashtags or the rankings or the fame. It's always been about the people.

"Yes," I say, and then I hit record.

Relationship Goals, Episode 1

Transcript

SHAY GOLDSTEIN: So I think we have to start with an apology.

DOMINIC YUN: We've been doing a lot of apologizing lately. I think we've gotten pretty creative with it, yeah?

SHAY GOLDSTEIN: That's true. I don't think I'll ever be able to accept another apology from someone unless it's done on the air during a public radio pledge drive. It's just not going to feel authentic.

DOMINIC YUN: But in all honesty, we're truly sorry to anyone who listened to *The Ex Talk* and thought we were together. We were part of the lie from the beginning, and we deeply apologize for that.

SHAY GOLDSTEIN: The honest truth, since we're all about honesty now, is that we kind of crashed and burned on public radio. And I realized I'd spent all my life on public radio, when our show had the most success as a podcast. Shout-out to our new distributor, Audiophile, who approached us with this idea for a new show. So this is *Relationship Goals*, and we're going to focus on all kinds of interesting relationships, not just romantic ones. We're going to try really hard to make it up to everyone who was a fan of the first show.

DOMINIC YUN: In case you want a status update on our relationship, we've been together for real for three months, ever since that pledge drive.

SHAY GOLDSTEIN: And it's going well. Dominic actually moved in yesterday.

DOMINIC YUN: It's your typical coworkers turned enemies turned fake exes turned cohosts turned real romantic partners kind of love story.

SHAY GOLDSTEIN: I know, I know, it's a little overdone.

DOMINIC YUN: And we can swear!

SHAY GOLDSTEIN: Fuck yes we can! And we have a familiar name helping us behind the scenes. Ruthie, you want to say hi?

RUTHIE LIAO: Hi, guys!

SHAY GOLDSTEIN: Ruthie's our fantastic producer, and you may remember her from both *The Ex Talk* and *Puget Sounds*, a local show she and I worked on back at Pacific Public Radio. She doesn't like being on the radio, so—

RUTHIE LIAO: Bye, guys!

SHAY GOLDSTEIN: We're trying to view this podcast as more of a hobby than a job, which means, yes, I'm still job hunting. Storytelling was always what I loved most about radio, and I'm curious about exploring it in other mediums. I've been taking classes, doing research . . . you know, just trying to figure out what to do with my adult life.

DOMINIC YUN: And I've been doing some work for a startup that's building a new platform for nonprofit fundraising.

SHAY GOLDSTEIN: He's great at it.

DOMINIC YUN: You are such a suck-up.

SHAY GOLDSTEIN: A cute suck-up?

DOMINIC YUN: Obviously.

SHAY GOLDSTEIN: Public radio will always have a place in my heart, but we're both really excited about this new venture. We hope you stick with us.

DOMINIC YUN: We're not sure where it'll go from here, but I think it's going to be a pretty good story.

SHAY GOLDSTEIN: And now, a word from our sponsors.

ACKNOWLEDGMENTS

For a long time, I wanted to write a novel about public radio, and I absolutely couldn't have done it alone. My agent, Laura Bradford, gave me some early encouragement and spot-on advice, and continues to be a stellar advocate. Thank you for helping me find my dream career. It feels surreal that I get to write books for a living.

I'm so grateful to have found the perfect home for *The Ex Talk* at Berkley and with Kristine Swartz. Kristine, your enthusiasm and expert editorial guidance have made this process so much fun! Thank you for loving my messy cohosts as much as I do. Thank you to art director Vi-An Nguyen for this stunning cover—I'm obsessed! Thank you, too, to the rest of the fantastic Berkley team: Jessica Brock, Jessica Plummer, and Megha Jain.

Erin Hennessey and Joanne Silberner—this book would not exist if you hadn't taken a chance on me ten years ago and encouraged me with your knowledge of public radio. Erin, you had coffee with me and told me all about KPLU when you knew next to nothing about me. Joanne, you were the highlight of my senior year at the University of Washington. I am wildly lucky to have learned from you both. Many thanks to the other journalists I had the pleasure of working with at KUOW, KPLU (now KNKX), and the *Seattle Times.*

Tara Tsai, you are my favorite person to talk to about romance novels and podcasts. Rachel Griffin, thank you for your compassion and for somehow always knowing the right thing to say. Kelsey Rodkey, thank you for the perfect title and for telling me to stop apologizing. Much love to everyone who read this book in part or in whole at various stages of its life: Carlyn Greenwald, Marisa Kanter, Haley Neil, Monica Gomez-Hira, Claire Ahn, Sonia Hartl, Annette Christie, Auriane Desombre, Susan Lee, and Andrea Contos. I never truly felt like I belonged until I met other writers, and in that vein I am also so grateful to Joy McCullough, Kit Frick, Gloria Chao, and Rosie Danan.

The readers, booksellers, librarians, bloggers, and bookstagrammers who've shouted about my books for the past few years—"thank you" will never be enough. Your creativity and generosity floor me on a daily basis. Every post, every photo means the world to me. To my family and especially to Ivan, thank you for being so excited about this one. Journalism and radio have been part of our story almost since the beginning, which makes it kind of perfect that my radio book is a romance.

Finally, thank you to all the podcasts that I refresh-refresh-refresh until the latest episode appears, the shows I can't imagine my life without, the hosts who feel like friends and make me laugh even on my worst days. I hope I did you justice and captured some of that magic.

Photo by Sabreen Lakhani

Rachel Lynn Solomon worked in public radio before her love of storytelling carried her to fiction. She's the author of several books for teens and adults and will tell anyone who'll listen that it really doesn't rain that much in Seattle, where she lives with her husband and tiny dog.

CONNECT ONLINE

RachelSolomonBooks.com

🐦 📷 RLynn_Solomon

Ready to find
your next great read?

Let us help.

Visit prh.com/nextread

Penguin
Random
House

No female was impervious to Sawyer Buchanon.

Except Jade. Even if he had a kind side, and he did, and even if she found him attractive—and who wouldn't?—he was a Buchanon. And her maiden name was on his father's naughty list.

He spotted her inside the dim room with the baby and raised both palms in a comical, supplicating gesture.

"What's this? You've ditched me for a younger man?"

"His toothless grin was irresistible."

Sawyer paused for one second as if her banter caught him off guard. She knew he considered her humorless and cold, which was for the best, but she wasn't always that way.

Crossing the room, Sawyer swooped Ashton into his arms. "You ready? Where's the squirt's bag?"

She reached for the backpack but Sawyer beat her to it, swung it over his opposite shoulder, and they headed out for the day.

The sight of the man with a baby in his tanned, muscled arms tugged at Jade's insides. He was a puzzle she couldn't fit into her tidy mental box.

Linda Goodnight, a *New York Times* bestselling author and winner of a RITA® Award in inspirational fiction, has appeared on the Christian bestseller lists. Her novels have been translated into more than a dozen languages. Active in orphan ministry, Linda enjoys writing fiction that carries a message of hope in a sometimes dark world. She and her husband live in Oklahoma. Visit her website, lindagoodnight.com, for more information.

Books by Linda Goodnight

Love Inspired

The Buchanons

Cowboy Under the Mistletoe
The Christmas Family
Lone Star Dad
Lone Star Bachelor

Whisper Falls

Rancher's Refuge
Baby in His Arms
Sugarplum Homecoming
The Lawman's Honor

Redemption River

Finding Her Way Home
The Wedding Garden
A Place to Belong
The Christmas Child
The Last Bridge Home

Visit the Author Profile Page at Harlequin.com for more titles.

Lone Star Bachelor

Linda Goodnight

HARLEQUIN® LOVE INSPIRED®

LOVE INSPIRED BOOKS

Recycling programs
for this product may
not exist in your area.

ISBN-13: 978-0-373-62279-5

Lone Star Bachelor

www.Harlequin.com

Printed in U.S.A.

Out of the same mouth proceed
blessing and cursing. My brethren,
these things ought not to be so.
—*James* 3:10

For my forever friend, Trisha Hayes. We've been
through a long journey together over many
years and many tears, laughter, music and kids.
Always, always, I knew I could lean on you for
prayer and love and enduring friendship.
And the turquoise jewelry ain't bad either!
Love you, sweet lady. This one is for you.

Chapter One

It was now or never. Walk up to that door and knock or drive back to the office and give the case to someone else.

From behind the wheel of her plain white Chevy Cruze, Jade Warren eyed the housing complex next to the smooth green golf course of Gabriel's Crossing, Texas. She wasn't a bit surprised that Sawyer Buchanon lived in such a nice place. His family's construction company had likely built the buff brick townhomes, something she would know if she'd done her computer homework. But the impulse to immediately drive to the river town and face the dragon had overshadowed her usual rigid work ethic.

Do the job. Do it right. Don't get involved.

Which was exactly why she shouldn't have accepted this assignment.

She *was* involved. She'd been involved for years. Being here, accepting this investigation, made her a traitor.

But frankly she was tired of chasing absconding debtors and deadbeat exes. She wanted a case with meat on the bones, something she could sink her investigating teeth into.

Most of all, she was curious about her family nemeses, the dreaded Buchanons.

To hear her daddy tell it, the Buchanons breathed fire and plotted the demise of anyone they didn't like. And they always won. She'd grown up despising a group of people she'd never met.

Until today.

A pretty redhead exited the front door of number 4, Sawyer Buchanon's home. Figures. Very little investigative skill was required to learn Sawyer liked women and they liked him back. His social media was loaded with messages and photos from beautiful females.

The shapely, jean-clad redhead hopped into the cab of a bloodred F-150 pickup complete with a big white toolbox across the back.

Jade waited until the woman pulled away, the truck's mufflers rumbling, before leaving her nondescript car to walk across the lush, manicured grass, up the clean-swept sidewalk past recently groomed boxwood to ring the doorbell.

Before she had time to put on her game face, Sawyer Buchanon, in gray athletic pants and white T-shirt, opened the door.

Jade thought she had prepared for this moment. She'd seen his photos. She knew he was very handsome and was determined not to react, not to become distracted from the case, or worse, become an idiot female and simper.

She swallowed and breathed slowly through her nose in a concerted effort to keep her expression cool and passive.

Photos didn't do the man justice. Messy midlength hair, vivid blue eyes and a morning scruff as black as his hair.

Every female cell in her body reacted. She held the reaction inside, tightening her mouth to a determined thin line.

Sawyer flashed a movie star smile, a little crooked and a lot breathtaking.

Jade clamped her back teeth against her cheek until pain shot from the roof of her mouth to the top of her head.

There. Better. He wasn't *that* good looking.

"Did you forget somethi— Oh, I thought you were Clare." He poked his head around the door and looked toward the driveway. "She just left."

Right. The redhead.

Jade stuck out a hand, her words intentionally crisp. "I'm Jade Warren, Paris Investigations. Is this a good time for us to talk?"

His smile faltered, replaced by a look of bewilderment. "You're the private investigator my father hired?"

"Yes. Is there a problem?" She braced for it.

"Does my dad know you're…?"

Her hackles rose. "A woman?"

"I was going to say pretty." He flashed the smile again, eyes alight with mischief, and stepped to one side. "Come in. I was about to have a Coke. Want one?"

She shook her head. "Too early in the morning."

"That's what I've been told." He led the way into the living room. The interior surprised her somewhat. Given his reputation, she'd expected a bachelor's lair but was met with clean, simple lines in tones of gray and white with splashes of maroon. Masculine. Tasteful. Jade settled on the dove-gray sofa. Directly in front of it was a big-screen television mounted above a small tiled fireplace.

While Sawyer disappeared around a wall for his caffeine, she took out a notebook and jotted a few lines.

He popped back into the room. "I have coffee."

"I'm good, thank you."

He held up a single-serving coffee pod. "K-cups. Only take a minute. Would you rather have hot chocolate? Cider?" He turned the packet up close to his eyes and pretended to squint. "Caramel vanilla cream?"

She loved caramel vanilla cream. So, apparently, did

his legion of girlfriends. Probably including the shapely redhead.

With a soft hum, she scribbled *player* on her pad. Now he was showing his true colors. "Do you stock every flavor?"

"Never know when you'll need them." He grinned. "I aim to please."

Jade didn't roll her eyes but she came close. *Give it a rest, Romeo. I know your kind. I even have the scars to prove it.*

"How nice." She didn't smile. "I'd prefer to get down to business if you don't mind."

"Okay." Coke can in hand, he stood in the doorway between the living room and whatever was behind the wall. Kitchen, apparently. "Shoot."

She wished he would sit down. From her place on the couch she had to look up and it made her feel inferior. At a disadvantage. He was a good six feet tall but not particularly broad. Just fit and lean with the right amount of shoulders. Strong and muscular as she'd expect of a man who made his living with a hammer and his hands.

Not that she noticed shoulders. She'd never known any worth leaning on.

Nor did she allow herself to be intimidated. Maintaining a businesslike tone, she held his gaze and absolutely refused to blink first.

"I'm here to investigate the vandalism plaguing Buchanon Built Construction projects. Your father shared some background with my boss and I have the police reports, but I'll need you to fill me in on details from your perspective."

"You'd do better to discuss this with Brady. He's the site manager and COO of Buchanon Built." A pair of eyebrows, as black as sin's underbelly, twitched with a hint of amusement. "But he's in Italy on his honeymoon. Lucky duck."

Jade flipped through her notes. "Brady. Your older

brother. A pet project of his burned to the ground on New Year's Eve."

The handsome face darkened. "Arson. Abby's house. He was building it for her as a Christmas makeover."

"Abby. Brady's wife."

"Fiancée at the time of the fire."

She scribbled a note. "Interesting, but your father is more concerned about the photo recently found after a break-in."

Sawyer made a noise deep in his throat. "Dad has it in his head that Dawson or me—Dawson's my twin—is somehow to blame for all this trouble."

"Why would he think that?"

"Beats me. You'd think he'd focus on Brady. After all, Brady's project was torched, not mine, but someone leaves a picture and Dad suddenly points at us. Me in particular."

"Why you over Dawson?"

"The hair. His is different."

"And this was apparent in the photo?"

Sawyer emitted a frustrated breath. "Yep."

"I'll want to see that photo and speak to your brother, of course."

He jacked a thumb to the south. "He lives next door."

"Yes, I know."

He looked discomfited. "Exactly how much do you know about us?"

She curved her lips for the first time, a cat's smile that had nothing to do with humor. "The more I know, the faster I can solve this case."

"Buchanon Built has dealt with a vandalism problem off and on for going on two years." He pushed away from the wall, his body language clearly indicating he doubted her. "Do you seriously think you can discover something the police and fire investigators can't?"

He had no idea how much fuel his doubts added to her determination. "They have other cases. You have my full focus."

The smile appeared again. He was good at that. Flashing those white teeth against Texas-tanned skin with stunning effectiveness. "And you'll have mine."

His entire focus? She doubted that, not with gorgeous redheads coming and going at random. Women crawling out of the woodwork.

She held his gaze and refused to acknowledge the zip of energy caused by staring into eyes that flashed like blue lightning and were every bit as mesmerizing.

Cam was like this, charming and magnetic. And dangerous.

She ducked her head, annoyed at the direction of her thoughts. The ugly business with Cam was eons behind her and that's where it needed to remain.

During her four-year stint as a police officer, before joining Paris Investigations, she'd interviewed plenty of nice-looking men and dozens of creeps. A pretty face and infectious smile did not sway her. Not anymore. Cam had taught her a painful lesson she wasn't likely to forget.

So save your smiles for someone else, Mr. Buchanon. I know your kind.

"Do you have anything to hide? Anything you'd rather the rest of the world didn't know?"

He blinked, startled by the vehemence of the question. Good. She'd knocked the grin off his face.

After sipping at his soda in contemplation, he ambled across the living room and sank onto a chair across from her. Lanky, agile and oozing manly appeal.

"Are we exchanging secrets?"

She cocked an eyebrow at him, keeping her stare as cool

as November. *Get this straight, buster. I know the ploys of a handsome man and I will never, ever fall for that again.*

"Okay." He lifted a hand in surrender. "I guess that would be a negative. In which case, my answer is no. No secrets. No skeletons. Except for a couple of speeding tickets and maybe that one other time."

She sat up straighter. "What other time?"

He chuckled and pointed his Coke, clearly trying to rile her. "Got you interested, didn't I?"

Jade's insides did a slow burn. Mr. Playboy refused to take her seriously.

"Mr. Buchanon, this is a legal investigation, not a contest, and certainly not a joking matter. Do you, or do you not, want to find out who is sabotaging your building projects?"

He sobered. "Sorry. It's just that the whole idea of hiring a PI is ludicrous. A waste of money."

A red flag rose. Did he indeed have something to hide? Some reason he didn't want her to discover? "You object to the investigation?"

"I object to wasting time and money."

Maybe. But Buchanons had plenty. Maybe the money comment was a smoke screen. "Will I have your cooperation?"

"You will, but I don't know anything that's not in the police reports."

Her lips curved again in a humorless smile.

"Let me be the judge of that."

Sawyer squinted at the woman sitting on his couch and rubbed a hand over the discombobulated feeling in his chest while mulling the previous ten minutes.

Jade Warren, for some reason, had decided not to like him, and he tried to understand why. When he'd seemed surprised at seeing her standing on his itty-bitty porch, she'd jumped to immediate conclusions and practically accused him of misogyny.

He bit back a grin. Sawyer Buchanon was anything but a woman hater.

Granted, he'd been surprised at the investigator's gender considering her profession, but he certainly didn't object. Just as he didn't object to women in the construction business.

Take Clare Hammond, for instance. A great trim carpenter, she beat him to the job every morning. Like today, while he'd still been slouching around the town house, Clare had dropped by to return a set of miter clamps he'd inadvertently left behind. She'd been on the job since six. What a work ethic! And she was easy on the eyes, too.

Sawyer also knew Clare took flack at times for being a woman in what was traditionally a man's world, and being pretty was not to her advantage on a construction crew. She had to work hard to prove she was as good at her job as the men. Even then, some crews frowned on having a female on the job site.

But not Buchanon Built Construction Company. When Dad said equal-opportunity employer, he meant it. If a woman could do the job, do it well in a timely fashion and take the inevitable joking that happened on every crew, she was hired. Dad was no dummy. All he had to do was look around at his own family. The Buchanon women were as strong and independent as they came, and Sawyer respected those traits, just as he respected all women.

He also adored them. A woman like Clare who could work him into the ground fascinated him. Women were, in his view, the most blessed gender. They made the world a happier, prettier, kinder place.

So if he had to hang out with someone prying into

his life, he'd rather have the vulnerable-looking blonde with the bee-stung mouth than some trench-coat-wearing, smoke-scented gumshoe with an attitude.

Not that Miss Jade Warren didn't have an attitude. She did. A very cold attitude that said she suspected him of something heinous, like sinking the Titanic single-handedly.

She sat on the edge of his sofa, as straight and stiff as a planed two-by-four, hand poised over a notebook. Not a cell phone as he would have used for notes. An old-fashioned notebook.

Except for the clipped tone and suspicious gray eyes that seemed to take in every element in his living room, Little Miss Magnum PI looked too soft and small to investigate anything. Maybe that was her strategy to fool the guilty.

If Sawyer was guilty of anything, she'd have had him in handcuffs by now. Her long eyelashes, mysterious and dark against pale cheeks, captivated his attention.

She flicked a glance up at him. His breath stuttered and a moth took flight in his midsection.

Whoa. Weird. Nice weird but still weird. He liked women but he could normally maintain coherent thought in their presence.

Jade Warren was different.

There was no good reason in the world for him to be attracted to her. She was too cold, too tight-lipped, too suspicious. But interest bubbled up anyway.

A mouth like hers was made to smile, and he wondered what it would take to make her laugh.

Not that he saw that happening in the next five minutes. Talk about chilly—and yet somebody needed to remind the woman of the outside temperature. Texas in summer scorched, but here she was in a nifty black business suit, tucked in and buttoned up as if she dared anyone to notice she was female.

Sorry to burst your bubble, lady. Even in long pants and sensible shoes—also black—you are all woman. Above the white button-down blouse was a pair of fascinating gray eyes. The color of his couch. Smoke and mystery.

Sawyer took a stinging gulp of Coke, letting the burn brand some sense into him. At the Huckleberry Addition, he had a massive built-in china hutch waiting for his hammer and expertise. He couldn't sit here and contemplate the novelty of a female private investigator who'd managed to both insult and interest him. Maybe more than interest him.

He glanced at his watch. "Ask me whatever you need to. But talk fast. I have to meet my brother at the building supply center in thirty minutes."

"We have a lot to discuss. I need more time with you than that."

He tilted his head. "Time's an important commodity for me, too."

"When can we meet again?"

Sawyer couldn't help himself. He grinned. "Are you asking me out?"

She glared icicles at him. The temperature in the room fell ten degrees. No wonder she wore a black suit. The chill emanating from her could cause frostbite.

Sawyer rubbed his bare arms and fought back a grimace. Prickly little woman, this PI. Pretty and prickly.

"Mr. Buchanon—"

"Sawyer." He held up a hand. "Before you pounce, I apologize. Joking around is my style."

"Not mine."

Sawyer bit back a sigh.

Well, wasn't she more fun than a dental drill? Maybe Dad should have hired a smoke-scented gumshoe after all.

Chapter Two

The Gabriel's Crossing Building and Supply Company spanned a full block and was one of Sawyer's favorite places to shop, if you called buying boards and nails shopping.

Employees knew him by name and catered to his needs as a trim carpenter specializing in beautiful cabinetry and other built-ins. To top it all off, the coffee and popcorn were free.

He stood next to the fragrant machines, munching hot, salty corn while waiting for Dawson. His twin had hit the neighborhood pool early this morning while Sawyer ran five miles around the golf course, their usual routine. Sawyer ran. Dawson swam. He'd not bothered to inform the know-it-all investigator of this fact. That she hadn't headed over to Dawson's condo was a good sign that she already knew their daily routines, an unsettling thought. Though he had nothing to hide, he wasn't wild about the idea of someone knowing his every move. Invasive. Like Big Brother or something.

"Sawyer, good morning. May I help you?"

A dark-haired woman in glasses wearing a red apron and carrying a tape measure approached. She'd worked here in the Building and Supply a long time but he could never remember her name. "I'm good. Thanks."

She paused in front of him as if she had something important to say. "I guess you're waiting for Dawson."

"Yep. As usual, I'm here and he's late."

"You're always so punctual. Can I get you anything while you wait? Popcorn or maybe a coffee?" When he hoisted his popcorn bag, she continued, "We have some new router bits you might want to see."

"Thanks, but no. I like to create my own custom designs."

Her smile faltered. "Oh."

She seemed disappointed and he didn't like to hurt anyone's feelings. "On second thought, if those router bits are handy, I'll have a look. Okay?"

The clerk perked right up. She smiled and pushed at her glasses. "I'll grab the examples for you. We have some pretty ones I'd love to have in my new home. When I get married, I mean." Her cheeks reddened.

He glanced at her name tag. Nora. "Are congratulations in order? You getting married soon?"

"Oh. Well. I hope so." She blushed a deeper crimson and flapped a hand in front of her face. "I'll get those samples."

"Thanks, Nora."

Still blushing and smiling, she hurried off.

Mouth dry from the popcorn, Sawyer poured himself a cup of coffee. He wasn't a big coffee man, but the other Buchanons lived on the stuff. Cut a Buchanon and he bled sawdust, coffee and family loyalty.

He stirred too much cream into the foam cup and heard his brother say, "Why not have a glass of milk?"

"Hey." He left the coffee sitting and turned to Dawson, whose black hair was still wet and shiny from his swim. He was a good-looking dude, even if Sawyer did say so.

The same height, with the same face, he and his brother were best friends, though their personalities were different.

Dawson was a calm, introspective guy who counseled family and friends with a gentle God-directed wisdom. Dawson was, in a word, sensitive, and noticed nuances and undercurrents in relationships that Sawyer invariably missed.

Sawyer was— Well, he was different. He'd rather make people smile.

"I had a visitor this morning."

"Yeah? Who?" Dawson confiscated the abandoned coffee cup and sipped.

"Private investigator."

The unflappable brother gave a facial shrug. "Dad warned us."

"He didn't warn us about one thing."

An eyebrow shot up. "Yeah? What's that?"

"She's a woman. A young, beautiful woman. Maybe thirty. About this tall." Sawyer indicated shoulder height. "Wavy blond hair to her shoulders. Kind of soft and vulnerable looking. Not your stereotypical PI."

Dawson saluted him with the cup. "You sure noticed a lot about her. You must be interested."

He was, and he couldn't figure out why. "You need to meet her before you form an opinion. Tough lady."

"Hard-boiled?"

"Cold as a grape Popsicle in January."

"Aw, poor Sawyer." Dawson pulled a silly face. "The lady wasn't charmed."

"Not one bit."

Dawson chuckled and toasted him with the cup. "Losing your touch, bro."

The salesclerk—Nora—came around an end cap struggling to juggle several blister-wrapped packages with four wooden cabinet doors. Sawyer leaped forward to help. "Let me carry those. That's too much for one lady."

"Thank you." She beamed up at him as he stood close enough to take charge of the wooden doors. "These are the new router designs. When I saw them, I thought of you."

Sawyer sorted through the stack, sharing each one with his twin. "Nice. What do you think, Dawson? Can we use some of these?"

Dawson put his finger on one. "This would look great in the Carter house in the Huckleberry Addition."

Nora, standing between the brothers, frowned up at Sawyer. "The Carter house? Is that a new one? I don't remember seeing any invoices with that name."

"It was a spec home until Charity sold it a couple of days ago. Now that we know the owner, we'll be coordinating on the final details with the Carters." Sawyer tapped the router design. "I agree with Dawson. This one's great, but maybe we could take samples of all of them for showing? You never know a buyer's taste."

"Sure!" she said. "We can do that. I'll go in the back and have the guys run some scrap boards for you to take along."

Dawson reached in his pocket and removed two master keys. "Almost forgot. Can you make a couple of copies from these?"

Her smile broadened. "Be glad to. Should I mark them so you'll know them apart?"

"Good idea." He indicated the project name for each key. "Thanks, Nora."

"Anytime." She started off but turned back, gaze falling on Sawyer. "If you need anything else, let me know."

She left them, and the brothers got down to business, going over their respective phone lists of supplies they needed for today's work.

"I think you have another admirer," Dawson said as they walked through the supply building.

"Who?" The private investigator flashed into Sawyer's head. Jade—pretty name, but hard as the jewel she was named for.

"Nora, dimwit. You need an update on your navigation system?"

"The clerk? Nah, she's a great employee. She helps everyone like that."

Dawson tossed the empty cup into a trash can. "She's never brought me samples to look at. Except that time she thought I was you."

"Nothing unusual about that." They were mirror twins. Dawson was right-handed and Sawyer a leftie. Each had an identical birthmark but on opposite shoulders. But many people still confused them because they were otherwise identical. They'd dealt with the twin confusion all their lives and had used it to their advantage many times, particularly during the ornery middle school years.

"Except she called me Sawyer and sort of gushed, getting all red like she did a minute ago." Dawson pitterpattered a hand over his heart.

"Give it a rest. After being grilled by the private investigator this morning, I'm not thinking about women." None except the PI.

"That bad, huh?"

"You'll get your turn. What I can't figure out is why the focus is on me."

"The photo was you."

True. No matter how he combed his hair, the part fell naturally to the left. Dawson's on the right. Otherwise, they'd never have figured out an identity. Weird that he didn't recall when or where the photo was taken.

"Just because a picture of me was found on a vandalized site doesn't make the discovery significant. Maybe the photo has nothing at all to do with the case."

"Convince Dad of that."

"Right," Sawyer said. "Dad and one female Sherlock Holmes."

The Red River Roost, a long, old-fashioned strip motel complete with a rooster perched in crowing posture above the flashing vacancy sign, looked a little tired but offered extended stays for a price that fit Jade's expense budget. Dale Trentworth, owner of Paris Investigations, squeezed every penny and expected his employees to do the same.

Jade knew all about pinching pennies, and the River Roost, as the manager called the place, wasn't too bad. Located in a residential area on the far side of Gabriel's Crossing, the place should be quiet and restful, and that was all she required.

She pulled her Chevy into the spot in front of Unit Three and got out, peeling off her jacket as she approached her room. To say she was sweltering in this black suit would be a gross understatement. She was a cooked goose, a roasted duck, a rabbit on a spit baking in the Texas sun. Sweaty and sticky, though the day was young, she tossed the jacket over her elbow.

She knew better than to wear black this time of year, but she'd wanted to appear professional and in control. If she'd arrived at Sawyer Buchanon's house in a dress and spiky heels, he might have turned on the charm and distracted her from her questions. Not that he hadn't tried anyway. The man was a born flirt.

She had not been moved. Not one bit.

Well, perhaps a little, but she'd handled him and his charisma. Even if the picture of his too-handsome face kept flashing behind her eyes, she was proud of her cool, competent reaction.

Now that she'd established her professionalism and complete lack of interest in Mr. Playboy Buchanon, the black had to go.

A glance at her cell phone indicated plenty of time to change before her next appointment.

What she wouldn't give to slip into comfortable jeans and a cool tank top, but first impressions mattered in this business. To be taken seriously, she had to work harder than a man. A glance in the mirror wasn't required to remind her of how she looked. Petite. Fragile. An easy mark.

She was neither fragile nor easy, not anymore. But her size wasn't likely to change, and unless she succumbed to plastic surgery. Neither was her baby-doll face.

Well, she was no baby doll. Sawyer Buchanon and his kind better understand that from the get-go.

She was tough and determined.

Fishing for her key, she glanced around, taking mental snapshots of her surroundings. Police work had taught her to be always on the alert, though Gabriel's Crossing, Texas, was about as calm and peaceful a place as she could think of.

Yet someone had sabotaged the Buchanons' work projects. Bad things happened in small towns, only on a lesser scale.

The small motel was sparsely populated this weekday morning. Beneath the awning in front of the office sat a battered green pickup truck with a riding lawn mower in the bed. From somewhere nearby, she smelled the clean, fresh aroma of cut grass.

A gray late-model Hyundai was parked in front of Unit Eight and a cleaning cart sat outside Unit Seven. Out on the street, a black SUV motored slowly past, tires hissing against the hot pavement.

A few doors up at Unit One, a young strawberry blonde exited her room, a chubby-cheeked baby on her hip. Her gaze caught Jade's. She looked worried, her bottom lip caught between her teeth, brow furrowed beneath wispy bangs. She also looked like a kid, sixteen, seventeen at the most.

Watchful but concerned, too, Jade offered a smile. "Cute baby."

Babies got to her in a big way. She'd wanted two or three. Cam hadn't wanted any. He'd made that painfully clear.

The teenager shifted the baby on her hip. "Thanks. Say hi, Ashton."

She lifted the baby's little hand and waved. Jade waved back, and the friendliness must have been the encourage-ment the girl needed. She glanced toward the parking lot, squared her shoulders and walked the few feet to Jade's door.

Glad she hadn't unlocked her unit, Jade took the girl's measure. She was an inch or two taller than Jade and too thin, her pale skin devoid of makeup. Dressed in jean shorts and a pink T-shirt, she wore cheap flip-flops and had a pink Cupid's heart tattooed on top of her left foot. No other obvious identifying marks.

Jade relaxed. The girl presented no threat that she could detect. She was just a friendly, nervous teenager with a baby wearing only a disposable diaper.

"I was wondering." The girl darted a worried glance at Jade but quickly looked down at her shoes. "I need a ride. Ashton's out of diapers and…" She let the words trail away.

"You don't have a car?"

The red-blond ponytail swished from side to side. "No."

A dozen questions flashed through Jade's mind. Where

was this girl's family? What was she doing in a motel? Was she alone?

She caught on the last one. "Are you staying here by yourself?"

"Me and Ashton." The girl focused on the baby and then on Jade. She licked her lips and swallowed.

Nervous. Embarrassed.

Jade logged every movement, assessing. As a cop, she'd dealt with plenty of runaways. Was this another?

"Where do you live?"

The girl shrugged, but her face flushed crimson. "We got kicked out and moved here."

"Kicked out of where?" Jade was being nosy but this girl had asked for a ride. No harm in requesting information in exchange.

"My mom's place. She let me stay for a while after I had Ashton, but—well, money's tight and she has her own problems. She said it was time for us to take care of ourselves."

Nice family. "You have no one else? What about the baby's father?"

The girl rolled her eyes and made a rueful sound. "He skipped out a looong time ago."

The baby started to fuss and squirm in his mother's arms. Sweat beaded on his upper lip. Instinctively, Jade reached out and grasped the little guy's thrashing arm and wiggled it.

"Are you too hot, precious?" she crooned. "You sure are a handsome boy."

The baby quieted instantly, his big brown eyes latched onto her face.

"I think he likes you," the girl said hopefully.

Jade laughed, itching to hold him as she made a quick decision. Walking half a mile to the nearest store for diapers would be miserable for both mom and baby.

"What's your name?"

"Bailey."

"Okay, Bailey. I'm Jade. I need to change clothes but I won't be long. Fifteen minutes or so, maybe. Take the baby back to your room and stay cool. I'll knock on the door when I'm ready and I'll drive you down to the Dollar Store."

Relief washed over the girl like a sudden summer rain. "Thank you so much. I can't pay you but—"

Jade waved her off. The girl probably didn't have two extra nickels. "I'm glad to do it. Ashton is adorable."

And you break my heart.

The key caught and Jade entered the small motel room, grateful for the blast of cool air chugging from the wall unit.

The room was clean, but that was about all she could say for it. Bed, TV, desk and cheap chair with a tiny bathroom. "All the comforts of home."

She didn't plan to be here long. The Red River Roost would do until she finished the investigation and returned to her nice apartment in Paris, Texas.

Resisting the urge to jump in the shower and cool off, she changed tops and jackets, opting for a white blazer and orchid button-down. Still professional, but definitely cooler.

From beneath the mattress, she withdrew her tiny laptop and booted up, taking a moment to check her email and run through some records sent by her boss, though nothing appeared pertinent to the Buchanon case. At least not yet.

As an afterthought, she pulled up Sawyer's Facebook profile. Social media was an amazing source of information to private investigators and police officers.

She scanned through the recent posts, pausing at one

with a puzzled frown. Sawyer had responded to a message with:

Praying for you, man. Hang in there.

In another, he'd posted a scripture.

No one had mentioned his religious affiliation, but Jade had experience with men who wielded scriptures like a weapon. Her father was one of them, battering her, her brothers and mother over the head with the Bible whenever the words suited his intent.

Granted, Sawyer's scripture had been encouraging, not scathing, but religious fanatics were always suspect in her book. Closing the lid, Jade slid the laptop back into its hiding place. She exited the room, still pondering the complexities of human beings, one in particular. She wondered if Sawyer's twin would prove as interesting.

Chapter Three

Buchanon Built Construction Company was housed in a warehouse on the edge of Gabriel's Crossing, not far from the railroad tracks and the downtown area. Every day at least four times, a train rumbled through town, shook the earth, rattled windows and made dogs howl. Townsfolk like Sawyer barely noticed unless they were stuck at the railroad crossing. Like this morning.

When Sawyer finally arrived at the warehouse with Dawson pulling in behind him, a row of familiar pickup trucks had parked at an angle in front. UPS and a flatbed lumber truck unloaded supplies through the end double doors, the clatter of their labor enlivening the quiet, sunny morning. Summer in Gabriel's Crossing meant construction work and plenty of it. Business for the Buchanon family was not good. Business was great.

Sawyer entered through the front door, stepping into the main offices where a U-shaped desk filled most of the room. Two of his sisters were behind the business center, already busy, and the ever-present scents of coffee and new wood welcomed him in.

"Did you bring doughnuts?" Allison asked. His petite sister could normally eat anything without gaining weight, but lately she'd put on a few pounds, mostly around the middle. She was hungry all the time.

"You'd be better off eating something healthy, Allison." Jaylee, stick thin, was super health conscious and happily nagged the rest of them on a regular basis about their food choices. They mostly ignored her.

"I am eating healthy." Allison patted her barely rounded belly. If he hadn't been reminded a hundred times, Sawyer wouldn't even know she was pregnant. "But baby Hamilton wants a doughnut with his milk this morning."

Sawyer held up a white box. "Uncle Sawyer to the rescue."

Allison sucked in a deep, appreciative breath. "My hero."

"I thought Jake was your hero."

"He is, but he's not here and you have doughnuts." She laughed, tossing her flippy dark hair.

"Did the poor guy already have enough of your pregnancy hormones and run away?" He knew better. Jake Hamilton was so thrilled over the expected baby he behaved as if he was the only man ever to experience fatherhood. Not that Sawyer would know a thing about that. Someday he'd like a passel of kids. It was the Buchanon way. But for now, he'd play the happy uncle and teasing brother.

"He and Manny are hauling bulls to the sale." Allison pumped her arm once. "Cha-ching. Gotta buy baby some pretties."

She reached for the doughnut box on the counter and flipped the lid open with an approving moan. "These are amazing. Which do you think is healthiest? The Bavarian cream? Does that count as dairy?"

Jaylee snorted. "If you're going to eat one, pick the one you like best. *Healthy* and *doughnuts* are incompatible terms."

Sawyer reached across the counter and took a chocolate-iced pastry. "Coke, popcorn and doughnuts. My breakfast of champions."

Jaylee swatted at him with a stack of paper. He laughed and added, "I promise to eat a salad for lunch. Anything I need to know before I head on over to the job site?"

"Dad's in the back. He wants to talk before you leave."

Beyond the office space was a conference area for family and vendor meetings and anything else that required a gathering place. Quinn, the family architect, worked there for peace and quiet and because he'd been a reclusive grump since moving home from Dallas a couple of years ago. However, since falling in love with Gena Satterfield, the local nurse practitioner, Quinn was a lot easier to be around.

"Sure thing." Sawyer sauntered through the doorway, mouth full of fried dough. Dawson followed.

When he saw the woman standing stiff as the Statue of Liberty at the end of a long table, he nearly choked.

The fiery attraction he'd hoped was a fluke seared up the back of his neck.

His father, standing next to her, waved them in. "Sawyer, I think you've met Jade Warren from the private investigation firm."

Sawyer battled the doughnut and managed to swallow down the thick lump.

The attraction was an entirely different matter. It raced through his bloodstream like molten lava. Nice. And weird.

He liked fun-loving, happy women with sunny dispositions and lots of laughter. Why did he find the serious, unfriendly Jade so compelling?

"Well, if it isn't Nancy Drew." He offered an intentionally flirty smile, hoping to loosen her up a little.

Her icy stare knocked the smile right out of him. She

nodded once, a head bob that was both dismissal and acknowledgment.

Did anything rattle Miss Prim and Grim?

"Let's have a seat," Dad was saying as he pulled out a chair for Jade. Sawyer would have done that. Wanted to do it. Instead he seated himself across from her and noticed she'd changed clothes. She was still buttoned to the top in a choke hold that could take out a sumo wrestler, but the light purple color looked good with her eyes.

Yeah. He was noticing way too much about a woman who really didn't want to like him.

He folded his arms on the tabletop and let his gaze linger on her deceptively sweet face while she talked in that crisp, no-nonsense manner that made him straighten his posture.

"Your father is creating a list of disgruntled employees." She flipped open the spiral notebook. "I'd like each of you to do the same for cross-referencing purposes."

Sawyer exchanged looks with Dawson and they both laughed. They still had the twin radar at times, knowing what the other thought. "Disgruntled? Would that include us brothers? We *stay* disgruntled."

"But Dad won't let us stop working." Dawson lifted his coffee cup in a salute.

Dan Buchanon smiled slightly. "My boys like to joke around."

"I see that." But she didn't crack a smile. "Does anyone come to mind immediately? Anyone who was fired, injured on the job, or caused a problem? No matter how small or seemingly insignificant the issue, I need to know."

The four men mentioned a handful of people but stalled out quickly. They ran a reputable business and treated employees well. Dan, a workaholic, could be tough and demanding, but Brady, Mom and the three sisters kept things running smoothly so that most employees loved to work for the Buchanons.

Everyone wanted to come to the Buchanon Built Christmas party and the Fourth of July cookout, the place where Dan handed out bonuses and gifts and goodies to show appreciation for the previous six months of success.

"This business goes back many years to Grandpa. Maybe our bad guy goes that far back, too." Dawson's usually serene face was troubled. "I'll give the list more thought."

Sawyer nodded. "Sure. I will, too."

"Have we provided enough to get started?" Dan pushed up from the table. He really was a workaholic. Sitting around for too long made him antsy.

Jade stood as well and tapped a pen against her notebook. "I want to see the vandalized sites today if possible."

"No problem." Dad aimed a finger toward Sawyer. "Sawyer will show you around. You can use the time to discuss anything in his past that may have set someone off on a vendetta."

"Dad! Come on. I'm not the guilty party here. And I have important work to do."

Dan held up a hand, his universal signal for "don't argue."

"Dawson can handle your load today." To Dawson, he said, "Call Clare Hammond to help out in Sawyer's place."

"Works for me." Dawson knocked back the last of his coffee and pushed to a stand. "Clare's a pro, almost as good as us."

Sawyer liked working with her, too. He could actually make Clare laugh, something he couldn't say for the PI. But maybe if he and Jade Warren spent some time together, if she got to know him better, she might loosen up. Maybe he'd even convince her that he was a good guy—a long shot, he thought with humor, but he was always up for a challenge.

And when had he ever refused a day off with a beautiful woman?

Jade's sensible shoes crunched on the gravel parking area outside the Buchanon offices as she made her way to her practical white Chevy. Even after driving her motel neighbor to the store and back, she'd arrived with plenty of time to spare for the meeting with the Buchanon boss. Now that she'd met the main man in person Jade felt better, more in control.

She wished her feelings were the same about Bailey Shaffer. The kid with the cute baby boy was barely seventeen and completely alone. No education, no job, no transportation. If not for public assistance, she and baby Ashton would have nothing. Bailey seemed like a sweet girl, and her love for Ashton showed on her face and in every action. She was a good, if too young, mother in a very bad situation.

Jade shook her head, knowing she should be focused on the job instead of the teenage mother. But she hurt for the girl and worried about her and the baby.

Sawyer Buchanon was behind her a few paces, having stopped to grab a doughnut from his sisters. He'd offered her one but she'd refused. She didn't know why. She loved doughnuts, especially the ones with chocolate icing and lots of sprinkles, but she didn't want Sawyer to think he could beguile his way under her skin.

Again, she couldn't put a finger on what it was about him. He ruffled her and she didn't like the feeling. It felt like attraction and that scared her. She had always been a sucker for handsome, smiling men until Cam Warren taught her a lesson she couldn't forget. She knew her weaknesses, so she had to be careful. She would not be a victim again.

"Hey, Jade. Hold up."

She stopped, one hand on her car door, keys ready. Sawyer ambled in her direction, the sun glinting on his black hair. He was built tall, like his brothers and father, lean, well-proportioned and fit, with long legs that ate up the ground in no time. She observed him as she would a suspect, wondering what kind of man lived inside that too-perfect body.

Her stomach clenched. Or was that flutters? Awareness flutters.

Annoyed to think it might be, she bit out a reply. "What?"

"Ride with me." He hitched his head. "My truck's over here."

"No need. I'll follow you in my vehicle."

His nostrils flared. He gave her a long, slow look that seared the ends of her hair. "Suit yourself."

Sawyer spun toward his big maroon pickup while Jade contemplated what she'd done. If she wanted to dig into the guy's past, she needed to spend time with him in his environment, get to know more about him than what was on his Facebook page.

Her refusal was a bad sign that he was causing her to react like a woman instead of an investigator. That simply would not do.

"On second thought, I might as well conserve fuel and ride with you." *Nice save, Jade.* And Dale would appreciate her sacrifice.

Sawyer spun back, boots grinding the gravel. He still didn't look happy, but Jade was certain she saw a triumphant gleam in his disturbingly attractive eyes.

Saying nothing, she grabbed her mini backpack containing camera, notebook, phone and wallet, and followed him to his truck. He opened the door, took her backpack and tossed it into the back of the double cab, and was about to help her up into the high passenger seat. She stared at his outstretched hand.

"I can do it."

His hand didn't budge.

She flashed a quick glance at his face. *Mistake.* Though he neither smiled nor spoke, he stood watching her, serene and easy, as if he helped women into his truck all the time. Which he probably did.

Ignoring him, if such a thing was possible, as well as his offered hand Jade grabbed the side of the door and started to boost herself up. She was woefully short.

Strong, masculine fingers steadied her elbow with exactly the right amount of pressure. Gentle. Steady. Dependable.

Pulse clattering, which annoyed her no end, Jade managed a terse "Thank you."

"No problem. It's the Buchanon way."

Whatever that meant.

These high cabs were a pain, but she was perfectly capable of helping herself. However, being treated with courtesy and respect was not a bad thing. She wanted that. Courtesy. Respect. But not the warm fuzzies Sawyer seemed to generate in her nerve endings.

As she settled into the oversize vehicle, Sawyer slammed the door, jogged around the front and hopped inside.

"Nice truck." Might as well start with his vehicle, always a good way to get a man talking about himself.

"I like it." He started the engine. A diesel rumble bubbled around them. "You want music?"

"I'm good. Whatever you usually do. Don't let me get

in the way." *Let me observe you in your natural habitat, like a lion or a grizzly.*

He flipped on the radio, and contemporary Christian music came through the speakers. He turned the volume to low. "You can change channels if you want."

She said nothing, but made a point to notice everything about the vehicle, jotting notes in her spiral book. The interior smelled like him—woodsy and male—and except for a pair of brown leather work gloves in the seat between them it was devoid of clutter. Unusual for a work vehicle.

She craned her head toward the truck bed. "Where are your tools?"

He kept his eyes on the road. "We pull a trailer onto the job site."

Somewhere between his house and now he'd lost his jaunty attitude and gift of gab. He was none too happy with her, and she was fine with that. He was, however, surprisingly polite about it.

They rode along in silence for a couple more minutes, through pleasant neighborhoods and into the heart of Gabriel's Crossing. The pretty little Texas town had been built near the Red River and, judging by the attention to curb appeal, probably belonged to one of those Main Street America organizations.

Large pots of geraniums and pansies decorated each corner with splashes of color, and brightly painted storefronts were well tended to show off everything from the latest boots and jeans to lawn mowers and lava lamps. A very good artist had painted a pioneer mural down the outside walls depicting a ferry crossing the river while men on horseback and families in wagons waited their turns.

"I don't know what good this will do."

She turned her attention toward him. Even though he

stared straight ahead at the street, Jade's stomach did that ridiculously annoying flutter thing. "Excuse me?"

"Visiting the damaged houses." He flicked a glance her way and then looked back at the road. Long, strong fingers lightly sprinkled with dark hair curled around the steering wheel at eight and two. Manly hands devoid of jewelry. A carpenter's hands. "All of them are repaired now and Abby's home is rebuilt. She and Brady put it up for sale."

Since their earlier meeting he'd shaved, a shame from a purely aesthetic perspective, but his smooth profile remained square-jawed perfection. A man ought not to look that good.

She swallowed and watched the passing town instead of Sawyer Buchanon, though her thoughts remained on him. Purely for professional reasons. He was her job.

"It's a new home. Why don't they live there?" she asked.

"Brady already had his own place out in the country when he and Abby realized they couldn't live without each other. They'll live in his house when they get back from Italy." He flipped on the signal light and slowed to turn. "You should see that place. It's spectacular. All kinds of golden wood and native rock. The house is huge, but then, so's my brother."

"I've heard that. He played football at Tech. Linebacker." She wasn't that much of a football fan but no one lived in Texas without being aware of the game.

Sawyer's gaze swung toward her, flashing lightning. He spoke easily but with a bite. "I've no doubt you know where all of us went to college, with info right down to our GPAs."

As a matter of fact, she did. She did not, however, think he would appreciate that information and since she wanted him to talk, she skipped right on past the comment.

"The police ruled out one suspect, Jake Hamilton. He's now your brother-in-law."

"Yeah. Pointing fingers at Jake was a mistake. He's all right. He treats my sister like a princess, and that's good enough for me."

"Then why did you suspect him as the vandal?"

He glanced over, eyebrow jacked. "Don't you already know this information?"

She flipped a page in her notebook. "I want to hear the story from your perspective."

With a button push, he silenced the radio. "Okay, then. In a nutshell. A hunting accident. Jake and Quinn were stupid kids, Quinn in college making a big splash as a pro-bound quarterback."

She knew all that, too, but let him talk. Everybody in Texas and most of America knew about the superstar football player. He'd been in the news, ESPN, *Sports Illustrated* and attended charity benefits constantly until the accident.

"He was up for the Heisman Trophy his freshman year."

"Sophomore, too. Quinn was the man with the golden arm and the big future until he and Jake decided beer and guns were a good mix. Mistaking him for a deer, Jake accidently shot Quinn."

Jade watched his profile, saw the tightening of his mouth and the way his Adam's apple bobbed. He still ached for his brother.

"Destroying his golden arm."

"Right. Quinn's had years of surgeries, rehab, physical therapy. He'll never be the same, but he's doing okay."

"I can see where that would generate some animosity, but why blame Jake for the vandalism?"

"My brothers weren't exactly excited when Jake and

Allison reconnected and fell in love. I think maybe Quinn and Brady were looking for a reason to blame Jake."

"Payback?"

"I suppose, but payback's not usually the Buchanon way." He lifted a finger and motioned toward a housing complex. "There's the Huckleberry Addition up ahead."

"Most of the vandalism has occurred here?"

"All except the time at Abby's house."

"Hmm." She scribbled in her book. "Her place was an anomaly, which may indicate a personal connection in that instance."

"Yes. Maybe. But if that's true, why are all the other crimes here in the Huckleberry Addition? We have other projects going on all the time. And why isn't Brady the focus of your investigation, considering the property was his makeover and the owner was his fiancée?" He pulled alongside a curb and stopped the truck.

"Fair question. My focus is on all areas, not you only." Definitely not. Not with the way her blood pressure spiked every time he beamed those electric eyes in her direction.

"Brady will get his share of attention when he returns from that honeymoon." She slid the backpack over her shoulder. "Unless I've already solved the case."

"I hope you can."

So did she. "Can we talk a minute before I see the homes?"

He paused, one hand on the door lever. "What about?"

"You."

His head dropped back and he groaned. "Dad won't be satisfied until you do, so go ahead. I have all day."

"Does that bother you?"

He hiked an eyebrow. "Does what bother me?"

"Spending the day with me."

Sawyer studied her for several uncomfortable seconds,

his expression serious. She expected some flirtatious remark, a come-on.

Instead, he said, "The jury is still out on that."

"Fair enough." She was disappointed and the reaction ruffled her. Why should she care one way or the other whether he enjoyed her company? He was a client, not a friend. "I'll need a list of all your friends, particularly women you've dated recently, along with their contact information."

"That's a bit invasive, isn't it?"

"Part of the investigation. Jilted girlfriends can sometimes harbor anger for a long time. You know the old adage. There is no fury like a woman scorned."

"Scorned?" He frowned and his eyebrows dipped as if she'd insulted him. "I'm not that kind of guy."

She'd be the judge of that. "Are you seeing anyone now?"

"Not anyone special, if that's what you mean. Are you?"

His tone was relaxed and conversational but Jade stiffened anyway. Her traitorous pulse jumped higher than a kangaroo on a trampoline.

With self-protecting snarkiness, she crossed her arms tightly and glared. "I'm asking the questions, if you don't mind. Who have you dated in the last month?"

Sawyer shifted in his bucket seat, bounced a fist against the steering wheel and, with a sigh, reluctantly mentioned two names.

He had to be lying. While assuring herself her interest was purely professional, she pressed. "That's all? Two?"

He gave her a puzzled look. "Clare and I are work pals, though, nothing serious there. We work together sometimes, so occasionally we grab dinner or watch a ball game. She's fun. Knows how to laugh and have a good time."

Was there something pointed in his remark? Did he think she was as dull as used dishwater?

With a sniff and an internal reminder that he was one of the subjects in this investigation, she tapped the other name on the too-short list.

"And Lacy?"

"Great girl. She golfs on the course near my house. We've played a few rounds. Gone out a few times."

The tension returned to her shoulders. "Are you still seeing her?"

"Not lately. Both of us have been too busy." He folded his arms over the steering wheel. "Is this really necessary? The women I know are good people. And I'm not all that. They aren't breaking into houses over me."

"Stranger things have happened."

He made a derisive hiss, like a tire going flat.

She asked a few more questions but Sawyer refused to say much about the women he dated beyond their names, even when she pushed back into his college days. He was popular. She knew that from his social media, but he didn't brag. If he'd had conquests or left a trail of angry broken hearts, he wasn't going to tell her. Jade found that both admirable and frustrating.

"I'm sure I'll have more questions later." She closed her notebook with a businesslike snap. "But for now, let's have a look at those houses."

"The interrogation is over. Big yea."

She hitched an eyebrow at him. "For now."

He exhaled a gusty breath, tilted his head back and looked toward the sky. "Great."

With a pinch of satisfaction at ruffling him, Jade pushed open the heavy door.

Sawyer came around to her side of the pickup but she'd already slid to the pavement, hitting with a jarring thud.

He noticed the abrupt landing but didn't say anything.

Her pride was getting the best of her. She should have waited for him. It was a long way down in these high-rise pickup trucks. Especially for a small person.

She straightened her blazer and her shoulders, but even with her best posture she struck Sawyer only about halfway up on his blue T-shirt. Right in that muscular bow of pecs and biceps.

"This was the first house hit," he said, "about a year and a half ago."

Jerking her attention to the house, Jade lifted her camera and snapped photos. The home he indicated, now occupied, was a beautiful modern brick with a double garage and bright red front door.

The other homes around the neighborhood were similar in style but unique enough to avoid the cookie-cutter look of some housing developments. Different colors or shutters, a few different designs. And the landscaping was the perfect blend of trees, small shrubs and smooth grass.

"The police report said the damage at this address was all cosmetic." She snapped more photos.

"Mostly paint and graffiti."

"Damage escalated with each attack. That has to be significant."

"I never gave it much thought, but I guess it did."

"One of the first things I looked at when I received the police reports." She'd laid them out end to end and created a spreadsheet, chronicling every bit of reported damage. "I graphed the escalation."

He flashed that smile. "Brainy woman. I like it."

She was, and she was also smart enough not to be led astray by a handsome face, blue eyes and a compliment. Even if he affected her blood pressure and didn't kiss and tell.

"Which other houses in this neighborhood were hit?"

"Come on. If you're up for a walk, I'll show you around."

"Of course." As a former cop, she stayed in top shape. A walk, even in the Texas heat, would not deter her.

Leaving the truck parked along the curb, they walked the area, four square blocks of beautiful Buchanon Built homes. Signs heralding their construction company stabbed the ground in front of several yet to be sold.

Sawyer's long legs outpaced her but when he realized she trailed him by several yards, he slowed, adjusting his speed to hers. In his relaxed manner, he chatted about the area, pointing out the attractive features like a real estate salesman.

He was easy in his skin, a confident man.

Across the street, a home owner with a toddler in tow exited one house and waved. Jade's thoughts zoomed to the young mother at the motel. She wasn't in Gabriel's Crossing to babysit teenage mothers but it wouldn't hurt to check on the pair after work, to make sure Bailey and Ashton had something to eat.

Sawyer lifted a hand and greeted the home owner by name.

"How are you doing, Maggie? Enjoying your new home?"

"Loving it. You guys do great work." She lifted the toddler into a car seat.

"Thanks. I'll pass along the compliment."

The woman waved again as she drove away.

Friendly. Attractive to women. Was Sawyer truly a nice guy? Or was his smile and friendliness a facade to get what he wanted? Like Cam's?

Troubled at the line of thought and the way she couldn't stop noticing Sawyer as a man, Jade forced her attention back to the houses. Do the job. Do it right. Focus on the investigation.

She asked questions, took photos, made notes and considered the location of this particular housing complex. They'd built on the edge of a rural area but close enough to town for convenience, a perfect location for those wanting expansive lawns and a little privacy without all those board fences. The kind of neighborhood where kids could safely play outside, roller-skate and ride bikes.

She'd love to live in a family-friendly place like this.

"Why this housing addition? Was there a problem with any of the nearby landowners? Did someone object to the city pushing out this far into the countryside?"

"Dad wrangled with the owner for a while over the price but in the end both parties approved of the agreement."

"Maybe. I'll need the previous owner's name and contact info."

"I think Leroy's already checked that out."

"Leroy?" She jacked a doubtful eyebrow. "The local police officer?"

Sawyer's easygoing nature disappeared. He bristled, eyes narrowed. "Leroy's a good cop and a great friend. He's done his best on this."

Here was another new side to Mr. Charm. Loyalty, willing to stand up for a friend.

"I didn't mean that as an insult. Leroy does a good job, but he's short-staffed, and a growing town stretches him to the limit. He could have missed something."

She raised the camera and snapped. A line of woods and a small creek flowed to the south of the houses. "This location is beautiful. I see the appeal. Do kids play in that creek?"

"Sure. It's very shallow. Perfect for tadpole fishing." He paused. "Ever been?"

She glanced at the sky, a pretty blue dabbled with cotton-ball clouds and with an egg-yolk sun perched halfway between morning and noon.

She wouldn't play his game. They were not friends having a chitchat.

"The only thing I'm fishing for is clues."

"You don't like to fish? To cast a lure in the water and get mocked by big, fat bass that swim around your line and laugh?" He made a casting motion and began to reel. With his left hand, she noticed. "And maybe, just maybe, if you hold your mouth right, you catch one off guard and—" He yanked back on his imaginary rod, pretending to battle a fighting fish. Suddenly his shoulders dipped and he relaxed. "Rats. Lost him."

She bit back a laugh.

Sawyer Buchanon was fun. No wonder women loved him. Caution would be her friend around this man.

"I haven't been fishing in years," she said. "Not since my brothers and I used to go to the lake on weekends. We'd rent a boat at the marina and play all day." Just the three of them, away from the stress of home. She smiled a little at the memory.

"Good memories, huh?" Sawyer's focus was on her face, interested. And she liked the feeling. "Do you water-ski?"

"I haven't in a long time. Do you?"

He tapped his chest. "King of the waves. Until Brady decides to make a sharp U-turn and dump me in the brink."

"That's mean."

"No, that's fun. The trick is to pay close attention so he can't lose me and, of course, to maneuver with my mad skills and precision—" He laughed to lessen the brag. "Challenge is the Buchanon way."

"I see what you mean. It sounds like fun." And she'd not allowed herself much fun in a long time. Oh, she went out with friends, had dinner and saw movies, but the outdoors had been her love as a kid. "You and your family spend a lot of time together? All of you?"

"Lots of time. We're our favorite people." His gaze slid over her. "I imagine you were good. At water-skiing, I mean."

"As a matter of fact, I was. Light and quick." She twitched an eyebrow and crossed her arms in a teasing challenge. "I think I could handle Brady's devious moves."

"I think you could, too." He grinned, his eyes all happy dancing. "Next time Brady takes the boat out, you should come with us. Two masters competing with the boat-rocking Brady."

The invitation was like ice water. What was she doing? Flirting with a client? With the kind of man she couldn't afford to like? And during an investigation, of all the in-appropriate times.

She dropped her friendly stance and stiffened. "I think we should concentrate on the investigation. Which of these homes is next on our list?"

He didn't say anything for a moment, but a tiny pucker appeared between his onyx eyebrows. After a long, thoughtful pause, he pointed to a pretty cream-colored brick. "That one."

They walked toward the house in silence. She was annoyed with herself. She was here to pry into his life, not let him pry into hers. At least she'd learned some useful information during the conversation. Nothing earth shattering but his family was close, he adored his brothers and he liked to fish and ski. He was an outdoors person. Like her.

She shut that line of thinking off so fast, she got a headache. Knowing more about him was a means to an end and part of her job. Nothing personal. Nothing personal at all.

Chapter Four

Much later, when they'd made the rounds of the Huckleberry Addition, Sawyer drove them back toward town. The private investigator intrigued him. One minute, when they'd discussed fishing and he'd done his best to be his usual enchanting self, she'd actually smiled. A second later, she'd bristled like a feral tomcat.

She didn't want to like him. He'd figured out that much, but he didn't know why. He wasn't the bad guy here.

He opened the pickup door for her and helped her up into the high cab. She didn't like that either, but his mama had raised him with manners, especially around ladies. Most women ate it up like a hot fudge sundae. Jade looked as if she wanted to throat punch him.

As he drove, he answered questions all the way. She was the most inquisitive woman he'd ever encountered. But every time he'd tried to ask about her, she'd shut him down.

The sun had moved to high overhead and his belly reminded him of the long gone popcorn and doughnut. He aimed the truck down First Street and pulled in front of the Buttered Biscuit Café.

Jade leaned forward, glaring out the windshield as if he'd driven her to a nudie bar. "What are you doing?"

"Eating. Private investigators eat, don't they?"

"I can grab something later."

He got out of the truck and went around, opening her door anyway. "You won't find a better lunch than the Biscuit's. Come on. I'll buy."

"I don't need anyone to pay for my meal."

A grin twitched his lips. "We'll fight over the check after you taste Jan's coconut cream pie."

She hesitated. "Homemade?"

He had her now. "With meringue three inches tall."

She didn't smile but she *did* capitulate. "Sold."

Score one for his team.

She let him help her down, another victory of sorts, though Sawyer didn't understand why they were in a battle.

He led the way inside, nodding to friends and a cousin as he found an open table. The café, as usual, was jammed and noisy with townspeople, most of whom he knew by their first names.

Jade walked alongside him, gazing around the small space with her usual intensity.

"Memorizing Jan's signs and slogans?" Every inch of wall space was crammed with signs or plaques, most of them snarky and clever.

She pointed at one. *Plenty of people have eaten here and gone on to live nearly normal lives.* "Pretty funny."

Then why didn't she laugh? "Jan's got sass but she sure can cook."

He pulled out a chair for her and stood, patient as Job himself. She could be stubborn. He could be patient.

Her full mouth flattened but she didn't yank away the chair and make a scene. Satisfied, Sawyer took the seat across from her and folded his arms on the laminated tabletop. He enjoyed seeing her straight on. She was nice to look at.

"Anything in particular sound good to you?" he asked.

Jade took a paper napkin from the metal container and shook it onto her lap. "You have recommendations?"

Sawyer studied the tiny mole—just one—to the left of her nose. He'd never noticed how appealing one single little beauty mark could be. "Plate lunch special."

She blinked. "What is it?"

"I didn't read the sign, but whatever it is will be good."

"Okay by me."

Nice. A woman who wasn't picky about her food, though Jade Warren was picky about everything else. Well, maybe not everything and maybe the word was *prickly* instead of *picky.*

Charla, an African American waitress with every bit as much sass as Jan, slapped two plastic menus on the table. "Hiya, Sawyer."

"Hey, Charla." He waved the menus away. "Don't need those. We'll have the special."

"Good choice. Roast beef and mashed potatoes. Jan's recipe." She retrieved the unused menus. "Drinks?"

"Iced tea for me." He shot a questioning look at Jade. "You?"

"Iced tea is good. Sweet, please."

Charla scribbled on her pad. "Who's your new friend, Sawyer?"

Now, that was a dilemma. He didn't particularly want the whole town to know he was being investigated by order of his own father. "Jade Warren, meet Charla Fredrick."

The two women exchanged greetings before Charla dashed to answer the call of "Order up." A new waitress, probably Abby's replacement, moved much slower.

Sawyer made small talk about the town and the people in the café until Charla returned with their tea glasses.

"We sure miss Abby around this place," Charla said. "Have you heard from her?"

"Yep. They're having the time of their lives."

"Good. She deserves that. You tell her I got her post-card from Venice. Such a pretty place. Is little Miss Lila doing all right with her grandma and grandpa?"

Abby's four-year-old daughter was staying with Sawyer's mom and dad while the newlyweds honeymooned in Italy.

"They're spoiling her, but you know Lila. She's a ray of sunshine and easy to spoil."

"She miss her mama much?"

"They Skype every night. I think Abby is the one suffering separation pangs. Lila's in her element."

"Abby's a good mama." Charla tossed her head, swinging giant pink earrings as if she dared anyone to argue.

"The best, and we Buchanons are all suckers for Lila."

"She does that to people. Precious child."

The waitress scooted away, returning in minutes with two steaming plates that she slid with expert ease onto the table.

"Tender roast beef, mashed potatoes and gravy, green beans and hot buttery biscuits." Sawyer rubbed his hands together. "Food of the divine."

Charla perched a hand on her ample hip. "Y'all need anything else?"

"Pie later."

"Coconut?"

Sawyer flashed a victory sign. "Two."

"Got it." She hustled away again.

Jade stared, wide-eyed, at her plate. "I'll never eat all of this."

"Take a carryout box home with you." He reached for the salt and pepper. "Where are you staying anyway?"

"The Red River Roost."

Oh, not so good. "You okay there?"

"Sure. Why wouldn't I be?"

"The River Roost isn't in the best area of town."

She got that look on her face again. The one that said he should mind his own business. "I can take care of myself."

He shrugged. So she said, but if she was his sister, he'd be concerned. Not that he considered her a sister. Not even close.

He frowned at the fluffy white insides of a steaming-hot biscuit.

She didn't like him, was suspicious as all get-out, but he was fascinated by her.

Now, what did that say about him?

Jade thought she should probably tell him to mind his own business, but Sawyer knew Gabriel's Crossing and she didn't. Forewarned was forearmed. If there were problems, she needed to know.

"What's so bad about that part of town?"

"Kind of run-down. More crime. The Roost is the type of motel where—" He leaned back in his chair and scrunched his face. "How do I put this delicately?"

"No need. I understand your point." She lifted a fork, not letting him see that his words troubled her. Not for herself, but for that lonely teen and her baby. "I was a police officer before becoming a private detective. I'm well trained, and like I said, I can take care of myself."

Sometimes she'd made a mess of things, but she'd survived and grown wiser from the experience. She didn't need or trust anyone's protection but her own.

Sliding her fork into the potatoes, she prepared to enjoy what appeared to be a delicious meal. Sawyer, she noted, had yet to begin. She shot him a questioning look. "Something wrong?"

One side of his mouth quirked up. "Grace."

"Oh." She lowered her fork and bowed her head but kept one eye on the man across the table, bracing for a major show so everyone in the place would know how devout he was.

Sawyer discreetly murmured a few words followed with "Amen." As he opened his eyes, she sat back, studying him while battling the slight guilt that she'd been focused on the man instead of the blessing.

When she'd left home, she'd left her faith behind. Not that she'd ever had much to begin with. She wasn't mad at God or anything like that. She was just…tired of the hassle.

But Sawyer Buchanon didn't fit her concept of loud, judgmental Christians. Those she knew and understood. This quiet faith, offered up with a smile and courtesy, bewildered her.

"What?"

She shook her head. "Nothing really."

"I offended you by praying?" Those magnificent eyes were serious but not apologetic. Could a man really have eyelashes that long and black?

"No. Your faith is your business."

"I take it you're not a believer?"

"Religion isn't my thing."

"Did I mention religion?" He tilted his head in the cutest way.

"Religion. Christianity. Same thing."

She took up her fork again and tasted a bite of tender roast beef and fought to suppress a moan. She'd always been an auditory eater, and this was seriously delicious.

Sawyer squinted at her, the fork in his left hand paused above the steaming, aromatic food. "Not hardly."

"What do you mean?"

"Religions are about rules and laws. Christianity is about my personal relationship with Jesus."

She'd heard that before but all this personal relationship stuff went right over her head. She knew faith didn't work like that. Her daddy had religion and claimed to be a Christian. She couldn't see the difference. *Do this. Don't do that.* If she stepped out of line, God would get her and she would suffer.

All she knew about faith was that her father twisted Bible verses to control his wife and kids.

If that was Christianity, she didn't want any part of it. Or any part of another smiling, handsome man who claimed, like Cam had, to be a man of faith.

Sawyer, quick mind that he was, instantly caught her anti-religion vibe. Somebody or something had turned her off the Lord. To him, and to every Buchanon old enough to think, her reaction was tragic. All the more because he liked her.

Something beneath the surface of the cool, serious PI intrigued him. She was much more than she'd let him see.

Yeah, and he must be sniffing too much sawdust.

Whatever. He'd take Mom's sage advice and live his faith instead of preaching it.

With that in mind, he shifted easily to her other interesting statement. "How long were you a cop?"

She sipped her tea, and for a second Sawyer thought she would tell him to mind his own business. Again.

She set the glass down and rubbed damp fingers on her napkin. In this heat, the tea glass condensed faster than Campbell's soup.

"Four years in Paris. Texas, not France."

Was that the hint of a real smile he spotted dancing

around her pretty mouth? Being a naturally happy guy, he couldn't help offering a smile in response.

Apparently, discussing her job was preferable to talking about God.

"You've probably had to say that a million times."

"At least. Mostly on the phone. People here in Texoma land know the *real* Paris is in Texas."

A joke. They were making progress. Pepped him right up. "Did you like being a cop?"

"Loved it. Most of the time."

"Then why switch careers?"

"Oh, you know." She shrugged, contemplating a biscuit and a pat of real butter. "Did you always want to be a carpenter?"

Changing topics. Nice diversion. Or was that a cop tactic to dig for info?

"No. When I was six I wanted to be Batman. Still do, but they tell me the job is taken."

A spark lit her eyes. "Your degree is in business."

He slapped a hand against his chest, pretending shock. "Are you saying Batman didn't have a business plan?"

This time she actually smiled. And the result knocked his socks off. He was tempted to look under the table to see if they were still there. Except he was wearing work boots.

"Seriously. Why a business degree if you planned to build things?"

"Dad was a stickler. All of us kids had to at least try college—preferably his alma mater, Tech. I liked college life and stuck around to get a degree." Mostly because of the good times, but he didn't tell her that part. "Even if I pound nails for the family company, I'm still a businessman. What about you? Did you attend college?"

He held his breath waiting for the cold shoulder.

"Community college classes in criminal justice and then

police academy and some investigation courses. I always knew what I wanted to do."

"How does one know such a thing? Especially you, being a woman." He held up both hands. "No insult intended, but you've probably taken some flack as a female in a male-dominated field."

She stiffened up. "I can handle myself."

"No doubt." One blast of that arctic stare and a lesser man would freeze in his tracks. "But it couldn't be easy."

"I had some run-ins. Guys who didn't want to ride with me. Who thought I couldn't hold my own and would get them killed. Suggestive cartoons in my locker. The basic hazing stuff."

A bite of green beans froze halfway to Sawyer's mouth. "Say that again."

She shrugged. "Harassment made me tougher. I wasn't about to wimp out after that."

"Still." He didn't like the idea of some creep shooting innuendoes in her direction. He and the brothers would bust some chops if anyone did that to their sisters. Which brought to mind her family.

"Didn't your brothers want to knock some heads?"

Her gaze was cool. "I didn't tell them. Why would I?"

A revealing confession. She faced the world on her own. "Because men stand up for their women."

"Let's get this straight, Mr. Buchanon. I don't need or want a man to take care of me." She tossed a wadded napkin onto the table. "Not now. Not ever."

Ouch. Raw nerve. Somebody had done a number on her. Somebody who needed a knot jerked in his neck.

Sawyer was normally a lover, not a fighter, but he wouldn't mind meeting up with the culprit. Preferably alone.

Chapter Five

The next evening Jade pushed back from the small wobbly, laminated motel desk and read over the notes she'd typed into a computer document.

She'd spent the day interviewing the rest of the Buchanon family, including Dawson, who reminded her constantly of his twin. They were both too good looking for words, but so very different in personality. To her consternation, it was the playboy twin she couldn't stop thinking about.

A psychological default, she suspected, and one which she would fight with all her might. She refused to be a stereotype, falling for the same kind of man over and over again.

Dawson had been her focus today. Sawyer could wait, though she would have to talk to him again soon, regardless of her misgivings. Dan Buchanon wanted her focus on Sawyer, and the big boss was the man paying the bill.

With seven Buchanon siblings and the two parents, she'd asked the standard questions and written a lot of notes, but nothing raised a red flag. Whoever was vandalizing the Buchanon properties covered their tracks well. At this point, she needed a clue. Any clue. Sawyer had been little help.

With a sigh, she clicked Save and spent a few minutes checking social media and public records. At Sawyer's Facebook page, she paused to read tags and new entries, not missing the number of women posting. He joked around a lot, posting silly memes and photos of his family, including one of a small girl with a walker. The dark-haired cutie with the infectious smile must be Lila, Brady's stepdaughter, the child with spina bifida.

Sawyer said the family doted on the little girl, which made sense. Any family with seven kids must enjoy children.

Her thoughts went to the teenage girl and baby in Unit One. Who doted on them? No one, it seemed. Sad. Troubling.

By the time she'd returned to the motel last night, their lights had been off and she'd left them undisturbed. This morning, she'd departed the motel early for an appointment.

Technically the teen and her baby weren't Jade's business, but she'd been a police officer. She didn't back away from getting involved.

Everybody had to eat, and right now, her quick drive-through lunch was gone. Today had not been a repeat of yesterday's impromptu lunch with Sawyer at the Buttered Biscuit, though the only reason she cared was the great food, *not* the company.

Since the motel operator had kept his promise and brought over a microwave and mini fridge, she decided on a trip to the grocery store. The appliances were tiny but serviceable and would save her money in the long run. Brownie points with her boss.

She stashed the laptop under the mattress and stepped outside. The heat had eased, as if the sun had turned off the torch. In another thirty minutes, the evening air would be pleasant.

A car pulled beneath the office awning and a man and woman, both in sunglasses, got out. The woman kept her head down and hustled inside while the man glanced around as if afraid of being seen.

They weren't the first clandestine couple she'd observed

sneaking into the motel. And from the number of come-and-go visitors to Unit Six, she suspected something shady, probably drugs or prostitution, was happening there.

Sawyer had been right about the area. She supposed every town had its back-alley section. Another reason to worry about Bailey and Ashton.

She was about to walk the short distance to Bailey's unit when her cell phone vibrated. Seeing the caller ID, Jade answered before the second buzz.

Breath tight in her chest, she blurted, "Mama? Are you all right?"

"I'm fine, honey." Tammy Clifton *sounded* fine. But was she really?

Since moving away from her childhood home—escaping would be the better term—Jade worried about her mother, but no amount of talk convinced Tammy Clifton to leave the Oklahoma town where she'd grown up. Southview was all she'd ever known, and fear held her there. Lots of fear.

"Are you sure? Is Daddy—"

Tammy interrupted quickly, "He's at work."

"Where?" In the past ten years, Hugh Clifton had been unemployed more often than not. This was, of course, the fault of every Buchanon who walked the face of God's green earth.

"Four Seasons Nursing Home. Maintenance."

Jade hoped the employment would last, though she heard the reservation in her mother's voice. The seeds of hope sprang eternal in Tammy Clifton but there were less of them with each passing year. "That's great."

"How are you, sweetie? When are you coming home?"

Never. Not if she could help it. Not after the fiasco last Christmas. "When are you coming to Paris to see my apartment?"

That answer was also never.

Her mother gave a soft laugh. "Oh, you know how it is around here."

"You could drive down by yourself, Mama. Paris isn't that far."

"Hugh would worry about me."

"Worry you'd leave and not go back." She couldn't keep the derisive tone from her voice.

"Now, Jade, don't start."

"Mama, women today don't have to put up with…the things you do."

"We're not going to discuss this. He's your father. Show some respect."

If Mama crammed *honor thy father and mother* down her throat one more time, Jade feared she'd scream.

"My generation is not as quick to give up on a marriage as yours."

So they were back to that. "You know why I left Cam."

Though there were things about the divorce her mother didn't know, things too painful to share, including the identity of the woman she'd found in her king-size bed—her favorite cousin, of all people, hideous judge of character that she'd been. She was wiser now, harder. Nobody would fool her again.

"Cam was such a good provider. He gave you the most beautiful home and car and anything else you wanted."

Jade barked a cold laugh. "He also put me in the hospital, Mama. I don't care how much money he made."

A sound of distress carried through the phone. "We've had this conversation before. No one is perfect."

"Some are downright impossible. You know what Cam did. And I know how Daddy is. Please don't pretend with me."

"Neither your father nor Cam are the monsters you make them out to be."

Her family still believed she'd done something to ignite Cam's anger that night. She had, though she hadn't known it at the time.

Little had she realized when she'd married Cam that she was following in her mother's footsteps, from one angry man to another. That psychological defect again. Now she knew better.

"I'm sorry, Mama. I love you. Let's not fight."

"I love you, too. That's why I called. To hear my girl's voice and know you're well and happy. You are happy, aren't you, sugar?"

Desperation coated her mother's words. She wanted Jade to have what she didn't though she refused to admit how unhappy she was herself. Admitting it would mean she'd have to do something about it.

"I'm great. How are my brothers?"

"Staying busy." Her mother's way of saying she didn't see them often enough. "Robby's wife brought the baby by a few days ago. I never dreamed being a grandma would be this wonderful."

Jade's heart stood still long enough to be reminded of what she didn't have. Of what Mama didn't know.

"Twila sends me pictures on Facebook and Instagram. Jeremiah's a cutie."

"You should come home and visit more. He needs to know his auntie Jade."

Jade sighed and rubbed a now pulsing right temple. "I won't listen to Daddy harp on me about Cam or the Bible or going to church."

Or watch him treat you like a second-class servant.

"Cam was in town yesterday. He asked about you."

Ah, so now they were getting down to the real reason for the phone call. Jade's grip tightened on the cell phone. "How can you take his side?"

"I don't agree with what he did, but six years is long enough to hold a grudge."

"You're talking to me about holding a grudge? What about our family's hatred toward the Buchanons? Isn't that a grudge?"

"That's different."

"How?"

"All I'm saying is that you need to forgive. For your sake if not his. Bitterness will make you old and ugly."

Cam the creep needed to repent before he deserved forgiveness, not that she'd give it even if he crawled over flaming glass and begged. Cam Warren would get nothing from her but animosity. Ever.

Rather than argue, she looked for a reason to end the conversation.

"Mama, I'm sorry to cut this short but I'm working a new case."

"Oh? Anything exciting?"

If you knew, you'd disown me.

"I can't discuss an ongoing investigation. Privacy issues and all that. Gotta run now. I'll call you tomorrow."

"Don't call during meal times. You know how that aggravates Hugh."

"I know, Mama. I know." *Walk on egg shells. Sacrifice your soul, your pride and your self-esteem. Anything to keep the peace.* "Bye now."

Disheartened but resigned, she ended the call.

Talking to her family always tied her in knots and left her feeling vaguely guilty. She wouldn't be able to relax for hours now.

Sliding the phone into her pocket, she started back inside her room but paused, gazing at Bailey's closed door.

She hadn't seen the girl yesterday or today. Was she okay? Did she need anything? Did the baby?

With determined strides she closed the short distance between rooms and knocked.

The door opened in seconds. With an inner groan, Jade

shook her head. The girl needed some lessons in self-defense.

Cop instinct took over. "Never open this door without asking who's on the other side."

"Oh." Bailey's eyes widened. "I didn't think."

"Not thinking can get you raped. Or killed. And then what would happen to Ashton?"

"I'm sorry." Head down, the girl's voice was whisper quiet, her distress obvious.

Jade reined in the lecture. She touched Bailey's shoulder. "I apologize for coming on strong, but you need to be more careful."

"Okay. I will. I promise. Sometimes I'm so stupid."

"Don't get down on yourself. We all mess up sometimes." Jade offered a smile to ease the strain. "I'm driving to the store. Want to come along?"

Bailey brightened. "Sure. Ashton and me are sick of this room."

She could only imagine. A little one needed space to move and play.

"We'll grab some sandwich fixings and stop at the park. How does that sound?"

The offer was a spur-of-the-moment thought but why not? Being a Good Samaritan was in a cop's blood, and the distraction might help to clear her mind so she could come up with a clue for the investigation.

"That would be awesome. Ashton loves the park but it's so far to walk. He's getting heavy."

"No stroller?"

Bailey shook her head. "A friend said she'd give me hers, but then she got pregnant again."

Jade kept her thoughts to herself as she took the baby from Bailey's arms and waited for the girl to grab a bottle and a diaper and follow her to the car. Bailey's flip-flops slapped the concrete.

They chatted companionably during the trip and Jade couldn't help digging for information about Bailey's family, her life, the high school she hadn't finished. She didn't know the local system but surely someone could help this kid and her baby.

When they arrived at the park, Jade pulled her emergency blanket from the trunk for Ashton to play on while the women organized their impromptu picnic on the concrete table. Over Bailey's protest, she'd bought baby food and a banana for Ashton and far more groceries than she'd intended.

They were finishing their sandwiches when a big maroon pickup truck pulled into the parking area next to Jade's car.

Her heart jumped. She stared. Was that Sawyer's truck? And if so, what was he doing here?

Sawyer leaned over the steering wheel and squinted toward two women sitting at a concrete picnic table beneath one of the huge pecan trees shading the city park. He'd thought the Chevy Cruze looked like Jade's and sure enough there she was, having a picnic.

That he also recognized her companion convinced him to hop out of the truck and say hello. Not that he needed much convincing, but it was nice to have Bailey as an excuse. Miss Sherlock Holmes had been on his mind all day and he'd not seen her one time. That he missed talking to her after yesterday's interrogations said he might have a loose board in the attic.

The thought made him chuckle. He, a carpenter, with a loose board. Better take a nail gun to that.

He sauntered across the grass, still vivid green from a recent cloudburst. Inside the shady park, the temperature dropped ten degrees, and he removed his sunglasses, hanging them on his shirt pocket.

As he reached the table, Bailey rose, Coke can in hand. "Sawyer? I thought that was you. Hi."

Jade, he noted, cut a sharp look between them. After her insistence that he was some kind of womanizer, she probably thought the worst. But she was way out of line there. He wasn't a womanizer and even if he was, Bailey was only a kid.

"Hey, Bailey. Long time no see. Where you been? We've missed you at Life Group."

Bailey turned three shades of crimson and lifted a baby from a pallet next to the table. "Oh, you know. After I had Ashton, I was kind of busy and…"

Her voice trailed away and Sawyer, being an astute sort of guy, caught the drift. The older boyfriend no one in their church's youth group had trusted must have skipped out and left her with a baby. And she was too embarrassed to come to church, expecting judgment. Sawyer hated that. Church should be the place to run to, not from, but he understood Bailey's anxiety. Some people who called themselves Christians could use a good dose of Jesus's love.

"Let me see that little fella."

Had he known about the baby? He couldn't remember for sure. And if he had heard, he felt like a jerk for not following up. As young as she was, Bailey needed church support more than ever.

She handed over the little one. Ashton gurgled, drooling a little, and patted Sawyer's face with a slobbery hand.

He laughed. "Anointed in baby drool."

Bailey laughed nervously. "I'm really sorry. He's cutting a tooth, I think."

"Let me see." Sawyer tugged the baby's bottom lip and peered inside. "Yep. Bottom gums are puffy and red. I think I see a little tooth bud down there."

Jade cut into the conversation, a slight dip in her forehead. "You two know each other?"

Bailey nodded. "Church youth group. Sawyer's one of the leaders."

"Really?"

From the chill in her voice, Jade was not impressed—whether with church or him, he had yet to figure out. Maybe both.

"Yeah," Bailey said. "He does a great job."

"No work required. I get to hang out with teenagers and have fun. Who wouldn't want to do that?" Sawyer eased a hip onto the table, still bouncing the baby. He was a cute little critter with big brown eyes, pale, barely there hair and an easy nature. "Nice evening for a picnic."

Bailey pointed to the food spread on the table. "Would you like a sandwich?" She shot a look toward Jade. "If it's okay with Jade, I mean. She bought the stuff."

The PI didn't exactly look enthusiastic but she waved a hand toward the various foods scattered across the table. "If you haven't eaten…"

Sawyer heard the hesitation and because he wanted to ruffle her feathers, he grinned. "I haven't. A sandwich sounds good."

He handed the baby back to Bailey and accepted a baby wipe in return. "He's a dandy, Bailey. Bring him to youth group on Wednesday. Introduce him."

Hope flared in the teen's eyes, but she only said, "I'll think about it."

After a minute, she carried Ashton to the swings a few yards away.

Sawyer swung his legs over the concrete bench and began rummaging in the sandwich fixings. Pepper jack, his favorite cheese. Shaved ham. Good choices.

Jade held out two slices of wheat bread. Sawyer took them and hoped for mayo.

"I didn't see you around today. Dawson said you interviewed him." He'd started to say *interrogated* but suspected the term might cause a cold front to move in.

She wasn't exactly warm but she hadn't kicked him out of the park, either. And she was feeding him. He must be making progress. The fact that he wanted to still befuddled him.

"Along with the rest of your family." She offered a squeeze bottle of mustard.

He shook his head. No mayo. He'd survive. "Learn anything useful?"

"No." The reply came with a frustrated sigh.

"It's early in the investigation yet. Don't get discouraged."

"You were the one who said I wouldn't find anything Leroy and the fire investigators hadn't."

"Yeah, well. I might have been grumpy. You caught me before I'd had my caffeine."

"I'll remember that."

While he chowed down on the ham and cheese, she zipped open a pack of Oreos and took one.

The squeak of swing chains drew his attention. He glanced at Bailey, sitting in the swings with the baby on her lap. One foot tapped the ground, moving them back and forth in a steady rhythm. She was only a kid. With a kid.

He finished his bite and swallowed. "How did you and Bailey connect?"

"She's living at the Red River Roost."

He jacked an eyebrow. "With who? Baby's daddy?"

He had a very clear memory of the boy she'd dated. Though he and others had tried to mentor the young man, the boy had been a loser, a thug with an attitude and no interest in changing.

"Alone. Her mom kicked her out of the house and the boyfriend disappeared. No job. No education. I don't want to think about what her life is going to be. Doesn't this town have resources for kids like her?"

Jade nibbled the edge of a cookie. Chocolate crumbs specked her upper lip. Sawyer had a remedy for that but he didn't figure she'd appreciate his thoughtfulness.

The woman distracted him something fierce.

"If it doesn't it should. Bailey used to attend youth group but when she started hanging out with an older boy, she stopped coming around."

One of the leaders should have followed up. *He* should have talked to her, but he usually left the girls up to the female leaders.

"She said he wouldn't let her."

Sawyer blinked toward Bailey and then met Jade's stormy gaze. "Wouldn't *let her* attend church?"

Her nostrils flared, the pouty mouth tight. "Typical male. The creep. It's all about what they want, never about the girl."

"Not all men are like that, Jade. No *real* man is."

With a huff, she crossed her arms. If she didn't have cookie crumbs on her face, she'd be scary. "Right."

Sawyer made a mental note. *Distrustful of the male species.*

He glanced at her left hand even though he knew from a sneak peek yesterday that she wore no rings. "Is that why you're not married? Too many creeps?"

"Let's just say once burned was plenty for me. I'm divorced." She uncrossed her arms and reached for another Oreo. "Thankfully."

Her pronouncement didn't surprise him. But beneath the defiance and anger, he detected hurt.

Someone had hurt her, and though she wasn't a bit of his business, seeing her pain made him mad.

Chapter Six

The next day Jade felt about as confused as a rat in a new maze. After she had basically labeled Sawyer and the entire male gender as nothing but user creeps, he had changed the subject as if not a bit insulted. The man was...baffling.

During a long conversation about the small town of Gabriel's Crossing, the investigation, and silly twin tricks he and Dawson had contrived to confuse people, she'd found herself warming a teeny bit. Maybe more than that.

"He definitely earned his reputation as a charmer," she muttered. She'd have to be careful not to lose her objectivity.

"Excuse me? Did you say something?"

Jade whirled toward the voice. Sawyer's pregnant sister, Allison, had come into the Buchanon Built conference room where Jade was plowing through piles of old records, some on the computer and others in file boxes. Except for Quinn Buchanon, who had bailed five minutes after her arrival muttering about working at home, she'd been alone for the better part of an hour.

"Sorry. Talking to myself."

"Don't apologize. I do it, too." Allison Hamilton patted her slightly round tummy. "Only now, Junior has to listen."

Jade allowed a smile though she knew the effort looked pinched. "Boy or girl?"

"We don't know yet. Whichever God sends will be a wonderful blessing."

A hollow ache started up. "No preference?"

"Well." The brunette shrugged one shoulder. The woman glowed. Glistened. "Between you and me, I'd love a little cowboy like his daddy. And I really want to decorate the nursery in cute little ponies and cartoon cows."

"No reason you can't do that for a girl."

"True, but if I have a girl, Jake has already decreed her a princess."

Jade's stomach tightened. Naturally, and Jake would get his way.

Rather than spew her negative thoughts, she turned back to the pile of records. Allison came alongside the table and peered at the stack.

"Finding anything useful?"

"Not really. Your family runs a tight ship. Few consumer complaints. Most of those required only minor adjustments."

"My dad is a stickler. He goes ballistic if one of the boys or a subcontractor messes up. Subs know Dad won't use them again unless the finished project is near perfection."

"Has he fired many?"

"A few."

Jade made a mental note. Someone surely resented a tough, exacting boss. Someone besides her father.

A moment of angst gripped her. Her father and the Buchanons had parted ways years ago. If Dad had wanted revenge, he'd have taken it long before now. Besides, he was an hour away and never came to Gabriel's Crossing. No way he could be involved.

"Can you think of any subcontractors who might hold a grudge?" *Please don't say my father.*

"Oh, that's why I came in here in the first place." Allison produced a manila folder. "Dad dropped this off for you. He said he and Mom had brainstormed some additional names and situations last night."

"Great." Jade accepted the folder, eager to dig in. Maybe this would be the info that broke the case wide open. She placed the folder on the table but, not wanting to be rude, left it unopened.

Allison crossed to the refrigerator in the far corner, reached in and took out an orange. With a sheepish shrug she said, "I'm starving all the time lately."

"I've heard that's normal."

"No kids?"

That hollow ache deepened. "No kids. Not married."

"Oh. Well, I highly recommend it—with the right guy." She peeled the orange with her fingers, sending up a strong citrus scent to compete with the lumber and coffee smells of the conference room. "If you're in the market, I happen to have two single brothers. Good looks. Good guys."

The jury was still out on the good guys part. Though she had to admit Sawyer had made a dint in her animosity last night at the park when he'd bounced Bailey's baby around and hadn't complained about being drooled on. Cam would have freaked out. Sawyer actually seemed to enjoy himself and he was genuinely concerned about Bailey.

Was there more to him than a pretty face and a flirty grin?

Interesting question, and one she would follow up on. For the case.

Jade responded to Allison's not-so-subtle matchmaking hint with an insincere smile. "Conflict of interest. I am investigating your single brothers."

Allison waved off the idea. "Dad is spitting in the wind on that."

"You think so? Then who should be the focus? Who's causing the problem?"

"I wish I knew." The pregnant woman reached back into the fridge, grabbed a carton of milk and another orange and said, "Hope you find something," before leaving the room.

Five minutes later she did. And the discovery nearly gave her a heart attack.

Her father's name, big and bold, next to Clifton Concrete, the name of his now defunct company, jumped off the list of lawsuits Buchanon Built had filed.

Pulse thumping, she frowned at the information. A lawsuit? Against her father? Dad had never mentioned a lawsuit. He'd said the Buchanons refused to pay for work rendered and bad-mouthed him to the other contractors. According to Hugh Clifton, Dan Buchanon was a wicked man who played favorites and discriminated against persons of true faith.

She couldn't ask her father for the whole story, either. He'd want to know why. Worse, if the Buchanons found out she was related to anyone on this list of possible suspects, she'd be in big trouble. Her boss, Dale, would take her off the case. He might even fire her for withholding that all-important piece of the puzzle.

She gnawed on her lip, thinking. She was a PI. She needed more information on what happened with her father. But she'd have to be very subtle or risk raising suspicions.

Folder in hand, she stepped out into the office area. Jaylee tapped away at her computer while Allison spoke to her mother. Karen Buchanon, an attractive blonde with a warm personality, looked up when Jade came into the room.

Choosing her words carefully, Jade said, "I have a question about some of the lawsuits on your list."

By asking about more than one, she shouldn't raise any red flags.

Moving to Karen's side, she pointed out several, asking astute questions. Any of these contractors, she told herself, stood as much chance of being the culprit as her father.

When she came to Hugh Clifton, she continued in her cool, professional manner, sounding, at least to her ears, completely objective.

Karen's pretty forehead puckered. "Clifton. Yes, I remember that contractor. Dan and I discussed him last night. His workmanship was shoddy, and he used cut-rate materials but charged us for top-of-the-line. At first, we didn't know about the cut corners. He was crafty. He made everything appear legit and had good references."

Jade's stomach sank. "Which you checked?"

"Yes. Apparently, he'd once run a reputable business in Oklahoma, but when the foundations of several new homes started shifting, Dan filed a lien, hoping the man would do the honorable thing and make repairs. When he refused, claiming financial problems, we had no choice but to take him to court."

"Foundations shifted?" Jade's stomach dipped low. This was not good. Not good at all. "Isn't that dangerous?"

"Absolutely. In the end, we were forced to demolish all four homes Clifton Concrete had worked on, and you can imagine how costly that was to everyone. We had to work very hard to keep our reputation as a trusted builder from being ruined."

"Didn't his company have insurance?"

"He defaulted on that, too, apparently. Nonpayment. The man had gambling issues, I believe, and was desperate for money."

Her holier-than-thou father gambled? Why had she not known this?

"Interesting." She was too stunned to say much else at this point. She needed to get away and breathe deep, to process.

"We never like to take a contractor to court," Karen continued, "but someone could have been badly injured in those homes. Not that the lawsuit recouped much of our loss."

Now she understood why her father's business had failed, why he'd sold everything he could and filed for bankruptcy. And why he hated the Buchanons. He blamed them so he wouldn't have to blame himself. And to keep his gambling secret.

Did Mama know? Should Jade tell her?

Rubbing a hand over her now aching forehead, Jade recognized the conflict of interest, but now, more than ever, she wanted to see this investigation through. She must discover if her father was involved in the Buchanon break-ins. Not for his sake. For her mother's.

Sawyer hummed a happy little tune as he yanked on the always stuck door leading into the Buchanon Built warehouse. The heavy metal screeched on its hinges, high-pitched and painful. Sawyer winced. He needed to fix that.

The screech turned two faces in his direction. His mom's and...*hers*. The PI tickling his thoughts.

He'd seen Jade's car parked outside. He knew she was here, digging into Buchanon business, courtesy of his father. As aggravating as the intrusion was, he didn't blame Jade. She was only doing her job. That she was also prickly and frosty at times only served to heighten his interest— odd duck that he was.

"Nancy Drew." He moseyed toward the big central desk

where his two sisters, his mom and the PI were hanging out. "How goes the investigation?"

Jade looked good, but then she'd looked good in that scalding black suit the first day they'd met. Miserable, but intriguing and oh so neat and professional. Last night at the park, in cuffed jean shorts and a pink T-shirt, she'd been downright human.

Very human.

"Progressing slowly." Did he perceive a slight thawing in her steady gaze? "You and I need to talk again soon. About the case, I mean."

Sweet. She *was* thawing. Things were looking up.

"I'm free this weekend." As soon as the words were out, he bounced a fist against his forehead. "No, wait. I almost forgot. I have plans."

Those finely tuned eyebrows lifted like the golden arches. "Big date?"

"The biggest. Four beautiful women at once, all who love me."

Three of those women burst out laughing. They never let him get away with anything.

"Sawyer," his mother chided. "Stop teasing her. Jade doesn't know how to take you yet."

Allison leaned over the U-shaped counter, her short hair flying around her pert and, of late, rounded face. "What Sawyer means, Jade, is that the family is going to the lake together on Saturday and he happens to have three sisters and a mom who love him *in spite* of everything." Allison splayed four fingers.

"Oh. I see. Four women." Jade did not look impressed.

"Don't pay any attention to him." Allison waved him off as if he were a gnat. "He's trying to endear himself with his juvenile sense of humor but failing miserably."

"Hey!" Sawyer pretended hurt. "See if I bring you any more doughnuts."

Allison came over and patted his cheek. "You will feed me. I know you will. You love me and I love you, Sawyer Mark."

He grabbed her in a gentle hug. "Got that right, cutie. Even if you are getting fat."

Allison laughed happily, bracketing her tiny tummy pooch.

He loved seeing his little sister this way, in love and expecting Jake's baby with so much joyful anticipation that she almost had Sawyer wishing he could find the right woman to marry.

Jaylee looked up from her computer. "What are you doing this weekend, Jade? You won't be working on the case, will you?"

"I will if anything new comes to light."

"Why not come to the lake with us? When the Buchanons are relaxed they talk more. Never know what little thing you might learn."

"I couldn't intrude on family time."

"You wouldn't be intruding." Now that Jaylee had come up with the idea, Sawyer jumped on it. "We take friends and colleagues all the time."

"All work and no play," Allison said, and Sawyer secretly blessed her. "Fun is guaranteed."

"Well, I don't know…"

He could see she was weakening, so he tossed in a hook loaded with bait.

"Jade skis," he said to his mother. "She thinks she can handle Brady's moves."

Allison paused in peeling an orange. "You ski?"

"Well, I used to. It's been a long time."

"Like riding a bike. Muscle memory." Sawyer held both

hands in front of him in water-ski position. "Brady's boat, skis, big water."

"But Brady's not back from his honeymoon."

"And guess who has his keys?" Sawyer tapped his chest. "Can you handle *my* moves?"

He realized how that sounded but didn't back down. Jade's gray eyes sparked at the challenge and maybe at the innuendo, too. "I think I can. The question is, can you handle mine?"

"Ah, the gauntlet has been thrown, the die cast, the challenge laid." He rubbed his hands together. "Bring it on, Sherlock."

To his disappointment, Jade was already shaking her head. Fluffy, pretty blond hair swished around her shoulders like a pale cloud.

"Thank you for the invitation but maybe another time. It sounds terrific, but I promised to hang out with Bailey on Saturday."

"Bring her along!" He glanced toward his mother. He'd told her about Bailey's situation, hoping she knew of resources to help the girl. "Right, Mom?"

Mom, bless her, was always on his side. "If Bailey's stuck in a motel room with a baby all day, she'll probably thrill at the chance for some recreation."

"I hadn't thought of that." But Jade was thinking about it now. He could tell by that tiny wrinkle in her pretty forehead.

"She's a teenager." Sawyer shamelessly used the girl to break down Jade's resistance. Was a skiing challenge really so important? "Bailey needs to have fun and we Buchanons are a regular fun-mobile. As well as a willing bunch of built-in babysitters. You would be doing Bailey and Ashton a favor."

"Well—" Her teeth caught her full bottom lip, gnawed a little. Such a pretty lip.

And she was weakening.

"Look at it this way, Jade. You get to help Bailey, ask us a million questions and have a terrific day on the lake with perhaps the greatest family this side of the Red River— unless you're afraid you can't live up to the Sawyer ski challenge."

He saw the smiles on his sisters' faces. They knew him too well and would probably give him a hard time about his persistence. He didn't care. Miss Magnum PI was a tough cookie, but after watching her with Bailey and Ashton, he suspected she had a very soft heart. One that he wanted to know better.

So he let the bait dangle. "Come on. What do you say? Help out a needy teenager. Stuff your face on Dad's barbecue. Battle my mad boating skills."

Without cracking a smile, Jade pointed a finger at him. "Since you put it that way, practice your driving, mister, because you're on."

Chapter Seven

The moment she told Bailey about the lake trip Jade stopped regretting her decision to go. The girl was ecstatic. You would think she'd won a trip to Disney World.

"This is the best day ever, Jade." Bailey bounced around the hotel room like the teenager she was, packing a backpack for Ashton. She'd been this way for two days. Jubilant. Planning. Behaving as if she'd never had a day of fun in her life.

Maybe she hadn't.

Jade settled in the one motel room chair with Ashton and a formula bottle while they talked. "I bought sunscreen and a little hat for Ashton yesterday."

She'd also intended to buy a new swimsuit, but Bailey bemoaned the fact that since Ashton's birth hers no longer fit and she couldn't afford a new one, so they'd both decided to wear shorts and tank tops. Ashton would be fine in a onesie.

Bailey paused in her mad packing to anxiously twist the end of her ponytail. "I hadn't even considered that. What if Ashton gets sunburned?"

"We'll be extra careful to slather him with this and then keep him in the shade as much as possible. Sawyer said the Buchanons bring the house, including an awning, a grill, chairs, you name it."

"They are so awesome." Bailey stuffed yet another diaper into the backpack. She had enough to stay a week. "Are you and Sawyer, like, a couple or something?"

The question blindsided Jade. She blinked at the girl until the question registered. "What? Sawyer and me? No. He's a client."

"Oh. I thought, after the park and now the lake, he must be crushing on you."

Jade laughed humorlessly. The idea of Sawyer crushing on her when he had a bevy of beauties vying for his attentions was ludicrous. The fact that this knowledge bothered her set alarms clanging. She knew better. He was the exact kind of man she would not fall for again. Shallow. Self-focused. Charming to a fault. Jade was determined that he would not think she agreed to the lake trip because of him. The trip was to enhance the investigation and for Bailey.

That she was almost as excited as Bailey was beside the point.

She checked the time on her cell phone. "He'll be here soon. Are you about ready?"

The question was barely out of her mouth when a heavy knock vibrated the door. Bailey rushed forward as if to let the caller in.

"Bailey. Caution."

"Right." The teen slowed to a walk, wiped her hands down the sides of her shorts before calling out, "Who is it?"

A muffled voice came through the door. "The chauffeur. Your carriage awaits."

Bailey yanked the door wide, giggling. "Sawyer, you're so funny."

Jade didn't roll her eyes but she wanted to. She'd recognized Sawyer's voice too but the teen had a long way to go to be street savvy.

Sawyer stepped into the room. Something in the center of Jade's chest reacted. Even baggy cargo shorts and a well-worn Red Raiders T-shirt didn't detract from his looks. But it was the way he greeted Bailey that really got her thinking. Like a big brother. The way he greeted his sisters.

He casually flopped a muscled arm over the teen's shoulders, gave a quick squeeze and released her with a cheery smile. "All ready for a great day?"

Bailey turned every shade of red known to humans. "I can't wait. I'm so excited."

No female, it seemed, was impervious to Sawyer Buchanon.

Except Jade. Even if he had a kind side—and he did—and even if she found him attractive—and who wouldn't—he was a Buchanon. And her maiden name was on his father's naughty list.

He spotted her inside the dim room with the baby and raised both palms in a comical, supplicating gesture.

"What's this? You've ditched me for a younger man?"

"His toothless grin was irresistible."

Sawyer paused for one second as if her return banter caught him off guard. She knew he considered her humorless and cold, which was for the best, but she wasn't always that way.

Crossing the room, Sawyer swooped Ashton into his arms. "You ladies ready? Where's the squirt's bag?"

Bailey reached for the backpack but Sawyer beat her to it, swung it over his opposite shoulder, and the four of them headed out for the day.

The sight of the man with a baby in his tanned, muscled arms tugged at Jade's insides. He was a puzzle she couldn't fit into her tidy mental box.

Once they were in the truck, driving north with a glittery blue boat pulling behind, Jade turned toward him. "What about the rest of your family? Are we meeting them somewhere?"

"They left earlier, all except Jake and Allison who will come later. Mom and Dad rise with the sun and like to set up camp before everyone else arrives."

"Nice of them."

"Strategy. Broken Bow Lake usually isn't too crowded, but you never know. We have a special spot."

Jade almost swallowed her tongue.

"Broken Bow?" she managed, hoping she sounded normal.

"Ever been there? It's a gorgeous lake. Clear and deep, lots of secluded coves and little islands to play on."

"A few times." Heart pounding in her throat, she swiveled toward the passenger window and watched the passing scenery.

Broken Bow was close to Southview. Too close.

Sawyer plopped into one of the many lawn chairs beneath the shady blue awning that stretched out along a narrow section of beach. Behind their day camp, thick, pine-scented forest shielded them from the rest of the world, and in front, a little cove of blue mountain water glistened in the sun. An occasional boat motored past in the distance but for the most part only Buchanon noises melded with the lapping water.

In the nearby shallows, Brady's stepdaughter wore a bright orange life vest above a pink tutu swimsuit and splashed with Charity's son and daughter, Ryan and Amber. Little Lila and the older Amber were tight, and Ryan took his job as big, protective cousin seriously. Nonetheless, the whole family, including Sawyer, kept a close eye on Lila, the special needs child.

Out on the lake, Brady's boat sliced across the sparkling current as Quinn pulled his fiancée and Derek, her nephew, on a tube. The boy stood up in the rubber conveyance and circled one hand over his head cowboy-style to yell, "Yahoo!"

The once surly Derek, like Quinn, had come a long way in the past few months.

"Ever been tubing?" Feeling pleasantly relaxed, Sawyer slowly turned his face toward Bailey. The needy teen twitched his heart, and from the way Mom and the sisters circled her with chairs, they felt the same.

"No, but it looks fun." Ashton bounced on her lap, patting chubby little hands on his legs.

"I'll take you around when Quinn comes in."

"Really?" Her face brightened, but every bit as quickly darkened. "Oh, I better not. I can't leave Ashton."

Jade, who stood nearby talking to Dad and Dawson about the case, must have overheard. She glanced around. "You go, Bailey. Have fun. That's why you're here. I'll look after Ashton."

"We'll all watch him." Charity reached for the baby. "I've wanted to get my hands on this little doll since you arrived. My kids are growing up too fast."

"We need more babies in this family." His mother eyed him. "You and your brother need to stop dragging your feet, find a couple of nice Christian women and give me more grandchildren."

"Can't find anyone who'll have us. We're too ugly," he said lazily. But the fact that he felt Jade's eyes on him during the exchange poked at a lonely spot. Recently that spot, along with his empty town house, had started to bother him. The fact that Jade had a problem with God, or appeared to, bothered him, too.

He leaned his head back against the chaise lounge and tipped a ball cap over his eyes. He had plenty of opportunities for dates. He was never alone unless he wanted to be. So why had this sudden wave of loneliness washed over him?

Sometime later Jade was still trying to relax as she stroked coconut-scented sunscreen over her arms. Being this close to home made her anxious. She didn't want to run into family, or worse, Cam. The chances were slim that any of them would show up in this particular spot on the lake, but she couldn't be certain.

Dan Buchanon had answered a handful of questions about the lawsuits she'd been checking into, but then Karen reminded them that this was a pleasure trip, not work, and the subject was closed. Dan had sheepishly retired to his fishing reel with Quinn. A lanky boy went with them and the three male heads now huddled above a tackle box in search of the proper bait.

Out on the lake, Sawyer had taken charge of the boat and pulled a tube carrying Bailey and Jaylee. There were so many Buchanons, Jade scrambled to keep them straight, but Bailey's grin was big enough to see from here.

Pleased at the girl's delight and glad she'd agreed to this outing regardless of her family's proximity, she sipped at a bottle of cold water and scribbled in her notebook. She was safe here. Her family wouldn't know she was consorting with the enemy.

Bothered by feeling guilty when she'd done nothing wrong, she tuned in to the conversation between Charity and Karen, hoping to glean something useful to the investigation. Instead, she heard a discussion of Charity's navy pilot husband and the concern that he was once more flying in a danger zone and had missed his usual phone call home.

Sawyer guided the boat to the nearby dock and cut the engine.

"Hey, Nancy Drew, come on. Your turn." He held up a water ski.

Her insides leaped. "It's been a long time."

"Excuses, excuses." He laughed, letting her know he teased. "Admit the real truth. You fear my mad boating maneuvers."

She stowed the notepad in her tote and started toward him. Lacing her fingers, she flipped her hands palm out and stretched like a champion warming up for the finals. "Bring it on, boat man."

Quinn hooted from the sidelines. "You better watch out, Sawyer. She looks serious."

"I'm shaking in my flip-flops."

He looked incredible standing at the boat helm, glorious eyes covered in dark shades and black hair glistening in the sunlight. A magazine ad.

He tossed her a life jacket. "Saddle up, cowgirl."

Ignoring the troubling quiver in her belly that she hoped was caused by the thought of skiing for the first time in several years and not by the man, Jade donned the jacket and waded into the shallows to put the skis on while Sawyer hooked the ski rope and prepared the boat.

The other twin ambled out onto the dock. "I'll spot for you."

A spotter. Good. For all his reckless-sounding bravado, Sawyer didn't forgo safety. She relaxed a little and hoped he was right about muscle memory.

Sawyer hitched his chin. "Ready when you are, Jade."

She settled into the water, knees bent, arms out and skis at the ready. "I demand a warm-up period."

"Got it."

She'd watched him drive the boat for Bailey and the other kids. He knew what he was doing, though their challenge loomed large in her head. Would he drive like a maniac? Would he dunk her in the brink to intentionally embarrass her and prove his masculine superiority?

The motor revved as the boat slowly began to move forward. Jade's adrenaline jacked. Her breath caught, released.

The wake lapped gently at her body, bobbing her up and down in the thick life jacket. Sawyer looked back over his shoulder and gave a thumbs-up. Grinning, she nodded, the thrill of being on the water again too good to resist as he accelerated and she began to rise.

In less than a minute she was on her feet, the wind whipping her hair as she sailed across the waves. Ten miles an hour. Twenty. Now twenty-five.

She tasted the lake spray, relished the cool air, the blinding glare of sun on water. In her peripheral vision, trees passed in a green blur.

A laugh burst free. She let out a whoop of joy.

Sawyer's head whipped around and his teeth flashed before he returned his attention to driving. He kept the speed steady, the trajectory straight, giving her time to adjust.

Quickly gaining confidence, she found her balance and began to move from side to side, only a little but enough to know she hadn't lost her skills. Living this close to the lake most of her life, she loved the water and was an accomplished swimmer, skier, boater. Sad that she'd stopped enjoying it. Until today.

She raised a thumb, indicating her desire to go faster. Her legs burned and her knees protested. She was out of shape but too stubborn and having too much fun to stop. Dawson lifted an answering thumb as he spoke to the driver. Again, Sawyer glanced over his shoulder. She raised her thumb, urging him to speed up. He seemed to consider for a second but turned back to the controls.

She was flying now, not another boat anywhere nearby.

It was as though they had the lake to themselves. The twins' voices floated back to her, but she couldn't make out the words.

Though her arms ached, she thrilled to the wind, the water, the speed. Confident, she swerved the skis to the left and then the right.

The action proved too much for her out-of-practice knees. She went down.

Lake water closed over her head. Automatically—that muscle memory thing—she released the rope and bobbed to the surface.

Sawyer had already cut the throttle and turned the boat back toward her. "You all right?"

The jokester was now all business. Face serious, intent.

"Great. This is amazing!" She started to swim toward the boat.

"Save your energy. I'll bring the rope back to you." In a maneuver that appeared easy but she knew wasn't, he guided the floating ski rope to within inches of where she bobbed.

As much as she didn't want to stop, she said, "My legs are burning. I should probably go ashore for a while."

"In the boat or on the skis?"

She grinned. "The skis. I'm no wimp."

He raised his hands. "No argument from me. Hang tight. I'll have you back up in a minute."

True to his word, she was on her feet and flying again in seconds. With precision, he delivered her to shore, killed the engine and hopped out to tie up the boat.

Water sports made her ravenous and the smell of grilling hamburgers made her stomach rumble. She glanced toward the awning fifty feet up on shore where Dan had taken over the grill and some of the Buchanon women laid out side dishes on a folding table.

More exhausted than she wanted to be, Jade plopped in the shallows and began to unlatch the binding. Dawson slogged past with a fist bump. "Nice moves out there."

Rid of the skis, she was shocked by her shaky knees but proud that she'd held her own.

Sawyer leaped off the dock and flip-flopped through the water. "Not bad for a girl."

She stuck her legs straight out. Binding straps left red streaks atop her feet.

"Fighting words, boat man." She glanced up at him, too tired and pleased to fight the pleasant hum in her bloodstream. "Why no fancy boating moves from you? I thought you had mad skills."

He shrugged a broad shoulder. "I took pity on you."

Normally, a comment like that would make her stiffen. Instead she laughed. "Coward."

"Well, yeah. But that was a warm-up. I'll get you before the day's over." He slipped into the water next to her, cargo shorts and all. Removing his flip-flops, he tossed them at the camp. They landed with a plop. "Seriously, you did good out there. I was impressed."

A happy balloon inflated in her chest. "Thanks. You made it easy. You're a very good driver."

He didn't answer, didn't even preen, and side by side they leaned back on their elbows and relaxed in the sun, water waist deep.

Two kids ran past and splashed them, squealing.

They both laughed and threatened revenge.

"I need water balloons," she said, pretending to take aim at the kids.

"Spoken like a Buchanon." His grin captured hers. Something dinged in her brain, but she ignored the warning.

He was a flirt as well as a client but she was allowed to have a good time on her day off. Wasn't she?

Quinn and his fiancée, Gena, approached, holding hands. "Are you through with the boat?"

"For now. Go ahead."

"I'm going to show Gena the island." Quinn indicated a patch of green a hundred yards down the shoreline. "Want to go with us?"

Sawyer shook his head and the other pair got in the craft and motored away.

"They look happy together." Did her voice sound wistful?

"Love has changed my brother." Sawyer levered up, rubbing the sand from his elbows.

Love had changed her, too, though not in the way Sawyer meant.

When she remained silent, thinking about the damage love could inflict, Sawyer said, "Not all relationships turn out like yours did, Jade."

He was treading on dangerous ground. He knew nothing about her relationship. Nothing. "I should hope not."

He stroked a finger down her arm and her breath caught in her throat. "I'm sorry."

It was the last thing she expected him to say. She softened, yearned.

Attracted and floundering, she searched for something mundane to say, though she couldn't take her eyes off his face. "Am I getting a sunburn?"

His mouth curved and a dimple erupted in one cheek. Her thoughts flew to kissing. Sawyer would be an expert.

"Sun-kissed." He tapped the end of her nose and winked. "Looks good on you."

Too close. Too appealing. Jade floundered for a snappy reply and found none. She could barely breathe.

Karen called from the awning. "Hey, you two. Burgers are ready when you are."

"Be right there." Sawyer waved a lazy hand but his gaze remained fixed on Jade.

She squirmed a little but didn't back away. Some powerful electric current seemed to freeze them in place. Hunger forgotten, the only thing she really wanted to do was lean into his strong chest and feel his arms around her.

She was one messed-up chick.

Sawyer's lips moved. "Ready?"

She certainly was.

He unwound his long length and bounced to a stand. For a moment, Jade felt disoriented. Then Sawyer reached a hand toward her. She accepted his strong carpenter's grip, and let him pull her up. He did so easily, as if she weighed nothing at all.

When he didn't let go, she didn't protest, didn't pull away. Perhaps she should have but she didn't. They walked together, Sawyer chatting in his easy way about his father's perfect burgers and his personal disdain for dill pickles.

Jade couldn't find her voice, so she let him talk. Her mind raced while her chest boiled with unwanted emotions. He was a client. She shouldn't hold his hand. He was a womanizer. She should run the other way.

None of those arguments made a bit of difference.

If any of the Buchanons noticed the hand-holding episode, they said nothing. When he let go, she felt the loss. Foolish woman that she was.

Somehow she managed to put together a hamburger, though she was acutely aware of Sawyer's nearness as he reached across her for mayo.

"You know, I've been thinking." Dan squirted mustard on a burger patty. "We haven't had any break-ins since Jade came on the job."

Karen, balancing a paper plate on her lap, said, "Then we better keep her around."

Sawyer's eyes captured hers, serious for once.

"Yes," he said. "I think we better."

Chapter Eight

"**Y**ou better come outside."

Sawyer was barely out of bed and still half-asleep, but from the grim expression on Dawson's face, he'd better wake up fast. His brother showed up on his stoop fairly often, considering they lived side by side, but this was different. A difference Sawyer suspected he wasn't going to like.

"What's wrong?" He chugged a long drink of Coke. The burn snapped him into focus. His eyes watered.

"You're gonna hate this." His twin pivoted on his blue athletic shoes and walked away.

Growing more alarmed with every step his brother took, Sawyer put the Coke can back inside and followed Dawson across the small lawn to the driveway where he'd left his truck parked last night. Halfway there, he stopped, squinted, barely believing his eyes.

"No way." A sick dread gripped his gut.

"The other side is worse."

Sawyer emitted a pained groan.

Sprayed in garish orange paint across the full length of his beautiful maroon truck were the words, "You'll be sorry."

He thought he might lose his soda right here on the front lawn. "Sorry for what? What did I do?"

"So much for our vandal backing off."

His head snapped around to stare at Dawson. "You think this is the same person?"

"Don't you? Surely we don't have that many enemies."

"Yeah. Yeah. Must be." Sawyer tilted his head back and stared straight up. The blue June sky didn't cheer him one bit. "What's on the other side?"

"Something you're going to want to cover fast." They walked around together.

Sawyer's body sagged at the desecration. Along with a collection of disturbing obscenities, someone had scrawled the word "Cheater."

"So, Dad's right. I am the focus of this nut."

"From the personal references? Most likely. Why'd you leave your pickup parked outside last night?"

After a long day at the lake, he'd dropped Jade and Bailey at the motel, come home and collapsed. The sun and water had wrecked him.

"I park in the drive half the time. This is Gabriel's Crossing." Safe, quiet, friendly. Neighbors helped neighbors.

"Better call Leroy and Jade."

Jade. She'd want to know.

He eyed the obscene graffiti. "I don't want her to read this."

"She's an investigator, Sawyer, a former cop. She's seen worse."

He perched both hands on his hips. "That doesn't mean it's a good thing. We Buchanons protect our women."

"'Our women'?" Dawson's look was mild but pointed. "I noticed you and Jade were pretty cozy yesterday. Am I missing something?"

"No, no. I was only—" Sawyer rubbed the back of his neck, perplexed. "Maybe."

"Hmpf."

That's all his brother said, but that was enough. For now.

His twin understood him as no one else did. Even when he didn't understand himself.

After a long, silent look passed between them, Dawson withdrew his cell phone and pushed one single number. Sadly, the police department was now on speed dial. While his brother explained the situation to the dispatcher, Sawyer growled in frustration and called Jade.

Before she arrived, he dressed, snapped photos of the damage and contacted the local body shop. He needed a paint job fast. Like, before Jade arrived.

Within thirty minutes' time, she came at him across his front lawn looking crisp, fresh and competent in a navy skirt and white top, her pale hair clipped up in some kind of mysteriously appealing glob at the back of her head.

The weirdest sense of relief came over him.

No greeting. No smile. No fond comments about the incredible time they'd had together yesterday—and it had been incredible. He'd gone to sleep with a happy face, a regular emoji man, aware that something positive was brewing between them.

"Show me." Today, Jade was all business, but Sawyer couldn't hide his grin. Her nose was sunburned, her cheeks kissed with pink.

"Can you take my word for it?" He'd moved the truck inside the garage out of sight. "The vocabulary is not... nice."

She cut him a no-nonsense glance. "Show me."

He'd known she would insist. Prickly PI. He poked at the remote and waited for the garage door hum to cease before leading the way inside.

Gentleman that he was, he took her to the driver's side first. She whipped a camera from her backpack and snapped a few shots.

"Did you see or hear anything?" she asked.

"I was dead to the world last night. Weren't you?"

"Yes." A pucker appeared in her brow. A pretty pucker he was tempted to smooth away. "What do you suppose this means? Why should you, if you are indeed the target, be sorry? What have you done to rile someone to this extent?"

"I've asked myself those questions for days." He lifted his hands in helplessness. "Nada."

She moved around the truck. He followed, watching her reaction.

Her face tightened. "Ugly business."

"Sorry you had to see that."

"I'm a big girl."

"So you keep saying." He leaned an elbow on the fender. "Still not something a lady should have to read."

She snapped photos, looked at the graffiti from various angles, tested the paint with the tip of her finger. "Dry."

"Spray paint dries fast, especially in this heat."

"Have the police been informed?"

"Leroy will be here when he can. He was out on a domestic."

She paused. Her nostrils flared. Anger darkened her face. Quickly, she spun away.

Sawyer's frown deepened.

What was that about?

Domestic calls made Jade's blood boil. Her blood pressure rose at the very mention of some muscle-bound oaf knocking around a woman or kids. Every cop instinct inside her wanted to take the call herself and toss the creep in jail. Permanently.

To work off the reaction, she rounded the truck several times and then moved out to the driveway and across the grass to look for evidence, careful not to usurp Leroy's role or disturb the crime scene.

Sawyer followed close behind. She felt him there, hovering, almost protective. The juxtaposition of the domestic call and Sawyer's concern that she shouldn't read swear words had her brain in a boggle.

"See anything?"

"Not yet." She took photos of the grass, the driveway, the street in front of his house.

He stood watching, hands on his hips, a distraction she couldn't afford. "Why are you doing that?"

"Later, I'll look at these enlarged. You never know what you might miss." When she'd finished in the front, she moved around to the side and then the back of the town house. What she saw stopped her in her tracks.

"Sawyer." She glanced over one shoulder and held a hand out behind her to stop his progress. "Don't come any farther. Someone's been back here. We want to preserve this."

His tanned skin paled. "Footprints?"

The impressions on the morning dew were light but they led right up to his window. She backtracked to where he stood.

"Someone walked through those woods—" she pointed "—across the edge of the golf course and looked in this back window."

His Adam's apple bobbed. "That's a guest bedroom. Mine's upstairs."

But his vandal didn't know that. Until last night.

This was personal. Very personal. Which meant his

graffiti artist might be a woman. "Is there any chance you have a stalker?"

"A stalker? Seriously?" He scoffed, a short, disbelieving laugh. "No."

"No one? Nothing unusual? No girlfriend who won't turn you loose? No phone calls that hang up? No notes or emails or Facebook messages that make you uncomfortable or seem out of place?"

"No— I— Well…" His usually happy countenance darkened to midnight. He pulled a hand over his face. "I've had a couple of odd emails and a few weird Facebook messages, but that's social media for you. Everybody gets them. I didn't give them a second thought."

She offered her coldest, most professional glare. "How long have you gotten these?"

He shifted, clearly uncomfortable. "A while."

"A while? You've had possible evidence all along and you've been holding out on me?"

"No! Not intentionally anyway. I didn't think they were important."

She looked toward the sky and made a frustrated growling sound. "I'll want to see those. All of them."

"Okay. Sure thing."

She clenched her back teeth. "Now."

Now didn't happen immediately. Leroy arrived and took his report before they had a chance to retire inside the town house.

Sawyer knew Jade was miffed and the delay annoyed her to no end. She was as chilly as Denali in January.

After Leroy left, Sawyer phoned his parents to give them an update and announce regrets that he wouldn't make it to church this morning.

"Would you mind picking up Bailey and Ashton? I invited her but—" He let the rest dangle. Mom got it.

"Are you sure everything is safe at your house?" she asked.

He was admittedly a little freaked out. "Yeah. I'm fine. No worries. Jade is here and we're going over some ideas."

No way he would tell his mother about the weird emails until he knew if they were meaningful. Having one female upset with him was enough.

"Will you be here later for dinner?" Sunday afternoons were a tradition at the parents' house. He didn't like to miss it.

"Don't know." He eyed Jade. She paced like a neat little lion around his living room, staring at everything as if he was hiding something. She was still fired up about the emails as if he'd intentionally kept them from her. "I'll ask Jade."

Jade's head whipped around, smoky eyes curious. His silly heart did a downbeat. He shot her a quick, if uncertain, smile, finished his conversation with Mom and rang off.

"Want something to drink?" His abandoned Coke had long gone flat. He ambled to the doorway between kitchen and living room. "Hot out there."

"Some water would be great."

"Got it." They'd come a long way. The first time she'd been in his house, she'd refused his offer of refreshment and dripped icicles all over the place. She wasn't really mad at him about the emails. She was worried.

Before he could get happy about that revelation, she appeared in the doorway. "Ask me what?"

"Are you eavesdropping on my convo with my mama?" He offered a smile so she'd know he joked, though he didn't figure she'd be amused.

"Hard not to." She crossed her arms but he detected a

softening around that pretty mouth and a sparkle in her gray eyes. "Ask me what?"

"The Buchanons get together every Sunday morning for church and at Mom and Dad's house for food and fun in the afternoon. You're invited."

He twisted the top on a frosty water bottle and handed it to her. Her fingers brushed his in the exchange and he had a flashback to the lake, holding hands, feeling a bit romancey.

"Thanks." She turned away with her drink, leaving him alone in the kitchen.

"'Thanks' isn't an answer." He popped the top on a fresh Coke and followed. "We had a great time yesterday, didn't we?"

"Yes. It was fantastic. Your family is very nice. The lake was perfect. I haven't enjoyed a day on the water in over a year." She actually smiled. "And your mad boating skills were impressive."

Would wonders never cease? She'd admitted what he already knew—she'd had a good time. And unless his radar had gone wonky, she liked him more than she wanted to admit, though he couldn't figure out why she resisted the idea. Was he that bad?

"You're a good skier," he said.

"So are you." Admittedly, he'd shown off to impress her when he'd had his turn on the water.

"We had fun together. You and me."

Her smile wavered. "We did. Thanks for taking me."

They stood staring at each other while some emotion pinged through the atmosphere. She'd accused him of holding back, but she was holding back, as well.

Divorce, he supposed, could do that to you. Distrust. Uncertainty. Lumping all guys into the same category. Was that the problem?

"So what do you say? Later this afternoon with the Buchanon clan?"

"Maybe. If I have time." She motioned toward his laptop. "Now let's see those posts and emails."

Sawyer sipped his soda and ambled to the couch.

He could be content with maybe.

Jade settled on the sofa next to Sawyer and his laptop. He smelled clean, like soap and water, though he hadn't shaved today. No time, she supposed, after discovering the graffiti on his truck. Not that she was complaining. The scruff only added to his tanned good looks.

"I deleted the emails but they should still be in my trash folder." He scrolled through the long list, and if he was bothered by having her look over his shoulder and pry into his personal email account, he didn't let on.

"Here. This one." He clicked on an email and she leaned in to read the rambling love letter. With her side touching his and his breath on her cheek, she struggled to focus on the email. All she had to do was turn her head and there he was, scruffy beard, blue eyes and manly face.

She cleared her throat and stared at the computer screen, too aware of him. "You have a secret admirer."

She wasn't surprised by that. Probably lots of girls crushed on him and never let on. But had this particular one taken her feelings too far and become a stalker?

Sawyer was shaking his head. "I don't buy the secret admirer idea. Buchanons shoot from the hip, straight and honest."

Did they? Really? She wondered what her father would say to that.

"You may be an upfront kind of person. That doesn't mean she is." Jade ran her gaze over the letter a second time.

"She calls herself 'your special girl.' Doesn't that bring

anyone to mind? Some girl you've given a pet name to? Some secret love you don't want your family to know about?"

She lifted her eyes and they were face-to-face, way too close. Not close enough.

Her heart did a painful rhythm. She battled to remember that Sawyer was a client and she was on the job.

Sawyer was clearly oblivious to the turmoil going on inside her. He flicked a glance in her direction and then back to the screen, all business. Which she should be.

"I told you. I'm not fond of secrets. Not that kind anyway. I don't date anyone my family wouldn't approve of."

Had his family approved of her?

She pushed that aberrant thought back into hiding. He didn't like secrets and she had plenty he didn't know about.

"You require your family's approval to date a woman? That sounds a bit archaic."

"I don't *require* anything. I want their approval."

Were the Buchanons controlling? Demanding? Forceful and judgmental when he didn't bow to their expectations? Like her father. "Family first?"

"Nope. God comes first. Family second."

The God issue again. "Will you be ostracized if you don't abide by their beliefs?"

He gave her the strangest look. "Seriously? Does my family seem that way to you?"

No, they didn't. They'd been warm and receptive and genuinely interested in her. They'd even gone to the trouble of bringing homemade oatmeal cookies because they'd somehow discovered those were her favorite.

"I'm trying to get a clearer picture of your family dynamics." True enough, but not because of the case.

"We're as transparent as they come, Jade. Plain and simple, we love and respect each other. We like to be together. We like serving God and our community as a family unit. It's the Buchanon way."

The Buchanon way sounded nothing like the Clifton way. Was their idea of Christian faith different, too?

Flummoxed, she turned to the screen and pointed. "Email this to me. I'll try to trace the source."

He gave her a strange look but didn't press. Instead, he followed her directions to forward the email. His fingers moved quickly over the keyboard, competent, as he seemed to be in so many things.

Fighting to remain professional, she said, "Let's have a look at the Facebook messages."

He logged in to his profile page, his shoulder rubbing against hers as he typed.

After their day at the lake, she'd lain awake in the motel for hours, reliving every moment, remembering the feel of her hand in his, the flash of his smile, the concern he'd shown on the water. He wasn't what she'd expected, a truth that messed with her head.

That he was handsome was a given, but more than looks fueled Sawyer's appeal. Was he for real? Was all this familial love and harmony on the up-and-up?

She watched his hands, strong and masculine, working the keys. He was, she knew, left-hand dominant, and a long scar ran between his thumb and forefinger.

"I didn't notice that yesterday."

"What?" He stopped typing.

"The scar." Without a second thought, she reached out and traced it with her index finger. His skin was firm and very warm. An unbidden zip arced up her arm.

Sawyer shifted slightly toward her. Had he felt it, too?

He turned his hand over, wrapped her fingers with his. His expression had gone serious, searching.

Jade swallowed. She shouldn't have touched him. They

were already too cozy, particularly since she couldn't stop thinking about yesterday. About him.

His gaze fell to her lips. He wanted to kiss her. And she wanted him to.

Was she so programmed to fall for the wrong men that she couldn't help herself?

She jerked her hand from his, swallowed thickly and moved toward the coffee table, ostensibly to retrieve her notebook but mostly to regain her equilibrium.

He'd given her more than a potential stalker to think about. A lot more.

Chapter Nine

Friday evening after work, Dawson dropped Sawyer at the body shop for his newly painted truck. His ride looked sweet again, shiny and unmarred by the obscenities he still wished Jade hadn't seen.

Thoughts of Jade were never far away. He was getting in deep with a woman who kept him at arm's length. Most of the time.

One minute Sawyer thought they had something going, and the next she was as cold as the tundra. In spite of everything, he liked her. He'd seen beneath the chilly detective's mask to the woman. She was smart and athletic, she knew how to play and her concern for Bailey and Ashton spoke volumes about her character. There was a good person under that stiff detective exterior.

Something more than this case troubled her, though. He was praying about it, about her. For her.

He regretted the near kiss, and not only because it hadn't happened, though he definitely regretted that part. Worse, their sparks had ignited her reserve and she'd backed out on the afternoon with him and his family.

He'd been bummed enough to talk to Dawson about her, about the way she blew hot and cold, about his own growing desire to be more than her investigation. His twin advised him to give her time and space. If something was there, she'd come around.

In the week since the graffiti incident, he had taken his brother's advice and kept things light and easy even though he'd been with her every day, a necessity for digging into his life, his friends, his college days, his work relationships. No stone was left unturned. As uncomfortable as the invasion of privacy was, he enjoyed the time with Jade.

The fact that he used the case as an excuse to buy her lunch, and as often as he could her dinner, which sometimes turned into long walks by the river—to discuss the case, of course—didn't shame him one bit. He hadn't even held her hand.

Focusing on the more important matter of faith, he had invited her to church, which led to a conversation about his personal relationship with Christ. This time she listened, asking questions in her astute detective manner. She'd said little and he didn't know where she stood, but she was thawing.

Like Dawson, Mom said she'd been hurt and that he should tread easy, both as an interested man and as a Christian. Living faith was a more powerful witness than talking about it.

He didn't figure he could tread any easier. If Jade didn't know he was a good guy by now, would she ever?

He cranked the truck engine, listened with pleasure at the diesel rumble and prepared to drive away. His cell phone buzzed against his hip. He left the vehicle in Park and answered.

"Sawyer here. Who's this?"

"Sawyer? This is Kinley. Something kind of weird happened today."

Kinley Aimes. They'd dated off and on last year. Gorgeous brunette who could dance like a pro. Nice girl. "Something weird? Are you okay?"

"I'm good, but I thought you should know a woman stopped by my work. She was asking questions about you."

The hair at the back of his neck tingled. Jade thought he had a stalker. Was his stalker now after his former girlfriends?

"Did you get a name?"

"She said she was a private investigator working on a case for your family. But her questions seemed off. She made me uncomfortable."

Jade? Why would she be talking to Kinley? Had he even given her Kinley's name? "Off? Like how?"

"She asked about us, about when we were seeing each other. I thought it was a strange conversation."

Oh. That made sense. Part of the investigation. Maybe she was ruling out stalkers. Not that he would enlighten Kinley on that front.

"Nothing to worry about, Kin. She's working for my dad, investigating vandalism to Buchanon Built properties."

"I've heard about that. But why is she asking about you? And why is she getting so personal?"

The word penetrated his thick skull. "Personal? How personal?"

"She didn't ask much about me or about the vandalism. She wanted to know about your temper."

"Me? A temper?"

Kinley laughed. "That's what I told her. You're the least tempestuous guy I know, but she was a little pushy and insisted on asking about your behavior. Were you the jealous type? Did you control where I went or who my friends were? Did you get upset if I talked to other guys? Had you ever hit me?"

Sawyer gripped the cell phone in a stranglehold. "She asked you that? For real?"

"Yes. It was a really strange moment, Sawyer. I'm sorry. I thought you should know someone is saying this kind of thing about you."

Somehow he managed to finish the conversation with the appropriate assurances and thanks.

As he pressed End, he stared out at the busy street, seeing nothing but trouble.

He didn't have a temper. He wasn't mean or abusive. But right now, he was running between bewildered and steamed.

He and Nancy Drew had some serious talking to do.

Jade sat cross-legged on the motel bed, computer on her lap and notes at her side. Her brain was exhausted and she needed a break but she'd learned some interesting things today. Some of which she should share with Sawyer. Some. Definitely not all.

She reached for her cell. He'd been different this week, careful, almost solicitous. He'd kept a friendly distance. Oh, he'd been Mr. Charm and Smiles, but he hadn't been the least romantic. He hadn't even held her hand. Not once.

Which was great. Fine. Dandy. Friendly and businesslike was for the best.

Even if it left her a little miserable and lonely at the end of each day. Especially on the evenings he or someone in his family swept Bailey and Ashton away for dinner or some church event. They invited her, too, but she always declined.

Jade rubbed her eyes and stretched. Why had she said no? Was she that afraid?

A knock sounded on her door. "Hey, Nancy. You in there?"

Her heart leaped like a circus flea. Sawyer.

She padded on bare feet to the door. "Who's there?"

"The Big Bad Wolf. Open up before I blow your house down."

She opened up.

He didn't smile. "We need to talk."

"I'm busy—"

"Now works for me."

Before she could react, he barged into her room and shut the door behind him. Mr. Charm wasn't happy. He bordered on anger. Maybe worse.

A breath caught in Jade's throat. She backed up a few steps and bumped into the built-in desk.

They were alone. She had nowhere to run. He was bigger, more muscular. And he'd caught her off guard.

Self-defense training floated through her mind. If he raised a hand, she'd fight back. She wouldn't be a victim again. She would not cower.

With much effort, she forced herself to straighten and clench her fists. Ready.

Sawyer tilted his head. His expression went from anger to confusion. "What's wrong with you? Why are you looking at me like that?"

She licked dry lips. "Like what?"

"Scared." Light dawned on his face. "Did you learn something? Did someone threaten you?"

He moved then and she let him, aware she was overreacting.

"No." To regain her composure, she turned her back, pretending to look through a folder on the desk. When she thought she had herself together, she whipped around, pasting on a pleasant expression. "What did you want to talk to me about?"

"Are you sure you're okay? You look—"

"I'm fine. Now what do you want?" There. Crisp. Professional. To the point.

If only she wasn't dressed in yoga pants and flip-flops.

He gave her a once-over, as if he still thought she had a screw loose, but settled with saying, "You paid a visit to a friend of mine today. Kinley."

How did he know that?

"I did. And to several other girls whose names you gave me." She reached behind and drew out the folder. "I have them all in here."

"Must be crowded."

She blinked, bewildered for a second before the joke settled in. "Oh. Funny."

"You don't look amused. And I'm not, either. Why are you bothering my friends with this? None of them would vandalize my truck."

"I can't leave any stone unturned, Sawyer. Even though you believe the best about your friends, people sometimes hide who they really are." She flipped open the folder. "Like your stalker friend. Her email is fake. So is her Facebook and other social media files."

"Is that so?"

"She uses a fake name, photos of lesser-known actresses as her profile pics and leaves no useful identifying information."

His frown deepened to a scowl. "Why would anyone do that?"

She shrugged. "A number of reasons. Privacy. Safety."

"Or to cover her tracks."

"If our perp is female."

"What if it's a man using this as a ploy to throw us off?"

The idea scared her to pieces. "Possible but doubtful. I see desperation, maybe unrequited love, feelings of rejection."

"That's stupid."

"There are a lot of women's names in my file."

"Friends."

"That's what I hear." Every last female she'd called or visited claimed she and Sawyer remained friends after they stopped dating. Did anyone really do that? Or were they covering up for him? For themselves?

"If you'd bother to ask, I have male friends, too." He pivoted to her fridge. "Got any Cokes in here?"

"No."

He huffed a weary, put-upon breath and crossed his arms. "All right, then. I need to know something. And I expect a straight answer."

She didn't like the look in his eyes.

"Why did you ask Kinley if I'd ever hit her? What's that got to do with someone spray painting my truck?"

Jade imitated his posture and crossed her arms. "Procedure."

"No." His head wagged from side to side. "I don't buy that. Something else is going on here."

"I spoke with five women today and asked them all the same questions." Unable to hold his gaze any longer, she dropped her stance and pretended to rummage through the file.

She felt him move across the motel room, felt his size and height in the small space. Though the hair rose on the back of her neck, she didn't turn around, didn't cower. If Sawyer's women spoke the truth, she had nothing to fear.

A strong hand touched her shoulder.

In spite of everything, she flinched.

"Why do you do that?" His voice had grown soft and was a breath away from her ear. His new-wood scent whispered around her like his voice.

She gulped. "Do what?"

The murmured words trembled.

"Jade." Slowly, he turned her around and took the clutched file from her death grip. "All these questions today about my temper and violence. Then tonight you jump as if you're afraid of me. If someone said I hurt them, they lied and I need to know."

She was already shaking her head. "No one."

"Then what's going on? I thought we liked each other. I'm not the grim reaper."

She forced a laugh. "I know that."

"Let's get something straight." His piercing gaze never left her face. "I don't hit women. Ever. I don't push them or slap them or force them to do anything they don't want to. And I'm offended that you would think that."

"I don't." She didn't. She really didn't. But the defense mechanisms had become second nature.

"Yes, you do. Or maybe it's not me. Maybe it was the jerk you divorced."

She went very still, barely breathing. Talking about the abuse made her vulnerable. She couldn't appear vulnerable to a client.

She turned her head to one side, away from his intensely interested gaze. If her heart beat any faster, she'd need a defibrillator. Paddles to the chest. Electroshock.

As gentle as a breath, Sawyer touched her chin and tugged her back to face him. "I said the magic words, didn't I? The ex."

She remained silent but tears prickled the back of her eyelids. She did not cry. She would not cry. Crying was a weak woman's weapon.

But Sawyer, with his gift for people, saw what she tried to hide. The expression on his face changed, melting her. Compassion, devastation.

Her family had blamed her. She'd provoked Cam. She

was stubborn, uncooperative, a bad wife. She got what she deserved.

"I'm right, aren't I?" His voice was so tender and understanding, she nodded.

His arms came around her immediately. He drew her to his chest, lightly, carefully.

"Oh, Jade. Sweetheart. I'm sorry." Long fingers caressed her hair, smoothing it over and over again as he had his niece when she'd scraped a knee at the lake. Gentle, protective, caring.

Letting down six years of carefully erected guard, she laid her head against his thudding, thudding heart and rested.

Sawyer was a peaceful man. He normally made friends, not foes. Somewhere along the line, he'd made a powerful enemy who vandalized his family's property. And now he had another. A man he didn't know. A man he'd like to get his hands on for five long minutes in a private setting. Man-to-man.

Carpentry had made him strong. He could do some serious damage if he wanted to. Right now, he wanted to.

As tenderly as knew how, he held Jade against him and stroked her hair, her back, and if he kissed the top of her head, he wasn't sorry. She needed comfort. She tried to put on a brave front, but she was wounded.

"Want to tell me about it?"

At first she shook her head no, so he didn't press. He simply held her. She made no attempt to move and seemed perfectly content where she was. So was he. Holding Jade was something he'd thought about often but he'd been waiting for the right moment.

He'd had something decidedly more romantic in mind. But for now, she needed him, and that was enough.

The room grew quiet until the only sounds were their mingled breaths and the outside noises. Cars passed in a hiss on hot pavement. A heavy unit door slammed nearby. Vague voices drifted through the paper-thin walls of the old motel.

Then she began to speak. Softly at first, almost as if to herself. She told of Cam, her husband of three years. Three years with a man who alternated between sweetness and gifts to control and anger. He'd bought her a new Mercedes the day after he'd knocked out a tooth.

"He promised it would never happen again."

He could feel her trembling. Even remembering the abuse was traumatic. "And you wanted to believe him."

"If I would try harder, it wouldn't happen. If I wouldn't make him angry. If I could be the good wife he expected me to be." Her words grew stronger, more defiant. "We were married two years before I realized the problem was him instead of my inadequacies."

"Why didn't you leave then?"

She pulled away from his embrace and crossed her arms again. Then, as if she realized she didn't need a defensive posture with him, she let her arms fall to her sides.

"Women keep silent. Submit to your husbands. A divorced woman is an adulteress, a Jezebel. I've had those scriptures forced down my throat since I was a child." She made a scoffing sound that pricked his heart. "My father insists I'm doomed for all eternity unless I return to Cam."

Somebody's theology was seriously twisted. "That's wrong, Jade. Those scriptures are in the Bible, sure, but the context is off."

She tossed her head. "Whatever. I don't really care anymore. I'm rid of Cam and religion."

"Good for you for tossing Cam. But don't throw Jesus out with the bathwater."

She backed away, face tight. "Don't preach to me, Sawyer. I've had enough of that to last a lifetime."

He raised both hands. "No preaching. Just remember that real men don't have to force their women to do anything. They sure don't hit them. Real men take care of women."

"I can take care of myself." She crossed her arms again, tight as shrink-wrap.

"You shouldn't have to. Not alone. The Bible says two are better than one because if one falls down, the other can help them up." He stretched a hand toward her. "Let me help you up, Jade."

"I'm the investigator. I'm supposed to be helping you."

He kept his hand extended, waiting, his chest hot with compassion and yearning. "We can help each other."

A dozen emotions flickered across her face until at last she softened. Slowly, she extended her hand and with her gaze pinned to his, reading him, making sure she could trust his motives, she moved back into his embrace.

Sawyer felt as if he'd conquered Mount Everest.

Chapter Ten

Sunday morning, Jade stood in front of the wavy motel mirror with a curling iron and a hairbrush. Somehow Sawyer, with help from Bailey, had persuaded her to attend church as a prelude to dinner at his parents' home.

The very idea formed a knot in her stomach so tight she'd need Houdini to untie it.

She enjoyed the Buchanons, having spent every day with at least one of them. And the lake trip had been terrific. The big noisy family was all right, cordial, even likable. But church? What had she been thinking to willingly subject herself to fire and brimstone so hot it singed her hair? Hadn't she had enough of that growing up?

Sawyer Buchanon was getting to her. That's all there was to it.

Check that. Sawyer had gotten to her. With his warmth and charm, he'd tunneled through her barriers and made her like him. Not that she fully trusted him, but she felt something she'd never felt before, not even for Cam in their early days before she learned of the monster hidden behind the smile and a bouquet of roses.

People, she'd learned the hard way, were not always who they presented to the rest of the world. Sawyer seemed like the real deal, but she wasn't foolish. He might be hiding something, the way he'd hidden the secret admirer emails. Sure, he denied he was hiding them, but she couldn't be positive.

Emotions would never rule her life again.

The curling iron clattered against the desktop. She turned it off. Should she go or not?

Long after Sawyer had left the other night Jade had pondered their conversation, a talk that had lasted into the late hours. She was still amazed that she'd told him about Cam. Not everything, of course. Some hurts cut too deep.

The fact that he'd tiptoed around her aversion to his faith, all the while displaying his in the gentlest way, didn't escape notice.

She wasn't stupid. She knew there were different kinds of Christians. The trouble was she'd blocked all mention of God out of her life after escaping Cam and Southview.

And then Sawyer came along.

Caution lights flashed like red and yellow fireworks inside her head.

Bailey would be disappointed if she backed out now.

"Bailey will be fine." She had friends at the Lighthouse Church and a nursery full of workers with tons of baby toys for Ashton.

She leaned into the funhouse mirror and stroked mascara onto her lashes.

Church was only a couple of hours. She could endure it. And Sawyer was probably already on his way.

But why should she have to?

Why indeed?

With a click, she recapped the mascara and went for her cell phone. In seconds, Sawyer was on the line. She opened her mouth to tell a lie when someone pecked on the door.

"Jade?" Bailey's voice came through the flimsy wood loud and clear.

"Just a second, Sawyer." Jade spoke into the receiver. "Bailey's outside."

She crossed the small space and opened the door.

"You don't look ready for church." In fact, Bailey looked exhausted and scared. "Is something wrong?"

Bailey nodded and burst into tears.

Instinctively, Jade pulled the young mom and her baby into her room, stepped out and scanned the area.

A tinny voice inside her cell phone said, "Jade. Is Bailey all right? What's wrong? I hear her crying. What's going on?"

Ashton whimpered, drowning out the rest of Sawyer's words.

Satisfied that the area was clear, Jade closed the door and shoved the dead bolt, before speaking to Sawyer. "I'll call you back."

Before he could argue, she pushed End and tossed the phone toward the unmade bed.

She guided the sobbing teenager to a corner of the bed and sat down beside her. "Talk to me. Did someone hurt you? Did someone break in? Are you sick?"

"Ashton."

Jade noticed what she hadn't before. A listless Ashton lay against Bailey's chest, his face flushed, his eyes glassy.

Jade placed a hand on his little forehead. "He's burning up."

Bailey nodded, tears streaking her young face. "I don't know what to do. He's never been sick."

"Did you take his temperature?"

"I don't have a thermometer." And she burst into fresh tears. "I'm scared, Jade. I'm a horrible mother. I don't know how to do this. He won't eat and he just lays there like he's dying. Is he going to die, Jade?"

Jade's years of cop training clicked in. Brusquely, with forced confidence, she replied, "Of course not. Babies get fevers easily."

She had no idea if that was true.

"He was fussy last night but when he finally stopped crying, I went to sleep, thinking he was okay. But he's not. He's not okay." Bailey's face contorted. "I'm a terrible mom. I should have stayed awake. He needed me and I was asleep! What if he had died?"

Jade put her arm around the distraught girl. She was exhausted, scared and too young to handle a baby alone. Jade didn't know a lot about babies either, and her first responder training didn't cover fevers.

"Let's calm down. Okay? He will be fine, but Ashton needs you to have a clear head right now." She kept her voice kind but firm and confident. "Deep breath. Blow it out."

Bailey shuddered in a chest full of air but sobbed on the exhale.

Carefully, Jade lifted the hot baby from his mother's arms. He felt limp and lifeless. Her adrenaline jacked a notch higher.

"We'll take him to the emergency room and get him checked out. Okay?"

Bailey nodded, wiping at her face with the backs of her hands.

"Tissue in the bathroom. Splash some water on your face too and we'll go." She didn't even know where the nearest hospital was but GPS would get her there.

The door to her unit shook under a pounding fist. "Jade. It's Sawyer. Let me in."

A familiar voice. Someone who knew the town and doctors. Thank goodness.

Baby in one arm, she slid the dead bolt. Handsome in slacks, shirt and tie, a harried Sawyer plunged inside. He took one look at Ashton and said, "He's sick."

Fighting the instant attraction, Jade snarled. "You don't have to be a detective to know that."

If Sawyer was insulted, he didn't let on, and she instantly felt like a jerk for barking at him.

"Hey, little man. What's wrong, buddy?" Sawyer placed a hand on Ashton's forehead. Worried blue eyes flickered up to hers. "He's burning up."

Grimly, she nodded. "We're headed to the ER."

Tissue pressed against her nose, Bailey exited the bathroom, spotted Sawyer and burst into fresh sobs. He crossed the room and folded her into his arms.

"Hey, we got this, little sis. We got this." He rocked her back and forth for a minute while Jade's insides turned over and her heart squeezed.

He released Bailey, dazzled her with a reassuring smile and guided her toward the door. "Get in my truck. I'll take you. We'll have this little guy fixed up in time for Sunday dinner."

Jade didn't argue. The baby was the important thing here, not her rather significant relief at discovering Sawyer Buchanon outside her door.

The Gabriel's Crossing Hospital sprawled on the south edge of town, three blocks from the fire station and fifteen minutes from the River Roost Motel. Sawyer drove there in ten.

Babies, he assured Bailey on the short drive, spiked fevers over the simplest thing. Ashton probably had a cold.

He'd conjured up all the calming things he'd heard his mother say to his sister when Ryan and Amber were babies.

Still, turning the teen and her baby over to Gena Satterfield, nurse practitioner, brought instant relief. Gena was a first-rate pro and practically family. She'd take good care of Ashton.

The nurse whisked Mom and baby away with her usual efficient cheer and left him and Jade to wait.

He sat next to Jade in a green vinyl chair, hands clasped between his knees, eyes shut as he prayed for Ashton to be okay.

"Bailey's too young to handle this alone."

Sawyer swiveled his head toward Jade. "She's not alone. She has us."

"For today. But what about the next time? What about the rest of her life?"

Her knuckles had gone white where she squeezed the chair arm. The episode had shaken her. Not so much, he thought, because of the sick baby but because Bailey lived alone, without family support. Like Jade, apparently.

"One thing at a time, okay?" He took the liberty of placing his hand atop hers. Even though the temperature outside was hot, her fingers were cold. "Let's get Ashton well. We'll figure out the rest from there."

He'd expected her to argue but instead, she chewed that intriguing bottom lip and momentarily took his mind off Ashton.

We, he'd said. As if Jade would be around to help. That she wouldn't be soured his stomach.

He tapped a message into his phone. His family would add Ashton to today's prayer requests.

"You're missing church again," Jade said.

"Jesus knows where I am. He was always more concerned about people's needs than a church building anyway."

She gave him a funny look and he understood. His faith didn't match her distorted view of God. He was praying for her. Had the whole family on their knees.

Admittedly, his heart had gone a little *bonk-bonk* when Jade opened the door with a baby in her arms. She'd looked soft and motherly, though soft wasn't a word Jade wanted anyone to use in her regard. She tried so hard to be tough.

He understood that, too, now that he knew about the ex-husband. If Sawyer ever met Cam Warren, they'd both need prayer.

He stretched out his long legs to get more comfortable and brought Jade's hand to rest on his knee, holding her there.

A man entered the emergency room, a towel held to his hand. A brunette woman followed, red purse under one arm.

"Chet?" Sawyer sat up straight, releasing Jade's hand. "What happened? Are you okay?"

"Aw, nothing serious. A little cut." Chet hitched a chin toward the woman now at the reception desk. "Livy thinks I need stitches."

Livy, a robust woman in glasses and sneakers, turned her head. "And a tetanus shot. Hiya, Sawyer."

"Livy." He offered a courteous nod. "Anything I can do?"

"Short of taking away his power tools? Not a thing." She shook her head as though disgusted with the whole male gender.

The two men exchanged amused glances before a scrub-clad nurse stepped out to take the couple back to an exam room.

The ER was slow this Sunday morning. Thankfully.

"Do you know everyone in Gabriel's Crossing?" Jade

reached for one of the dog-eared, battered magazines lying on an end table.

"Mostly. The blessing of a small town."

"Or the curse. You likely know your stalker. Maybe see her every day."

His stomach clenched. The stalker hadn't been on his mind—until now. *Thanks a lot, Jade.* "Disturbing thought."

His cell phone buzzed. Sawyer looked down. "From Dawson. The family had prayer for Ashton. Wants to know if they should come down here."

"Why would they do that?"

"The Buchanon way. Doesn't your family come running when you need them?"

Her jaw tightened. "I'm an adult. I don't need them to come running."

The adamant response convinced him all was not well with her family. He couldn't imagine. "You're not close?"

"Close enough."

She turned prickly again and he knew he'd stepped on troubled territory. She had brothers. She'd shared that much, and they'd once skied together. But not in a long time.

Something had happened.

"I wouldn't want to be without my family around. They're awesome people."

"Not everyone has that, Sawyer."

"I'm sorry."

"Me, too." Her bottom lip quivered, vulnerable. She turned her head away.

Sawyer wanted badly to comfort her. Jade could seem alone in a crowded room. He wanted to wrap her in his arms the way he had at the motel last week. To feel her heartbeat against his, her breath against his neck.

She pricked his heart, and he was still trying to wrap his head around the way she made him feel.

His phone chimed again. He read the message. "They'll wait dinner for us."

"They don't have to do that."

"But they will." His thumbs moved over the keyboard. "I told him we'd let them know as soon as Gena comes out with news about Ashton."

She went back to her magazine, though he could tell from the way she flipped pages that her mind was elsewhere.

Time ticked past, marked by the commercials on Sunday-morning television programs.

He spotted them before Jade did and an inner smile moved to his lips.

"What are you smiling about?"

He hadn't known she was watching.

He pointed toward the glass doors.

Jade's face grew incredulous as the parade of Buchanons streamed into the waiting area. His parents, his brothers and sisters. Even Brady and Abby, back only one or two days from their honeymoon, were here.

He'd known they would come. No amount of reassurance would keep them away.

Sawyer stood, aware of how blessed he was to have this giant bunch of people who loved him. No matter his failures and quirks, they were there for him. Bailey didn't have that kind of support. Neither did Jade.

"Any news yet?" His mother came straight to him for a hug. She smelled like summer flowers, familiar and cheering.

"No, but Gena's got him."

Quinn nodded, pride shining on his face as vivid as

Abby and Brady's Italian glow. "Best doc in town, even if she's a nurse."

Jade looked from one Buchanon to the other, apparently stunned by the overwhelming support. "But you were at church…"

"We spoke to Pastor and asked for prayer before leaving. He understands family emergencies."

Mom's statement seemed to confuse Jade even more. "Ashton and Bailey aren't your family."

"Family of God. They need us. We're here." Dawson flopped into one of the green chairs, long legs identical to his twin's in navy dress slacks. The rest of the family scattered around the small waiting area, taking up all the vacant seats.

The quiet waiting room was suddenly less cold and anesthetic.

Sawyer and Jade filled in the details they knew about Ashton's illness, and then they settled in to wait, chatting about this and that, mostly about Brady's honeymoon. Anything to pass the time.

Dad, with his usual workaholic energy, paced the room and stared out the window a few times.

Brady and Abby snuggled together on a love seat to exchange loving looks and to share honeymoon photos with Charity and Jaylee.

"Want to see these, Jade?" Jaylee patted the corner of her chair. His youngest sister was so thin, petite Jade easily fit in the extra space.

The distraction, Sawyer thought, was good for her. And he enjoyed watching her with his family.

By the time Gena finally ushered Bailey and Ashton to the waiting room, the nurse practitioner was smiling. Bailey looked less frightened.

Sawyer stood. The rest of the Buchanons rose with him, a wall of protection and support. "What's the verdict?"

"Ear infection." Gena held a prescription in one hand. "Baby fever reducer and antibiotics should fix him up. He'll probably sleep most of the day." She settled a steady look at Bailey. "And his mother should do the same."

Sawyer reached for the Rx. The tension in his shoulders eased.

"I'll take that." He winked at Bailey. "Your hands are full."

His mama, God bless her, slipped an arm around the teenager. "You're coming home with us, honey. We'll look after Ashton so you can get some rest. After you have a good dinner."

"Oh, I couldn't."

"Why not?"

"I—" The yearning on the girl's face was undeniable.

"Don't argue with Mom." Sawyer shot Bailey an easy, encouraging smile and a quick wink. "She always wins."

The Buchanon women flanked the young mother. Charity lifted the baby from her arms and laid him over one shoulder to pat his little back. "Both of you need rest and we're all at Mom's house today anyway. We'd love to watch this little prince while you catch a nap."

At times like this, he adored his big sister.

"Trust me, I know how crucial sleep can be when you have a sick child." This from Abby, who'd weathered many illnesses alone with her special needs daughter until she'd met Brady and been enveloped by the Buchanon clan.

"I *am* really tired," Bailey admitted. "But Jade—"

"Jade's coming, too." Sawyer knew an advantage when he had one. Jade wouldn't let Bailey down.

Bailey nodded, relief hanging on her like a robe. "Okay, then. Thanks."

Before Jade could utter a word of protest, Sawyer took her elbow and ushered her to his truck.

Who were these people? Were they for real?

Sunday afternoon at the Buchanon home was like nothing Jade had ever experienced. Even the few friends who had invited her to their homes as a teenager didn't have families like this one.

The sprawling split-level home on Barley Street rocked with laughter and conversation. The smell of bacon-wrapped chicken from Dan's patio smoker had everyone salivating and groaning while they waited for side dishes to be completed.

Feeling at loose ends, Jade hung around the long bar separating a huge kitchen from an even bigger family/dining room. With seven kids, she supposed the enormous space and the long, banquet-style table were warranted.

Bailey, too exhausted to wait for dinner, had been put to bed in something called "the apartment" off the garage. Apparently, Abby and Lila had lived there for a while when their house was being built and in the subsequent days after the fire destroyed the new home Brady had built for her.

As soon as the girl and baby were settled, the Buchanons formed a huddle in the family room. Jade stood on the perimeter, curious as she listened to a discussion of Bailey's situation.

They expressed concern and tossed around ideas. Not once did she hear anyone malign the teenager for being an unwed mother. No one spouted dire scriptures about her sinfulness. No one condemned her to punishment and misery.

Allison, sitting next to her husband, Jake, bracketed her baby bump. "I can't imagine being alone with my baby, no support, no family to call in times of stress."

"Social services can only do so much." Quinn massaged his damaged shoulder.

"No social service can offer love and a promise to be available anytime, anywhere."

"But we can." Karen looped an arm with her husband's. "We're in the perfect position to give it. Aren't we, Dan?"

The older Buchanons made a handsome couple. Tall and dark like his sons, Dan's slight paunch didn't detract from his looks and blonde, middle-aged Karen was beautiful.

It wasn't their looks, though, that intrigued Jade. It was the way Dan treated Karen with respect and admiration, as an equal, instead of like a brainless doormat. And Karen clearly admired her husband. They formed a team, banded together for a common goal.

Nothing like her parents, for sure.

"Another rug rat around here is exactly what this big old house needs." Dan's expression grew tender as he gazed from Karen to little Lila pushing her walker around the patio outside. "We're going to miss our Princess Lila around here."

Brady laughed. "She won't be that far away, Dad."

"Still gonna miss hearing her giggles."

"Yes, we are." Karen patted Dan's arm. "So the issue of Bailey and Ashton is settled. We'll ask them to move in with us while she finishes school and gets on her feet."

Jade blinked at Karen's statement. While she finished school? That was more than an afternoon of kindness. That was long-term. "You'd do that?"

"Welcome to the Buchanon menagerie, Jade." Sawyer's smile spoke of his familial pride. If the Buchanons were for real, he had a right to be.

Dan clapped his hands once, as if that finalized everything. "Now that we have that settled, who's hungry?"

Collective cheers went up as the group stampeded

toward the dining room table. Jade stood there, dumb-founded. By them. By their generosity. By their sheer numbers.

Sawyer snagged her elbow as he passed. There was so much noise, feet and chairs shuffling, laughter and tomfoolery, she didn't catch much of the conversation.

But she let him lead her into the fray, her brain whirling with a paradigm shift.

Was this the way life was meant to be lived? Was this how Christians were supposed to act?

Sawyer jostled her left arm and handed over a big bowl of potato salad, his dimple showing. Quinn teased Brady and Abby about living on love, though Brady's plate was piled high with shrimp and vegetables. Charity made a joke about Dan singeing his eyebrows over the smoker while a smiling Karen called him the hero of the barbecue.

They weren't perfect, as she knew from her investigation, but they were happy and kind and loved each other.

Regardless of her reserve, she liked them. Every last one, but the man on her left more than all, more than she'd intended.

Maybe families were supposed to be like this, and maybe, just maybe, the Buchanons were not the evil, vengeful creatures her father claimed them to be.

Chapter Eleven

A sunny afternoon by the family swimming pool turned to cooler evening and a touch football game on the lawn. At dark, someone flipped on the porch light for one last game. June bugs buzzed the light, beating their brains out on the side of the house.

Men, women, kids, the whole gang except for Sawyer's pregnant sister, galloped and dodged, laughed and cheated in their usual outrageous manner. Even Bailey, after a very long nap, joined the fun. It was good, Sawyer thought as he watched her, to hear her laugh and play like the teenager she was.

With a pat of her growing belly, Allison opted out of the rough-and-tumble game, volunteering instead to stay inside with Ashton. Even though the baby mostly slept, waking only for a bottle and some fever reducer, Allison declared her need of practice.

Jade genuinely seemed to have a good time. And when she bashed into his side with a fearsome block, Sawyer purposely went sprawling on the thick grass.

Laughing the way he'd always wanted to hear, Jade shot out a hand.

He slapped her palm and wrapped his fingers around hers. "You're tougher than you look."

She tossed blond curls, sassy as she yanked him to his feet. "Told you."

They grinned at each other, out of breath, until one of his ornery brothers shoved him from the back.

"Got a good one there, brother." Brady twitched an eyebrow toward Jade.

Sawyer blew off the statement with a joke, though he suspected his big brother was right. "Not bad for a nosy girl."

Jade elbowed him in the ribs. He *oofed* and moved forward, pretending there was more damage than there was.

Dawson jogged up beside them. "Early start in the morning. I'm heading home. Meet you at the Miller house at seven?"

"Us, too," Brady said. "We're still playing catch-up from being gone so long, and I'm meeting the mayor for breakfast. Zoning issues."

Sawyer readjusted from play to work and mentally checked his schedule, glad Brady handled the business end of things. Give him a slab of wood and a hammer any day over schmoozing the mayor. "Gotta stop at the Building Supply first."

Monday began a new workweek, always a busy day.

The party broke up as the adults gathered kids, toys and wet towels from the backyard and tromped inside.

"I'm grateful we didn't have any break-ins this weekend." Positioning himself next to Jade, Sawyer followed the crowd.

"Perhaps you'll have no more construction site damage. The vandal seems to have focused on you personally."

He made a frustrated noise. "Don't remind me."

"You *are* taking the precautions I suggested, aren't you?"

"Sure." Mostly. He was a man. He was annoyed and angry, not afraid.

Whatever the vandal's motive, Sawyer refused to believe someone wished him physical harm. Still, being the target of anyone's fury nagged at him. Who? Who could be doing this? Was it someone he knew? Someone he liked and thought liked him?

Mom came at Jade with a foil-wrapped packet and a Tupperware container. "Sawyer said you have a fridge and a microwave."

"That's very nice of you. Thanks, and thank you for inviting me this afternoon."

His mom patted Jade's shoulder. "You had a rough start to the day. I'm glad the afternoon turned out better."

"Me, too."

"Don't worry about Bailey and Ashton. We'll take good care of them. Tomorrow, I'll bring her by the motel to pick up her things and check out."

"You're very kind. She appears to be in good hands."

Sawyer frowned. *Appears to be?* That was a strange way to put it. Sawyer had no doubt that his mom and dad would be the underpinnings Bailey needed to get her life back on track. But then, Jade was a private investigator, and her suspicion meter never took a day off.

After a few more minutes of conversation, they said their goodbyes and started the drive to the motel.

Jade was quiet on the ride, focusing her attention out the passenger window. He wondered what she was thinking, what she thought of his family, of him.

"I hope the Buchanon clan wasn't too much for you."

She swiveled to face him. "They're very nice."

"Overwhelming?"

"In a good way."

"Yeah, they're awesome. Loud, annoying, nosy but pretty amazing. I'm a blessed man."

"Yes, you are."

The softly spoken words turned his head. In the soft light of the dashboard, Jade's profile was pensive.

"You worrying about Bailey?" His right hand found hers in the darkness.

"A little." She shifted, her capris whispering on his leather upholstery. "She's a good kid, Sawyer. She needs this boost your family is willing to offer, but I have to ask. What do they get out of it?"

He blinked, frowning at the odd question. "I'm not sure I follow."

"No one is that altruistic without reason. What's their motive?"

"Okaaay." He let go of her hand and made the turn into the motel parking area. "If you need a reason, here you go—Hebrews 13, Matthew 25 and a dozen other scriptures I can't remember. God tells us to share what we have with those in need. To take care of our neighbors."

"That simple?"

He wasn't ready to let her go but she opened the passenger door, lighting the interior.

"That simple." He hopped out, speeding around the truck in time to catch her before she hit the ground. He laughed softly as she stumbled against him. Good timing as far as he was concerned.

He dropped an arm loosely over her shoulders and walked her to the door. This area of town wasn't the best and he fretted to know she came and went alone, but she'd stiffen up all prickly again if he said anything.

Only a few cars passed on the street adjacent to the River Roost, though two of them bounced with loud bass music that set his teeth on edge. Somewhere nearby, probably uptown at the main intersection, an eighteen-wheeler downshifted. A dog barked. The warm summer night pulsed, the area around the motel dark except for the flashing vacancy sign.

When they reached Unit Three, Jade unlocked the door and turned to say good-night. "I enjoyed this afternoon. Thank you."

So stiff and formal. Was she nervous? Afraid that he'd kiss her? Afraid he wouldn't?

He certainly wanted to. "Thanks for hanging out with the wild bunch. You held your own pretty well."

Her bee-stung mouth curved. Sawyer's pulse bumped against his collarbone.

Before he could think of a single reason not to, he leaned slowly down and kissed her. Lightly. Tenderly.

Jade's lips were sweet and soft, the way he'd imagined, and she smelled like barbecue and sunshine.

For the briefest second, she tensed, but every bit as quickly she relaxed and tiptoed up to meet him.

Yeah. This was nice. Better than awesome.

He had that *bing-bong* sensation again, his pulse ratcheting, chest warming. His mind chanted her name.

Reluctantly, figuring he should quit while he was ahead, Sawyer ended the kiss and backed away with a quiet "Good night."

In the shadowy light, Jade's eyes were wide but soft and shining. She looked thunderstruck, the way he felt.

"Good night, Sawyer."

She stepped inside, flipped on the light and closed the door in his face. Sawyer waited until he heard the dead bolt slide before he walked away.

Jade couldn't stop touching her lips. Sawyer, as she'd known he would, kissed like a pro. Like a man who'd kissed dozens of women.

Kissed in a way that made her want to snuggle closer and kiss him again and again.

Heart thudding, she peeled back one slat in the window blinds and watched him walk to his truck, watched the vehicle back up, swing around and drive away, headlights sweeping the motel and disappearing into the night.

He'd kissed her with such tenderness, she'd almost wept. But he hadn't pushed for more. He hadn't taken advantage. He hadn't asked to come inside, expecting more than that one devastating touch of his firm, supple, amazing lips.

He had no idea what that simple act of restraint meant to her.

Dropping the foil-wrapped food and her handbag on the bed, Jade crossed to the wavy, scarred mirror and leaned in, hardly recognizing herself. The tough detective had turned to mush.

She looked soft and vulnerable, the way she didn't want to be. And yet, she couldn't deny the rhythm of happiness pulsing through her bloodstream.

She'd allowed Sawyer to invade her citadel, to smile his way into her heart, to share his incredible family. She felt more for the tall carpenter with the movie star looks than she'd ever intended to allow. Danger was all around, but she'd succumbed to his charm.

Like she had with Cam.

She pressed both hands to her face, reliving the kiss and battling her inward demons. Nothing like Cam.

Nothing like Cam.

Sawyer wasn't all charm and no substance. At least, he didn't appear to be. Cam would never have driven Bailey and her baby to the hospital. Cam wouldn't have stopped at the motel door with only a kiss.

She was falling for Sawyer Buchanon. Falling for a charmer.

Sawyer and his family messed with her head. Were they really such good people, altruistic and caring?

What if they knew who her father was? Would they still invite her to their home and freely offer their friendship?

How would they react if they knew she'd deceived them?

Her conscience pinged.

Like Sawyer, the Buchanon family had been nothing but warm and welcoming. She should have been upfront about her family background from the first day.

But if she'd told them the truth, she could have lost the case…and with it, the opportunity to know Sawyer.

Maybe that would have been a good thing.

With a groan, she put the leftovers in the mini fridge and then flopped onto the bed.

Sawyer was more to her than a pretty face and an intriguing case.

He would hate her if he knew she'd lied. Not in words but in deed.

No, he wouldn't. Not Sawyer.

Mind spinning with a mixture of confusion, longing and all the reasons she shouldn't get involved with Sawyer Buchanon, and all the reasons she already was, Jade relived the day's events, snagging on the conversation in Sawyer's pickup truck.

He'd claimed his family had offered assistance to Bailey because of their faith. He had mentioned two scriptures, neither of which was familiar to her. Not surprising since she had never read the Bible for herself. Never wanted to read about the angry, vengeful God who was eager to punish her for every misstep.

But the Buchanons spoke of God as loving and merciful.

Jade rolled to one side and reached into the top drawer of the bedside table. A Gideon Bible lay inside. She'd seen it every time she'd opened the drawer. Seen the book and ignored it.

Now, she withdrew the brown hardback Bible, racking her memory for the mentioned scriptures.

"Hebrews 13." Finding the index, she flipped to the page and read the entire chapter. She snagged on the first two verses about brotherly love and again at verse sixteen. "Do not forget to do good and to share, for with such sacrifices God is well pleased."

The Buchanons wanted to please God by doing good— a motive with which she could find no fault. Everyone wanted to please God, but she'd grown up thinking to do so required perfection and far greater sacrifices than treating others well.

She'd learned the hard way that she could never be perfect. Nobody could be.

Intrigued, she flipped the pages and read the entire Gospel of John. Some of the scriptures were familiar, but she was shocked at how many were not.

Her interpretation of God shifted. Jesus came to heal hearts, to forgive mistakes and erase wrongs. He displayed mercy and compassion to those who asked.

He came not to condemn but to love and forgive.

Jade's eyes teared up. She blinked away the moisture. She was tired, that was all. She should put away this Bible and go to sleep.

But some force tugged at the place deep inside that had been empty, and she read until she fell asleep with the Gideon Bible on her chest.

Early the next morning she headed to Southview, to the familial home she'd vowed to ignore for as long as possible.

Stubborn to a fault. Begrudging. Unforgiving. That was her.

The drive took less than an hour. Jade used the time to pray, something she hadn't done since Cam had beaten her unconscious and left her bleeding on the bedroom floor of their expensive suburban home.

For such a long time, she'd believed God hadn't heard her sobs and pleas for help. But perhaps she'd been wrong. Cam hadn't killed her. He'd broken her in body and spirit but the event had given her the courage to finally leave him. And she'd survived.

She'd awakened this morning with yesterday's revelations on her mind. She remained confused and uncertain, but if she'd misjudged the Buchanons and God, maybe she'd misjudged her family, too.

Regardless of their differing opinions, she loved her family and missed her mother and their talks. Missed her enough to take this morning away from the Buchanon investigation and drive to the Clifton home in Southview.

Maybe she'd been too hard on her family, even her dad. Perhaps she could mend the rift and take steps toward a more positive, healthy relationship. Like the one the Buchanons shared.

When she arrived at the ordinary wood frame house on Connor Street, only her mother was home. The house looked the same as always, tired and worn, but the interior was spotless, the floors shiny, nothing out of place, the way her father liked things. Mama looked the same. Though she was not allowed to work outside the home, she rose before Daddy every morning to fix her hair and makeup, cook breakfast and to make sure the house was perfect—Daddy's socks and dirty towel picked up, his ashtrays emptied and polished.

Daddy couldn't abide an unkempt woman or a messy house.

Even with finances stretched to the limit, Hugh Clifton

demanded perfection in his home and expected Mama to make it happen. According to Daddy, the Bible said that a wife was subject to her husband's authority and her only role in life was to marry, bear children and take care of the house, and she better keep her mouth shut and do it right. Control was his middle name.

As a child, Jade hadn't recognized his need for power, his complete domination over his wife and children. Now she did.

Jade hugged her mother hello and pushed the resentful thoughts aside. She'd come to mend, not to rehash old wounds.

"Jade, honey, I'm so happy to see you. I thought—" Tammy shook her tidy blond head. "Never mind. Let's get some tea and catch up on all you've been doing."

Jade followed her mother into the kitchen and sat at the small round table, watching as Mama bustled around, smiling and happy.

Her conscience throbbed. Could something as simple as a visit bring her mother this much pleasure?

"How have you been, Mama? Really."

"Wonderful as always."

As always. A telling phrase.

"But I don't want to talk about me." Ice rattled from the old-fashioned trays and clinked into glasses. "Tell me about you. About what you've been doing. About your friends. Everything."

Jade accepted the tall glass of amber tea and sipped. "Life is busy. I have a few good friends I go out with sometimes. And I love my work as a private investigator."

"I'm still surprised when you say that. My little girl investigating criminals." Tammy faked a shudder. "Such a dangerous business. I pray for your safety every day."

Jade wanted to scoff but kept her expression straight.

She'd been in far more danger married to the man her parents had chosen than she'd ever been in law enforcement.

"I'm perfectly safe, Mama, and if I run into a problem, I'm trained to handle myself."

"But you're pretty and feminine and smart as a whip. Surely you could find a more ladylike occupation."

Jade clenched her back teeth, schooling her words. Mama would never understand. To her, a woman's place was in the home. "I like what I do. I'm happy being an investigator."

And a gorgeous, witty man calls me "Nancy Drew" and is showing me what real faith looks like.

"Then I'm happy for you, no matter what your daddy thinks." They shared a conspiratorial look. "We still have a few secrets, don't we?"

"Yes, we do." Like the time Mama had covered for her so she could attend her junior prom.

Warmed, she reached across the table and squeezed her mother's fingers. Mama had guarded her children against their father's moods and secretly pinched pennies from the grocery budget for the extras every teenager craved, simple little things that Hugh felt were unnecessary.

But even Mama had failed to protect Jade from Cam. He'd been a member of the church, the son of an elder, and the most likely to succeed in their high school.

He'd proven them right in that respect. He now owned a shopping mall, among other things. But he no longer owned her.

Sawyer's smiling face flashed in her mind.

Sawyer. Kind and real, charming and funny, a man who went out of his way for other people.

In a gush of words, she admitted, "Mama, I've met someone."

"Someone?" Tammy looked at her over the glass. "As in a man?"

"Yes."

Her mother leaned back in her chair, the concern on her face evident.

"Aren't you going to ask about him? If he's a good man? If he's a Christian?"

"Is he?"

"Yes. The best kind, I think. Not like Daddy."

"Jade!"

"Because of Sawyer, I prayed today, really prayed, and last night I read the Bible for the first time in my life."

Her mother scoffed. "You've read the Bible since you were a child."

"No, Mama. Daddy gave us verses to memorize." *A foolish child is a grief to his father and bitterness to her who bare him.* "Verses he chose. Verses he used to control us. I never read any of the Bible for myself."

The truth of the statement settled over her mother. Tammy's fingers whitened against the glass of amber tea. In a hesitant murmur, she asked, "Are you…in love with this man?"

A spark went off inside Jade, igniting a thought she'd only begun to consider. *Love.* A big word. A bigger emotion and a giant responsibility.

Like fog over the river, love was slowly creeping in, wrapping gentle fingers around her heart.

"I don't know yet. Maybe. I think he cares for me, and he has the most wonderful family."

Her mother's face softened. "Does he make you happy?"

"It's early, and I'm being cautious this time, but yes, he does. I feel alive again when I'm with him. I feel like I matter, as if I'm important."

Tammy took in a long, deep breath and exhaled, letting the corners of her eyes crinkle. "Then good for you."

"You're not mad at me anymore about leaving Cam?"

"I never was mad, honey, only confused and sad, but after we spoke a few days ago, I realized six years is long enough. You have every right to move on with your life and if that includes this man, then I'm glad for you."

"No matter what Daddy thinks?"

"He'd be upset if he knew, but we'll keep this between us for now. Your father doesn't need to know."

"No, he doesn't." At least, not yet.

They exchanged the secret smile again that warmed Jade all the way through. She was glad she'd come. Glad to see Mama. "Is he at work?"

Tammy cast a nervous glance toward the door. "He went to town for a while."

"What happened to the job at the nursing home?"

"You know your daddy. Maintenance work is below him. Hugh owned his own company. He'll never be satisfied with menial employment."

Jade's mouth tightened but she didn't say the obvious. Any work was better than nothing. "So he's unemployed again?"

"Temporarily." Tammy emitted a tired sigh. "He'll find something to tide us over until he gets his company going again. He always does."

Tide them over. For as long as Jade could remember, they barely got by—the fault of every Buchanon on the planet, of course.

Jade longed to ask about the lawsuit Dan Buchanon filed against Clifton Construction some years ago. As confident as she was that Sawyer's "special girl" was also their vandal, a pinch of doubt lingered. If her own flesh and blood was involved in the vandalism, seeking revenge for perceived wrongs done to Hugh Clifton and his company, she needed to know. Discovering the truth was her job.

She had to find out before Sawyer learned she was Hugh Clifton's daughter. Maybe he would understand but what if he didn't? What if he despised her deceit? He was, he'd told her on more than one occasion, an upfront kind of man. No secrets.

And she had too many.

Readjusting the napkin beneath her tea glass, Jade determined to get the truth and share that truth with Sawyer. Somehow.

"Was Daddy always…" She wanted to say *angry, vengeful, volatile,* but those words would upset her mother, so she rephrased. "What was Daddy like when you first met?"

Mama's expression brightened. "He was the handsomest man I'd ever seen. Sweet and funny."

"Daddy? Funny?"

"Oh, yes, he had a great sense of humor. All the girls were after him, and I was so flattered when he picked me. I fell hard."

Jade propped her chin on her fist and leaned in, intrigued by this revelation. "Tell me about your courtship. How did he treat you?"

She wanted to ask if he was controlling and abusive even then. She needed to know if all men began with smiles and ended with slaps.

"He sent me flowers and candy and was forever telling me how pretty I was." Mama touched her sleek French knot. "He loved my long blond hair and said I should never cut anything so beautiful."

"And you never have."

"Why would I when long hair makes my husband happy?" Mama sipped her tea, nostalgic. "I'd never met such an attentive, charming man, and when he proposed, I jumped at the chance to be his wife."

Charming. A word that scared Jade.

"Was he ever…rough with you when you were dating?"

"No. Not once." Mama picked at the napkin beneath her glass.

"What happened?" She didn't have to elaborate. Her mother understood what she was asking: *When had the slaps and shoves begun?*

Tammy grew pensive, staring across the kitchen at the ancient refrigerator they'd had since Jade was a child. "Life hasn't been easy for your father. When he lost his company—"

"Even before then, he didn't treat you right." Although Hugh hadn't hit her in the early days, Tammy Clifton had been ridiculed and put down and made to appear stupid and inadequate for as long as Jade could remember.

His cruel words and the tension in their home had been the reason Jade jumped into marriage with Cam. She'd thought Cameron Warren was all the things her father wasn't. Now she knew her father had been kind and loving in the beginning, too.

Was Sawyer the same? Was he another case of Jekyll and Hyde?

She didn't want to believe it, but she was too smart not to be cautious.

"Things happen in a marriage, I guess," Mama was saying. "Disappointments. Misunderstandings. Inadequacies. I considered his jealousy a compliment. He didn't want to share me."

"But he was wonderful when you dated?"

"Yes, he was, and someday, when he gets his company going again, he'll be the man I fell in love with."

Would he be? Or was there something elemental broken inside her father?

"What's going on in here?"

The male voice stunned them both. They turned toward the barrel-chested man entering the kitchen.

How much of their conversation had he overheard?

Mama hopped to her feet, flustered, guilty. "Hugh, look who's here. Our Jade drove all the way from Paris to see us."

Jade didn't bother to correct her mother's mistake. She'd driven from Gabriel's Crossing, not Paris.

"Hi, Daddy." Out of habit, she stood to her feet. Daddy commanded respect from his children.

He swept a glance across her but spoke to his wife. "Get me some tea. It's hot out there."

At his curt tone of voice, Jade thought of the way Dan Buchanon treated his wife, of his affectionate tone, his appreciation for the things she did. Brady and Jake treated their wives well, too.

She had been, she knew, soured on men as husbands, though rationally she understood that not all husbands were harsh masters over their servant wives. Not like her father.

Even now, Tammy hurried to do her husband's bidding, taking ice trays from the freezer in a rush. As she held them over the sink and broke out the cubes, she looked over one shoulder. "How was your meeting?"

Jade watched her father's face. She knew the signs, felt the crackle of tension. He was in a bad mood. No big surprise there.

"A bust." He sat down across from Jade. She slid back onto her chair, disappointed that there would be no lovely family reunion. She shouldn't have expected one.

Tammy bustled to Hugh's side with the filled glass.

He pushed it away. "You know I like plenty of ice."

Temper prickled the hair on Jade's neck. For her mother's sake, she kept her lips clamped tightly.

The fridge opened and closed and ice plopped. "Sorry, honey. I was so excited to see Jade, I wasn't thinking. Is this better? Would you like something to eat with it? I made oatmeal cookies, your favorite."

Without responding, Hugh took the glass and drank deeply. "Stupid bank won't float the equipment loan."

"Why not?"

"Bad economy, financial risk. Even though I explained the bankruptcy again for the hundredth time, they didn't budge." He slammed the glass against the tabletop. "Sorry Buchanons. This is their fault."

Her mother jumped. She hovered around the table, on her feet, wringing a dish towel in her hands.

Anger bubbled in Jade's chest. She tamped it down, kept her tone conversational. This was her opportunity and she wouldn't ruin it with a fight.

"Why, Daddy? Why is this the Buchanons' fault? Wasn't that a long time ago?"

Steel-gray eyes slanted toward her, hard and cold. "Do you see any concrete trucks in the driveway? No, you don't. Thanks to them, I sold everything the bank didn't take."

"I know, Daddy. I know, but help me understand what happened."

"Why bother? They're like a cancer. Once they invade, they suck the life out of a man."

"But that was years ago. Why does it matter now?"

Her mother paused behind her chair to squeeze her shoulder in a silent plea to stop talking.

She couldn't. While keeping her knowledge to herself, she pushed the topic, needing to know, needing to settle in her heart the issue of which was the guilty party.

"What did the Buchanons do that was so terrible?"

"Ran me out of business. Bad-mouthed my hard work, told other builders not to use my company. You know all that."

"Maybe they thought they had good reason."

Her mother's fingers tightened on her shoulders, tightened and held.

Hugh's eyes narrowed to slits. "What are you talking about, girly? What good reason could they have for ruining a man except they're plain evil?"

"The lawsuit."

Her father's face reddened to purple. His eyes bulged. "Don't you come into my house disrespecting me."

Honor thy father and mother ran through Jade's head like a knife blade. Any moment now, Hugh would blast her with all the scriptural reasons why she was wrong and he was right. A child should never have an opinion, especially a female child.

Jade softened her tone but didn't retreat. She'd faced scarier men during her cop days.

"I don't mean disrespect, Daddy. I'm only trying to understand."

"Then understand this. Dan Buchanon is a worthless piece of trash who stole everything we ever had!" His voice rising with his body, he leaned across the table to jab a thick finger in Jade's face. "Don't you ever let me hear you defend him again. Now shut your mouth or get out!"

Icy cold and heavyhearted, Jade rose from the table, set her half-emptied glass in the sink and hugged her mother goodbye.

So much for thinking she could mend fences.

Chapter Twelve

> You kissed that blonde witch. I saw you. She came on to you, pushing up against you, trying to lure you inside the motel. She disgusts me. Stop seeing her. My love is strong, but I cried myself to sleep last night. Does that make you sad? Like the paint on your truck? Did you cry? Are you sorry? Sorry you cheated? I forgive you, my darling. Forgiveness is the price of love. Don't do it again. You'll have to pay.

Sawyer gazed in fascinated horror at the rambling pink letter found under his truck's wiper blade.

Who was this person? And how did she know he'd kissed Jade outside the River Roost last night?

His fingers tightened on the sheet.

"She admits spray painting my truck! This, this—" He was sputtering as he found the signature on the back page halfway down. The same person who wrote the rambling emails. "Special Girl."

The idea that someone might be watching his every move had him turning in a slow circle, suddenly paranoid. The only other people he saw on his quiet residential street were two men on the golf course and the older widow, Mrs. French, three houses down watering her flowers.

His neighborhood remained peaceful. No signs of a mad stalker, though now that he knew she'd been to his home, peeked in windows, left a note on his windshield and watched him kiss Jade, he could get seriously freaked out.

Anyone who wrote secret, bizarre notes and vandalized property out of "love" couldn't be emotionally stable. Was she insane? Dangerous? Outright evil? Or simply mean and vindictive?

He jabbed the office number into his phone.

"Speak." Quinn was never one for long hellos.

"Is everyone okay over there?"

"Sure. Why wouldn't we be?"

Sawyer turned another slow circle in his driveway, aware that his adrenaline had jacked and hair rose on the back of his neck. "I found a note on my truck."

"More graffiti?"

"No, an actual handwritten note under the wiper blade. Rambling, creepy. She knew I was with Jade last night and wasn't at all happy. She made some veiled threats."

A beat passed. "Are you in danger?"

"Probably not." He gave a short laugh. "She says she loves me. Me and my pretty face."

"So she paints your truck and leaves threatening notes. Some love."

"Tell me about it."

"You have no idea who this woman is?"

"None. Jade says she uses a false profile on social media."

"Eerie. Unsettling. You think your admirer and the vandal are connected?"

How could they be? This woman claimed to love him. Love didn't destroy. And yet she'd painted his truck with obscenities.

"I'm not sure. Maybe. Maybe not. Jade thinks it's possible, even though I haven't heard directly from this woman until now and the vandalism has been going on for a couple of years."

"Either way, better call Leroy."

"Yeah. Yeah." Sawyer shoved a hand over his hair. "I'd rather Mom didn't know about this. She'll worry about me."

"Got it. And, brother—"

"Yeah?"

"Watch your back."

A chill prickled Sawyer's spine as he hung up. He gave the police chief a quick call and then dialed Jade. That he wanted to see her anyway was a bonus, but right now the focus was this nutty, rambling, semicoherent letter that went on for two miserable pages.

Jade answered on the third ring. "Hello."

"Hey. It's me, Sawyer."

"I know." She didn't sound too friendly.

"You okay? Is everything all right?"

"Why wouldn't I be?" Her speech was terse, snappy.

Okaaay. Was she angry about last night's kiss? Regretting it? Wishing he'd go away?

Sawyer titled his head back and stared at the fluffy white clouds. He spotted Moses with a staff, like he might have during a game he and his twin had played as boys. Find the picture in the clouds.

He wished he could as easily find a balance with Jade.

"Can you come over to my house? I need to show you something."

"I'm busy. Is this related to the case?"

Whoa. Sherlock was back, cool and professional.

"Yes, but what happened to the woman I was with last night?"

"Excuse me?"

He squinched his eyes shut. "Did I do something to upset you?"

"Of course not. I'm out of town visiting family. This is a bad time."

That explained her brusque tone. She didn't mean anything by it. She was preoccupied.

"I found a bizarre note on my windshield."

"From Special Girl?"

"How did you guess?"

She didn't humor him with a response. "Call the police."

"I did."

There was a pause on the other end of the line.

He heard a noise in the background that sounded like traffic.

Did her family live in the middle of a busy highway?

"I'll be back into town tonight, around seven. I'll come by your place then, have a look at the note and discuss business."

"Can we discuss happy things, too?"

Silence.

"Jade."

"Yes."

"I want to see you again. You. Not Nancy Drew."

She hung up without responding.

Sawyer stared at the cell phone for fifteen seconds, puzzled by her cool, curt behavior. After her dogged attempts to solve this case, Sawyer thought she'd be thrilled to have a new clue.

Not that *he* was all that happy about the latest installment. Having a demented secret admirer gave a man serious pause.

But ever the optimist, Sawyer looked on the bright side. Jade was coming over tonight. He didn't understand why she'd suddenly become distant when he thought things were really taking off between them, but maybe she had other things on her mind. A person got distracted around family. He certainly did.

"Admit it, man." With the pink note in hand, he sat down on his front porch to await Leroy. "You're falling for her."

With a laugh, he nodded, aware that if his stalker was watching him talk to himself, she'd think he was as nutty as her.

He wished Jade was here now. Last night, he'd fallen asleep with her taste on his lips and their wonderful afternoon on his mind. His dreams had been sweet and filled with her.

He was falling for a woman who only liked him on alternate Sundays. Or less.

Nah, that wasn't true. She was only trying to maintain her professional distance. When she interacted with his family and with him on a personal level, she was warm and fun. Real warm.

He revisited last night's kiss and her reaction. He wasn't naive. She'd felt something, too. Something *bing-bong* big.

Love. He'd been in *like* a hundred times, but love had evaded him.

Beautiful Jade had him by the heart and he didn't mind one bit.

Now, if only she would cooperate.

Jade's back ached with tension as she guided her Chevy across the Red River Bridge. The swirling muddy water below mirrored her thoughts and emotions.

Her father would never change. Why did she think a few prayers and her new attitude toward God and family would make any difference?

But she wanted it to make a difference so badly. She wanted a family like Sawyer's. She wanted to believe God cared about her.

The radio played country music but she barely noticed.

Sawyer had called. Something about a note from his secret admirer.

Simply hearing his voice had cheered her. She wanted to believe Sawyer was nothing like Cam or her father.

After today, how could she ever be sure?

From Mama's description, Daddy was sweet and charming before the marriage…the way Cam had been. Charmers, both of them, like Sawyer.

Men presented one personality when they wanted a woman. Once they had her, they turned to monsters.

Like multicolored beads on a string, a few cars and trucks motored past. When a faded blue Dodge Ram came into sight, her stomach tightened.

Her brother Bo drove a truck like that. She squinted as the truck sailed past, recognizing Bo in the driver's seat and Kurt next to him.

What were her brothers doing near Gabriel's Crossing?

She punched off the radio, needing to clear her mind of thoughts of Sawyer so she could really think. This bridge connected Oklahoma and Texas. Bo and Kurt could be heading home from anywhere. Their presence could be perfectly innocent. Or they could have been in Gabriel's Crossing for a more sinister reason—to avenge their father, to punish the Buchanons, to destroy another Buchanon Built property.

Gripping the steering wheel in a choke hold, she accelerated toward Sawyer's house.

He met her at the door, all smiles and sweetness. Clean shaven and smelling really good, he wore slacks and a button-down shirt as if he'd planned an evening out.

"You made it."

Nerves about to snap and trying not to ask where he was headed, she blurted, "Was there another break-in today?"

Expression puzzled, he shook his head. "No. Why?"

"Are you sure?"

"Positive."

She gave a curt nod. Get the note, get out and let him be on his way. That was a better scenario anyway. The more she was with him the more she wanted to be.

"Show me this note you received."

"Hey, slow down, Nancy." He took her hand and tugged her through the door. "I've waited all day to see you again. The note can wait."

Inside the house was quiet, dim and cool, a welcome respite from Texas heat.

She was here on business. She was an investigator. He didn't know the truth about her family.

"But you're going somewhere." She struggled for cool professionalism but Sawyer's touch distracted her, warmed her, made her yearn to be with him on a personal level.

He chuckled softly. "No, I'm not. Come here. I want to show you something."

There was nothing she could do but follow as he led her through the tidy living room into the dim kitchen-dining area. Jade stopped in the doorway, stunned.

She noticed then what she'd been too preoccupied to observe when he'd first opened the door. The house smelled as good as Sawyer, only the scents were food.

And the dining room had been transformed into a cozy, romantic setting for two.

A chunky candle glowed white atop a small linen-covered table set with cherry-red placemats and silverware. Across one gleaming white plate, he'd placed a long-stemmed red rose. Soft instrumental music floated from somewhere.

Jade's heart bumped against her rib cage. "Sawyer, what are you doing? What's going on?"

"Surprise." His voice was soft and gentle.

"This is for me?" He wasn't going out. Nor was he expecting some gorgeous redhead for dinner. He'd done this for her.

If she hadn't been a wreck before, she was now.

"For us. You sounded upset on the phone. Stressed. Uptight. I thought a nice, relaxing dinner…" His words dwindled, his expression a mix of pride and uncertainty.

The uncertainty endeared him to her even more.

"It's beautiful." And romantic. Way too romantic. She loved it.

Oh, dear.

"I should really see that note." Her tone wasn't the least bit cool and professional.

"Gave it to Leroy. We'll look at a copy later. Right now you need to relax." His strong carpenter's fingers found her shoulders and massaged. "Tight as Dick's hatband." His laugh was soft against her ear, sending shivers. "I have no idea what that means but Dad says it."

She gave herself to his talented fingers and let her head loll forward. She shouldn't, but he was right—today's confrontation with her father and the disappointment that followed had tied her into a thousand hard knots.

"You went to visit your family today. Did something happen to upset you?"

His radar was right on.

"Something always happens with them. My dad—" She bit down on her lip and shook her head, stepping away from his delicious touch, reluctant to share her problems with a man who came from the perfect environment. "You wouldn't understand."

But he was having none of it. "Try me. I'm a pretty good listener and a great shoulder if you need one."

Leaning on Sawyer's broad shoulders sounded wonderful. She couldn't allow herself to be that weak and needy.

Two are better than one. Wasn't that what he'd told her? Because if one fell down, the other was there to give a hand up.

Was that the way marriage was for his parents? Partners. Helping each other? Or was such a relationship nothing but a romantic fantasy?

"Come and sit." He pulled the chair away from the table. "I'll fix your drink and you can tell me all about it. Then we'll let the stress burn up in that candle flame while we enjoy the dinner I slaved over for hours." He flashed his teasing, breathtaking smile. "Deal?"

When he put it like that, how could she refuse?

After seating her, he moved around his kitchen with ease. He glanced in the oven and gave a pleased hum before bringing two tall drinks to the table. A sprig of mint garnished each glass.

"I hope you like blackberry tea."

She'd never had it but she took a sip. "Light, refreshing. Perfect." Like him. Too perfect.

He slid two salad plates onto the table and joined her, his handsome face shadowy and romantic in the candlelight as he leaned toward her. "Want to tell me what got you so upset?"

She sighed and sat back, hands in her lap. "My father and I had words. We always do. That's all. Not worth discussing."

"I'm sorry." He smoothed out his napkin and jabbed a

fork into the green salad. "Fathers can be exacting some-times."

"Not yours." She picked up her fork and began to eat.

"Oh, yes, he can. He and Brady butt heads on a regular basis, and I've had my moments with him."

"But you get along so well together."

"Well, sure we do. We're family. We disagree and then we kiss and make up and have a cookout." The corner of his mouth lifted. "Maybe not the kissing part so much any-more, but we fix the problem and move forward."

"My family doesn't do that. They hold grudges for-ever. With each other. With everyone else. Especially with those who've done them wrong." The truth hovered on her tongue, a winged creature demanding to fly.

"Want to talk about your argument? What started things off on the wrong foot?"

"I don't want to talk about it all." She lifted a bite of mixed salad. "This dressing is delicious. Did you make it?"

"No, but I made the money that bought it."

She laughed outright, feeling the day's stress slowly seep from her shoulders. Sawyer had that effect on her, as if being with him made everything all right.

"Whatever you have in the oven smells incredible. Did you make the money that bought that, too?"

"I did. But I also baked it, with a little help from my baby sister." He rubbed his palms together and intoned like the best maître d'. "Slow-baked salmon with lemon and thyme, served alongside parmesan asparagus."

"Sounds fancy."

"Are you suitably impressed?"

"I haven't tasted it yet."

He laughed. "Spoken like a Buchanon."

While she absorbed that tempting phrase, the oven

beeped and he hopped up to plate and serve the meal, taking time to refill her glass before he rejoined her.

She had never seen her father fill her mother's glass. Certainly, Daddy had never cooked a meal or prepared Mama's plate. Not in her lifetime.

With the candle flickering between them, they talked as they ate. To her relief they moved from the subject of her family to Bailey and Ashton who were now settled in Karen and Dan's extra apartment.

"I'll miss having the pair of them right down the walkway from me."

"Which means you'll have to come to more Sunday dinners so you can see them."

"I'd like that."

"Church, too?"

"Maybe." Jade sipped her tea. "Your interpretation of God is different from the way I was raised. But I like yours better and I've been reading the Gideon Bible in my motel room, trying to decide…which is the real God?"

"Good question. Mine is, of course." The grin flashed but he was serious. "Keep reading that Bible, Jade. Read the first four books of the New Testament. Watch Jesus at work, the way He treated people, the love and compassion He displayed."

"But that was Jesus."

"Christ said, 'If you've seen me, you've seen the Father.'"

"The Bible says that?"

"Yep. Don't get me wrong. God is a god of justice and can't tolerate sin. He doesn't have an attitude of 'anything goes,' but above all else He loves. In fact, He's the embodiment of love." Sawyer lifted one shoulder in a mini shrug. "Sorry, if I'm coming on too strong. I'm pretty passionate about Jesus."

She waved her fork, showing him that he hadn't. "You've given me a lot to think about. And pray about. I appreciate your input. But can we get back to Bailey and Ashton?"

Talking about religion was something she'd avoided for a long time. Sawyer and his family had opened her eyes to an appealing Christianity but she needed time to process and study for herself. Never again would she take anyone's word for what the Bible said.

"Absolutely."

His lips curved, blue eyes aglow in the candlelight. Sawyer was devastatingly handsome, and once she'd worked her way beyond the happy-go-lucky facade, she discovered a man of intellect and deep character. Who would have guessed there was so much behind that movie star face?

"I stopped by Mom's this afternoon to check on them. Ashton is a heart grabber." He thumped a fist against his chest. "Gets me right there."

"You like kids." She'd seen the way he played with his nieces and nephews, the way he listened to their chatter and made them feel important. He'd even toted each in turn on a piggyback gallop around the backyard and tossed them around in the swimming pool.

Sawyer Buchanon would make a terrific father.

"Adore them. Want a few of them myself someday. Maybe not as many as Mom and Dad had…" His gaze held hers over the flickering candle. "How about you?"

So much for sidestepping difficult topics. From religion to babies—a tough transition. A cloak of the past shrouded her for a brief moment while she sought balance. She lowered her eyes to the salmon, surprised at how much she'd eaten.

Sawyer couldn't know how the question of children stirred painful memories.

"Hey." He reached across the table and tilted her chin upward. "Did I say something wrong? You don't like kids?"

"I love kids." Her lip trembled. She bit it but not before Sawyer noticed.

His brow puckered. "Why do you look so sad? What's wrong?"

She didn't talk about the loss. Never had, not even to her closest friends.

Two are better than one. Bear one another's burdens.

Suddenly, the need to share her heartache was overwhelming and the dim lighting provided a cover that fostered intimacy. She could tell him. Sawyer was a good listener.

Jade sat back in the chair with a heavy sigh, a deep ache in her soul throbbing for release.

Keeping her voice cool and professional, while her heart rattled against her rib cage, she said the forbidden words. "I had a miscarriage a few years ago, courtesy of my ex."

Sawyer's scowl deepened. "What do you mean, *courtesy* of your ex?"

Her pulse pounded so hard, she thought her collarbone might snap. "He didn't want children. He was furious when I told him. We had a huge fight. He won."

She tried to sound matter-of-fact, but her lips trembled again and tears burned the back of her nose.

Slowly, slowly, Sawyer put aside his fork and rose to his feet, coming around the table to kneel next to her chair. He took her hand, warming it between both of his.

"Are you saying what I think you are?"

She licked dry, dry lips. Candle flame flickered as if her inner turmoil stirred the air. "He beat me unconscious. When I came to, I called 911. Cam was gone. An ambulance took me to the hospital. I lost the baby."

At the time, she'd blamed herself. She'd known he didn't

want children. She'd foolishly thought he'd change his mind when he learned she was pregnant. Now, she knew better. Cam was selfish, angry and broken, and nothing she did would fix him.

Sawyer growled low and deep, a primal sound, before tugging her into his arms where he rocked her back and forth like a child. A wall of fear and caution began to crumble as she rested in his accepting embrace.

Compassion poured from him. He murmured comfort and words tender enough to melt the coldest iceberg.

This man melted her, made her feel safe and valued.

The tears came then. Tears she'd held back since the kind-faced physician in Southview had confirmed her suspicions of miscarriage.

"Cry, my love. It's okay. I've got you."

He let her cry while he smoothed his hand over her hair, down her back, murmuring, making promises not to let anyone ever hurt her again. She wished he could keep that promise, that she dared trust him.

She'd learned the hard way not to depend on a man. A woman had to protect herself. But in this moment, the words soothed a raw, aching wound, and she let them pour over her like warm rain.

When the torrent passed, she shuddered a few times and tried to pull away, embarrassed, though strangely relieved, as if the tears had washed out toxins she hadn't known were there. "I'm sorry. I never do that."

Had she ever let herself cry for her lost baby?

"Don't apologize. I'm here for you." Sawyer cupped her face and kissed away the remaining tears before finding her lips with his.

The kiss was gentle and compassionate, but leashed passion hovered in the wings. His heart ricocheted against hers, his restraint meaning more to her than he'd ever know. She'd never met a man with self-control, one that thought of her first and himself second.

Sawyer was a different kind of man, and the truth of that both thrilled and terrified her. Would he always be this way, or would he change?

He eased back a little, held her face close to his and whispered, "I'm falling in love with you, Jade." His breath brushed her lips in a soft, self-deprecating laugh. "I guess that's obvious."

The rattle in her chest shot into her brain. Her blood pressure jacked. Adrenaline flooded through her body. Fight or flight.

With every fiber of her being, Jade wanted to believe he was the man he presented to her tonight. She wanted to believe he wouldn't change with the first disagreement.

But would he turn into a monster when he discovered who she really was? That her family might be the cause of his family's problems?

As much as she wanted to let go and feel all the beautiful emotions banking up inside like a brewing summer rain, she couldn't take the chance.

Requiring every ounce of willpower she had, Jade levered away from Sawyer's tempting arms, thanked him politely for the nice dinner and, over his bewildered protests, escaped into the hot, muggy Texas night.

Chapter Thirteen

$\sim$

Jade slept little that night. She sprawled on the bed listening to the humming pipes in the next unit and loud music thump from the adjacent street while wondering what she'd gotten herself into.

Sawyer loved her? Really?

Reliving those moments in his arms was torture and pure delight.

With a groan, she flipped on the light, took her computer from beneath the mattress and opened the Buchanon file.

Then, and only then, she remembered the reason for her visit to Sawyer's house. Not to tell him her sad story. Not to be wined and dined with a romantic dinner. Not even to hear him say those beautiful words that replayed in her head like a melody.

The note from Sawyer's stalker. In her haste and confusion, she'd forgotten all about the note.

Frustrated, she slapped a hand against her forehead. The note could be information vital to solving this case and relieve her fear that her family was involved in the break-ins. The note could lead to the stalker, the vandal.

She was losing her perspective, her professionalism.

Sawyer and a volley of rampant emotions compromised her ability to do her job.

She needed to finish this investigation, find the culprit and get away while she still had a brain cell left in her head.

Next to her brother's name, she typed, Spotted Bo near Gabriel's Crossing. Could he have written the note and left it on Sawyer's truck to draw attention away from himself, the true vandal? She had no proof that the stalker was real or even that the person who wrote the note was a woman. Bo could have done the damage to Sawyer's truck as well as vandalizing the Buchanon properties. He could be using the stalker concept to throw investigators off the scent. Was her brother clever enough to concoct such a scheme?

Stomach sinking, she admitted the awful truth. Between the three of them, her brothers and her father could easily be to blame. And her job was to find out and report them to the police.

The next morning, Jade rose after less than three hours of restless sleep, gritty-eyed but determined. She texted Sawyer and asked him to meet her with the note. Sawyer probably thought she was nuts, the way she'd run out on him last night.

Sawyer's reply named The Buttered Biscuit Café in fifteen minutes. Good. A neutral location in public. No way would she return to his town house and the rush of romantic emotions, but she must complete this investigation. She *had* to learn if her family was involved.

Taking her time in the shower, Jade procrastinated, putting off the inevitable moment when she'd have to face Sawyer again.

She'd been anything but professional last night. Today, she would be. Cool. Confident. Professional.

By the time she finally walked inside the café, she was

late and the room was thick with people and delicious smells, bacon and Jan's cat-head biscuits. Jade's mouth pooled with hunger as she found Sawyer among the crowd.

He waited at a square table next to a window, iced orange juice in front of him. The blinds at his elbow were closed against the morning sun and he spotted her immediately. He didn't smile.

Guilt clenched at her as their gazes met and held. He looked puzzled…and hurt. She'd done that. She'd stolen the laughter from a happy man.

She yearned to tell him everything, to spill out the truth the way she'd told him of the miscarriage, to make him smile again. To admit she was falling in love with him, too.

Don't take the chance. Don't be vulnerable. Don't be a fool.

Excusing her way past the filled tables, she approached him. He stood, gentlemanlike, which only compounded her guilt.

"You okay?" he asked, softly.

His look of concern almost did her in. Why did he have to do that? Why did he have to appear concerned for her well-being after she had performed her Houdini act and disappeared?

A little voice in her head whispered, "Because he's the real deal."

She glanced down, away from those piercing eyes. "I'm fine."

"Are you sure? You look tired." He pulled out a chair and gestured. "Sit. I ordered your breakfast."

There he went again. Considerate and thoughtful. Or was he being controlling and pushy?

The thought scared her. "No need. I only came for the note."

The waitress appeared with coffee and poured without asking. "Pancakes and bacon will be up in a minute. Want anything else with that? The blackberry syrup is on the table."

Dumbly, she shook her head. He'd ordered foods she loved. She was hungry. She might as well eat.

The strain at the table nearly palpable, she searched for something to say. "Pancakes with blackberry syrup are my favorite."

"I know. Bacon, too."

He'd remembered their passing conversation about favorite foods? He was an omelet man, Southwestern style with plenty of jalapeños and onions and an unbelievably huge glob of hot salsa.

Charla flashed by and deposited two steaming plates on the table. "You all need anything else?"

Sawyer lifted an eyebrow toward Jade. She shook her head.

"We're good for now, Charla. Thank you."

Charla gave his biceps a playful tweak. "Don't forget to leave me a big tip. You know I'm worth it."

He laughed, and Jade was grateful for the feisty waitress.

After Charla bustled away, last night pulsed between them, unspoken. While they ate, they talked of mundane things, impersonal, distant, the way she wanted them to be. Though her thoughts were on last night and how bewildered he must be, Jade focused on the note and the investigation, digging deeper into even the most innocent friendships he shared with women.

She prayed there was something in his past relationships, anything that would stir a personal vendetta.

It had to be that. It simply had to be. The alternative was too upsetting.

All the while, her blood thrummed with the fear that

her brother, not an unrequited lover, had written the note and spray painted Sawyer's truck.

Installing crown molding above a set of custom-built birch cabinets in the Carter house should have kept Sawyer's mind off Jade Warren. It didn't.

Finish nails in hand, Sawyer mulled Jade's bizarre behavior from last night and this morning's return to the cool, impersonal detective. A detective who had kissed him like she meant it.

What had happened?

One minute, he'd said the three gargantuan words he'd never said to anyone and the next she'd bolted like a startled rabbit. He'd thought they were beyond that.

Nail between index finger and thumb, he slammed the hammer down...onto his hand.

With a yelp, he dropped the tools and shook his clenched hand. He hadn't hammered himself in years.

"What's going on with you today?" Dawson, working from the other wall, paused midhammer.

Sawyer glared at the insulted skin, already beginning to bruise. "Nothing. Why?"

"You're too quiet. Makes me suspicious. Now you're banging your hand like an amateur."

"Got a lot on my mind." He retrieved the finish hammer and slipped it through the loop on his tool belt.

Nails rattled as Dawson withdrew a handful from the box on the counter. "The stalker?"

"Partly."

"Ah." His intuitive twin pinned him with a look, nodding sagely. "Jade. Want to talk about her?"

Sawyer scowled. "No."

Jade had effectively given him the cold shoulder. He

wasn't one who liked to discuss being rejected, especially when he didn't know why. Not even with his twin.

Unless his girl-guy radar was seriously out of whack, Jade liked him. A lot. Or she had. Last night she'd been enjoying herself, once she'd relaxed from whatever had happened with her father. Then she'd shared a deep, painful event with him, one that had him wanting to comfort her and take a hammer to her ex. She liked him. She trusted him with her pain. Something special was growing between them.

And yet all she'd wanted to talk about this morning was the case, his former girlfriends, his unknown stalker.

He was tired of the whole mess, tired of looking over his shoulder, of wondering if every friend he spoke to was sabotaging him behind his back. Most of all, he was tired of Jade's hot and cold behavior. She was enough to give him a head cold.

He didn't like living this way.

"I can finish this up if you want to knock off for the day." Dawson flipped over a length of molding and positioned it along the wall.

Sawyer ran a hand over the back of his neck and winced. The thumb throbbed like a gangsters' set of Bose subwoofers. "Thanks. I think I will. I'm worthless anyway."

"I'll lock up, but don't leave your saw."

They'd had too many things stolen, even a landscaper's skid-steer, which was later recovered in the woods. How the vandal had started and moved the large piece of equipment without being seen baffled them all.

Sawyer removed his tool bag and tossed the overloaded leather onto the counter with a loud *thunk*. "Bathroom cabinets tomorrow?"

"If you're up to it." Dawson's grin teased. "Go see Jade. Let her kiss that thumb and make it all better."

"Stuff it, Dawson." Though the idea didn't sound half-bad.

Outside he slapped the sawdust from his clothes and loaded his saw and other major tools before hopping into his truck.

The thumb throbbed. His head hurt, and yes, his heart hurt.

In town, he stopped at the IGA for milk and contemplated a fast-food dinner. He could always go over to Mom's for a home-cooked meal.

Nah, Mom would know something was wrong. Her mother radar never took a day off. And he wasn't up to cooking again. A sandwich would have to do.

He really wanted to see Jade.

Was he ever messed up!

He flipped on K-LOVE Radio, hoping the positive music would encourage him, and as he drove, he prayed. God knew what was going on even if Sawyer was in the dark.

The big diesel pickup rumbled into the garage and he cut the engine and walked out to the mailbox on the curb.

His *Master Builder* magazine lay curled inside along with a couple of bills. "And enough junk mail to destroy the Brazilian rain forest."

As he walked toward the front door, he scanned the new magazine and distractedly jiggled his key into the lock.

Inside, he tossed the mail onto a side table, flipped on the light…and froze.

His living room looked like a monument to ransacking. Tours on the hour.

End tables turned over, lamps smashed, pictures torn from the walls and frames broken. His television was muted, news of a bombing flickering, and red paint scrawled across the walls and his fifty-two-inch TV screen.

I warned you.

Guts knotted, neck tense, he listened for a hint that the perpetrator was still inside his home. Nothing. All he heard was his own heartbeat, loud, rapid.

His adrenaline leaping like a Jack Russell terrier, Sawyer backed out of the house and went to his truck, dialing 911 as he went. Hammer in hand, he returned and explored both floors.

Whoever had done this was gone.

He stalled out at the bottom of the stairs, sucked oxygen and considered if he was relieved to be alone or furious to have not found the culprit.

Jaw tight, he pressed ten on his cell phone, Jade's speed dial number.

Yeah, he'd put her on speed dial.

After too many rings that told him she wasn't excited to talk to him, she answered. "Hello."

"You'd better get over to my place right away."

She must have heard the urgency in his voice because she didn't argue. "What happened?"

"The stalker paid me a visit. It isn't pretty."

A sharp intake of breath. "Get out of the house."

"No need. It's clear."

"You shouldn't have checked."

"Too bad. I did." He was a man and he wanted to know who was doing this to him. "I have a hammer."

She snorted. "Call the police."

"I already have."

"On my way."

She arrived in less than five minutes and burst through the front door without knocking.

He whirled at the sound, hammer aloft and then, annoyed to be jumpy, lowered the weapon. He'd never before considered his tools as weapons, but yeah, they came in handy.

"Are you all right?" Nancy Drew was all business. He didn't like it.

"I am. My house isn't."

Her eyes roved over the topsy-turvy clutter, settling on the television. He saw her mind work through the details.

"Is she saying the note from yesterday was a warning?"

"What do you think?" The first disturbing paragraph was indelibly imprinted in his brain. He'd been warned in no uncertain terms to stay away from Jade.

"She warned you about—" Jade's cheeks reddened "—me."

"About kissing you. Which I don't regret one bit."

Jade cleared her throat, tugged at the neck of her button-down shirt. "Yes."

"She knows you were here last night and apparently, she's angry."

Their eyes locked and he wondered if she was remembering last night the way he was. A romantic dinner for two, candlelight, kisses that tasted sweeter than the ice cream she hadn't stayed around to enjoy.

A night that started so well and ended so badly. A night when he'd told her he was falling in love. The big L word. L-O-V-E.

And she'd made appropriate noises that she might feel the same.

But somewhere the whole conversation had gone south and never returned.

"Which means she's watching your house, maybe following you."

Sawyer slapped both fists on his hips and growled low in his throat. "I hate this."

"You haven't touched anything, have you?" Jade jotted notes into her little notebook and snapped photos. "Leroy might be able to get some prints."

"We've been vandalized so often in the last two years, I know the drill. I've touched nothing except that light switch by the door and the refrigerator handle."

"Why the fridge?"

"I don't like hot milk."

The hint of a smile whispered against her lips. "Is the rest of the house like the living room?"

"This is the worst, but she paid my bedroom a visit. Might as well have a look."

Though reluctant and embarrassed to let Jade see what the demented vandal had done, he led the way to his bedroom.

Once inside, she drew in a long breath and let it out slowly. "Very personal."

"Tell me about it."

Rose petals covered his bed and a single red rose lay limp, twisted and broken on his pillow. Someone, not him, had turned back the blue duvet, and the sheets were rumpled. Had someone been sleeping in his bed?

Jade emitted a small gasp. "Is that the rose…?"

Their gazes bumped before she turned her attention back to the bed.

"From your plate last night? That I bought for you?" If he sounded miffed, so be it. This morning, he'd tossed the rose in the trash in a fit of self-pity. "Yes, it is. She crushed it."

"Unrequited love is a powerful motivator. Someone you've rejected wants your attention very badly."

"None of this makes sense."

"Stalkers often don't. Their thinking is twisted." Jade snapped a couple more photos before heading back down the stairs, talking as she went. "I've been doing research on the mentality of stalkers, trying to get inside this person's head."

"Scary place to be."

"You're more right than you know." She stopped in the dining room and glanced at the table, now devoid of last night's romantic dinner.

"Want to sit in here and have a Coke while we wait for the police?"

She hesitated long enough to bother him before nodding. "You have any of that blackberry tea left?"

He smiled a little at that. The whole night hadn't been a failure. "Coming right up."

While he prepared the iced tea, she settled at the table with her camera and notebook in front of her. She scribbled something and then looked up at him.

"Your stalker is moving closer, getting more personal, angrier, more dangerous."

Invading his bedroom already reeked of crazy to him. He didn't want her any closer than that.

"Nice to know," he said wryly. "Thanks."

"I've been researching stalker profiles and their mentality. I'm seeing key characteristics here. You need to know what you're dealing with."

"Okay. Clue me in." He handed her the tea glass, popped a fizzy Coke for himself and leaned against the bar a few steps from the table to listen. "What I know about stalkers might cover a pinhead."

"Fortunately, most people never need to know." She flipped a page in her notebook as if looking for something. "Stalkers are obsessed with the object of their affections." She glanced up. "That would be you if, indeed, you were dealing with a stalker."

Grimly, he nodded. "Aren't I the fortunate one?"

"She wouldn't take no for an answer and she'd truly believe her victim loves her. Stalkers live in a fantasy world when it comes to the other person."

"You mean this woman thinks if she keeps this up, we'll be together?" That was seriously sick.

"Exactly. She doesn't see this as harmful to you. She thinks she's proving her love and if she hangs on, you'll come around."

Coke burned as Sawyer took a swallow. "Hard to do when she conceals her identity."

"In her fantasy, you know who she is and you love her."

"That's crazy."

"Probably. The profiles say she's delusional, a loner with low self-esteem and someone with few relationships, which makes her all the more desperate to have you, the object of her desire. And she's smart, smarter than average. Any of that ring a bell? Conjure up a name?"

"Not even a little ding."

"You need to tell your family about today's incident. All of them. I can talk to them, if you'd prefer."

"I'd rather Mom didn't know. She'll worry."

"Stalkers are nothing to mess around with, Sawyer."

Hair stood up on the back of his neck. "Are you saying she might hurt my family?"

Chapter Fourteen

Jade saw the fear in Sawyer's eyes, not for himself but for his loved ones. He looked as fierce and protective as a SWAT team.

No wonder she was falling in love with him. A man like Sawyer would not let his people down. Not when it mattered.

"She might, but for the most part and for now, you, not your family, are her focus. As long as she believes she has a chance with you, you'll remain the person on her radar."

The corner of his mouth lifted, though he was anything but amused. "Tick her off again and we can't predict what she'll do. Is that it?"

"Actually, I have a good notion of what the stalker might do, and it scares me, Sawyer." Scared her deeply. Sawyer could be in danger. A lot of danger.

Enraged stalkers had been known to murder their victims.

An awful thought suddenly slammed into her brain and prickled the hair on her arms. The stalker could be watching the house. She could know, right now, that Jade and Sawyer were alone together. At this very moment, some crazy woman could be plotting her next move.

Sawyer could be in danger because of his feelings for Jade. Because he'd kissed her. Because he loved her.

The truth hit her so hard, her knees threatened to give way. Sawyer Buchanon loved her. He hadn't been playing at romance last night. He loved her.

If she cared—and she did—she should get out of his house and leave him alone. For more reasons than one.

She paced to the front window and peered out. "I wonder why the police haven't arrived?"

"They were working a car accident out on the bridge." Sawyer tossed his empty soda can into the trash can. "I told the dispatcher not to rush. The house isn't going anywhere. And I'm safe."

"You may not be."

He froze midmove. "You think she's still around? Just waiting?"

"I think she might know I'm here and that knowledge could be dangerous. You have to avoid any situation that might send her over the edge." She fought the quiver in her voice. Staying cool was hard when someone she cared for might be in jeopardy. "Please, Sawyer. Take this very seriously and be careful. I don't want—" she glanced to one side, words falling to a whisper "—anything to happen to you."

Sawyer's heart leaped. He heard what she didn't say. No matter what had spooked her last night, she cared for him.

He crossed the space between them in three seconds, gently took the notebook from her, placed it on the table and tugged her hands into his. He longed to hold her close and forget about this crazy stalker business.

"I don't like this, Jade. You could be in danger, too. That scares me more than anything."

She pulled her hands away. Her lips trembled the slightest bit. "I trained as a police officer. I can take care of myself."

Her usual bravado was not convincing.

"You shouldn't have to. This nasty business is my fault and I won't have you in harm's way because of me."

"All right then, we're in agreement."

"Good. You'll let me protect you."

"No."

"No?" He tilted his head, bewildered, frustrated. She could be so annoyingly self-reliant. "But you said we're in agreement."

"That we can't see each other."

"What? No! I didn't agree to that. I can't." She'd admitted she had feelings for him, but now she didn't want to see him. What sense did that make? "I'd rather you take yourself off the case and go home to Paris. You'll be safer there anyway until this stalker business goes away."

She shook her head. "No. I'm too close to stop. And trust me when I say this 'stalker business,' as you call it, won't go away by itself. She probably knows I'm here right now, and we both know I'm the cause of today's furious attack. But you're the one she's after, not me. I'm perfectly safe."

He wanted to argue but couldn't. The stalker was smart, smart enough to know about the romantic dinner, smart enough to know Jade was more to him than a business acquaintance.

"So what do we do?"

"We avoid each other as much as possible, and we can never, ever be alone together again."

He let two beats pass while the words soaked in. "What exactly are you trying to say?"

"Sawyer, I care about you." She reached out and then seemed to change her mind and let her hand fall. "But that's not important."

"It's the only important thing in this conversation."

"No. This is business, an investigation. I'm getting paid by your family. If I allow my personal feelings to interfere—"

"They already have."

"That has to end here. Now. Today."

"Is that what you want?"

"That's what has to be. We'll work together until this case is resolved but in the meantime we have to be more… professional."

"Professional?" After he'd kissed her? After he'd thrown his heart at her feet? "I'm starting to empathize with my rejected stalker."

"That's not funny."

"You got that right. I don't feel like laughing at all. I want to be with you, Jade. I have feelings for you. Strong feelings. You can't ignore that."

Feelings. Such a mundane term for the tsunami of emotion filling him up from the inside out. But for now *feelings* was the safest term. At least to his heart.

"I know, and I—" At the very second he thought she might admit to feeling the same, Jade stopped, frustrating him all over again. "We can't let this go any further. Being apart is for the best."

"For who?" He was getting riled up. Mad. Ticked. Hurt.

"For all concerned." Jade picked up the notebook and held it between them like a shield. She straightened as tall as a small woman could, her usually full lips prim and tight as she spoke. "I don't think things between us can ever work out, Sawyer, on any level and for many reasons. We should end it now and move on."

"Because of this crazy stalker issue? You'd let some nut job come between us?"

"It's more than that."

"Then explain it to me. And be very clear, because I must be stupid." He banged a fist against his chest, directly over the throbbing ache. "Tell me you don't care for me. Tell me that, and I'll walk away and never bother you again."

She glanced down, voice barely a whisper. "I can't."

"Then what's the deal!" He slammed that same fist into his palm.

Jade flinched. Her gaze flew to his face, eyes widening, pupils dilating until the gray formed only a thin ring on the outer edges.

He'd scared her. For one fraction of a second, she'd thought he would raise his fist and hit her.

His eyes dropped shut. His pulse banged with regret. *Jesus, forgive me.*

Softening his demeanor, Sawyer stepped close again, voice lowered to a hush. "This isn't about the stalker, is it? This is about your ex."

She had secrets in her eyes as she shook her head. "You are in danger, Sawyer. I won't be the cause of a tragedy."

"Okay. Granted, but you're holding something back."

She crossed her arms, shut him out. "I don't know what you mean."

"You're afraid to trust me. You're afraid I'll turn into your ex. That I'll hurt you. I wouldn't. Not ever."

It killed him to know she'd been hurt so deeply, that because of her ex she'd lost her trust in men, had lost a baby. A baby that would have been a little girl with her blond beauty or a little boy with her strength. A baby he would have adored.

She looked vulnerable and alone, though she didn't have to be. Not with him. Didn't she get it? He'd take care of her. He'd make her happy. He'd be the man her ex wasn't.

Sawyer couldn't help himself. "I love you, Jade. I'll never hurt you. We can work this out."

Her mouth dropped open the slightest bit. Her chest heaved. Emotion swam in her usually cool gray eyes.

Sawyer opened his arms and waited, vulnerable, accepting. If she rejected him, he'd live. He wouldn't want to but he would. But he had to hold her this one last time.

Just when he thought she might turn and walk away, she moved forward and leaned her head against his chest. Simply leaned.

He wrapped his arms around her and sighed deeply.

Now they were getting somewhere.

Jade nearly crumbled as Sawyer held her like a child against his thudding heart. She shouldn't have capitulated, but the hurt on his face had nearly done her in. She loved being here, near him, listening to his life source thrum for her.

"I'm not afraid of you, Sawyer." Granted, she'd flash-backed to Cam raising his voice and then his fist. But only for a second.

She wasn't afraid *of* Sawyer. She was afraid *for* him.

"I never want you to be. I want—"

She couldn't let him say it. "You wouldn't. I know that. But there are other reasons."

She loved Sawyer Buchanon, but if she said the words that bubbled and danced in her throat, she'd be lost forever.

A thousand emotions rolled through her. Love. Longing. Fear.

"We can work this out, Jade. Whatever it is." The words rumbled in his chest and tickled her ear, his voice full of emotion she couldn't let him feel. "All you have to do is tell me. We'll face it together."

A thousand conflicting emotions swamped Jade. She loved him. He was a good man.

She wanted so badly to cling to him and pledge her love. But she was afraid for him, too.

They couldn't be together. Too many barriers stood between them, and would remain even when the stalker issue was resolved—if there was indeed a crazed stalker. Part of her believed it. Part of her didn't, and those were facts she couldn't share with Sawyer. If he knew everything, would he want her then?

Her brother Bo could have ransacked this house. He could have written the note. He could have dumped the rose petals as a smoke screen. Those were exactly the things their father would encourage, applaud. "An eye for an eye," he'd say. "They owe us an eye."

No matter what else happened, the issue of her family remained. Her family. His enemy.

"I wish… If things were different…" She squeezed her eyes tight as Sawyer's heart thudded faster against her ear. "But they're not."

"They will be once we find out who this stalker is. We must be getting close or she wouldn't have upped her game."

Jade raised her head and soaked in his beloved face. "No. Nothing will change, Sawyer. We're too different. We won't work."

"What are you talking about? We have tons in common. The outdoors, skiing, funny movies, kids. We both love kids."

The words seared her like a blowtorch. They were good together on so many levels. "Our families are worlds apart."

"I'm starting to think you're grasping for excuses, looking for a way to let me down easy." He bracketed her face with both hands, pleading with eyes so blue and wounded, she almost capitulated.

She couldn't. Wouldn't. Especially now when he was in danger.

"Nothing unfixable," he said. "I care for you. You care for me. We'll work out the rest as we go."

Jade backed away, watching as his arms fell to his sides. If she had any integrity at all, she'd end this now.

"There are things you don't know."

"They won't matter."

Frustrated not to be able to get through to him, she dropped her head back and groaned. "Yes, they will. They will!"

"Try me."

"You'll hate me."

But that was what she wanted. Right? If he hated what she'd done, the lies of omission, the truth of who she was, he'd let her walk away from any hope of a relationship... and he'd be safe.

She licked dry, dry lips and blurted, "You don't know me. Not really. My maiden name is Clifton."

She waited to see if the name jarred his memory.

"Is that supposed to mean anything to me?"

"Your family and mine are enemies."

He tilted his head, a scowl narrowing the space between his eyebrows. "What are you talking about?"

"Hugh Clifton is my father." When he still didn't react, she went on. She might as well lay it all out. He'd learn the truth sooner or later, especially if her family was involved in the break-ins. "Clifton Concrete. Four Buchanon Built homes had to be demolished. A lawsuit."

Behind the puzzled face, Sawyer's mind worked and she knew the moment the name computed. "You're—?"

"Yes."

And before the initial shock wore off, before he could spew all the horrible things she knew to be true about her father, she turned and walked out of his life.

Chapter Fifteen

Dawson burst through the town house door less than a minute after the police car pulled into Sawyer's drive and ten minutes after Jade's bewildering departure. Sawyer turned toward his brother, leaving the officer to his investigation. He knew nothing about dusting for fingerprints anyway.

"What's going o—" Dawson froze in the doorway as he surveyed the topsy-turvy living room. "Whoa."

"You can say that again." Sawyer held up a hand, noting the throbbing bruise on his thumb. Was it only this afternoon he'd whacked it with a hammer and left work early? "But don't."

"What happened?"

"Other than my house being burglarized and the woman of my dreams telling me to leave her alone—permanently— nothing at all." Sawyer didn't try to hide the sarcasm. "I'm having a great day. A great week." If it got any better, he'd skip the next one and move right on to another month.

Dawson ignored the obvious destruction of personal property and homed in on the real problem, the one bumping around inside Sawyer like a lone tennis shoe in a clothes dryer.

"You and Jade had a fight?"

"A fight? Not exactly." He pinched his temples with thumb and finger. "I'm not sure."

"Did someone bonk you on the head? You're not making sense."

Sawyer rubbed his chest. The ache got worse. "That's the problem. None of this makes sense. A demented stalker who thinks I'm in love with her. Jade bolting on me because of something I barely remember."

Equipment jiggled as the police officer stepped around them and headed for the stairs. Sawyer grimaced. Gabriel's Crossing was a small town. Everyone would know about the rose petals by nightfall. He'd better steer clear of the Buttered Biscuit for a few days.

Dawson followed his gaze. "What's up there?"

"Rose petals, all over my bed."

Dawson's forehead scrunched up. "I hope Jade put them there."

"She didn't."

"Weird." Dawson blew out a long gust, a look of sheer yuck on his face. "Way weird."

"Tell me about it." Sawyer dipped to one side to holler up the stairs. "Hey, Jim. Can we start clean-up down here?"

A disembodied voice replied, "Go ahead. I've finished dusting for prints."

Dawson tipped an end table upright. "Don't change the subject. What happened between you and Jade?"

"I cooked her a romantic dinner." Shaking out a giant black trash bag, Sawyer placed it in the center of the room. Some love this stalker had for him. He was about to lose some valuables.

"You cooked and she bolted. What happened? She get indigestion? Food poisoning? She's hating on you for bad cooking?"

"Not funny. Everything went great. I told her I might

love her, we talked, ate, laughed, and then she ran out on me. I thought it was nerves or something. Then today, things got worse. Way worse."

"Whoa. Halt. Hold the phone." Dawson stared at him over the top of a busted lamp. "Back way up. You told her you *might* love her."

"Yeah, something like that."

"Do you?"

Sawyer rubbed that ache again. "I would if she'd let me. Every time I get close, she pushes me away."

"Bad breath? Body odor?"

"Would you stop? This is serious."

"Sorry. You're right." Dawson eyed the lamp, shrugged and placed it next to the trash bag. "Maybe she doesn't feel the same way about you."

Oh man, he loved that lamp!

"I think she does. She said she cared and that if things were different, blah, blah, blah. Then, as if it was the biggest problem in the universe, she went into this white-faced admission that her family and ours are some kind of enemies. Like Romeo and Juliet or something."

"Who is her family?"

"I barely remember. Must have happened when you and I were at college." He squatted next to the fireplace where a clock had shattered on the hearth. His clock, for crying out loud! "Apparently, her dad and our dad had issues at some point in the past."

"Nothing new there. Dad has issues on a regular basis. That's where Brady, Mom and Charity work the spin."

"This was more than that. I remember when Dad had to completely raze some finished homes for structural defects. The finger of blame pointed at the concrete company."

"Her father's concrete company."

"Right. Hugh Clifton."

"Don't remember him." Dawson pointed at the scattered clock parts. "That clock is a goner."

"I love this clock." With the glass face now shattered, Sawyer traced his finger on the scripture reference. John 15:5 had become his life verse after Mom sent the clock with him to college as a reminder to keep his eyes on Jesus and off the world. Every time he'd been tempted to get a little crazy—and college presented plenty of opportunities—he would look at that scripture.

"Yeah, me, too." Dawson clapped a sympathetic hand on his shoulder and then left the room, returning with a broom and dustpan.

They scooped the clock guts onto the tray, working in silence for a few beats.

"So, you're upset with Jade for not telling you about her father from the start?"

Sawyer paused, a dismantled candle in one hand. Was he? "Maybe a little. The part about her dad's business doesn't bother me that much, but I don't like that she held back on me. She should have been straight up with all of us before she became our investigator."

His brother took the candle and tossed it into the garbage bag. "Hugh Clifton has nothing to do with the vandalism or trashing your truck, so I don't see a conflict of interest."

"Maybe Jade thinks he's responsible. Otherwise, why would she be so freaked out?"

"Ask her."

He rubbed the back of his neck. "She's the one that left. Shouldn't I take her at her word? We're done. Over. Move on. Quit being a hardhead who can't comprehend that a woman doesn't want him."

"Is that what you want to do?"

Hadn't he asked Jade the same thing? "No. I can't even muster the energy to be mad. Not about her family issue. Not even about the way she high-tailed it out of here as if I'd developed a severe case of Ebola."

"Doesn't sound to me as if that's what she wants, either. I think she's running scared."

A watercolor painting that reminded him of Broken Bow Lake lay facedown on the floor. He picked it up, saw the frame was loosened but the painting intact and gently stood it against the couch. This was something he could fix.

He wished fixing Jade were as easy.

"Her ex abused her."

Dawson, broom in hand, paused. He didn't have to speak for Sawyer to know his opinion of a man who hit women.

"There you go then. You gotta show her how a Buchanon man loves."

"I thought I was doing that."

"She trusted the guy enough to marry him. Then he betrayed her with his fists." Dawson's eyebrows lifted as he blew out a gusty breath. "Understandable if she harbors a lot of hurt. She needs proof that you're different. More time, more tenderness, more roses and dinners."

"You think the family issue is a smoke screen for what's really bothering her?"

"The only way for you to find out is to talk to her." The other twin waved a hand around the ransacked room. "I got this. Go ahead. Give her a call and ask to meet up and talk this thing out."

Dawson the peacemaker, the mediator, the wise twin. Maybe he had a point.

"Thanks." Energized and hopeful, Sawyer whipped out his cell and stepped into the kitchen.

The phone buzzed in his ear. He let it ring until voice mail kicked in. "Jade. It's Sawyer. We need to talk. Call me."

In his vivid imagination, Sawyer saw her staring at the phone, unwilling to answer. She was still upset. She didn't want to talk to him. Yet.

Dawson suggested time and patience. Okay. He could be patient.

Until tomorrow.

Jade dreamed about spiderwebs. They were everywhere. In her hair, on her arms and legs, sticky and confining.

Somehow she knew she was dreaming. If she could wake up, the spiderwebs would go away.

Deep in her subconscious, she struggled toward the surface, struggled to wake up. Fluttering her eyes, she strained toward the light. The spiderwebs grew tighter, more frustrating.

She tried to run, battling the tangled webs.

Cam was coming. He'd hurt her. She twisted, tried to scream, but she couldn't get away.

A dream. She was dreaming. *Wake up. Wake up!*

She tossed her head back and forth.

Out of the darkness, Cam appeared. Fear froze Jade in place. Her legs wouldn't move. She couldn't run. He came at her, fists raised and the familiar expression of rage. She could hear him rambling, calling her a liar and a cheat. He was going to hurt her again. Kill her baby. Kill her.

She cringed, awaiting the blows, the crack of bone, the taste of blood.

And then his face morphed and Sawyer stood there, a knife in his chest. Blood ran down his Texas Tech T-shirt. He stepped toward her and suddenly the knife appeared in his hand.

By now, the white lacy spiderwebs encased her like a mummy. She was paralyzed.

Sawyer raised the knife and gently, tenderly began to cut away her strictures. The webs stuck to his hands and tried to enslave him, too, but he slashed away the bonds, refusing to stop.

"I've got you," he kept saying. "It's the Buchanon way. I've got you."

Dear, wonderful man.

"Sawyer," she whispered.

Someone screamed.

And Jade jerked her eyes open, fully awake. Her heart thundered. The dream dissipated like water vapor. She breathed a deep sigh of relief. It was a dream. Only a strange dream.

She tried to sit up but couldn't. As in the dream, she was frozen in place, immobilized.

What was wrong with her? Why couldn't she move?

She heard a sound. Mice? She braced for a rodent to race across the bed. Slowly, she turned her head, expecting beady rat eyes to look back.

But the bloodshot eyes staring at her were brown... and human.

Startled, Jade jerked and tried again to sit up.

The woman laughed, though the sound was anything but pleasant. "Stupid. Stupid. Stupid. You're not going anywhere."

The only body part Jade could move was her head. Something was very wrong. Something terrible had happened to her.

She glanced down. Her cover sheet was gone. Silver duct tape bound her wrists and bare ankles. Ropes stretched from one side of the bed to the other, crisscrossing her chest, her legs, her stomach like spiderwebs.

"Oh, no." The adrenaline burst hit her. She fought against the ropes. "Let me up. Who are you? What are you doing?"

But she was afraid she knew.

The woman leaned over her, eyes glittering and a six-inch buck knife in one hand. "You know who I am. You know what you did. I warned you. I warned you both."

Scared out of her mind, Jade catalogued the woman's description. If she got out of here alive, she'd need to describe her attacker.

If she got out of here alive.

She forced herself to breathe slowly and focus.

The woman was average height and weight, dark brown hair yanked back in a ponytail and black-framed glasses. Oval-shaped, ordinary face. A short, slightly flared nose. Freckles on her arms. No scars. No tattoos. No piercings. Not even her ears. Her captor was the kind of woman Jade had passed on the street a hundred times without noticing much at all.

"I don't know what you mean," Jade said. "Why are you here? What do you want? I don't have much money but you can have it." She motioned toward the desk with her chin. "My backpack is over there. My wallet is inside."

"You trying to buy me off? Love can't be bought. He's worth everything." The woman's face became menacing. "A trick. You think you can give me money and I'll walk away? I've invested too much. Sawyer is mine, not yours." She leaned closer and spat a swear word in Jade's face. "You can't fool me."

"Right. You're right. Nobody can fool you." Jade's mind raced in tandem with her pulse. She could think of no way out other than negotiations. She had some training. She could try. "Let's talk about this."

"Talk, talk, talk. You think I want to talk to you? You

tried to take him from me. But I won't let that happen. We're getting married."

Keeping her voice friendly, Jade said, "Congratulations. I'm happy for you."

"No, you're not. I saw you." The woman sneered. "All snuggled up with my man. He gave you a rose. Just like on that TV show. You got the rose. Well, I got one, too. Now you're trying to ruin everything. You took my rose. He bought it for me. I watched him at the flower shop, and I was so happy. But I won't have it. I won't let you steal what's mine."

The woman rambled, her words jumbled and fragmented.

Something had tipped the balance. The woman was out of control.

Jade tried to control the blood pumping through her veins at a crazy speed. She needed to stay calm. She needed to think. She was trapped. Her only hope was to convince the woman they weren't enemies.

"What's your name?"

"Nora Tipton *Buchanon*." Nora tossed her pony tail and touched the tip of the knife to Jade's nose. "Remember that name. Sawyer is mine. Or he will be once you're out of the way."

The woman whipped around and began to pace the room, mumbling and muttering. "She has to go. It's all her fault. The wedding must go on. She stole the rose. Kill her. Get rid of her."

Fear was a live snake slithering up Jade's spine, wrapping around every nerve ending. She considered a scream for help, but Nora would plunge that knife through her chest before anyone responded. If anyone ever did.

She wished Bailey still lived in the motel. She'd hear the screams and investigate.

No, that was stupid. Bailey could get hurt. She was a

kid. Bailey and Ashton were right where they needed to be, safe with the Buchanons.

Whatever happened here today depended solely on her training and wits.

She licked her lips, searching for the right words. Her throat was as dry as Sahara sand.

"Tell me about the wedding, Nora. Who's your maid of honor?"

Ignoring the question, Nora paced to the window, peeked out and then paced back to the bed, only to repeat the motion twice more. She seemed lost in her own world.

"I'm always there for him. He said so. He told me. 'You're something special, Nora.' That's what he said. I knew then. He loves me. Sawyer's the handsomest man in the world and so sweet."

Yes, he was, and Jade was a fool for running out on him.

She pretended ignorance. "You're in love with Sawyer Buchanon?"

Nora, halfway across the room, spun around and screamed, "*He* loves *me*! We love each other. That makes you angry, doesn't it?"

Calm, Jade, cool and professional. "No, of course not. Why would it? I barely know him."

How did this woman know Sawyer? Had they dated? She didn't recall Nora's name on any list of friends or girl-friends anyone had given her.

Behind a pair of glasses, Nora's eyes bugged and her face distorted. "Don't try to trick me. You think you're so smart, but I'm smarter. I see what you're trying to do to Sawyer and me. You want to crash the wedding. You want to stand up and object."

Keep her talking—get on her side.

"I'm not in your way, Nora. You can have him. I barely know the man. He's a client. I'm only the private investigator hired to find you." Jade tried for a shaky smile. "But I never guessed you were involved. You've been too clever for me."

A smug look settled over the woman's face. She eased back a little and focused on the empty wall as if watching a movie screen. "I was, wasn't I? And too clever for those one-horse cops and the Buchanons to figure out that sweet and helpful Nora from the Building Supply could get inside all those houses without anyone ever knowing."

The Building Supply. Sawyer went there nearly every day. Was that why Nora had focused on him? He was outgoing, friendly and nice to everyone. Were his visits enough to make Nora spin a fantasy that Sawyer's business stops were romantic trysts?

"How did you do it? How did you get inside? You must have devised a brilliant plan to fool everyone the way you did."

Nora pondered for a moment and then turned the knife over and stared at it. She slid a finger and thumb down either side, all the way to the point. "I guess it doesn't matter now if you know."

The words chilled Jade's very marrow. Telling the whole truth didn't matter because Nora planned to kill her. She was as good as dead.

Her body began to quake with the knowledge. The bed shook. Sweat beaded on her face and back, under her bindings.

Help me, God. Sawyer says You're good. He says You love me. If Sawyer is right, calm my mind and show me what to do. Send help. Do something. I'm so scared.

"Tell me all about it," she managed to say. "I admire cleverness."

"I *was* clever, wasn't I? So very clever. No one suspected a thing." The shiny, sinister blade gleamed in the light. "He shouldn't have been with that Lisa girl. Not after all we'd been together. She was snotty to me, and because of her, Sawyer wouldn't talk to me. He didn't even notice me."

Nora's grip tightened around the knife. She glared down at Jade as if blaming her for Lisa's behavior.

Jade braced for the worst, praying. Praying that God would forgive her sins and take her to heaven. Praying that she wouldn't die in the next moment.

"That wasn't very nice," she managed through teeth that had begun to chatter. "I'm sorry that happened to you. Maybe it was a mistake, a misunderstanding."

Crazed eyes roamed the room, unable to settle. "I showed her. I showed him. They can't get away with treating me like trash." She laughed her ugly laugh. "I had fun wrecking those houses. No one suspected me at all."

Keep her talking. Let her brag. "How did you get inside?"

Nora's attention stopped on Jade, a flitting housefly glance. "Every time one of the Buchanons came to the Building Supply to have a key made, guess who made a copy?"

"You. I'm amazed. Impressed. You're brilliant, Nora. The Building Supply is fortunate to have someone of your talents."

"I've been there ten years and I know everyone and everything. I know when the Buchanon crews take a day off. I know who is working where. I read the invoices. I even learned to drive the machinery so I would be indispensable. It came in handy when I moved their Bobcat last year. Everyone in town talked about that for days."

"And the fire."

Nora's face pinched. "That was Abby's fault. I saw her in the café talking to Sawyer. Cozy. She hugged him."

"But she married Brady."

"Because Sawyer wouldn't have her. I saw to that. I burned her dream house down and she had to move in with Brady."

Abby had done no such thing, but Jade was not about to argue. The woman's mind twisted facts to suit her fantasy. She was truly insane. Dangerously insane.

"Once you're dead, Sawyer will need comfort. He'll come to me. We'll finally be man and wife. Bride and groom." Nora hummed the bridal chorus and swayed, a soft, bizarre smile curving her lips.

Think, Jade, think.

"Sawyer isn't interested in me, Nora. I'm only the private investigator his father hired." Sawyer's Nancy Drew. "Naturally, I've had to interview him, but that's all."

As if Jade's words penetrated her insanity, Nora faltered. She blinked, confused, uncertain.

Thank You, God.

Then Jade's cell phone began to ring. Nora spun toward the desk and grabbed the device.

Her shriek shot Jade's blood pressure through the roof. "It's him. He's calling you. You lied. You lied!"

"No, no. Nora, listen to me. He's calling about the case. About his house being broken into. That's all. The call is not personal."

Hang up, Sawyer. Please don't leave another message.

The ringing stopped. A minute passed while Jade held her breath and prayed, and Nora stared down at the smartphone with hate.

A beep sounded.

Oh, no. No, no, no! Sawyer had left a message.

Nora moved closer to the bed, knife menacing as she pressed the voice mail icon. "What's your password?"

Jade considered making one up to delay the inevitable, but a lie would anger Nora more. "There isn't one."

Nora put the phone on speaker. Sawyer's voice came on. "We have to talk, Jade. Whatever happened, we can work it out. Call me."

The demented stalker shrieked loud enough to drown out the cars on the outside street, drew back and, with all her might, threw the phone at Jade. "You have to die. You have to die!"

Chapter Sixteen

Sawyer's sleep was anything but restful. He'd prayed, wrestled with the fact that his house had been burglarized and some crazy woman was still running around loose, all while trying to figure out where he'd gone wrong with Jade.

Not a single resolution had come his way.

This morning, with his second Coke and a bowl of Cheerios in front of him, he propped his bare feet on the couch and considered repainting the living room sooner rather than later. He'd taken off from work to complete the clean-up and figure out if his television was salvageable, but a fresh coat of paint sounded like a positive start. Anything to help erase the nagging thought that some malicious maniac had rummaged through his things and left bizarre declarations of love on his walls. And was capable of striking again.

Now he understood the word *violated*.

He glanced at his cell phone. No return call from Jade. When he'd phoned Allison at the office, Jade had not yet checked in the way she normally did.

She must really be upset with him.

Be that as it may, his brother was right. They were going to talk.

He tapped in her number. After another series of buzzes, he left a message. Again.

Frustrated, he loaded the television into his truck and dropped it off at the repair shop before stopping at the Building Supply to look at paint samples.

While he sifted through the colors, a sales clerk walked past. "Can I help you, Mr. Buchanon?"

He half expected to discover the ever-helpful Nora leaning over his shoulder.

"Oh, hi, Anna. I thought you were Nora. She always seems to be around when I come in."

"Nora's out sick today."

"Sorry to hear that. Tell her I asked about her." He peeled a card from among the many in his hand. The color reminded him of Jade's eyes. Five gallons should do the trick. "I like this. Can you mix a five for me, satin finish?"

"Sure. We'll need a few minutes."

She left with the color chip and Sawyer roamed the building, a man's paradise, especially when that man was a carpenter. Today his mind wasn't on saw blades and power tools. It wasn't even on the stalker.

He couldn't stop thinking about Jade. Some inner nudge told him to try once more to reach her.

Probably his wishful imagination, but maybe she was thinking about him or ready to talk and too proud to make the first move.

Pausing in the plumbing aisle, he whipped out his phone and stared at her name. After a few seconds, he slid the device back into his jeans pocket and went in search of his paint. He'd give her a little more time, maybe invite her out to lunch.

He stopped by the Buchanon Built warehouse, more

than halfway hoping to find Jade there. He didn't, and even a phone call from the business phone to her cell went unanswered. Yeah, he'd asked his sister to make the call.

The inner nudge to make contact grew stronger. Was something wrong? Was Jade okay?

"Nobody's heard from her today?"

"Not yet." Allison thumbed absently through a stack of mail while they talked. "She may have driven out to one of the houses without stopping here first."

"That doesn't make sense. She's studied those thoroughly, and since I'm the only one getting visits from our vandal these days, I doubt our construction sites are the target anymore."

He didn't like using the word *stalker* in front of his sisters. Taking Jade's advice, he'd warned them, though, about what had happened at his house and made them promise to be extra diligent. If something happened to anyone in his family because of him... The thought didn't deserve completion.

Allison put a hand to her back and stretched. Her tummy got a little rounder every day. "I hope she's not sick all alone at the motel without anyone."

He couldn't fathom being alone in sickness. Family always showed up in droves. Mama and Allison with food. Jaylee with green tea or something equally as revolting. Charity with a humidifier and an armload of medicines. Even his brothers popped in to give him a hard time.

Jade had no one.

Not true. She has you.

If he was looking for an excuse to see her, he'd found one. "After I grab a few paint supplies from the back, I think I'll head over to the motel and make sure she's okay."

"Great idea." Allison's smile was knowing, but then

he didn't exactly hide the fact that he had a thing for the pretty PI.

Feeling better than he had since he'd walked into his wreck of a living room, Sawyer grabbed some brushes and rollers, dumped them in the bed of his truck and headed to the River Roost and the rough side of town.

As he pulled off the street and onto the gravel parking area, he spotted Jade's white Chevy in front of her unit, next to an old brown pickup.

She was still at the motel? This late in the morning? And not answering her calls?

Yep. She must be under the weather.

He stepped out of his truck and gazed around the run-down area. Intense summer sun beamed on the dingy, shaded windows and the River Roost seemed quiet and peaceful. Nighttime was a different matter, and the reason he worried about Jade staying here alone.

As he approached the unit, he thought he heard a voice, but when he knocked the sound went silent. He waited. No one answered.

The TV maybe?

Mouth pressed into a firm line, he knocked harder. "Jade? I know you're in there. Your car's here. Are you sick?"

All remained quiet while he listened and the sun baked the back of his head. He raised his hand to knock again.

Before he could, Jade's voice permeated the wall. "Go away, Sawyer."

He leaned in, cupped both hands around his mouth and yelled, "Not until we talk. Not until I know you're okay. Are you sick?"

"No. I'm okay. Go away."

Her voice sounded funny. "Open the door. Let me see for myself, and then if you still want me to leave, I'll go."

"Please, Sawyer, listen. Leave. I don't want you here.

We can *conduct business* later." Her tone was especially adamant. "I can't talk now."

Business? She knew he wasn't here on business.

An eerie awareness crept over him, prickled the hair on his arms. His gut screamed a warning.

He whipped around and scanned the area. Nothing. No one.

"Open the door, Jade."

Her reply was a frantic plea. "Go away! You have to leave."

Something was definitely wrong. "Open up now or I'll get the manager to let me in."

From the interior he perceived movement, a shuffling of footsteps. The lock clicked and the knob slowly turned.

He put on his best smile. "Now we're getting somewhere."

The door opened. A woman appeared. A familiar brunette woman who didn't look a thing like Jade. "We certainly are."

He blinked, bewildered. "Nora? Where's Jade? What—"

Sawyer's brain tried to make sense out of what he was seeing, but the next few seconds jumbled together like a junk drawer. He heard Jade cry, "Run, Sawyer! Run!"

But the warning came too late. Nora caught Sawyer off guard, grabbed his arm and yanked.

He stumbled into the room and fell to his knees as Nora slammed and relocked the door.

"What's going on in here?" He started to get up. Nora moved between him and Jade. The handy helper from the Building Supply held a knife the size of Florida.

Sawyer froze.

The fog of bewilderment dissipated. Sheer terror took over.

Jade tied on the bed. Nora holding a knife.

And he was on his knees, helpless.

If God be for you, who can be against you?

He wasn't alone. He wasn't helpless.

Sawyer drew in a slow, calming breath and prayed with all his mind for wisdom. And courage.

Slowly, he raised his hands above his head and played dumb. "Will someone fill me in? I'm kind of lost."

Very lost. But smart enough to know he and Jade were in deep trouble.

The saleswoman frowned. "You know what you did. I listened to her voice mail." Her face crumbled. "You're cheating again, Sawyer. After all we've been to each other. Over and over I've forgiven you. You're weak. You can't help yourself. These women won't leave you alone." She spun toward Jade and then back to him. "Like her. She seduced you. She's the reason."

Sawyer's heart stuck in his throat. Nora was his stalker? *Nora?* Pleasant, helpful, overeager Nora?

Cautiously, he rose to his feet, hands high, careful not to set the woman off.

He flicked a glance toward the bed.

"Jade," he murmured softly. "Are you hurt?"

"No." She held his gaze with particular intensity. "Nora has somehow gotten the wrong idea about you and me. I've been trying to explain that we are only business acquaintances. We are not romantically involved. Tell her, Sawyer."

"Is that true? Is she lying?" Nora stepped closer to Sawyer. He smelled sweat mixed with a sickly sweet perfume. Behind the glasses, her pupils had dilated to their fullest, obliterating her irises. Black, empty holes. "You can't keep cheating. I love you too much. I have to settle this once and for all."

Was the woman on drugs?

"Tell her, Sawyer. She needs to hear from you that she's the one, not me."

Aware of the message Jade was trying to send, he softened his tone and focused all his attention on his stalker. Nora thought Jade was a threat to her romantic fantasy. Convincing her otherwise was up to him.

What he did and said in the next moments could save Jade's life.

Lord, forgive the lies I'm about to tell.

"Absolutely true, Nora." He reached a hand toward her, cajoling, sweet-talking. If he'd ever had an ounce of persuasive charm, he needed to use it now. "Miss Warren is a private investigator hired by my father. I didn't want her around in the first place." That much was true. He hadn't wanted *anyone* on the job. "I thought hiring her was a waste of money."

"I want to believe you." Nora waved the knife in a circle. "You've hurt me so many times. All those women. You have to choose between these sleazy girls and me. You love *me*, Sawyer. I'm the one. The only one. I can make you happy." She pointed the gleaming blade toward Jade. "Not her. Never her!"

Sawyer watched Nora's every erratic movement, gauging, thinking. If he could catch her off guard, if he could go for the knife...

Nora might be crazy but she was smart. Angling her body to keep an eye on Sawyer, she stormed toward the bed and pressed the knife against Jade's jugular.

In a deep, guttural voice, she demanded, "Never, ever her. Do you hear me, Sawyer?"

Fear knocked against his knees. He nodded, afraid to look away from the woman, away from Jade's throat. If she moved that knife the slightest bit, he'd take action. He'd have no choice.

"Tell Nora how you feel, Sawyer," Jade urged, face white with terror. "Tell her she's the only one. She's concerned about the wedding."

Wedding? With him?

He swallowed, understanding what he had to do. Jade was in mortal danger. So was he unless they could convince Nora that she, not Jade, was the object of his affection.

"Nora, listen to me. Listen, sweetheart." He held both arms out to his sides, forcing a relaxed and pleasant stance. His heart was knocking through his shirt. "You're my special girl. I'm your man. Remember? You don't need to be jealous over Jade. She's nothing to me."

The words hurt but he had to say them.

Slowly, Nora lifted the knife from Jade's throat and turned to face him. Her lips quivered. "You gave her a rose. You cooked her dinner. Candles. I saw the candles."

The chill in his soul branched out until he felt cold all over. Had she watched them through his window?

"The rose was for you, sweetheart. I was only showing it to her. To be sure a woman as special as you would like it. I'm a guy. What do I know about flowers?"

"Really?" Nora blinked in rapid bursts. "You did that for me?"

"Absolutely. You're my special girl. Only you. No one else." He opened his arms, vulnerable, welcoming and cunning. "Come here. Let me hold you. I'm sorry if you misunderstood. I never meant to hurt you."

Nora's eyes widened and something shifted in the crazed depths as she looked with longing at the waiting embrace. Her chest rose and fell, her breathing loud in the room.

"You still love me?" A silver tear sparkled on her bottom lashes. "Truly?"

Now he was getting somewhere. She was softening.

"Let me show you how much." He tapped his chest. "Come to Sawyer, darlin'. I need to hold you, to feel your heart beat against mine."

If he hadn't been so scared, he'd have rolled his eyes. Never in his life had he ever made such a cornball statement.

Slowly, as if mesmerized by the prize before her, Nora edged toward Sawyer, away from Jade. The knife hand relaxed, fell to half-mast.

Blood roared against Sawyer's temples with enough force to take down a building. He had a plan. He prayed it would work. If it didn't, he and Jade were both dead.

He kept his focus on Nora and the knife, but in his peripheral vision, he saw the intensity with which Jade watched the scene being played out while she remained helpless. Once Nora's back was turned, she strained against the ropes, wiggling to get free.

He dared not look. Not yet. Not until Nora was in his embrace. He held the woman's gaze, willing her to come to him.

"I love you, Sawyer. You've made me the happiest woman in the world." A smile, rivaling the Joker's, spread her lips.

She walked into his chest and with a moaning sigh, wrapped her arms around his waist. He could feel the knife hand fisted against his back.

Nora raised her face to his. "Kiss me, my darling. Seal our love at last."

The idea revolted him. He wasn't sure he could.

Jade's life depended on it.

He'd never been much of an actor, but he closed his eyes, thought of Jade, and kissed Nora. She moaned again, kissed him long and hard, and then she buried her face in his neck. "Wonderful. Oh, Sawyer. My darling. At last."

Slowly, keeping her close, Sawyer released the hug and rubbed his hands over her upper arms. She tensed but he kept his stroke light and romantic, caressing her skin, gazing as tenderly as he could into her manic eyes.

After a few seconds, she shivered and raised her hands to his chest. The knife pointed inward, toward his thundering heart.

What do I do now?

The wedding. She wanted a wedding.

"Let's talk about our wedding." Get her talking. Keep her talking. Gain her trust. "We have plans to make. Should I rent a tux? Do you have your dress?"

She nodded, her face going dreamy. "Oh, yes. I ordered it online. A lacy gown like Duchess Kate's. I saved forever to buy exactly the right one."

"You'll be beautiful in it." Along with the prison orange. "I can't wait for that day."

Carefully, he bracketed her face with both hands and tipped his forehead against hers. "All this time, I thought I was out of your league. Now here you are. Mine at last."

The words seemed to work. Like chocolate in the Texas sun, she softened, melting into him, relaxing. She believed him.

He would only have a few seconds while his body blocked her view of the knife. He had to move fast.

Adrenaline jacked into his bloodstream. His blood pressure spiked.

He kissed her forehead, and one by one her eyelids. As if hypnotized, her eyes remained shut. She moaned softly.

Now!

In a move he'd learned from wrestling his brothers, Sawyer spun away, grabbed Nora's wrist and twisted.

Her scream shocked his eardrums. She went wild. Incredibly strong for an average woman, she kicked and fought like a mad mule.

They tumbled against the bed, slammed into the nightstand. A lamp thudded to the carpet.

He felt a stick, a sting, and vaguely heard Jade's shout but couldn't make out the words.

Nora heaved against him, raising her knee. He dodged, threw her off balance and finally wrestled her down and sat on her back with his full weight of nearly two hundred pounds.

Repeatedly, he slammed her wrist against the carpet until she released the weapon. She bucked and raged, calling him every vile name. Threatening to kill him. To kill Jade. To kill his whole family.

Sawyer grit his teeth. *That* was never going to happen.

He shoved the weapon out of reach, yanked Nora's arms behind her back and looked around for something to tie her. If he could get to his shoelace or his belt... Better yet, he needed Jade's ropes.

All were out of reach.

"Sawyer, the lamp cord. Hog-tie."

He flashed a grim smile at Jade. "Smart girl."

In seconds, Nora's ankles and wrists were bound, though her mouth never stopped. She spat, screamed and reviled in between bouts of declaring her obsessive, undying love.

That kind of love he could do without.

Sawyer untied Jade and quickly called 911. Then he did what he'd wanted to do for two days. He wrapped his arms around her. "You're shaking."

"That's you."

"Adrenaline rush."

"You weren't scared?"

"Out of my mind." He grimaced, thinking of the woman

on the floor, screaming obscenities. Above the din, he said, "Make that terrified."

While he waited for his pulse to return to normal, he searched Jade for wounds, for blood or bruises. Her wrists were striated red and raw. He lifted them to his lips and pressed gentle kisses there.

"Sure you're okay?"

"Yes, but you're not." She touched her fingers to his shoulder. "You're bleeding."

Texas red blood formed a softball-size circle on his shirt.

"A scratch." He shrugged away her concern and tugged her close. He kissed her lips, her hair, the red place on her neck where the knife had pressed. Oh, that red place. It broke him in half.

Nora's screams grew louder. "Liar. Cheater. I hate you!"

Ignoring the insults, he breathed in Jade's living, breathing essence.

She was safe. Nora hadn't hurt her. Jade was unharmed. *Thank you, Father God.*

"I'm okay, Sawyer. Really."

He pulled back and pressed his hand against his shoulder. "I'm getting blood on you."

Jade tugged away his hand and lifted his shirtsleeve. "Sawyer." She hissed through her teeth when she saw the wound, and then went into the bathroom for tissues. "You need stitches."

"Pressure works." But he let her minister to the cut and murmur over him in tender tones.

On the floor far enough away from them to be rendered harmless, Nora sobbed. "Liar. Liar."

Over the noise, sirens wailed and drew near. Rapid response. One of the blessings of a small town.

Jade tugged his sleeve down to cover the wadded tissues. "Promise you'll have the paramedics take a look."

"Sure." Whatever. He'd had worse nicks. A carpenter and his power tools sometimes tangled. "Gotta direct the police inside." He pointed to Nora. "Watch her."

"Gladly." Jade stuck a foot on Nora's back and grinned as Sawyer unlocked the door and stepped out into the heat. Jade. His super woman.

Fifteen long minutes, many questions and a bandage later, Leroy and a burly officer hauled the sobbing, incoherent woman away. Sawyer was stunned to learn Nora was the single perpetrator of every Buchanon break-in, including Abby's house fire. The woman was smart, conniving…and mad as the Hatter.

As the police cars pulled away, Sawyer stepped back into the motel room. He and Jade were alone at last.

They were finally going to have that talk.

Chapter Seventeen

His black hair stood out in a dozen directions, his shirt was bloody and his face scratched.

To Jade, Sawyer had never looked more wonderful.

Her motel room, however, was a mess. The lamp damaged, the bed rumpled, ropes and duct tape scattered about, and drops of Sawyer's blood on the carpet next to a wad of tissues and bandage wrappers.

None of that mattered now. Nora was in custody, the truth of her crimes revealed. She and Sawyer were safe.

The door clicked shut behind him. He stood with one hand on the knob staring at her.

"You're the most beautiful sight I've ever seen," he said.

Her lips curved. "So are you. I—"

Lightning fast and with a groan that could only be relief, he swooped in and kissed her, lingering again on her neck where the knife had pressed.

Touched but giggling at his vehemence, she tried to pull away. She'd been in intense situations before. He hadn't. Not this intense. "You're the one who got hurt."

He shook his head and murmured against her skin, sending her pulse into orbit. "I lost ten years of life when I saw that knife at your throat. I'm so thankful—"

"Me, too." She tugged his head up and held a hand on each side of his jaw. Dear, gorgeous, brave and wonderful man. "I prayed. A lot. I prayed and God heard me."

"Yeah?" Hope flared in his beloved sapphire gaze.

"God was with me. I felt Him." She gulped back a tear. "He gave me the right words to say to Nora. And He sent you."

"Somehow I knew you needed me." He tapped his chest. "Inside, I knew. It was as if God was urging me to come here. I couldn't get away from the nagging need to see you. Immediately."

"I finally understand what you've been trying to tell me. God is not angry, He's not mean. He's a good, good Father like you said." Humbled by the revelation, she touched two fingers to her heart. "I feel His love. I've never had that before."

He tugged her hands to his lips, kissing one finger at a time. "Do you feel mine, too?"

She swallowed, emotion bubbling up inside. "Yes, I do. So much, I want to cry. It's…incredible."

Still holding her hands, he guided her to the chair and knelt before her. Emotion bubbled in him, too. She could see it in his face and feel it through his trembling fingers.

"We need to have a serious talk. About us." For once, he didn't smile. "If you kick me to the curb this time, I'll get the message. But first we get everything out in the open."

"I'm not kicking you anywhere." She was thankful for his perseverance. If he'd given up on them, she'd be dead by now.

He turned her hands palms up and traced her lifeline. "Are you saying—?"

"I've been afraid of trusting anyone, Sawyer, particularly a man, and specifically one like you." He loved her. She wasn't afraid anymore.

"One like me? What does that mean?"

"Charming and smooth with women. Too good looking for words."

"Stop." He tilted back, grinning. "My head can only swell so much without an explosion."

"Don't be thrilled. Those were not traits I admired."

He faked a cute wince. "Ouch."

"Hear me out. It gets better." She patted his forearm. "You were different. Still charming and handsome, but you have something that surprised me. Character. Integrity. Kindness. I couldn't believe you were for real. I didn't know what to do with you."

He sat back on his heels, contemplating and, bless him, understanding. "So you kept waiting for the other shoe to drop. For me to turn into Frankenstein."

"Irrational, I know, but I needed to be in control. With you, I was losing control. I was afraid of letting anyone get that close again."

"Because of your ex?"

"Him. My father. The church I grew up in. They were all harsh and controlling. My mother is still under my father's thumb. His word is law, and believe me, his is a judgmental, angry law."

"So you expected all men to be like them?"

"And all Christians. After Cam, I never gave anyone a chance to get close enough to learn differently. Now, I understand how wrong that was." She'd been as judgmental as her father.

"I'm not your ex or your father or any other loser who dared hurt you. The Christians I know are good people, well-intentioned souls. Imperfect but trying to be like Jesus. And I promise here and now, no man is ever going to hurt you again. Not as long as I'm breathing."

"I believe you." Sawyer was one of the good guys. With

all her soul, she believed that. Jade blinked back grateful, happy tears, loving this man with an intensity that made her tremble. "Over and over, your actions have proven you to be the real deal. Then today, you stood up for me. You put yourself at risk to protect me."

"And I always will. I—"

She pressed her finger to his lips, silencing him. She knew what he was about to say. He loved her. But until he knew everything, she didn't deserve to hear those beautiful words.

"Don't say anything more until you hear me out. I have a confession. Okay?"

He kissed her fingertip and grinned. "As long as you aren't going to run out on me again."

"I won't, although you may want to run out on me."

His eyebrows dipped together in a vee. "Why?"

"My family."

"I don't care about the past or the lawsuit or any of that."

"That's not what I mean." She took a deep breath. "I haven't been completely open with you."

"Okay. I'm listening."

"I passed my brother's truck out on the bridge and feared my father had sent him. I thought they might be responsible for the vandalism."

"Seriously? You thought your family devised the break-ins and set fire to Abby's house?"

Nodding numbly, she caught her bottom lip between her teeth. She couldn't read Sawyer's expression, but he had every right to be upset.

"Why didn't you tell me about this? Or my dad?"

"They're my family, Sawyer. I couldn't point fingers at them unless I was positive."

He studied her for several long seconds while her heart pounded and her mouth went dry. Had she lost him?

"Family loyalty?"

"That sounds stupid coming from me. But as messed up as they are, they're still my kin and I love them."

"What would you have done if they'd been guilty?"

She wanted to leave no doubt of what she would have done. She and Sawyer didn't need that kind of suspicion hanging between them like toxic fumes.

"Let me show you something." Going to the desk, she flipped open the little laptop, scrolled to her email and opened a file marked confidential. "Read this."

He peered over her shoulder. "It's to your boss. Are you sure I should see this?"

"Yes."

Silent as stone, he read the email and then clicked each of the attachments.

"All the files, my suspicions and every piece of evidence is there, including my father's and my brothers' names, addresses, the sighting on the bridge, the lawsuit records and their ongoing hatred of any mention of the Buchanon name. Everything."

His head swiveled toward her. "You were turning the case over to your boss."

"Sending this to Dale held me accountable. If my family was guilty, I had to know first, but I also had to do the right thing. For the case. For me. For your family."

Sawyer straightened, a smile slowly moving from his lips to the crinkled corners of his eyes. "And for us?"

"If you can forgive the deception."

"If there is one thing a Buchanon understands and respects it's family loyalty. It's the Buchanon way." He took her hand, reeled her in. "And I'm a real forgiving guy."

She fell for his tender words, hook, line and sinker. The bait was too delicious to turn down. "There's something else you need to know."

One black eyebrow shot up. "More confessions?"

"Uh-huh. Just one." She fiddled with the front of his shirt. "And I think you'll like it."

For once, the chatty man had nothing to say. He simply waited. But his heart pounded beneath her fingers.

"Sawyer Buchanon, you take my breath away. You fill the empty place inside me. You showed me how to believe when I couldn't. And I can't imagine my life without you in it."

"Keep talking." His voice rumbled in his chest, deep and emotional. "I like this a lot."

"I love you, Sawyer." She tilted her face up to his, a breath away from his lips. "Want to find out where this love thing might take us?"

"Oh, darlin'," he said in his best Texas drawl. "I'm already there."

Epilogue

Five months later, Jade made the trip from Paris to Gabriel's Crossing to attend the marriage nuptials of Quinn Buchanon and nurse practitioner Gena Satterfield. Today wasn't her first nor would it be her last time making this trip. Between the two of them, she and Sawyer racked up more miles than a frequent flyer.

Things were progressing well in their relationship. Very well. As her faith deepened, so did her love for her Buchanon man and his for her.

She'd never imagined a Buchanon would hold her heart in the palm of his hand. But hold it he did, and ever so tenderly.

On this momentous occasion three weeks before Christmas, Sawyer was one of Quinn's groomsmen along with his other two brothers while their dad stood as best man. The handsome Buchanon men, in black tuxes, white shirts, red ties and sprigs of holly and pine as boutonnieres, had decorated the church front as much as the red bows, greenery, white lights and candles.

Jade had soaked up the beautiful, faith-filled ceremony that sealed two people into covenant marriage for all eternity.

Forever sounded good these days.

After the wedding, guests moved into the fellowship

hall, gorgeously festooned in Christmas colors. Jade, along with Bailey, made the rounds tasting the finger foods and the hot chocolate bar, and now waited for Sawyer to join her following more wedding photos.

A pianist softly played while guests roamed the room and chatted. The wedding, while not elaborate, seemed perfect to her.

But then weddings touched a sentimental spot she normally kept hidden, and Jade battled misty eyes as she sat at a white covered table with the handful of Buchanons who weren't in the wedding party, some she was meeting for the first time.

Bailey sat to her right, feeding grapes to Ashton. She'd thrilled at serving as keeper of the guest book and looked young and lovely in a red tartan dress with black leggings.

Allison, so pregnant she required help to get out of a chair, sat across the table with Jake, her watchful, hovering cowboy to his wife's left.

"Didn't you love that moment when the pastor said for Quinn to kiss his bride?" Abby, with her brunette hair and dark eyes, looked pretty in a belted burgundy sheath.

Jade nodded. Everyone had laughed and *ahhed* when Quinn whipped out a sprig of mistletoe to hold above Gena's head as they kissed. "The perfect Christmas touch."

"But completely out of character for Quinn." Jaylee, the ultra-fit sister, sleek as a cat in green velvet, nibbled on a small skewer of fruit.

"Which added to the surprise. Gena has mellowed him." Allison shifted positions, one hand to her immense belly. A curious expression moved across her face.

Jake frowned and leaned toward her. "You okay, babe?"

She batted her eyelashes at him. "I would be if I had some more hot chocolate and a cookie."

The former bull rider was up and moving before she completed her request.

Allison followed him with an adoring gaze. "He's the best."

Jade loved watching them together. They were endearingly devoted.

A pair of strong hands suddenly gripped her shoulders. Before she could whip around with an elbow to the solar plexus, Sawyer's warm voice whispered against her ear. "Miss me?"

Smiling from the inside out, Jade placed her hands over his. "Immensely. Can you finally join us for good?"

"All done." He took the saved seat on her other side, picked a chocolate-covered strawberry from her plate and munched.

As they talked and ate, enjoying the piano music while the bride and groom received guests and stared at each other with sappy happiness, more Buchanons stopped at the table.

Brady, the tallest of the brothers, scooted a chair up beside his wife and kissed her cheek. "Where's our princess?"

"Talking to Alabama." She pointed toward a tawny-skinned woman, Gena's office nurse who looked stunning in her Christmas-red maid of honor gown. "Lila's recruiting her to make her famous rocky road brownies for your grand opening."

"Aw, my little publicist."

Brady was in full swing with his yearly Christmas home makeover. Along with the Buchanon brothers, a passel of volunteers worked long and hard to make someone's dreams come true. Little Lila was not to be left out.

"Thank goodness we don't have to worry about an arsonist burning down the project this year," Abby said.

"We can thank my girl over here for that." Sawyer pointed a canapé at Jade and then popped it into his mouth.

"I'm relieved the case is solved, and Nora is no longer a threat to any of you or your property."

Sawyer tapped the top of her hand. "Or to you."

Yes, there was that. Jade still shivered to think how close she'd come to being killed by the insanely obsessed woman.

Karen, busy greeting guests, overheard the conversation and leaned in. "Nora is a sad, sick soul. Completely broken."

"You wouldn't say that if she'd hurt Jade or me."

Karen gave him a look. "Sawyer."

"I know, Mom. Compassion. Mercy. Even for Nora. God and I are working on it." He rose and hugged his mother. "You and the women's ministry are doing a good thing."

"I still can't believe her own family refuses to see her. She needs to know *someone* cares."

Karen and her friends visited Nora each week at the psychiatric hospital, baked goodies, sent cards and prayed for her. Jade admired the woman's ability to forgive and to love the unlovely. Like Sawyer, Jade was working on the forgiveness thing. Both with Nora and with her own family, particularly her father.

With a final pat to Sawyer's shoulder, Karen swirled back into the crowd, and the group broke up to move about and celebrate the occasion with guests.

The piano player slipped into lively Christmas tunes. Jade soaked in the festive, loving atmosphere, happy to be beside Sawyer as they chatted and laughed.

She squeezed his arm and he smiled down at her.

Someday, she wanted a wedding like this. Not exactly like this, of course, but a celebration surrounded by loved ones.

"Hey, why the sad look?" Sawyer dipped down to look into her face.

"Did I look sad?"

"For a second. You okay?"

"I was thinking about how different your family is from mine."

"You worry about your mother."

She did, of course. Mama was a doormat. A battered wife who wouldn't complain. "She won't leave Daddy no matter how he treats her."

"But she did drive down to Paris with you to shop. That's progress."

Leave it to Sawyer to find the positive. "And we're praying together on the phone, something we've never done."

"Keep praying. You might be surprised at what God can do with your mom…and your dad. He's still in the people-fixing business."

"You're so awesome. No wonder I have a mountain-size crush on you."

"Yeah, well, Gena's getting ready to toss the bouquet. Get on over there and catch it."

"Is that a hint?"

"Catch that bouquet and find out."

"Ooh, mystery man." Laughing, Jade sauntered over to the gathering of single ladies, where she caught nothing but a sharp high heel on top of her foot.

Afterward, giggling with Bailey and Jaylee, she limped toward Sawyer and waited for the bride and groom to make their departure. Holding hands and laughing, Quinn and Gena ran the gauntlet of artificial snowflakes and wildly ringing jingle bells.

"My brother surprised us all," Sawyer said as they started back inside the church. "As reclusive as he was for so long, I figured he'd sneak off and get married without so much as a witness."

"Love changes people."

His tender look melted her. "I'll say. You hated me and now look at us."

"I can't believe you didn't hate me in return when you found out my maiden name."

"It's not the Buchanon way." He winked. "We're lovers not haters."

He'd been supportive, not angry or resentful. And when her father had said horrible things to her when he'd learned she was dating a Buchanon, Sawyer had been there, comforting, loving, in his Buchanon way.

She tiptoed up to kiss him and was really settling in well when a shout arose. They both whipped around.

Jade's police training jumped to the surface. "What's wrong?"

Jake Hamilton, his face white as paste, cleared a path. Allison waddled beside him.

"Don't let him panic, Sawyer." Allison gazed around the crowd. "Where's Mama?"

Jake spun around on his polished boots, clearly in the midst of a panic Allison didn't want him to have.

Sawyer put a hand on the other man's arm. "Hey, bud. Settle. What's up?"

"Allison's in labor!" The cowboy scooped his wife into his arms and took off in a trot. "We're having a baby!"

Later that night, Sawyer gazed at the tiny baby sleeping peacefully in the hospital nursery. The corridor was packed with Buchanons roaming in and out, up and down.

The new mom was doing great. The dad not so much. According to rumors, he'd turned a few shades of green during delivery and slithered down a wall, and now sat next to Allison's bed with an ice pack on the back of his neck.

The cowboy was going to make a terrific dad.

"She's beautiful, Sawyer." Jade gazed through the glass at the very small bit of humanity. "All pink and perfect."

"I hope Jake doesn't teach her to ride bulls."

They chuckled together, exhausted but full of wonder at this day's occurrences.

"First a wedding and now a baby, all in one day."

"God is good to us Buchanons." Sawyer slipped his arm around the woman beside him. Love flowed today like the mighty Red River, pulling them all into its tender current. His insides were the consistency of grits—roughed up but mushy. "Someday, not too far down the road, I want a baby like her. Or two or three or seven. Don't you?"

"I'd like to get married first."

He tilted his head downward. "Is that a proposal?"

She gave him a gentle poke in the ribs. "That's your job, mister."

"Will you say yes if I ask? You didn't catch the bouquet."

She laughed. "Ask and find out. I may not be superstitious."

He was confident of her answer, but she needed the words. Words he had, plenty of them, crowding his heart and spilling out his mouth.

"Cruel." He sighed dramatically. "But so smart and beautiful. How can a man resist a woman such as you?"

Not caring one bit that he was in a hospital and half the world could see and hear, Sawyer took his love by the shoulders, turned her in his direction and stared into her eyes with all the emotion bubbling in his chest.

"I love you." He'd said the words many times but even a million wouldn't be enough.

Her smile widened. "I love you, too."

"That's good. Real good." Still in his wedding clothes, though he'd shed the jacket, he went to one knee right there in the maternity ward with hard tile digging into his bones. "Love is a good start, but we both know it takes more, and I promise you those things. A lifetime of commitment and respect, of working together with God at the center of everything we do."

"You're going to make me cry." Tears glistened on her lashes.

"You're the woman I've prayed for, the one I've waited years to find, my other half. Marry me, Jade. Today, tomorrow, next year. Just say you'll marry me."

Her lips curved as a single tear slipped down her cheek. His icy Nancy Drew had thawed so beautifully.

"Yes," she whispered. "Forever yes."

Dawson's voice cut through the medicine-scented air. "Hey everybody, look! Sawyer's proposing to Jade."

The corridor erupted with noise and footsteps as his family surged around them. Cell phones snapped photos and captured video.

Sawyer dropped his head. "No privacy in this family."

Brady whacked him on the back. "You're in a public place, knothead. What did you expect?"

"Leave him alone, Brady. He's trying to be romantic." Dawson shaped a heart with his fingers and grinned. "Go ahead, brother. Do your thing."

And so Sawyer rose to a stand and pulled his new fiancée to him, tilting her lips to his to seal their promise. She sighed against his mouth, sending shivers of pleasure up his spine.

Applause erupted. Someone whooped. He vaguely heard a nurse admonish them to be quiet.

His mother and dad and sisters and brothers, all the people he loved most in the universe, were here as witnesses. And Jade was in his arms.

A wedding, a baby and a proposal all in one perfect day.

He dipped back in for another kiss, his heart full of love and thanks and praise. God was good. Life was blessed.

And that, he thought with a smile, was the way he wanted it. Now. Forever. Always. He and Jade together, the Buchanon way.

* * * * *

Dear Reader,

As I finish up the Buchanon series with Sawyer's story, I hope you've enjoyed our time together in Gabriel's Crossing, Texas. Like most families, the Buchanons have their share of troubles but their Christian faith and family loyalty hold them together.

I set the Buchanon series in what is known locally as Texoma or Texoma Land, the Red River border area where Oklahoma and Texas meet. Though many people think of these states as flat, dry plains, Texoma is a beautiful area of forests, lakes, mountains and friendly small towns. If you ever have a chance to visit Texoma in the autumn, the scenery will take your breath away and the warm people will leave you with a smile.

I love to hear from readers. Connect with me at my website www.lindagoodnight.com or on social media. Be sure to sign up for my newsletter so we can stay in touch!

Until my next books, be well and happy.

May God bless you,

Linda Goodnight

SPECIAL EXCERPT FROM

*Nell Stoltzfus falls for the new local veterinarian in town,
James Pierce. But their love is forbidden since he's
English and she's Amish. If Nell follows her heart,
will love conquer all?*

Read on for a sneak preview of
A SECRET AMISH LOVE *by* Rebecca Kertz,
available July 2017 from Love Inspired!

"You said your *bruder* was called out on an emergency,"
Nell said. "What does he do?"

"He's a veterinarian. He's recently opened a clinic here
in Happiness."

The strange sensation settled over Nell. Despite the
difference in their last names, could James be Maggie's
brother? "What's his name?" she asked.

"James Pierce." Maggie smiled. "He owns Pierce
Veterinary Clinic. Have you heard of him?"

"*Ja.* In fact, 'twas your bruder who treated my dog,
Jonas."

"Then you've met him!" Maggie looked delighted. "Is he
a *gut* veterinarian?"

Startled by this new knowledge, Nell could only nod
at first. "He was wonderful with Jonas. He's a kind and
compassionate man." She studied Maggie and recognized
the family resemblance. "How is he a Pierce and you a
Troyer?"

"I am a Pierce." Maggie grinned. "Abigail is, too. But
we don't go by the Pierce name. Adam is our stepfather,

and he is our *dat* now." Maggie's eyes filled with sadness. "I was too young to care, but James had a hard time with it. He loved Dad, and he'd wanted to be a veterinarian like him since he was ten. He became more determined to follow in Dad's footsteps."

Nell felt her heart break for James, who must have suffered after his father's death. "You chose the Amish life, but James chose a different path."

"And he's doing well," Maggie said. "My family is thrilled that he set up his practice in Happiness."

Later that afternoon, James arrived to spend time with his family.

She recognized his car immediately as he drove into the barnyard. James stood a moment, searching for family members. Nell couldn't move as he crossed the yard to where tables and bench seats had been set up. Soon, James headed to the gathering of young people, including his sisters Maggie and Abigail.

Nell found it heartwarming to see that his siblings regarded him with the same depth of love and affection. James spoke briefly to Maggie, clearly delighted that he'd handled his emergency then decided to come. She heard the siblings teasing and the ensuing laughter. Maggie said something to James as she gestured in Nell's direction.

James saw her, and Nell froze. Her heart started to beat hard when he broke away from the group to approach her.

Don't miss
A SECRET AMISH LOVE
by Rebecca Kertz, available July 2017 wherever
Love Inspired® books and ebooks are sold.

www.LoveInspired.com

LIEXP0617